HENRY FI

Literary
General Editor: Richard Dutt
Lancaster U

CW00818729

This series offers stimulating accou... ... ... careers of the
most admired and influential English-language authors. Volumes
follow the outline of the writers' working lives, not
in the spirit of traditional biography, but aiming to trace
the professional, publishing and social contexts which
shaped their writing.

A list of the published titles in the series follows overleaf.

Published titles

Morris Beja
JAMES JOYCE

Cedric C. Brown
JOHN MILTON

Peter Davison
George Orwell

Richard Dutton
WILLIAM SHAKESPEARE

Jan Fergus
JANE AUSTEN

James Gibson
THOMAS HARDY

Kenneth Graham
HENRY JAMES

Paul Hammond
JOHN DRYDEN

W. David Kay
BEN JONSON

Mary Lago
E. M. FORSTER

Clinton Machann
MATTHEW ARNOLD

Alasdair D. F. Macrae
W. B. YEATS

Joseph McMinn
JONATHAN SWIFT

Kerry McSweeney
GEORGE ELIOT

John Mepham
VIRGINIA WOOLF

Michael O'Neill
PERCY BYSSHE SHELLEY

Leonée Ormond
ALFRED TENNYSON

Harold Pagliaro
HENRY FIELDING

George Parfitt
JOHN DONNE

Gerald Roberts
GERARD MANLEY HOPKINS

Felicity Rosslyn
ALEXANDER POPE

Tony Sharpe
T. S. ELIOT

Grahame Smith
CHARLES DICKENS

Gary Waller
EDMUND SPENSER

Cedric Watts
JOSEPH CONRAD

John Williams
WILLIAM WORDSWORTH

Tom Winnifrith and Edward Chitham
CHARLOTTE AND EMILY BRONTË

John Worthen
D. H. LAWRENCE

Literary Lives
Series Standing Order ISBN 0–333–71486–5
(*outside North America only*)

You can receive future titles in this series as they are published by placing a standing order. Please contact your bookseller or, in case of difficulty, write to us at the address below with your name and address, the title of the series and the ISBN quoted above.

Customer Services Department, Macmillan Distribution Ltd
Houndmills, Basingstoke, Hampshire RG21 6XS, England

Henry Fielding

A Literary Life

Harold Pagliaro

Alexander Griswold Cummins Professor
Emeritus of English Literature
Swarthmore College, Pennsylvania

First published 1998 by
MACMILLAN PRESS LTD
Houndmills, Basingstoke, Hampshire RG21 6XS
and London
Companies and representatives
throughout the world

ISBN 0–333–63322–9 hardcover
ISBN 0–333–63323–7 paperback

A catalogue record for this book is available
from the British Library.

This book is printed on paper suitable for recycling and
made from fully managed and sustained forest sources.

10   9   8   7   6   5   4   3   2   1
07   06   05   04   03   02   01   00   99   98

Printed in Hong Kong

Published in the United States of America 1998 by
ST. MARTIN'S PRESS, INC.,
Scholarly and Reference Division
175 Fifth Avenue, New York, N.Y. 10010

ISBN 0–312–21032–9

To

Blake
Robert
Susanna
John

Contents

Preface

My aim in the book that follows is to inform those who are near the beginning of their Fielding studies and to engage readers among advanced students as well. Though not exhaustive, the biographical sketch I offer in the first and fourth chapters is meant to be thorough. My discussions of the plays, which are often unfamiliar even to specialists, are shaped to remind the reader of dramatic action at the same time providing contextual and formal commentary. Discussions of the novels and other prose fiction generally attempt to locate the works historically and to analyse some of the conjunctions of literary technique and content, Fielding's synergy of form and meaning. In addition, these chapters on the drama and prose fiction keep Fielding the man very much in sight. I hope my book may help readers to appreciate enough of Fielding's life, art and times to make the journey through it worthwhile.

In writing the following chapters, I incurred an enormous debt to Fielding scholarship, as a look at my notes will indicate. Without this authoritative silent assistance, I could not have completed the book.

I owe special thanks to Martin Battestin, William Appleton and John Richetti for reading early drafts of the major sections of the book. Professor Battestin helped me to improve the chapter on Fielding's life; Professor Appleton made useful comments on the chapter treating the eighteenth-century London theatre and Fielding's plays; and Professor Richetti suggested ways of revising the chapter on the novels. I am grateful for their help.

Finally, I wish to express deep appreciation to my wife, Judith Egan, for patiently reading the entire manuscript for clarity and consistency of style.

Errors of fact or judgment that may remain are, of course, mine alone.

HAROLD PAGLIARO

1

A Biographical Sketch, 1707–50

Henry Fielding was a man whose vital presence one can sense in his works but whose complex nature it is hard to synthesize. Tall and well built, strong-featured rather than conventionally handsome, he was sometimes a bully but more often an entertaining friend, whether in a grave or happy mood. He indulged his strong appetites for love, gaming, food, wine and snuff. He enjoyed success as a playwright of comedy, a theatre manager, a lawyer, a magistrate and a novelist; and he wrote extensively in several genres besides drama and prose fiction. He was passionate and gentle, conventionally 'masculine' and yet complex in his attitudes towards sex and gender, learned and down-to-earth, often in need of money and a spendthrift, highly sensitive to criticism from others and firm in his convictions, proud of his aristocratic ancestry and protective of the poor, in religion latitudinarian and intolerant of Catholics and Jews, sexually self-indulgent in his youth and a doting husband, brilliant both in rational discourse and in the dramatic art of burlesque, severe in his recommendations for criminal punishment and charitable as a magistrate. Fielding was above all deeply moral, believing that a compassionate human community, centred on loving marriage, was an ideal that should guide our actions. By and large, he lived according to his beliefs. But at times his own strong passions and appetites, which typically energized his principles, might undercut them, if only briefly. And at times the demands of the workaday world, in which we all struggle, showed him to be a pragmatist who acted without obvious reference to his deepest moral convictions. Though his vision of the world grew darker over the span of his relatively short life, it never overpowered his cherished belief in the fulfilment of a loving humanity. He rather modified the vision in the terms of loss owing to time's passage, and worse, what he found to be the unregenerate nature of too many among us. In all this, he enjoyed an essentially optimistic zest for life up to the end.

Fielding was born at Sharpham Park, near Glastonbury, in Somerset, on 22 April 1707. He was well connected on both sides. Through his father, Edmund Fielding, born in January 1679–80, a military man who rose to the rank of Lieutenant-General, Fielding was related to the Earls of Denbigh and Desmond.[1] The first were English, and the second Irish, peers, so that the extended family had interests in both countries. Edmund's father, John (1650–98), was the youngest son of George, Earl of Desmond; Edmund's uncle William (1640–85), John's oldest brother, was Earl of Denbigh. The Fieldings were descendants of an old family from Leicestershire and Warwickshire, who spelled the name Feilding. Owing to papers forged by Basil, 2nd Earl of Denbigh (*c.* 1608–75), later members of the family and the rest of the world mistakenly believed (until the late nineteenth century) that the Feildings were related to the Habsburgs of Germany. Fielding proudly used a seal that included their imperial eagle.[2] Fielding also enjoyed a more immediate sense of family pride. Among his paternal relatives was Lady Mary Wortley Montagu (1689–1762), daughter of Basil, 4th Earl of Denbigh, and grand-daughter of Edmund's uncle William, the 3rd Earl. Lady Mary was widely admired during her life for her intellectual independence and learning, and later for her Turkish Embassy Letters, published a year after her death, in 1763.[3] During his early days as dramatist, Fielding sought his older cousin's advice and support, which she willingly gave.

John, Fielding's paternal grandfather, like so many younger sons, entered the Church, and after his marriage to Dorothy Cockayne, moved to Dorset, in south-western England, where he and his wife reared a large family. John flourished in the Church, being first Vicar of St Mary's, Puddletown, which was a village four or five miles north-east of Dorchester, very close to Higher Bockhampton, Stinsford Parish, where the novelist of 'Wessex', Thomas Hardy, was to be born in 1840. Later, John became Prebendary of Salisbury, with multiple livings, and finally .Archdeacon of Dorset. His hopes for an Irish bishopric, realistic enough given his service in the Church and his family connections, were never fulfilled, and he lived out his life at Salisbury.

The Goulds, Fielding's mother's family, were substantial landowners in Somerset and Dorset. They included a wealthy London merchant, Richard Davidge, who was Fielding's great-grandfather, and several distinguished lawyers, chief among them Sir Henry Gould (1643–1710), Fielding's grandfather, who rose to become Judge of the King's Bench in 1699. Fielding's grandmother, Sarah, Richard Davidge's daughter, married Sir Henry in February 1676/7. Their daughter, also named Sarah (1682–1718), was Fielding's mother; it was probably in 1706 that she and Edmund Fielding were married, and without her family's consent, it seems. Where and how the couple lived for the first few years of their marriage is unknown. Though Edmund had been promoted to the rank of major, and was promoted rapidly thereafter, he was almost certainly short of money. Ultimately Sarah's parents helped them, Sir Henry providing Sarah with £3000 in trust for the purchase of an estate, which by the terms of his will was to be held in his daughter's sole possession. At this time at least, the Goulds had their doubts about Edmund. Shortly before he died in 1710, Sir Henry bought an estate for Sarah in East Stour, a few miles from Shaftesbury in Dorset, about 25 miles south-east of Sharpham Park as the crow flies. He paid £4750 for the property. But the two trustees of Sir Henry's estate, one of whom was Davidge, Sarah's brother, would allow only the allotted £3000 towards the purchase, with the result that Edmund had to make up the difference, for which he received title to a proportionate part of the estate.[4] Davidge himself, Sir Henry's only son, inherited Sharpham Park.

Wherever Edmund and his wife may have lived between the time of their marriage and their move to East Stour, Sarah returned to Sharpham Park to give birth to her first three children: Henry, the oldest (22 April 1707), and his sisters Catherine (1708) and Ursula (1709). It seems natural that the young Sarah, who may have had no settled household and whose husband was subject to military orders, should come to her mother and father at Sharpham for the lying-in. The ancient house itself had great character, and its setting was impressive. Fielding spent his very earliest years there, moving to the estate in East Stour in 1710. But he continued to see his grandmother, Sarah Gould, at Sharpham Park until she settled in Salisbury in 1719, after which time he visited her often in the cathedral city.[5]

Sharpham Park and its surroundings had a marked influence on Fielding, as we shall see. The estate had come into the family from Richard Davidge in 1657. From very early times until 1539, with the dissolution of the monasteries, Sharpham Park had been part of Glastonbury Abbey, legendary for its associations with Joseph of Arimathea, who is said to have come from the Holy Land, bringing relics, including the Grail, and establishing a religious society there shortly after the crucifixion. The Abbey was also associated with King Arthur, Glastonbury being another name for the Isle of Avalon where, according to one tradition, Arthur and Guinevere were buried, as the twelfth-century William of Malmesbury records.[6] Davidge acquired Sharpham Park from the Dyers, the family to which it had been granted by the Crown at the Dissolution. Though there had been a house at Sharpham Park from early times, it was elaborately rebuilt by Richard Beere, Glastonbury's distinguished Abbot from 1494 to 1524. 'Like other contemporary abbots Beere felt the need for a place of retreat not too far from the monastery . . . [The rebuilt house] remained intact after the Dissolution, but it was unfortunately completely refashioned in 1799.'[7] It is to date the centre of a working farm.

Fielding's biographers, Cross, Rogers and Battestin, all remark on the richness and beauty of his birthplace, which inded seems to have been chosen by some good angel for the author. The Abbey's ancient associations with Christianity – which include not only St Joseph, but St Patrick and other prominent church-men – and with King Arthur, Avalon and the Holy Grail make it an epitome of the England of legend.[8] A dramatic feature of this landscape, with its evocative history, is Glastonbury Tor, a majestic, lonely hill nearby; this is a place of worship dating probably from pre-Christian times and a hillfort from the Early and Middle Iron Ages to the sixth century AD.[9] St Michael's tower rises from the top of the Tor, a ruin in Fielding's day. It was restored in the late eighteenth century, as it had been many times before. Curiously enough the tower seems to rise higher when one views it from the flat land from which the Tor rises than it does from the top of the hill itself.

Below the Tor is Chalice Well, where the Holy Grail is said to have been buried. When King Henry's commissioners came to Glastonbury in 1539 to confiscate the Abbey and its land, they found the Abbot, Richard Whiting, at Sharpham Manor, where they questioned him about his loyalty to the Crown. Later, they carried him to London, to the Tower, for further interrogation. At first the intention seems to have been to charge him with treason, but for want of evidence it was decided, with unintended irony, to charge him instead with the robbery of many of the Abbey's valuables. He was tried at Wells, near Glastonbury, quickly found guilty by an intimidated jury, dragged on a hurdle up the Tor and hanged. Then he was beheaded and quartered, the head being placed over the gateway of the Abbey and the four parts displayed at Wells, Bath, Ilchester and Bridgwater.[10] Having survived civil and religious disputes over many centuries with Saxons, Danes and Normans, Glastonbury Abbey was finally taken by England's own king.

From the top of the Tor, about 500 feet (150m) above sea level, one may observe:

> just as Fielding had when a boy, the ruins of Glastonbury Abbey; on all sides he would have seen a landscape diversified by villages, hills, lawns, and woods; to the northwest the Mendip Hills, extending to Weston-super-Mare; to the westward the river Brue winding through distant meadows until it joins the Parret, the Quantock Hills with clouds trailing over them, and, if the day were clear, a wide sweep of the Bristol Channel, islands, and shipping even. It was Stert Island in Bridgewater Bay that closed the prospect, a short distance beyond where the united waters of the Brue and the Parret find their home. There on the slope of Tor Hill, Fielding placed the mansion of Squire Allworthy,[11]

master of Paradise-Hall in *Tom Jones*. To be sure he included a few of the features of other landscapes for his idealized setting, but the view of Glastonbury and its environs as seen from the Tor gave Fielding the essential Eden of his great novel.[12]

Unfortunately, we know very little directly about Fielding's boyhood.[13] There is evidence in the novels and elsewhere in his writings that he was deeply affected by the Dorset countryside in which he lived until he was sent to Eton in his twelfth year. In addition, we know just enough about his mother and father, his grandmother, Sarah Gould, and her sister, Mrs Cottington, Fielding's great-aunt, and about others who figured in his early life to speculate at least plausibly as to certain aspects of his boyhood temperament. His mother, who returned to Sharpham to deliver her first three children, and whose father bought the East Stour estate for her, was obviously close to her parents in ways that suggest she would herself have been a loving parent. Her first born, Henry, most probably enjoyed the nourishment and influence of her loving care, which is likely to have included in addition to warm affection a certain independence of spirit. After all, she was confident enough of her own judgment that she risked the consequences of marrying without her parents' consent, no slight matter for a woman of her class in eighteenth-century England.

The young mother had help in rearing her children: Anne Delaborde, a French governess hired especially to look after the girls, but whose spoken French may have provided the foundation for Fielding's later command of the language; Frances Barber, a nursery maid; and a staff of household servants, which Edmund and Sarah could not afford, but maintained nevertheless. Though Lady Gould and Mrs Cottington were not permanent residents at East Stour, they contributed their loving support to the Fielding household. With Edmund away much of the time, sometimes doing his job and sometimes enjoying himself as a man about town, Fielding was often surrounded by women and girls during the first eleven years of his life – mother, five sisters (Anne, aged three, died in 1716), governess, nursemaid, grandmother and great-aunt – until the last sibling, Edmund was born in April, 1716. And in fact he was reared in a largely female household until his protected childhood was cruelly ended with his mother's early death in April 1718.

Fielding's father, Edmund, was commissioned ensign in 1696, before fighting in the War of the League of Augsburg, 1689–97. During the early years of the War of the Spanish Succession (1701–13) he served with distinction under Marlborough, and took part in several actions, including the Battle of Blenheim in 1704, a resounding triumph for the allies. Edmund was a courageous soldier who seems to have been well regarded by his fellow officers. He was also a congenial man whom women found attractive, as he did them. Unfortunately, his inclination to live well kept him in debt most of his life. The expenses of the East Stour estate as Edmund ran it are not likely to have been covered by the small returns in rent. But they were nothing compared to his losses at the gaming table and, later, in 1720, in the South Sea venture, a joint-stock operation that failed. In addition, after the early years of his marriage, he enjoyed trips to London and elsewhere, which were one way and another costly.

Generally speaking, Edmund was an affable and fair-minded man, in some ways admirable. He was responsible and efficient in doing his work as a military officer, a rural justice of the peace, and acting-Governor of Jersey, for example. But he was often an absentee husband whose self-indulgence must have left his wife feeling uncertain about their financial security and about his marital fidelity as well. His son must also have experienced this neglect. We have good evidence that shortly after the death of his mother, when he was eleven, Fielding was wilful and uncontrollable, full of overtly expressed resentment for authority. Generally amiable and friendly, he was to be passionate about many things all of his life, sometimes losing his temper when he might have curbed it. Nevertheless, his rebellious state of mind following his mother's death was especially intense. Apart from the terrible loss itself, it may have owed something to his place in a household of younger girls and older women, who seem to have spoiled and encouraged him to behave as he would. And it must have owed something as well to Edmund's infrequent paternal presence and his questionable behaviour, as husband and financial manager, the effects of which Fielding would have experienced at least obliquely. But his rebelliousness was brought to full expression by his father's remarriage within ten months or so of his mother's death.

It was not only the haste of the second marriage that brought things to a crisis. The household at East Stour heard that the new Mrs Edmund Fielding, Anne Rapha, a widow, was an Italian who had kept an eating house in London, and that she and the children of her previous marriage were Papists. Anne was indeed a Roman Catholic, but she was not Italian, and neither had she kept an eating house. A short time later, in May, Mrs Cottington, who had been taking care of all the Fielding children since their father's departure for London some months earlier, was informed by Edmund that he and Anne were soon to move to the East Stour residence. Angry that Edmund could so soon have forgotten her beloved niece Sarah, and concerned that the Catholic step-mother would impose her religion on the children, Mrs Cottington predicted the worst to them and encouraged rebellion. Bad days followed the arrival of the newlyweds, but things were for a time patched up by Edmund's decision to move to London, after sending his oldest son, Henry, to Eton, and arranging for his daughters and their brother Edmund to live with their grandmother in Salisbury where she had taken a house. Edmund no doubt loved his children but, after a brief trial at East Stour, he seems to have wanted to begin his new marriage unencumbered by them.

We would be left to guess how the young Henry Fielding behaved during this period of upheaval were it not for the court records of a suit and countersuit. The first was an action brought by Lady Gould against Edmund, arguing, in the strongest terms, for her custody of the children and for the children's right to the remainder of the estate at East Stour, by alleging their father's bad behaviour, including his appropriation of income from the East Stour farms. The second was a complaint by Edmund against Lady Gould, in which he disavowed her various charges of culpable and irresponsible behaviour. Hearings and other procedures dragged on for more than a year. Meanwhile, Edmund sought and failed to regain custody of his children, and Fielding ran away from Eton to his grandmother's, though whether of his own accord or prompted by her is uncertain. In either case, he and the other children were caught up in the complex dispute in immediate ways. Eventually, Chancery decided in favour of Lady Gould, awarding her and other trustees control of the children and of the East Stour estate. Though the matter was thus settled legally, its emotional currents continued to be felt.

When witnesses for the two sides testified they inevitably contradicted each other, but their statements make it clear that young Fielding was deeply affected by the recriminations that intensified, in a public forum, the family's already irrevocable division, even though he had by then chosen his grandmother over his father. His behaviour during this period was outrageous. It seems hardly surprising that he was said to be 'very much subject to passion'. But several of his actions indicate an unusual loss of self-control. In a letter to his grandmother, he refers to his baby brother Edmund as a 'shitten brat'. It was said of him during this same period that he 'spit in the servants' faces'; he was said also to be 'guilty of committing some indecent actions with his sister Beatrice', not yet five years old. It appears that he and his favourite sister Sarah also experienced an incestuous connection of some sort.[14]

Apart from Fielding's use, in *Tom Jones*, of the Somerset and Dorset countryside in which he spent his earliest years, a few indications about his early education before he left East Stour for Eton, and a sketchy knowledge of his family, we know nothing much about the young Fielding until he emerges in the court records, full of overwrought vitality owing to the family troubles, beginning with his mother's death. We can hardly overlook this first living glimpse of the boy, but it should not lead us to excessive conclusions. Hyper-reactions like Fielding's in this instance are no doubt revealing, and they may even be in some sense representative. But they are likely to be radically modified over the long run, especially in capacious minds like his.

There is good reason to believe that Fielding had a sensitive and passionate nature. His contemporaries tell us he felt things keenly. He also had an eruptive temper, which more than once resulted in brawls with other men. But we are much less certain about his moderating tendencies. How did 'charity' or 'objectivity' or 'introspection' or time modify his passionate side? There are no definite answers to these important questions, but we can accumulate information and opinion about Fielding that contribute to our sense of the man. For example, Arthur Murphy, his first biographer, makes suggestions about certain of his capacities and attitudes, telling us that Fielding was shrewd in judging other people, contemptuous of 'the understandings of the generality of mankind', full of the knowledge of life, hard-working and hard-drinking, and capable of imagining (of becoming?) that ideal combination: the good man (having 'benevolence, honour, honesty, and charity') and the great man (endowed with 'parts and courage').[15] Without believing Murphy entirely, we can keep what he says alive in our minds, ready to have it modified or reinforced by other evidence.

Fielding's plays and novels are hardly precise mirrors of his life, but their treatment of certain subjects and themes is suggestive. In the plays, for instance, Fielding's rebellious sons (in some sense like himself?) are routinely preferred to self-indulgent or tyrannical fathers, like Young Wilding in *The Temple Beau*. (Incidentally, so are Fielding's rebellious daughters.) But then Wilding's father turns out to be a good-natured man, and in fact Fielding's plays and novels generally include loving and indulgent, as well as selfish and tyrannical, fathers. Does this balanced treatment imply Fielding's balanced view of his own father? Tom Jones (like Fielding himself?) is a sympathetically treated young hero who is passionate and headstrong, and yet loving, honest, steadfast, and morally sound in the long run. But Fielding also invents less intense male characters, who are likeable, if not as sympathetic as Tom: for example, Merital, Malvil and Wisemore, also in *The Temple Beau*, his very first play. Does the range of his sympathetic male characters imply that Fielding's imagination is generous, and not confined to self? As playwright and novelist, Fielding often uses incest to complicate the development of plot and character, as in *The Wedding-Day*, *Rape upon Rape*, *Joseph Andrews*, *Tom Jones* and (only briefly and implicitly) in *Amelia*. In these works, incest surprises us by its unforeshadowed appearance, survives (or is recollected) briefly as a dreaded threat, and then takes its place among unfulfilled possibilities. Does Fielding's frequent use of the subject suggest both his fascination with it and his unconscious need to make it no more than an inevitable and yet harmless aspect of human relations? Even without definite answers, these questions enrich our knowledge of the man.

Fielding's solid grounding in Greek and Latin and his love of classical literature probably had their real beginnings at Eton, where he was a student from 1719 to perhaps 1724. But before then, he is said to have begun to learn Latin from John Oliver, curate of St Mary's, Motcombe, who travelled the three or four miles to his pupil in East Stour several times a week. Murphy had taken Oliver to be the model for the gross Parson Trulliber of Fielding's *Joseph Andrews*. But Cross and Battestin point out that the 'sensible clergyman of the same name who in *Shamela* (1741) exposes the true character of Richardson's celebrated heroine' is a much more likely characterization of Fielding's first teacher.[16] Fielding's mastery of the classical languages, which he displayed without show during his life as an author, and his rapid advancement in the study of the law during his years in the Middle Temple, suggest that he was an apt pupil from the beginning. He seems to have concentrated his tremendous energy in the activity of the moment, whether at work or play. Later, as an author, his rapid composition would reflect the same concentration.

Though Fielding's marble bust is on display at Eton, along with busts of other illustrious Etonians, like Thomas Gray and Robert Walpole, the college records tell us very little about his student days there.[17] Just across the Thames from Windsor Castle, Eton was established by Henry VI in 1440, a collegiate church dedicated to religion and education. Henry's aims included the education of 'poor and indigent' scholars at the expense of the foundation, with the best students among them to be granted scholarships to King's College, Cambridge. In addition to these Collegers – scholars on the foundation – there were other students known as 'commensales' who, as their name suggests, took their meals in the Hall. In accordance with Henry's intention, they received free tuition, but otherwise paid their own expenses, for food, lodging and other items.[18] Over time, as the total number of College scholars and non-College students grew, so that all could not eat together, many of those living in town rather than at the College took their meals at inns and boarding houses. More accurately identified as Townies rather than as Messmates (commensales), they were known as 'oppidans', those who live in the town. Fielding was among these, an oppidan.

Unfortunately we have only a few direct references to his Eton days, chief among them being the Chancery records, telling us when he arrived and when he ran away, and a few comments from his father about the cost of Fielding's education there. Edmund says it cost him £60 to £70 a year to keep his son at Eton.[19] That would have included lodging, board, tuition and other expenses. Maxwell Lyte gives us a list of a half-year's expenses at Eton in 1719 for William Pitt, Fielding's contemporary at the College. It comes to a few pence over £29. Another of Pitt's half-yearly bills, dated 1723, totals almost exactly the same amount.[20] If Edmund did not exaggerate what he laid out for his son, we may suppose Fielding lived quite well in the town, spending at least as much as his classmate, Pitt, and probably more. The conclusion sorts well with what we know of Fielding's lifelong habit of letting money run through his fingers.

Though we have no exact information about the Eton curriculum during Fielding's years at the school, we know that it was intended primarily to teach the religion of the Church of England and the classical languages and literatures of Latin and Greek. In addition, we can with some assurance infer its general content by comparing William Malim's *Consuetudinarium* (1560), which includes the daily routine of school life at the time, with a document covering more or less the same ground, drawn up over 200 years later, between 1768 and 1775, by Thomas James, an Etonian who later became Headmaster of Rugby.[21] In the sixteenth century, besides religion, Etonians studied – roughly in the following order, from the First through to the Sixth Forms –

Cato, Vives (the Spanish classicist), Terence, Lucian and Aesop
(not in Greek, but in Latin translation), Cicero's epistles, Ovid's
Tristia, the epigrams of Catullus and Martial and Sir Thomas
Moore, Ovid's *Metamorphoses*, Horace, Caesar's *Commentaries*,
Cicero's *de Officiis* and *de Amicitia*, Virgil, Lucan and Greek grammar. The curriculum was almost exclusively classical, devoted
not quite entirely to Latin literature. Greek was introduced late,
and at first only the grammar was studied. Its gradually enlarg-
ing place in the Eton curriculum owes much to the early seventeenth-century interest in Greek religious texts. In fact, the first
publications of the Eton press were small books in Greek, followed by an edition of the works of St John Chrysostom, in eight
volumes, 1610–13.[22]

From Thomas James, we learn that during the second half of
the eighteenth century the curriculum was still heavily classical.
But Greek grammar was introduced in the Second Form, Church
Catechism in Latin in the Second, and Greek Testament in the
Fourth. The Fifth and Sixth Forms included Geography, Algebra
and Euclid. The classical literature, much of it the same as in
Malim's day, covered more Greek authors; in addition to Virgil,
Horace and Ovid, the Upper School read Homer, Lucian, the
Greek Testament and Aristophanes. In both the sixteenth and
eighteenth centuries, Latin composition, in verse and prose, was
part of the daily routine. By the eighteenth century students were
able to read Greek, and they were expected to model Greek iambics
as well.[23] Though Murphy had no first-hand information about
Fielding's learning at Eton, he offers a traditional view to which
Fielding's later work gives credence:

> At this great seminary of education, Henry Fielding gave dis-
> tinguishing proofs of strong and peculiar parts; and when he
> left the place, he was said to be uncommonly versed in the
> Greek authors, and an early master of the Latin classics; for
> both which he retained a strong admiration in all the subsequent
> passages of his life.[24]

Work was demanding, and corporal punishment was still usual,
both for violation of school rules and for careless scholarship.
Later, in his characterizations of Thwackum (*Tom Jones*, III, v)
and Roger Strap (*The Jacobite's Journal*, 7 May 1748), Fielding
satirized cruel masters who lash students with the birch rod.[25]

He himself had experienced their harsh treatment. But there were good times too. According to the report by Thomas James, Monday, Wednesday and Friday were full school days, but Tuesday was a full holiday, Thursday a half holiday, and Saturday a holiday after four o'clock.

In his last months at Eton, Fielding must have been a strong young male on the verge of manhood, full of energy and spirit. He might have spent his free time at one of the many activities the Eton boys enjoyed, including cricket, battledores, football and swimming, or he might have gone to the pony races in South Meadow on the College property, or to the Christopher, a house where the boys drank punch.[26] And given the command of classical, French and English literature evidenced in his plays and essays only a few years after his Eton days, one may well suppose that he spent much of his free time reading.

William Pitt and George Lyttelton were at Eton during Fielding's time, but we do not know how close he was to them at school. We may surmise from his later friendship and his loyalty to their political ideology when they entered the House of Commons, in 1735, that they had all been friends at Eton; although the college connection itself may have been reason enough for supporting their position in some of his very late plays, like *Eurydice Hiss'd* and *The Historical Register for the Year 1736*, and in other writing as well. Another point is that Fielding would have recognized that writing in support of his friends' policies was a way to earn a living. But in addition to friendship, the old school tie and money as reasons for supporting their Broad-Bottom politics, one may understand that Fielding found their political position itself congenial, recognizing as it did that Whigs and Tories (and their factions) were alike corrupt in their everlasting scramble for power and that a dispassionate address to issues could alone improve government.[27] For Fielding such a view would have been realistically constructive – the only possible way, however unlikely of accomplishment – rather than hopefully idealistic. The distinction says a good deal about how his mind worked.

He liked to think of himself as a comedian in the tradition of Lucian, Cervantes and Swift, whose primary role, Fielding said, had been to instruct, not to divert.[28] He cherished this high sense of purpose throughout his career as playwright, and with some justice. To what extent he took this sense from Eton, we cannot know. The school had shown a deep interest in comedy from early times. Fielding could not have known that Nicholas Udall, Headmaster, 1534–41(?), had written the earliest English comedy now extant, *Ralph Roister Doister*, which was performed there.[29] But he would have experienced Eton's keen interest in theatricals, which the boys, sometimes helped by their teachers, produced not only in Long Chamber, on the school grounds, but also at the boarding houses, where the oppidans lived.[30]

Unlike Gray, whose long correspondence with fellow Etonians and whose 'Ode on a Distant Prospect of Eton College' commemorate his attachment to the school, Fielding leaves us to guess about what Eton meant to him. But we can be sure from his works that he carried a great deal of learning when he left, and he enjoyed using it for the rest of his life. Though he disliked Eton's formidable disciplinary authority, he was obviously able to manage it, or he could not have flourished as a student there. His self-control at school must have been better than it had been during the period following his mother's death and his father's remarriage.

After Eton, Fielding did not return to his grandmother's home in Salisbury, though he was still under her care legally, and he visited her often. He seems to have gone to London where, upon witnessing the execution of Jonathan Wild by hanging, on 24 May 1725, he 'was shock'd at the Barbarity of the Populace'.[31] Wild's criminal life was to become the subject of Fielding's narrative of the underworld, *The Life of Mr. Jonathan Wild the Great* (1743). Though Fielding may have stayed in London long enough to spend some time with his father, his official place of residence by the summer of 1725 was a house rented for him by Edmund, in Upton Grey, Hampshire. Why Edmund chose to send his son to the north-eastern edge of the Hampshire Downs we can only guess. In a poem he wrote in 1728, 'A Description of U—n G—, (alias New Hog's Norton) in Com. Hants.', Fielding makes it plain that he did not like the place.[32] Apart from the title itself, any number of the poem's 50-odd lines tell the story. As Alexis, Fielding woos Rosalinda: 'In such a place how can *Alexis* sing?/ An Air ne'er beaten by the Muse's wing!/In such a Place what subject can appear?/What not unworthy *Rosalinda's* ear?' (ll. 11–14). Such depreciation of Upton Grey might have been only conventional, but in the title and elsewhere in the poem, Fielding's voice is pointedly mischievous: 'On the House-Side a Garden may be seen,/Which Docks and Nettles keep forever green' (ll. 29–30).

Though some Rosalinda may have distracted his mind from his dislike of Upton Grey, she must have done so only fleetingly. For by September 1725 Fielding, with a man servant, was in the Dorset coastal town of Lyme Regis, a picturesque village sloping to the sea, in pursuit of a young heiress, Sarah Andrews, his cousin by marriage. Her father, a wealthy merchant and landowner, had died when she was not three years old, and her mother soon remarried. Chancery placed Sarah under the guardianship of Andrew Tucker, her uncle by marriage, with whom she lived in Lyme Regis. Fielding's interest in her was intense, and he wanted to marry her. She was not only rich, but good-looking. Unfortunately, her uncle had other views: he wanted his son to marry Sarah.

Things got out of hand, probably because of Fielding's impetuosity. When Sarah's guardian made it clear he was not to court the young beauty, Fielding tried to abduct her on the way to church one Sunday, but he did not succeed. Battestin reports that records of the Lyme corporation show that before matters had thus come to a head, Andrew Tucker had appeared before the Mayor 'and solemnly declared on his oath that he is in fear of his life or of some bodily hurt to be done or to be procured to be done to him by Henry ffielding Gent'.[33] Maybe Tucker accused Fielding falsely, but it is not unlikely that his tempestuous nature got the better of him as it had with at least two others during 1725.[34]

Having written and posted a parting insult to the Tuckers, Fielding left Lyme Regis on the Monday following his failed abduction. That was the end of his affair with Sarah, who was married the following year, though not to her cousin John Tucker. Tradition has it that she never forgot the depth of Fielding's love for her. What he may have felt at the loss we are left to imagine, though probably his crude imitation of part of Juvenal's *Sixth*, an angry satire against women which dates from this period, expresses some of his frustration. It seems clear that if he was able to master his dislike of punitive authority at Eton well enough to become an accomplished student, he did not yet know how to control himself in matters of the heart.

We know little of Fielding's whereabouts between the time of his departure from Lyme Regis and the spring of 1727, when he is known to have been in London. He spent the next ten years there working chiefly as a playwright, with one notable interruption abroad and several longish periods on the farm in East Stour, after his marriage.[35] On 16 February 1728, his first play, *Love in Several Masques*, was performed for the first time, having been accepted the previous year. It was unusual to say the least that an unknown playwright, only twenty years old, should have had a play produced by one of the great patent theatres, Drury Lane. Fielding seems to have taken his good fortune in stride, probably regarding himself at the time as a gentleman amateur of drama, and not as a professional playwright.[36] Certainly he left London just when things seemed to be going his way. About six weeks after his first play was staged, Fielding registered at the University of Leiden, in Holland, as a student of literature, where he probably continued his classical studies, chiefly Latin. His stay at Leiden, from March 1728 to April 1729, was broken by a visit to England, from the summer through to the early winter of 1728, and he may have ended his time abroad with a tour of France and Italy for three or four months after he left the university.[37]

He probably returned to London by September 1729, in time for the beginning of the new theatre season. If indeed he left for the continent thinking of himself as a gentleman amateur, he must have come back to England with other ideas, for he brought with him portions of two new plays he had been working on, *Don Quixote in England* and *The Wedding-Day*. He was soon to establish himself in London as a dramatist, but also as a poet and as a prose essayist who might argue in a partisan way for a price. By the mid-1730s he had become his own theatre manager. During his very early years in London, he was very likely a libertine lover; and he enjoyed food, wine and night-time conversation both then and for the rest of his life. By the time he married in November 1734, he had cultivated a wide social acquaintance among men and women in varied walks of life, and he had made a reputation as a playwright and, less publicly, as an essayist who wrote on political and literary subjects.

It is well to recall his extreme youth when this rich decade of his life began. In some degree it extenuates his high living during the period: wine, women, gaming and late hours. But it also leaves us having to acknowledge a remarkable self-discipline, energy and maturity in one so young. By 1737, he had become the most productive and successful living playwright of the day. His audiences found many of his plays, especially his burlesques and topical political satires, highly entertaining. And certain of his essays, sometimes published anonymously but recognized by insiders as his, helped to make his satirical voice a matter to be reckoned with.[38]

During this first period of Fielding's adult life, he had to cope with the fact that his father was unable to support him in a way the eldest son of an aristocratic family might expect. Eighteenth-century society was so ordered that, generally speaking, one succeeded only through family influence or the influence of a patron, or both. The very fact that Fielding was well connected helped him, no doubt, but in a very real sense he had to make his own way. Even though he struggled to earn a living, he was ambitious to succeed on his own terms, as the author of sophisticated conventional comedies and as an independent-minded essayist. But he also recognized the need to write plays his audiences would pay to see, and essays partisan editors and publishers would buy or commission. Always an idealist at heart and a pragmatist in dealing with the world of circumstance, he managed with few exceptions to accommodate the distance between his own strong preferences and sheer necessity without real loss of principle. With rare exceptions, his voice was his own, even when he wrote with the market in view. His unique exuberance left its mark on almost all his work. He must have enjoyed making the world take notice. Even when he experienced failure, his spirits were never damped for long. Though Murphy did not meet Fielding until much later than these early years, what he says of him shortly after the return from Leiden suggests a vitality that sounds right: 'The brilliancy of his wit, the vivacity of his humour, and his high relish of social enjoyment, soon brought him into high request with the men of taste and literature.'[39]

As Fielding worked to establish himself, he tried his hand at several kinds of writing, and he sought preferment in several places. No doubt in an attempt to get his first play, *Love in Several Masques*, accepted, he was in touch with Lady Mary, probably some time in 1727, to ask her advice. (I discuss the remarkable acceptance of the twenty-year-old's play by the managers at the Theatre Royal, Drury Lane, in the next chapter.) In the same year, hoping to win favour, he also wrote two poems that have survived only as titles. Both celebrate George II, his coronation on 11 October, and his birthday, 30 October: 'The Coronation. A

Poem. And an Ode on the Birthday. By Mr. Fielding'.[40] In 1728,
Fielding's *The Masquerade, a Poem* was published; it was a satire
on balls, masquerades, and other ruling pleasures of the town.
In 1729, he wrote over 500 lines of an unfinished epic burlesque,
modelled on *The Dunciad*, satirizing Alexander Pope, apparently
to satisfy Lady Mary, by then Pope's enemy. Nevertheless the
lines are full of vitality. The young Fielding clearly relished his
own literary powers.

The attack on Pope includes hits at both his poetic art (perhaps more to please his cousin than himself) and his politics.
Pope was in sentiment a conservative, but in no political sense a
Tory; Fielding was a Whig, though often enough in opposition
to Walpole's policies.[41] But Fielding was an anti-Scriblerian only
in his choice of target in these verses. Like Pope, Swift and other
members of the Scriblerus Club, he was a traditionalist in taste
and learning; an Ancient, not a Modern. When he brought out
the printed version of his play *The Author's Farce* (1730), he
attributed it to 'Scriblerus Secundus', as if aligning himself with
the Scriblerians. Earlier, he had mischievously implied a literary
kinship with Swift, claiming that 'Lemuel Gulliver, Poet Laureat
to the King of Lilliput', was the author of *The Masquerade*. Indeed,
as Fielding grew older, he became increasingly conservative,
though never without a freshness of perspective that kept clear
of fixed positions.

Before he reached the age of 27, he had written 17 plays besides
Love in Several Masques, including short burlesques staged after
the mainpiece on the evening's programme: *Don Quixote in England*
(1728; not staged until 1734); *The Wedding-day* (1729; staged in
1743); *The Temple Beau* (1730); *The Author's Farce* (1730); *Tom Thumb*
(1730); *Rape upon Rape* (1730); *The Modern Husband* (1730); *The
Letter-Writers* (1731); *The Tragedy of Tragedies* (1731); *The Welsh
Opera* (1731); *The Grub-Street Opera* (written in 1731, but not performed); *The Lottery* (1732); *The Old Debauchees* (1732); *The Covent-
Garden Tragedy* (1732); *The Mock Doctor* (1732); *The Universal Gallant*
(written in 1733, staged in 1735); and *Deborah* (1733, lost).[42]

As I mentioned earlier, Fielding was also busy in other ways;
he wrote poems and essays, and he sought preferment. He was
probably the author of 'The Norfolk Lanthorn' (1728), a ballad
in triplets, and of three essays – 'On the Benefit of Laughing'
(1728), 'The Physiognomist' (1730), and 'On Hunters and Politicians' (1730) – all of which satirized Walpole.[43] Yet during this

time, he appeared at the minister's levee, asking for favours; and he dedicated a play to him, *The Modern Husband* (1732), in fulsome terms. By the end of 1733, he had also written 'An Epistle to Mr Lyttleton occasioned by two Lines in Mr Pope's Paraphrase on the first Satire of the 2d Book of Horace' (published by Isobel Grundy in 1972), in which he takes issue with Pope's attack on Lady Mary in firm but moderate terms. (Fielding's moderation must have owed something to his respect for his fellow-Etonian Lyttelton, who was a friend of Pope's.)[44]

During this period, Fielding also wrote epilogues to three plays: *Orestes* (1731), by Lewis Theobald, Pope's original Prince of Dullness; *The Modish Couple* (1732), by James Miller, over which the court and the opposition took sides furiously; and *Caelia: or, The Perjur'd Lover* (1732), by Charles Johnson, which closed on opening night. In addition, he wrote 'A Dialogue between a Beau's Head and His Heels', ten quatrains for a rollicking nonsense song, in the first of which Head says to Heels,

> Ye indolent Dogs! do you dare to refuse
> So little a Walk, in a new Pair of Shoes?
> My legs too, methinks, might have gratefully gone,
> Since a new Pair of Calves I this Morning put on.
>   Fa, la, la, la, &c.[45]

With all this activity, which besides writing included getting his plays produced (and his plays and other work published), rehearsing and revising, we are left to wonder how he had time to burn the candle at both ends as he did, especially given that he eventually became his own producer and theatre manager. He must have slept short hours and written at high speed. Murphy may exaggerate only slightly when he says of Fielding's short pieces for the theatre, 'They were generally the production of two or three mornings, so great was his facility in writing.'[46] Despite a growing reputation, his early efforts to find support from a patron came to nothing, except for Lady Mary's continued interest in him.

In the early 1730s, after the season ended, Fielding would leave London, often returning to Salisbury, East Stour and other West Country places, where he saw family, met old friends, and made new ones. Salisbury, Wiltshire's county seat, famous for its thirteenth-century cathedral (the tallest in England), was then and is still a handsome little city. It was a second home to Fielding. There, his paternal grandfather, John, had lived within the Cathedral Close until he died, about ten years before Fielding's birth. And his grandmother had lived in Salisbury since his Eton days, and so did the woman he was to marry, Charlotte Cradock. Though Fielding knew Charlotte by 1730, he had not yet fixed his attention on her. He seems at first to have been equally friendly with her sister Catherine, and he flirted with other Salisbury beauties as well. In 1732, he was in love with 'D W', the Dorinda he refers to in the early lines of 'An Epistle to Mr Lyttleton'. But she refused him, leaving him deeply disappointed.[47] Just when he turned to Charlotte, apparently preferring her to her sister, we do not know. Both of the Cradock women were said to be attractive, though soon after 1730 Charlotte was injured when a carriage overturned; the accident left her nose scarred after surgery. Fielding's choice of Charlotte as the model for his heroines Sophia Western, as he tells us in *Tom Jones* (IV, ii), and for Amelia Booth as well (*Amelia*, XI, i), makes it clear that the injury did not mar her beauty for him. The couple were married in Charlcombe near Bath on 28 November 1734, away from Salisbury, perhaps because Charlotte's mother was staying at Bath for her health at the time.[48] The bride brought with her a dowry 'which did not exceed fifteen hundred pounds'.[49] And when Mrs Cradock died, in 1735, Charlotte inherited everything else her mother had, Catherine having been cut off with next to nothing for reasons we do not know. Neither do we know the value of the mother's estate, though whatever its size it would not have been enough for Fielding.[50]

The Fieldings' marriage was both very happy and very sad. The two young people loved and admired each other, and they enjoyed each other's company. But Fielding cannot have been easy to live with. Apart from his lavish spending, which often left them desperate for money, he drank hard and he sniffed tobacco (or sometimes chewed it). As Rogers says, 'His character was lovable but his habits were probably irritating in the extreme; he led not the calm and genteel existence of an Edwardian man of letters, but the hectic routine of a resident house-dramatist.'[51] One hopes that he moderated his habits for Charlotte's sake.

They had at least three, and probably five, children. The three of which we are certain are Charlotte, born 1736, Henry, born 1741–42, and Henrietta Eleanor, born 1743.[52] It is likely that the

Fieldings had two other daughters, Penelope, born 1737–39 and Katherine, born 1738–40.[53] Of the five, only Henrietta Eleanor (Fielding called her Harriet) survived to adulthood, and she lived only four months after her marriage on 26 August 1766.[54] Charlotte and Henry were indeed unfortunate parents, and both felt the losses of their children keenly. Murphy seems right in saying of Fielding the husband and father, 'Though disposed to gallantry by his strong animal spirits, and the vivacity of his passions, he was remarkable for tenderness and constancy to his wife, and the strongest affection for his children.'[55]

They had endless money troubles. Despite Charlotte's dowry and inheritance and Fielding's income, principally from the theatre until 1737, and then from other writing, to which was added support from friends in the government's opposition, the Fieldings were always in debt. A good deal of money passed through Henry's hands. It came in at no even rate, which would have been reason enough to make a plan for living systematically within his means. But he never did so. No doubt his family suffered as a result, but we can only guess what Charlotte may have felt or said.

Their marriage was to last only ten years. By 1741, Charlotte was ill, probably with consumption. Fielding was deeply concerned for her over the remaining three years of her life, during which time she seemed to improve and then lose ground. They continued to be very close, as they had been from the beginning. Once, two years before her death, he left her in Bath, where they were living at the time (1742), to go to Bristol on legal business. He had been gone for over a week when a letter from his good friend James Harris arrived at the Bath residence. Using it as an excuse for a visit, Charlotte carried the letter to Bristol. In his reply to Harris, Fielding expresses his overwhelming joy at seeing her.[56] By 1744, Charlotte's condition had become acute:

> To see her daily languishing and wearing away before his eyes, was too much for a man of his strong sensations; the fortitude of mind, with which he met all the other calamities of life, deserted him on this most trying occasion; and her death . . . brought on such a vehemence of grief, that his friends began to think him in danger of losing his reason.[57]

But he tried to help himself by seeking the company of friends and of his sister Sarah.[58] It was like him to find consolation in the society of others and in his own sense of his great loss, rather than in the comforts of religion.

Almost from the time their marriage began, Fielding's professional life required his rapid accommodation to new circumstances. In 1734, prior to his wedding day in November, three of his plays were performed: a revised version of *The Author's Farce* (15 January), *The Intriguing Chambermaid* (also 15 January), and *Don Quixote in England* (15 April). Of these, only *The Intriguing Chambermaid* was a real success.[59] For some time thereafter, Fielding's dramatic career was marked by various uncertainties. The Drury Lane management had gone through difficult changes, there had been a war between actors and management, and the patent theatres had became less and less interested in mounting new plays, which were expensive and risky. They preferred successful old plays, with which the actors were already familiar. Though Fielding's *An Old Man Taught Wisdom*, a new ballad farce staged at Drury Lane as an afterpiece on 6 January 1735, was a success, his future as a dramatist was to take him in new directions. He was without a sure connection in any established theatre, and worse, a play for which he had high expectations, *The Universal Gallant*, staged on 10 February 1735, proved to be a devastating failure.[60]

When Fielding published *The Intriguing Chambermaid* on 15 January 1734, he included with it a complimentary poem said to have been sent to him by an unknown hand; the unknown poet expresses the wish that Walpole, 'Studious still of *Britain's* Fame', will reward Fielding.[61] But like the dedication to *The Modern Husband* two years before, this second broad hint did not dispose Walpole to help. Two months later, in a political shift (at least in the object of his pleas for assistance if not in his private convictions), Fielding dedicated *Don Quixote in England* to a prominent opposition member recently dismissed from the government by Walpole: Philip Dormer Stanhope, 4th Earl of Chesterfield.

At about the same time Fielding apparently began to make anonymous contributions to *The Craftsman*, the opposition's chief serial publication. But it is hard to gauge the significance of this change of position. Battestin argues that in 1734 Fielding began a more or less systematic support of the opposition, much of it accomplished by satires on the government and on Walpole himself.[62] His view rests to a considerable extent on attributions to Fielding of Letters to *The Craftsman* from 1734 to 1739.[63] But

Fielding's partisan (as distinct from his merely political plays) date from a somewhat later time, 1736, according to Goldgar and Hume.[64] Though Battestin and Hume are not quite agreed as to the date of Fielding's political shift, they agree that it was emphatic and that it was not irrevocable: good feelings (perhaps only a willingness to mollify each other) survived between Fielding and Walpole. Some time between 1741 and 1743, Walpole subscribed to Fielding's *Miscellanies*, buying ten sets at a cost of twenty guineas, an apparently generous act.[65] And Fielding, in 1754, in *The Journal of a Voyage to Lisbon*, says Walpole was 'one of the best of men and of ministers'.[66]

Fielding's effective absence from the theatre (probably from March to December of 1735), his return to the city for the season of 1735–6, and his political alignment with the opposition may have had more to do with conditions of the London stage in the mid-1730s than with politics, though it would be wrong to suppose that his new position was hypocritically or cynically maintained. He had Eton friends who were coming to the fore in what was known as the Broad-Bottom movement of the opposition, especially George Lyttelton and William Pitt.[67] Fielding was loyal to them, and he found their ideas congenial. But there were other considerations. In 1733 and 1734, the London theatre had changed radically (for a variety of reasons), and Fielding, who had until then done well at Drury Lane and the other major houses, lost his venue. Just how he went about planning his next move we shall probably never know. Hume conjectures that when he returned to London in the winter of 1735–6, he tried the established theatres once more, and when he was turned down, decided (probably step by step) to become his own theatre manager at the offbeat Little Haymarket.[68] There, for two seasons, he wrote and produced partisan burlesques and topical satires that were enormously popular. These include *Pasquin* and *Tumble-Down Dick* in 1736, and *Eurydice*, *The Historical Register for the Year 1736*, and *Eurydice Hiss'd* in 1737.

These plays were in varying degrees anti-ministerial, as the next chapter makes clear. Fielding was no doubt serious about their political content, but their comic vitality, which made them successful and helped his friends in the opposition, must have given him great satisfaction. Though he probably never gave up the idea that he would write traditional five-act comedies, he had really discovered his greatest talent: writing and producing burlesque and topical satires. These were all exciting original pieces, and they earned him money and reputation. Fielding's luck had taken a turn for the better.

In early 1737, his horizon was looking bright indeed. He even began to think of building his own theatre, but later decided to renovate the Little Haymarket instead.[69] Unfortunately for him, Walpole for several years had been sympathetic to legislation that would give him control of the stage, by limiting the number of theatres and by requiring the censorship of plays. Fielding must have been aware of the minister's aims, but their formal defeat, in 1735, may have led him to misread what was a continuing danger.[70] The unfortunate fact is that Walpole got his way with the passage of the Licensing Act, in 1737, which accomplished both his purposes.[71] Having achieved a unique theatrical success, Fielding was denied any real chance of its continuing.

He was by no means the only playwright whose work had offended Walpole's government. 'Between the end of January and late May [1737], approximately 100 performances of plays openly hostile to the ministry were staged at three of London's four theatres – an average of nearly one a night.'[72] Nevertheless, Fielding's popular success, the bite of his inventive satire, and his known speed of composition and production probably made him the greatest threat in Walpole's eyes.[73] Whatever the case, government censorship effectively stopped him from producing his most successful kind of play, and he was denied access to the Little Haymarket. He might have changed the nature of his dramatic career and carried on in the theatre, but he decided against that course. In May 1737, when he was 30 years old, he looked in another direction.

Though Fielding was to continue writing almost to the day he died, and to gain greater fame for his novels than for his plays, his publications never brought in enough money to support himself and his family, in part at least because he spent more than he had. In this habit he was unthinking; not so much selfish as generous to a fault. But he always felt the need for money. It was probably this uncertainty that made him decide on a career in the law, though part of the reason may well have been the prestige of the legal profession, reinforced by his pride in the Gould tradition: his maternal grandfather and his uncle became distinguished lawyers, and his cousin Henry was also on the way to a successful career. Two other cousins were also lawyers, in the Middle Temple, like all the Goulds in the profession. On 1 November 1737 Fielding was admitted to the Society of the Middle Temple as a special student, a status that exempted him from the Society's residential requirement and allowed him to live with his family. He was to prepare for the Bar for the next two-and-a-half years.[74]

According to Murphy, Fielding worked hard at reading the law, though he mixed his labour with recreation:

> His application, while he was a student in the Temple, was remarkably intense; and though it happened that the early taste he had taken of pleasure would occasionally return upon him, and conspire with his spirits and vivacity to carry him into the wild enjoyments of the town, yet it was particular in him that amidst all his dissipations nothing could suppress the thirst he had for knowledge, and the delight he felt in reading.[75]

This view of his diligence as a student seems to be supported by the evidence of his legal writings.[76]

In addition to study during this period, a good bit of Fielding's energy was taken up with writing letters for *The Craftsman* and with founding another journal, *The Champion*, in the winter of 1739–40. With the help of his friend of Little Haymarket days and earlier, James Ralph, Fielding nursed *The Champion* through hard times to success. Interestingly, an anonymous two-part essay appearing in one of these periodicals, *The Craftsman*, nos 613 and 615 (8 and 22 April 1738), provides further evidence that Fielding was a close student of the law during his student days. The essay is entitled 'Letter on the laws pertaining to libel and the liberty of the press'. In attributing the anonymous piece to Fielding, Battestin says:

> Methodically, [the writer] examines individual cases pertaining to the *Doctrine of Libels*, his intention being to prove that through an unconstitutional application of legal precedents the oppressive arbitrary powers of the Star Chamber have been transferred, in effect, to the judges, of the King's Bench, who are mere creatures of the Establishment . . . [Thus], in a manner anticipating Fielding in his legal pamphlets, [the writer] applies his already impressive knowledge of the law to argue his case cogently.[77]

By the time Fielding was admitted (early) to the Bar, on 20 June 1740 – his knowledge of the law having been attested by his uncle Davidge Gould, a Master of the Bench at the Middle Temple – he had experienced an abruptly truncated success in the theatre, established himself as a political, and to some extent a moral, essayist, and completed a rigorous legal training. Rich in themselves, these activities brought him face to face with a wide range of his contemporaries. With some, relations were intermittent, impersonal, and not often friendly, like those with Robert Walpole (1676–1745) and, of quite another sort, with Colley Cibber (1671–1757), playwright, actor and manager of Drury Lane. In different ways both men were powerful; at times, Fielding sought their help, and at other times he satirized them. He enjoyed many closer relations of various sorts – with relatives, like his favourite sister, Sarah (1710–68), the novelist, and his cousins Lady Mary (1689–1762) and Henry Gould (1710–94) – and with friends, who were often also his business associates. Among these were William Hogarth (1697–1762), the painter whose eye for the ridiculous Fielding no doubt found compatible with his own, and Hogarth's fellow student and colleague John Ellys (1701– 57), who selected the paintings for Walpole's country house at Houghton and did portraits of numerous contemporaries, but not of Fielding as far as we know. Fortunately, Hogarth left us with a likeness, although hardly a portrait.[78]

Fielding also knew many men and women of the theatre, including John Rich (1692–1761), manager of Lincoln's Inn Fields and Covent Garden; Henry Giffard (1694–1772), actor and owner-manager of Goodman's Fields, who provided Fielding with an example of entrepreneurship he could follow at the Little Haymarket; Barton Booth (1681–1733) and Robert Wilks (1665?–1732), who with Cibber managed Drury Lane, accepted Fielding's first play, *Love in Several Masques*, and turned down others, like *Don Quixote in England*; William Rufus Chetwood (d.1766), for about 20 years prompter at Drury Lane and the author of *General History of the Stage* (1749); Kitty Raftor, later Kitty Clive (1711–85), whose wonderful voice helped Fielding's ballad operas to succeed (and whose portrait Ellys painted); Charles Macklin (*c.* 1700–97), who acted in several of Fielding's plays, among them the revised *Author's Farce* and *Don Quixote in England*, and who in his varied career also worked as an acting coach and manager; Theophilus Cibber (1703–58), actor, son of Colley and husband of Susanna (1714–66), an actress; Susanna was the daughter of the well-known composer Thomas Arne (1710–78), Fielding's fellow-Etonian, who wrote music for some of his plays; Colley's daughter, Charlotte Charke (1713–60), actress, playwright, and (briefly) theatre manager, who left Drury Lane to play Lord Place in Fielding's *Pasquin* (she often played men). By the time Fielding was admitted to the Bar, in June 1740, it seems he also knew David Garrick (1717–79), who had come to London with Samuel Johnson in 1737 and was to become the most famous actor of the age. For on 15 April 1740, Garrick's play, *Lethe*, made use of two characters (Lucy and her husband) from Fielding's 'Miss Lucy' plays: *An Old Man Taught Wisdom* (1735) and *Miss Lucy in Town*. The second of these, the last of Fielding's to be premiered during his lifetime, was staged on 6 May 1742. The play may have been co-authored by Fielding and Garrick, though Fielding owned the copyright.[79]

Fielding enjoyed other friendships with collaborators. Unusual among these, both for the variety of the collaboration and for the duration of the friendship, was one with James Ralph (c. 1705–62). It began at least as far back as February 1729–30, the date of publication of Fielding's *The Temple Beau*, for which Ralph wrote the prologue, and it continued through the days of the Little Haymarket, though not, it seems, including the last year, 1737, and on to *The Champion* (1739–40) and the later numbers of *The True Patriot* (1745–6).[80] Ralph had no great literary gifts, but he was an indefatigable hack, in verse and prose. He had attacked Pope and the Scriblerians in *Sawney, an Heroic Poem occasioned by The Dunciad* (1728), which he claimed was a defence of those Pope had satirized there. *Sawney* was no better than Ralph's blank-verse descriptive poems *The Tempest* (1727) and *Night* (1728). Benjamin Franklin, who travelled to England from Philadelphia with Ralph and lent him money, includes him among his close friends – all free-thinkers – who are 'lovers of reading'. But he gives Ralph's poetry low marks, assuring us at the same time that Ralph's confidence in his poetic gift was not checked by the emphatic recommendations of his friends to give it up.[81]

It may have been a combination of Ralph's intellectual independence and his sociability – Franklin 'never knew a prettier talker' – that first drew Fielding to him.[82] Though Fielding was loyal to his friend, it does not seem likely that his high opinion of Ralph, which apparently marked the beginning of their friendship, could long have survived. Ralph's limitations must soon have been as obvious to him as they were to Franklin. Their partnership in the management of the Little Haymarket was very likely a nominal one, with Fielding making all the important decisions.[83] And Ralph's assignments for *The Champion* and *The True Patriot* – he seems to have been responsible for the political articles – were probably commensurate with his talent and experience, which in the difficult world of hack writing were considerable. But it would be surprising if Fielding had found Ralph's free-thinking mind attractive over the long run.

Among other London friends and acquaintances – some allies, others rivals – was Lewis Theobald (1688–1744), whom I have mentioned as one of Pope's chief objects of ridicule as the first Prince of Dullness in *The Dunciad* (1728). Like Ralph, Theobald had made his way by hack work: writing essays, translating plays by Aeschylus and Sophocles, and works of other Greek authors, and by playwriting. He also improvised pantomimes for John Rich, manager of Lincoln's Inn Fields. But it was as a solid Elizabethan scholar that he came to prominence. Theobald had the temerity to give the world a correction of Pope's edition of Shakespeare (1725), without a word of censure for the editor himself, in *Shakespeare Restored: Or a Specimen of the Many Errors, As Well Committed as Unamended, by Mr. Pope . . .* (1726). Is it any wonder that he irked Pope? Ralph's motive in publishing *Sawney* was almost certainly to annoy Pope into giving him a dubious fame by placing him among the dunces. This Pope did in *The Dunciad* of 1729. But Theobald's fate was unjust in that his correction of Pope's Shakespeare was a work of dispassionate scholarship, however eager the scholar himself may have been to make a mark.

Though Fielding befriended his drinking companion Theobald by contributing the epilogue to his *Orestes*, which was premiered on 3 April 1731, he satirized his Shakespeare commentary in *The Tragedy of Tragedies*, and he ridiculed him in other ways elsewhere. It is not easy to find the motive for such inconsistency. Probably those who lived by the pen in eighteenth-century England felt easier about such literary backbiting than we may ordinarily suppose. Battestin suggests that Fielding's contribution of the epilogue may have been a way of courting Walpole, with whom Theobald had a well established relation as a pro-ministerial propagandist.[84] Whatever the reason, it would probably be wrong to attach great importance to Fielding's inconsistent treatment of Theobald.

Fielding's life in London was enriched by many other friends and adversaries. Among the friends were Aaron Hill (1685–1750), playwright and drama critic (an admirer of both Fielding and his father), who commented acutely on Fielding's *Pasquin* and other works; and Thomas Cooke (*c.* 1702–56), a translator of Hesiod and Plautus, a pro-ministerial essayist and playwright, who apparently added a scene to a pirated performance of *Tom Thumb* and composed an uncomplimentary verse portrait of Fielding before the two became friends, perhaps through their mutual cronies Ralph and Theobald. In 1732, Fielding contributed to Cooke's monthly publication *The Comedian*, a magazine favouring Walpole, after Cooke had praised *The Modern Husband* (the play, it will be recalled, that Fielding had dedicated to Walpole).[85]

Among Fielding's London adversaries were many voices that spoke in such publications as *The Grub-Street Journal*, *The Daily Gazeteer* and *The London Journal*. One interesting adversarial voice was that of John (Orator) Henley, whom Fielding satirized as Dr Orator in *The Author's Farce* and elsewhere; Henley returned the favour in several publications, including *The Hyp-Doctor*, where he ridiculed plays to which the government had taken exception. But when Fielding died in Lisbon in 1754, it was Henley who delivered the only known funeral oration on him.[86]

Fielding had friends not only in London but in many other places, including Bath, Salisbury and East Stour where he owned a share of the family property until 1739. Among his friends in the south-west of the country were the Colliers, Arthur, Jane and Margaret, who were the children of the philosopher, the Reverend Arthur Collier (1680–1732). Fielding had probably known them from the early 1720s, when he was sometimes with his grandmother, Lady Gould, in Salisbury. Young Arthur (1707–77) was, like Fielding, a lawyer. And Margaret Collier was to join Fielding and his second wife on his last journey to Lisbon in 1754, though by then the relationship had soured. Another country friend was William Young (1702–57), the model for Parson Abraham Adams in *Joseph Andrews*, who from the early 1730s was curate of East and West Stour and Master of the nearby Gillingham Grammar School. Fielding enjoyed a close friendship with this amiable classical scholar, who seems to have had little in the way of practical sense. In need of more money than he could earn in Dorset, he followed Fielding to London in 1740, where he tried without much success to support his family by writing.[87] Fielding also got to know the son of the famous latitudinarian Bishop of Salisbury, Gilbert Burnet (1643–1715); the son, Thomas (1694–1753), was a distinguished lawyer, whose companionship Fielding enjoyed on the Western Circuit, especially as he began his legal career.

One of his closest friends was the wealthy and learned James Harris (1709–80), who lived very near the Cradocks in the Cathedral Close in Salisbury. His intelligence and kindness won Fielding's heart. By the time Fielding asked Harris to enter into an exchange of letters, on 8 September 1741 – a rare initiative for him – they had known each other for years. Fielding writes to Harris:

> I solemnly declare, I can never give Man or Woman with whom I have no Business . . . a more certain Token of a violent Affection than by writing to them, an Exercise which, notwithstanding I have in my time printed a few Pages, I so much detest, that I believe it is not in the Power of three Persons to expose my epistolary Correspondence.[88]

Harris and Fielding were close for the rest of Fielding's life. He contributed to Fielding's *Covent-Garden Journal* and *True Patriot*, assisted him in money matters, helped Sarah Fielding, Henry's sister, in various ways, and wrote the first (though not the first published) life of his friend.

Besides his career in the law, which included his work as a barrister and later as a magistrate, Fielding spent the rest of his life writing, chiefly essays and novels. Many of the essays of this period were political, conveying little of the moral sense that informs much of his other work. He probably felt more at home as the arbiter of taste and morals than as the spokesman for a political ideology; nevertheless he sometimes writes in support of faction, either out of conviction or the need for money. As has been said, though his plays did not become clearly partisan until 1736, he seems to have written partisan essays as early as 1734. In 1739–40, backed by some London publishers, he established *The Champion; or, British Mercury* (later called *The Champion: or, Evening Advertiser*), in which he wrote as Captain Hercules Vinegar, a British hero who had put down the sword to take up the pen. Fielding's intention in planning *The Champion* was not

political. He wanted to write witty moral pieces on social, philosophical, religious and literary subjects, and only an occasional
political essay. But his mounting debt, along with the taste of the
town, which called for partisan argument rather than the essays
he wanted to write, forced his hand. Thereafter, he became active
against Walpole, writing pro-Patriot essays for his journal, until
the minister intervened, one infers, from a few essays in *The
Champion* in the late spring and early autumn of 1740, which clearly
imply that Fielding has been offered money for his silence and
more money if he would change sides. In addition, he seems to
acknowledge that he was paid to withhold publication of a book.[89]

B. M. Jones, who has made the most intense study of Fielding's law career to date, notes that 'more than half of the articles
[in *The Champion*] definitely attributed to Fielding contain explanations or discussions of points of law, and sometimes a whole
article is devoted to the subject'.[90] Obviously the law was much
on Fielding's mind during these years, and one may suppose
that his interest in politics was to a great extent limited by financial
concerns. Accordingly, Fielding may not have found it hard to
leave more and more of the work of the periodical to Ralph and
others. Indeed, in 1741, he attended the assizes on the Western
Circuit, wrote independently of *The Champion*, and effected a
complete political turnabout in an essay, *The Opposition: A Vision*,
which both satirized the position he had in many ways supported
and championed Walpole and his policies.[91] Though the shift
represented by *The Opposition* is uniquely stark, it is only an
extreme example of Fielding's political activity, such as it was,
from the earliest days of his literary career, when he courted
Walpole's favour at the same time that he sometimes made him
the object of ridicule. Fielding's deepest moral sense was rarely
expressed in partisan terms. His typical view was that both sides
were morally at fault. Though he wrote for money, and made
no bones about it, his morality easily survived these nominal
betrayals. Besides, he may have begun to recognize that Walpole's
long career had overseen a national stability no other politician
was capable of securing.

Unfortunately, Fielding was hit by a series of misfortunes within
a year of his first attending the assizes on the Western Circuit,
where he was never to earn much money. In May 1741, he was
detained by a bailiff in a sponging house, the first step on the
journey to debtor's prison; friends agreed to stand good for the

money he owed, but Fielding was not released for about two weeks.[92] A month or so later, his father died, and quite apart from the sense of personal loss, he must have been deeply disappointed that Edmund's considerable estate, a good portion of which was left to him by his third wife, Eleanor Hill, was in disarray, and what remained of it was appropriated by his fourth wife, Elizabeth Sparrye, whom he had married only a few months before.[93] Impoverished as he was, Fielding was sorely in need of a stroke of luck; but he lived on without it.

Fielding must have called on all his energy at this time, to judge from the quality and the amount of his writing. In addition to his contributions to *The Champion* in 1740 and 1741, he published a translation of *The Military History of Charles XII. King of Sweden* (1740); *Of True Greatness. An Epistle to The Right Honourable George Dodington, Esq.*, (1741), written in effective heroic couplets, distinguishing between greatness, false and true; *The Vernoniad* (1741), a mock epic in heroic couplets, purporting to be a translation 'from the original Greek of Homer', which satirized Walpole for his ostensible delay in dispatching help to the naval hero Admiral Edward Vernon; *An Apology for the Life of Shamela Andrews* (1741), a parody of Samuel Richardson's enormously popular novel *Pamela* (1740), in which a servant girl resists the advances of her master until he offers to marry her (a treatment of 'virtue' and its 'reward' that Fielding derided); and *The Opposition. A Vision* (1741), the piece mentioned above, in which Fielding changed political sides, arguing in favour of Walpole's policies and against the opposition's.

During this same period, he was also at work on *Joseph Andrews*, published early the following year, 22 February 1742. If at this time Fielding, who was very much in need of money, wrote with the energy of desperation, the quality of his work does not show it. In fact his greatest work, *The History of Tom Jones, a Foundling*, lay ahead (February 1749), as did his last novel, *Amelia* (December 1751). Fielding was never to be free of anxiety about money, and from 1742 onwards he was beset by problems of ill health, both his family's and his own. He himself tells us, 'I was last Winter [1741–2] laid up in a Gout, with a favourite Child [Charlotte] dying in one Bed, and my Wife in a Condition very little better, on another.'[94]

In February 1742, Walpole resigned, forced out of office after years of his sagacious control of a majority in Commons, almost all the while enjoying the strong support of Queen Caroline and of King George II, which he had to the very end of his minis-try.[95] Despite his having taken Walpole's side in *The Opposition*, Fielding returned to the support of his old friends, Lyttelton, Dodington and the Patriots, who ultimately participated in a new Broad-Bottom government led by Henry Pelham. Thereafter Field-ing was generally loyal to the new ministry, probably feeling most comfortable in that political stance. But he could not afford to rule out writing partisan essays for money.

From 1742 to 1747–8, Fielding wrote a range of pieces, in some degree political. These include *A Full Vindication of the Duchess Dowager of Marlborough*, (1742), in which he argues on behalf of the ageing Duchess (1680–1744), who had precipitated a pamphlet war by commissioning a self-serving 'account of her conduct' which vilified many important people. In going to the Duchess's defence, Fielding aligned himself with Chesterfield and Pitt, two of her favourites, who at the time were part of a new Whig opposition; *Some Papers Proper to be Read before the R[oya]l Society* (1743), a piece in which Fielding parodies an essay that had appeared in *Philosophical Transactions of the Royal Society*, and in the process satirizes John Carteret, Lord Granville, then the King's chief minister, for policies on the continent disapproved by his friends Chesterfield, Pitt, Dodington and Lyttelton; and *An Attempt towards a Natural History of the Hanover Rat* (1744) which, like *Some Papers Proper to be Read*, parodies *Philosophical Transactions* and satirizes Carteret. In 1745, he published *A Serious Address to the People of Great Britain*, *The History of the Present Rebellion in Scotland*, and *A Dialogue between the Devil, the Pope, and the Pretender*; and he began *The True Patriot: and The History of Our Own Times* (33 numbers, 5 November 1745 to 17 June 1746). All four of these works of 1745–6 address issues deriving from the Jacobite rebel-lion known as the 'Forty-Five', the last serious threat by a Stuart to the Protestant monarchy.[96]

The last period of Fielding's political journalism, from June 1747 and to November 1748, saw the production of *A Dialogue between a Gentleman of London ... and an Honest Alderman of the Country Party* (1747), *A Proper Answer to a Late Scurrilous Libel* (1747), and *The Jacobite's Journal* (49 numbers, 5 December 1747 to 5 November 1748).[97] Generally, the two pamphlets (*A Dialogue* and *A Proper Answer*) and the numbers of *The Jacobite's Journal* support and defend the administration of the Pelhams during a time of anxiety (possibly an intentionally exaggerated anxiety) about a new Jacobite uprising, which it was feared might be supported by a French invasion even after the threat of 1745 had passed. (Peace with France was not concluded until October 1748.) In the *Jacobite's Journal*, speaking ironically as a Jacobite, John Trott-Plaid, Esq., Fielding propagandized for the administration; supporting the King to be sure, but more particularly supporting the policies of the ministry, and doing so as if its interests and the Crown's always coincided. He often enough found ways to defend his friends in the Pelham camp, to attack their enemies and his own, and to identify persons and institutions in which he made it clear one might find Jacobitism flourishing. *The Jacobite's Journal* can be witty, and it seems to have served its purpose of holding the opposition at bay while the ministry pursued its own Continental policies, which led ultimately to a peace treaty with France and the other warring nations. But it also drew the most slanderous personal abuse Fielding had ever experienced. He had hardly been objective and kind himself as he wrote about others behind the mask of impartial patriot and moral arbiter. For a variety of reasons he must have been happy to see the last number of *The Jacobite's Journal* appear on Saturday, 5 November 1748. Perhaps as a reward for his service to the Pelham ministry, he had by then been appointed to the Commission of the Peace for Westminster (on 30 July 1748). But he did not begin to hold court in the house he thereafter made famous, at Bow Steet, until 2 November, a few days before the *The Jacobite's Journal* ended its run.[98]

It will be useful to touch briefly on some of Fielding's work of the 1740s not yet mentioned, or only fleetingly referred to, before considering the first of his five years as magistrate. To do so is to reinforce the sense of his complex activity during this period that saw his struggle to establish himself as a barrister, his anguish over the loss of his daughter, in 1742, and of his wife, in 1744, and the beginnings of his own illness with gout. Besides his numerous political essays, he was diligently at work on his novels, adding *The Life of Mr. Jonathan Wild the Great* (1743) and *Tom Jones* to *Shamela* and *Joseph Andrews*. Though *Amelia* was not published until 1751, Fielding was probably at work on it not very long after taking up his duties as magistrate, in the summer of 1749.[99]

During this extraordinarily busy decade, Fielding's reputation as a novelist grew. *Shamela*, his parody of Richardson's novel, drew little critical attention, in part at least because the learned world had not yet decided what it thought of *Pamela*.[100] But after the appearance of *Joseph Andrews* and *Tom Jones*, Fielding was, with Richardson, at the centre of a division of critical opinion that persisted beyond his lifetime. On one side were those who found the 'low' characters in Fielding's novels quite acceptable because they were drawn from 'nature', giving legitimate pleasure to the reader; and on the other, those who thought his 'low' characters morally offensive and likely to be dangerously attractive, especially to the young, and more especially to young women. On 31 March 1750, Johnson's *Rambler*, No. 4, without ever mentioning Fielding, makes a strong case for the danger to youth of 'improper Combinations of Images':

> Many writers for the sake of following nature, so mingle good and bad qualities in their principal personages, that they are both equally conspicuous; and as we accompany them through their adventures with delight, and are led by degrees to interest ourselves in their favour, we lose the abhorrence of their faults, because they do not hinder our pleasure, or, perhaps, regard them with some kindness for being united with so much merit.[101]

Johnson found another reason for preferring Richardson, one that has survived better than his moral indictment: 'Sir, there is more knowledge of the human heart in one letter of Richardson's than in all *Tom Jones*.'[102] Though in one form or another this distinction is still alive among critics, it is not really useful unless one considers first whether 'knowledge of the human heart' may not be differently represented by each author; but more of that later.

Fielding's response to *Pamela* throws light on his own nature and initiates the illuminating division of opinion that followed. In *Shamela*, he turns Pamela inside out, having read her sustained compulsion to equate virginity with honour as a manipulative (immoral and reductive) effort to control her world. Accordingly, he gives us a Shamela who is the *disclosed* Pamela, acting with a full consciousness of her sexual management of those around her. In doing so, Fielding mischievously implies Richardson's complicity in Pamela's immorality or his culpable ignorance of it. Fielding might as well have said that her own maker has either concealed the dark truth about his creature, or that he is unaware

of it. In *Joseph Andrews* (where he quickly relegates the exposure
of Pamela to the background) and in *Tom Jones*, he continues to
write with a hearty openness of which Richardson disapproved.
The two were worlds apart, and temperamentally opposed. It is
not surprising that Richardson offered a moral judgment of his
own, saying that 'The virtues of Fielding's heroes were the vices
of truly good men.'[103]

Some of the best minds of the age took sides. Johnson reprimanded Hannah Moore, author of *Coelubs in Search of a Wife*,
because he heard her 'quote from so vicious a book [as *Tom
Jones*]'.[104] Johnson's friend, the musicologist Charles Burney,
explained that the Doctor's real objection to Fielding was 'his
loose life, and the profligacy of almost all his male characters'.[105]
Dr Burney's daughter, Fanny Burney, in her preface to *Evelina*,
tells us she is 'exhilarated by the wit of Fielding'. Fielding's cousin,
Lady Mary, says, 'This Richardson is a strange Fellow. I heartily
despise him and eagerly read him, nay, sob over his works in a
most scandalous manner.'[106] She seems also to have shared some
of Johnson's and Richardson's doubts about Fielding's heroes;
writing to her daughter, she says, 'I wonder [Fielding] does not
perceive Tom Jones and Mr. Booth [of *Amelia*] are sorry scoundrels. All these sort of books ... place a merit in extravagant
Passions, and encourage young people to hope for impossible
events to draw them out of the misery they chuse to plunge
themselves into.'[107] But Lady Mary inscribed her copy of *Tom
Jones* with quite a different opinion of the book, calling it '*Ne
plus ultra*'.[108] Perhaps she reserved one evaluation for her daughter,
Lady Bute, and another for herself.

By contrast, Boswell is unequivocal in his objection to Johnson's
view of the novelists:

> It always appeared to me that [Johnson] estimated the compo-
> sitions of Richardson too highly, and that he had an unreason-
> able prejudice against Fielding. . . . Fielding's characters, though
> they do not expand themselves so widely in dissertation are
> as just pictures of human nature, and I will venture to say
> have more striking features, and nicer touches of the pencil ...
> I will venture to add, that the moral tendency of Fielding's
> writings, though it does not encourage a strained and rarely
> possible virtue, is ever favourable to honour and honesty, and
> cherishes the benevolent and generous affections.[109]

Though there may be some truth in Johnson's opinion that 'splen-didly wicked' men corrupt the world, the view hardly applies to Fielding's heroes, who are deeply moral in a sense Johnson disregarded or would not accept. In any case, Boswell's more balanced opinion has prevailed, as Edward Gibbon in his own way predicted it would. Writing at a time when everyone thought the Fieldings were English connections of the Habsburgs, Gibbon said, 'The Romance of Tom Jones, that exquisite picture of human manners[,] will outlive the palace of the Escurial and the Imperial Eagle of the house of Austria.'[110]

In addition to the many works of the 1740s already cited, Field-ing wrote others. He was incredibly busy throughout the decade. In 1742, a collaborative work by him and William Young appeared, an annotated translation from the Greek of a comedy by Aristophanes, *Plutus, the God of Riches*. Between 1742 and 1745, he had three plays produced: *Miss Lucy in Town* (1742), *The Wedding-Day* (1743), and *The Debauchees: or, The Jesuit Caught* (1745). In 1743, he published his *Miscellanies*, in three volumes, which include, among other works, various poems, *A Journey from This World to the Next* (to be discussed later), two plays (*Eurydice* and *The Wedding-Day*), and *Jonathan Wild*.[111] He also helped his sister Sarah with a few suggestions for her anonymously published novel *The Adventures of David Simple* (May 1744). To the second edition, he added a preface, noted on the title-page, with his name assigned to it. The preface praises the novel, denies he wrote it – the book had been attributed to him – and points out disingenuously that he could not be the author because the book might have had 'a Tendency to injure me in a Profession [the law], to which I have applied with so arduous and intent a Diligence, that I have had no Leisure, if I had Inclination, to compose any thing of this kind'. It may be true that lawyers who were novelists would have seemed unprofessional to their eighteenth-century colleagues, but obviously Fielding had the 'Inclination' to write novels, and his prodigious energy would have provided him with the 'Leisure' for writing *David Simple*.[112]

He had another axe to grind in the preface. He had been accused of writing a scurrilous poem, *The Causicade* (1744), inspired by:

the resignation of Sir John Strange from the office of Solicitor-General . . . [In the poem], many of the Judges and more

prominent members of the Bar come in for ridicule and offensive references, and each of them was made to utter a pan-
egyric on himself as the most fit person for the vacant post.[113]

Fielding angrily disavowed any knowledge of *The Causicade*'s
authorship. Though he naturally hoped for the approval of his
colleagues in the law quite independently of any wish to defend
himself against accusations that he had written *The Causicade*, he
may nevertheless have been stimulated by the false charges to
begin writing an ambitious legal work, *An Institute of the Pleas of
the Crown*, which he announced for publication early in 1745. It
never appeared. Murphy tells us that after Fielding's death, two
folio volumes on the subject were in the possession of Fielding's
half-brother John.[114]

After Walpole died in 1745, the distinguished physician John
Ranby (1703–73) published an essay taking issue with the handling
of the former minister's last illness by members of the College
of Physicians. Ranby's essay started a paper war. Though Fielding had poked fun at the medical trade from his early days as
author, and continued to do so throughout his career, he admired
Ranby.[115] Maybe for the sheer fun of it, he entered the fray with
a clever spoof of the medical brotherhood, *The Charge to the jury:
or, The Sum of the Evidence, on the Trial of A.B.C.D. and E.F. All
M.D. For the Death of one Robert at Orfud, at a Special Commission
of Oyer and Terminer held at Justice-College, in W[arwi]ck Lane, before
Sir Asculapius Dosem, Dr. Timberhead, and Others, their Fellows,
Justices, &c.* The title well conveys the spirit of the piece.[116] In
1746, Fielding published *The Female Husband: or, The Surprising
History of Mrs. Mary, alias Mr. George Hamilton*, 'Who was convicted
of having married a Young Woman of Wells and lived with her
as her Husband. Taken from her own mouth since her Confine-
ment.' About this piece, it will be enough to repeat what the
man who knows Fielding best and likes him very well, Martin
Battestin, has to say: 'In this case of unnatural sexuality Fielding
found the hint for the shoddiest work of fiction he ever wrote.
Fiction it is, for despite the claim of authenticity on the title-
page, the story is almost wholly the product of the darker fancies
of his imagination.'[117]

In the following year, 1747, Fielding published *Ovid's Art of
Love Paraphrased, and Adapted to the Present Time*, Book I, and he
contributed a preface and Letters XL–XLIV to his sister Sarah's

*Familiar Letters between the Principal Characters in 'David Simple',
and Some Others.* Of the five letters, two are by women, Prudentia
Flutters and Lucy Rural, who exchange views about the city and
the country; two are by Valentine (a report to David Simple on
such matters as politics and the theatre, and a love letter to
Cynthia); and one, modelled on Montesquieu's *Lettres Persanes*
(1721), is by a French Gentleman who describes English customs
through foreign eyes in such a way as to induce the English
reader's fresh view of them.

The preface to his sister's book is more interesting, in two ways.
First, Fielding considers the means by which a story may be told
and decides, almost certainly with his rival Richardson in mind,
that 'no one will contend, that the epistolary style is in general
the most proper to the novelist, or that it hath been used by the
best writers of this kind'.[118] Then, repeating what he said in the
preface to *David Simple*, that he is 'allied' to the author, his sister,
both in 'friendship' and 'relation', he goes on to characterize and
to praise women's intellectual capacities, especially their ability
to read human nature. This high evaluation is only partially
accounted for by his prefatory mission, to help the sale of Sarah's
book. He had earlier shown unmistakable signs of respect for
the minds and talents of Sarah, Lady Mary and Kitty Clive, among
others. But a more impersonal and therefore more telling sign of
his respect is that he had endowed many of the female characters in his plays with strong minds and other enviable gifts, like
vitality, wit and self-knowledge: for example, Lady Matchless in
Love in Several Masques, Bellaria in *The Temple Beau*, and (in her
own way) Mrs Modern in *The Modern Husband*. Though Fielding
no doubt saw men and women as distinctly different from each
other, biologically and emotionally, the range of his female characters makes it clear that he was no reductive male chauvinist in
his view of women. Not only did he recognize that they could
be as intelligent and spirited as any man, he also understood
that each had a unique psyche and intellect.[119]

Fielding had a great success with *Tom Jones* – *Amelia* was less
popular – but he continued to need more money than he could
earn by writing. His appointment as magistrate brought with it
a potential for squeezing income from the criminal wretches
brought before him, but he would not exploit it with the result,
Fielding says in his Introduction to *The Journal of A Voyage to
Lisbon*, that he 'reduced an income of 500 l. a year of the dirtiest

money upon earth, to little more than 300 l; a considerable portion of which remained with my clerk'. To this information, Fielding adds in a note that a predecessor, Sir Thomas de Veil (1684?–1746), 'used to boast that he made 1000 l. a year in the office'. Fielding's note goes on to explain that he 'received from the government a yearly pension out of the public service-money'.[120] B. M. Jones comments on the magistracies:

> Originally gentlemen of standing had performed the duties [of justice of the peace] without payment, as in country districts; but in London, where the criminal classes of the whole country were by this time beginning to congregate, the work of the magistrate was continuous and arduous. It had proved impossible to find sufficient gentlemen to undertake the onerous and sordid work, and a practice had grown up of allowing the Westminster magistrates to repay themselves by fees taken from persons charged before them. In consequence, only inferior men could be induced to accept the office, and then only with the object of enriching themselves.[121]

During Fielding's five years in the office, he changed its nature radically. One might say that he began this work by means of a geographical strategy. With the help of the Duke of Bedford, he secured a place as justice on the Middlesex commission. By this means, he served in adjoining jurisdictions so that criminals could not escape the law simply by moving beyond the limits of Westminster. (The City of London proper was outside Fielding's jurisdiction.)[122] Then he methodically set about cleaning things up. In addition to eliminating the extortion of his predecessors, he heard cases tirelessly, with an eye to justice and his own sense of fair play. His views of punishment as a deterrent to crime were severe by our standards, though not at all unusual then. But he often dealt leniently with those who were not an obvious threat to society, such as 'destitute widows of clergymen, the "deserving" poor, a beautiful young girl bedded on her wedding night in a crowded room, a boy of twelve taken up for theft whose mother desperately pleaded for his release, a mother of three children charged with stealing a cap'.[123] Among his other accomplishments as magistrate, Fielding found support from the government for the establishment of a detective force that proved very effective in reducing crime (the Bow Street Runners), 'the first peace-officers to make a serious study of the art of detecting and running down criminals'.[124] Finally, by means of his writing and other activities, he promoted legislative reforms, the removal of some of the causes of crime, the reform of defects in the criminal law, and various changes in the operations of prisons.

Fielding's publications during the years of his magistracy include *A Charge delivered to the Grand Jury* (1749), *A True State of the Case of Bosavern Penlez* (1749), *An Enquiry into the Causes of the Late Increase of Robbers* (1751), *Examples of the Interposition of Providence in the Detection and Punishment of Murder* (1752), *A Proposal for Making an Effectual Provision for the Poor* (1753), and *A Clear State of the Case of Elizabeth Canning* (1753). Here I shall discuss the first two of these, leaving the works published in the 1750s to the final chapter. *A Charge* is an instance of the practice of informing a grand jury of its duties after it is sworn in and before it begins its business of hearing cases and identifying, on its own initiative, offences to be examined. Fielding must have been aware that his various public demeanours – author of burlesques, political satirist, vituperative essayist – might for some make his magisterial voice ludicrous by contrast. But 'in his *Charge* Fielding betrays no consciousness of past or impending animadversions on his position as magistrate . . . [The piece] is a masterly and assured model of its kind, confident and dignified in tone, precise in application, rich in legal allusion, and thoroughly at ease with the perspective of judicial tradition.'[125]

A True State of the Case of Bosavern Penlez is Fielding's defence of the execution of a man found guilty under the Riot Act of 1715. The case is extremely complicated, involving a range of factors: social, criminal, legal and political.[126] Though Penlez was executed after being convicted of participation in a riot by due process of the law (in which Fielding had early on played an important part), public opinion favoured his release for a number of reasons, including the following. The riot started after a sailor who had been robbed at a bawdyhouse returned with hundreds of his shipmates and set fire to it and other such houses in the neighbourhood, a series of actions many found acceptable, and some commendable. Penlez, a civilian who joined the rioters only after he got drunk, was a young man with no criminal past, the son of a clergyman; many hundreds of sailors and civilians were involved in the riots, but only Penlez was hanged (along with 13 sailors and a sailor's wife who were executed for crimes other than participation in the riots of 1–3 July 1749). Penlez was accused of theft when evidence was first heard against him, but he was not tried for theft because the presiding judge thought it unnecessary; of the three civilians tried for violating the Riot Act, one was acquitted, while another, John Wilson, was found guilty and pardoned (and, as I have said, Penlez was found guilty and hanged). Two of the chief witnesses against Penlez were husband and wife, the husband being the reputed proprietor of one of the bawdyhouses attacked by the rioters. It is hard to understand why so few rioters were arrested during the riots: Penlez 'was one of seven [four sailors and three civilians] arrested. One of these escaped, one died in prison, the indictments of two were found _ignoramus_, one was acquited, one pardoned and Penlez himself hanged.'[127]

On the other side it should be said that the rioting – which lasted three days, Saturday to Monday, 1–3 July 1749 – along with the burning of houses, was a serious matter. The fires posed an immediate danger to the city, and the rioting itself threatened the peace of the community. The situation required the close attention of Holborn's High Constable, Saunders Welch, and his men, and later of Fielding and other highly placed persons. It was brought under control satisfactorily, except, perhaps, for the unauthorized use of troops.[128]

Early reports by the press on the handling of the riots were favourable, but they soon gave way to partisan evaluations of the impending execution when it became clear that public sympathy for Penlez was running deep. Penlez had been convicted on 6 September 1749 and he was executed on 18 October. By this time Granville Leveson-Gower, Lord Trentham, brother-in-law of the Duke of Bedford (one of Fielding's patrons), was preparing for an election to retain his seat for Westminster. The opposition took advantage of the situation to brand Trentham, Bedford, Fielding and the ministry with a variety of nasty charges, among them that Trentham (or Fielding) had callously blocked the petition to a merciful king for Penlez's pardon and that Fielding's inclination to protect bawdyhouses made him unsympathetic to Penlez, who destroyed them. The published assaults against Fielding, Trentham, and others believed to be responsible for Penlez's execution were massive.[129]

This tangle of accusation was perhaps reasonable in its origins: why _did_ the administration execute Penlez? But it was exploitative in its political applications. In *The Case of Bosavern Penlez* Fielding tries to cope with the problem he and his patron faced. Given both the popular support for Penlez, which included hundreds of petitioners, among whom were the jury that convicted him, and the magnitude of the political aftermath to the trial, his job was not easy. Not surprisingly, Fielding's essay has a double purpose: to exonerate himself for his part in the case (which was to hear evidence against Penlez and to make the decision to commit him to Newgate until the grand jury convened) and to show that Trentham and the ministry had not behaved improperly in allowing the execution to proceed. Fielding argues from the history of the law that the Riot Act of 1715, which Penlez violated, neither breaks new ground nor calls for harsher sentences than antecedent laws, as its opponents were contending; that depositions from respected constables and members of the watch (which he quotes in full) make it clear that Penlez participated in the riot and that he stole some linen; and finally that the law must be enforced if an ordered society is to be maintained. Fielding's argument sounds clear and accurate, and he appears to be sincere in the belief that Penlez's execution was justified, the alternative being to 'suffer a licentious Rabble to be Accuser, Judge, Jury, and Executioner'.[130] But he is not convincing when he tries to explain that Wilson was pardoned and Penlez executed because Penlez was a thief.[131] In fact Wilson's pardon, along with Fielding's suggestion that Penlez would also have been pardoned if he had not stolen some linen, undercuts his whole argument, which is that enforcement of the Riot Act, ultimately a venerable and just law, is necessary for the preservation of order. However grateful Fielding was to Bedford, he must have written this piece without relish.[132]

One other important matter occupied Fielding's time during the second half of the 1740s: his second marriage, to Mary Daniel, and the prelude to the marriage. Mary had been his and Charlotte's cook-maid. After Charlotte died in 1744, Fielding's sister Sarah came to run the household for him and his very young children, Henry and Harriet. Whatever domestic stability this arrangement might have brought was undone by Fielding's attraction to Mary, which may have had no other basis than that she was young and available. Making love to one's servant and getting her with child was an old story in the eighteenth century. (The fanatical resistance of Richardson's Pamela to her master's addresses and his changing view of her status derive a good deal of their significance from her implacable rejection of this commonplace.) But marrying one's servant was unusual to say the least. However complicated his feelings may have been, Fielding's ultimate view of his and Mary's predicament required his decisive action. On 27 November 1747, Fielding married Mary Daniel in the sixth month of her pregnancy; his friend Lyttelton gave the bride away.[133] We can only surmise that Mary's feelings too must have been complicated, and that she accepted the marriage as the best available solution. Given the relatively fixed class-structure of the eighteenth-century world, she may even have been grateful (and maybe resentful as well). Inevitably there were those who believed Fielding had done the right thing and those who mocked him for having married his whore. To spare Mary (and himself) as much embarrassment as possible, Fielding rented a house in suburban Twickenham, where she would have relative privacy, and he moved back and forth between there and London as his responsibilities required. The trips must have been painful because he was suffering severe attacks of gout at the time.

Sarah left the Fielding household, though her affection for her brother survived his affair with Mary and the marriage that followed, of which we catch glimpses from time to time. In the spring of 1747/8, for example, Mary seems to have helped Fielding in one of his more unusual ventures: the establishment of a breakfasting-room, where for the price of a cup of tea, coffee or chocolate, the patrons could enjoy a puppet-show at no extra charge.[134] And we shall see that in the last stages of Fielding's illness, Mary accompanied him on his final journey to Lisbon, showing both a generous willingness to help him during his last days and a concern, sometimes an annoyance, over the way in which he handled his affairs.

Five children were born of their marriage: three daughters who died in infancy or early childhood – Mary Amelia, baptized 6 January 1748/9, Sophia, christened 21 January 1749/50, and Louisa, christened 3 December 1752 – and two sons who lived well into the nineteenth century: William, baptized 25 February 1747/8, died 1 October 1820, and Allen, christened 6 April 1754, died 9 April 1823.[135] Though his children by Charlotte, especially Harriet, were dear to him, we hear of his tender love for the children of his second marriage in *The Journal of a Voyage to Lisbon*, as he was about to leave for Portugal:

On this day [Wednesday, 26 June 1754], the most melancholy
sun I had ever beheld arose, and found me awake at my house
at Fordhook. By the light of this sun, I was, in my own opinion,
last to behold and take leave of some of those creatures on
whom I doated with a mother-like fondness, guided by nature
and passion, and uncured and unhardened by all the doctrine
of that philosophical school where I had learnt to bear pains
and to despise death.[136]

When he departed, he left William, Sophia and Allen behind,
never to be seen by him again. He probably had a special fondness for his and Charlotte's Harriet, but obviously he loved his
children by Mary too.

The years between 1750 and his voyage to Lisbon in June 1754
were full. Despite increasing problems of health, Fielding was
intensely busy with the magistracy; a business venture with his
half-brother John (the operation of a general brokerage house
called the Universal Register Office); the publication of *The Covent-
Garden Journal*, a twice-weekly paper which, although intended
to solicit customers for the brokerage business, took on a life of
its own; the completion of his last novel, *Amelia*; and other matters. We shall see in the final chapter that he accomplished all
this work suffering not only the pain of his own last illness but
the loss of a son, a daughter, and three of his sisters. Between
his deeply felt experience of love and death and his exuberant
energy for work, Fielding experienced an unusually full life in
his short term of 47 years.

2

Fielding in the Theatre

Between 1728 and 1737, by which time he was only 30 years old, Fielding became England's most successful living playwright. During that decade he wrote over two dozen comedies of various kinds, many of which he revised, either to meet the exigencies of continuing production or of publication. About a third of the plays are five-act traditional comedies or serious social satires – mainpieces – like *Love in Several Masques* and *The Modern Husband*. The rest are shorter works – afterpieces – which typically followed a five-act play on the programme. The afterpieces include burlesques like *The Welsh Opera*, farces like *The Lottery*, and topical satires like *The Historical Register for the Year 1736*. In some of his plays of all these kinds except the traditional comedies, Fielding used the dominant convention of ballad opera, which John Gay's *Beggar's Opera* (1728) had made immensely popular; airs are sung throughout the course of the play, with lyrics by the playwright, set to melodies everyone in the audience would recognize.

Fielding almost certainly wanted to excel as a traditional comedian, at first perhaps unconsciously modelling himself after his most successful predecessor William Congreve, whose influence was very strong in the repertory of the time. But neither Fielding nor anyone else could match Congreve's masterful wit. George Farquhar, a playwright whose comic vision was closer to Fielding's, might have been a better model, though the tides were then running against the kind of play he wrote, and they were few. Ultimately Fielding wanted to write comedy with a moral and social purpose, comedy that instructed.[1] But his ready gift (and his opportunities) lay in the direction of loosely structured short plays that were topical and iconoclastic. These owed something to the vigorous satire of Aristophanes, whom Fielding at the time admired, but they have a vitality unique to Fielding. When the Licensing Act of 1737 effectively ended his career as

playwright, he was moving in the direction of 'the intimate satirical revue',[2] as one critic suggests; or, as another says, towards
'topical cabaret'.[3]

Fielding's movement away from traditional comedy, towards
mocking burlesque and travesty, was in important ways the result
of experiment. He gradually discovered his immediate strength
as playwright, and he drew upon it. But the movement was also
determined by the conditions of the theatre in which he worked,
where there was little or no market for new five-act comedies.
The established houses were conservative in this regard, stick-
ing pretty much to limited repertories with a long history of
success. These included plays so often acted by a company that
they required little or no rehearsal time, and generally speaking
no new scenery or costumes. The cost of putting them on was
small compared to the cost of readying and mounting a new
play.[4] Given the situation, many have found it surprising that
the very young Fielding's first play, the five-act *Love in Several
Masques*, was accepted by Colley Cibber and his fellow theatre
managers of Drury Lane. Why should they have accepted a conventional apprentice piece from an unknown author? Though
we have no certain evidence on which to base an answer, many
have assumed until recently that Fielding's cousin, Lady Mary
Wortley Montagu, got Drury Lane to accept the play. She had
read a sketch of it and had encouraged Fielding to finish it; in
addition, he dedicated *Love in Several Masques* to her when it
was published.[5] But the conclusion is by no means certain. Lady
Mary's influence may have helped, but it seems doubtful that
her recommendation alone could have accounted for the acceptance. A glance at London's theatre world in the Restoration and
early eighteenth century helps one to understand the issues at
stake and the odds against getting a new play produced in the
late 1720s. It also provides a sense of the complexities, at least
some of which Fielding must have weighed, before deciding to
become a professional playwright, beginning in 1729–30 after his
Leiden days.

In the summer of 1660, Charles II, only recently crowned,
issued a patent to two of his friends, Sir William Davenant and
Thomas Killigrew. These franchises gave them an effective monopoly of the theatre in London, though various forms of dramatic entertainment offered intermittent competition. Killigrew's
company, technically part of Charles's household – the King's

players – at first performed at the converted Gibbon's Tennis Court, and later at the Theatre Royal in Bridge Street (1663). Unfortunately, the Bridge Street playhouse was destroyed by fire in 1672. So in 1674, the King's men settled in a new Theatre Royal, in Drury Lane. But more hard times were ahead.

In 1661, the other company, under Davenant's more enterprising mangement, the Duke of York's men, performed their plays in an up-to-date theatre, with changeable scenery, at Lincoln's Inn Fields; in 1671, they moved to an even better equipped theatre in Dorset Gardens where, unlike Killigrew's company, they enjoyed a measure of success. Unfortunately, by 1682, the King's players, despite their share in the monopoly, were in such financial trouble that they had to negotiate a union with the more successful Duke's men. The Bridge Street fire had hurt them badly, but so had bad management, and consequently, a poor box office and internal feuding.

Though this union worked well enough for over ten years, it was never a real success. Troubles arose in which patentees, actors and outside shareholders contended for what each group thought was its fair share of profits. They wrangled among themselves, formed new alliances, built new theatres, and experimented with different forms of entertainment like opera and pantomime. They also sued each other and called upon the Lord Chamberlain, head of the King's household (and who traditionally governed theatre activity in London and Westminster), to decide disputes.

By the summer of 1714, with the accession of George I, two facts dominated London's theatre world. First, the conservative forces of the patent monopoly had gradually won a new control of the market by the trials and errors of competition, recourse to legal authority, and political influence.[6] Second the theatre's turbulent past had left many questions unanswered either because they had been settled *ad hoc* only, without reference to abiding principles that alone could make the future secure, or because it was unclear despite the effective monopoly what new competition might be allowed its chance. There were many theatrical entrepreneurs who tried to circumvent the monopoly or to become a part of it.

For example, a licence had been granted to Vanbrugh and Congreve, on 14 December 1704, to establish a company at Queen's Theatre (later King's) in the Haymarket (completed in 1705). It threatened the two patent theatres with strong competition that never materialized for a variety of reasons, but it took years for its relative failure to become evident. Its acoustics were poor, so that 'scarce one word in ten could be distinctly heard in it',[7] and its location was well west of the other theatres, an inconvenient and costly coach ride away. But its acoustics were improved, and it was gradually given over entirely to music, including Italian opera, which had a great vogue for a time.[8] On 9 May 1719, the Lord Chamberlain issued a warrant establishing the Royal Academy of Music, which had its home in King's. It was patronized largely by the well-to-do, but it needed additional money from the Crown and the nobility to stay afloat.[9] Nevertheless King's indeed survived, and its Royal patronage represented a powerful interest in the world of the theatre.

Another issue that made for uncertainty in London's theatre was the status of patents, originally understood to be held in perpetuity and assignable to heirs or sold, but for various reasons suspended and reissued as licences or patents for a term of years or at the pleasure of some authority of the Crown. When George I ascended in 1714, the Drury Lane managers, Colley Cibber, Barton Booth and Robert Wilks, dropped their Tory partner and invited Richard Steele to join them because they needed his strong Whig connections in the new government.[10] He had no trouble securing a limited patent. But the patent itself raised another question, for its wording seemed to give him complete discretion to run the company; did it follow that the traditional authority of the Lord Chamberlain was in this instance suspended? For a time it seemed so, but a series of legal manoeuvres made it clear that the immediate power lay with the Lord Chamberlain, though questions, as usual, were left unanswered.[11] Indeed, such tugs of war were an old story by the time Steele became a patentee. When in 1694 actors and managers had a dispute over shares of the profits, it was settled by the Lord Chamberlain's issuance, in March 1695, of a licence to a group of prominent actors to set up a new company, Thomas Betterton, Elizabeth Barry and Anne Bracegirdle among them.[12] But it was a licence at the pleasure of the Lord Chamberlain, who could suspend it at any time. Who would invest in such a doubtful enterprise?

These and other troublesome issues made the theatre a precarious business. It was not clear when or how some new decision might affect the patent companies: for instance, when might the Lord Chamberlain or another arm of government intervene?

Neither in fact was it entirely clear that a theatre needed a licence to operate in London. Theatres had opened in the suburbs – among them two in Richmond Hill (1714) and one in Greenwich (1709) – and in 1720, a theatre opened in London, the New Theatre in the Haymarket, apparently without a licence or patent. The Little Theatre, later called Little Haymarket to distinguish it from the King's Opera House nearby, mounted 'illegitimate' productions, like rope-dancing and acrobatics; but it also performed standard repertory pieces occasionally, and in 1728, a pirate production of *The Beggar's Opera* was performed there. It probably did not offer strong competition to Drury Lane and Lincoln's Inn Fields, not day-to-day, at least, because it was not occupied by a single company, and neither, as far as we know, was it managed as the patent theatres were. Various troupes and companies made use of it for short periods, and what competition they offered was hit or miss.[13] But the theatre with its parade of occupants was very much there, an unpredictable reality.

However unsettled things were, the effective monopoly of the two patent theatres by the 1720s gave the London stage the appearance of a settled domain. In some senses it was settled precisely because the managers, especially at Drury Lane, were conservative, relying on old plays, tried favourites, to keep them going, and turning down new plays, which were chancy and of course expensive to produce. The actors in the patent houses were for their own reasons sympathetic to the managers' conservatism. They did not like to learn new parts which they might play once only, or perhaps a few times and never again. In this climate, the chances of getting a new play accepted were not good when Fielding first arrived on the scene in 1727, especially given his strong preference for writing conventional five-act comedies, which meant getting a play accepted by one of the two legitimate houses.

He was young, intelligent, well educated, confident, proud of his birth, full of vitality, attractive and ambitious. His plays make it clear that even as a young man he had a sense for the mind's quick workings in human confrontation. He was in certain ways inventive and capable of rapid composition. Yet at one level of mind he must have thought only remotely, if at all, about a career in the London theatre. More likely he thought of his first play as an isolated venture, which he undertook as a gentleman amateur, or as a first step not to be immediately followed by another. Certainly he left London and went abroad soon after

Love in Several Masques was produced. By the standards of the day, the play neither failed nor succeeded, running four nights as it did. He might have stayed and tried his hand again. But on 16 March 1728, about a month after the play's first performance, Fielding was registered in the faculty of Letters at the University of Leiden. It is reasonable to suppose that the move to Leiden had been planned a good deal earlier than this date, and approved, or at least accepted, by his father or his grandmother, either or both of whom might be paying the bills. In any case Fielding's first venture into the world of the London theatre – and what may appear like his abrupt departure – did not deter his return to it in the late summer or early autumn of 1729.[14] No one knows why he went to Leiden, or why he returned to become a professional writer of plays. He probably needed money.

Whether Fielding's good connections helped him to get his first play produced and thus, perhaps, encouraged him to become a serious playwright, we do not know for sure. As I have said, Cross, Rogers and others believe that Lady Mary, his cousin, successfully intervened at Drury Lane on his behalf. Hume thinks it unlikely: 'She was not a professional playwright; nothing in her letters suggests theatrical involvements; and Drury Lane did not work that way. If gentry could get a work staged by dropping hints to management, many more new plays would have been on the boards.'[15] Hume's view seems generally right. None of the managers was a pushover. Colley Cibber – playwright, actor, Poet Laureate, autobiographer, and the most influential of the three managers of Drury Lane – had a reputation for turning down plays with a peremptory no. But at the very end of his informative, lively, self-serving, commonsensical *An Apology for the Life of Mr. Colley Cibber*, after discussing the reasons for turning down novice plays and the frequent unpleasant aftermath of such rejections, he says:

> Yet this was not all we had to struggle with; to supersede our right of rejecting the recommendation, or rather the imposition of some great persons, whom it was not prudence to disoblige, they sometimes came in, with a high hand, to support [the playwright's] pretensions; and then, *coute qui coute*, acted it must be.[16]

No doubt such occasions were rare or, as Hume says, 'many more new plays would have been on the boards';[17] but they were not unheard of. Lady Mary was probably not 'some great person', but she had influence among such persons, including Walpole at this time. Maybe Hume is right to say Fielding's first play was accepted only because the Drury Lane managers and senior actors liked it; many of them, Cibber included, no doubt saw in it parts they wanted to play.[18] But Fielding's Whig connections probably helped them to see things his way, at least this once.[19]

Fielding returned to London from Leiden, probably by September 1729, the beginning of the theatrical season. He may have travelled briefly in France and Italy before returning to England.[20] At 22 years of age, full of hope and energy, and without much money, he was ready to launch his professional career as a writer.[21] Despite the difficulties of making his way, he would have found London an exciting city. It was then a greater metropolis in relation to the rest of the country than it is now in terms of population, commerce and the arts. Only Bristol maintained a trade independent of the capital. All the other cities, towns, and villages sent their products to London, either for immediate consumption or for processing and export.[22] Excepting the university presses at Oxford and Cambridge, all English publishing was concentrated in London. Its population at the time – about 700 000 counting the City, Westminster, Southwark, and the growing suburbs – included a huge number of poor who earned a bare living as day labourers at the docks and elsewhere. A much less numerous group – merchants, shopkeepers and craftsmen – made up a middle class, wide-ranging in terms of income and taste. The relatively few landed families of wealth lived in the country, coming to the city for the winter season. It was largely from this group of gentry and nobility, who like Fielding himself moved back and forth with the seasons, that the London theatre had drawn (and continued to draw) its audiences; although from the late seventeenth century, the middle classes began to attend as their various tastes were met by sentimental comedies like Cibber's *Love's Last Shift* (1696), Steele's *The Lying Lover* (1703) and *The Conscious Lovers* (1722), and the Reverend James Miller's *The Man of Taste* (1735), all of which catered one way and another to bourgeois expectations.

One sees from Fielding's plays that he had prepared himself for a career as playwright by studying the work of his English predecessors and contemporaries. This he continued to do. He had also read the comedies of Aristophanes, Plautus and Terence, as well as the plays of the French comedians, especially Molière. Along with his attraction to the lively, teeming world of London, which he knew and loved, and his perhaps misleading experience of *Love in Several Masques* (neither a success nor a failure, but after all accepted and produced by Drury Lane), his preparation as a student of drama must have encouraged him in his professional commitment. In addition, he had further prepared himself for the return to London by completing a traditional five-act comedy, *The Temple Beau*, and by writing substantial portions of two others, *Don Quixote in England* and *The Wedding-Day*.

Until he married Charlotte Cradock in 1734, we do not know where Fielding lived in London. Because the principal theatres were located in the respectable West End – an important exception was Thomas Odell's newly opened theatre (1729) on Ayliffe Street, Goodman's Fields, north-east of the Tower – it is reasonable to suppose Fielding lived in one of the West End parishes, St Martin-in-the-Fields, just north of the Strand at its western end, or the adjoining Parish of St Paul's, Covent Garden, just north-east of St Martin's. Battestin's list of Fielding's London residences or likely residences supports this view.[23]

The London theatre of the early eighteenth century – stage, props, lighting, actors, audience, finances – was in many ways a special institution, which we can reconstruct historically.[24] Despite variation, the chief playhouses shared a common design; there was, in effect, a typical theatre. It had a proscenium arch, and the part of the stage that extended beyond it, towards the main seating area – the pit – was the locus of most of the action. A curtain was opened to signal the beginning of the performance, but only after the prologue had been spoken; and it was not closed until after the epilogue. Movable, changeable, scenery, often elaborate, was located inside the proscenium. Regarded as part of the spectacle, these scenes, on separate shutters in the wings and at the back, were changed – closed and removed, while others were opened – in full view of the audience, and their changing marked a transition in dramatic action: 'a change of scene'. The stage was typically empty of sets between acts, when singing, dancing or other entertainment filled the interval. Doors leading to and from the stage were mounted on both sides of the proscenium. Because the theatre building was entirely enclosed, lighting was essential. Overhead chandeliers holding many candles did most of the work, but oil lamps supplied additional light. By the middle of an evening's bill, theatres could be uncomfortably warm.

In the first part of the season, early September to some time in October, the chief theatre companies played only two or three times a week. Thereafter, as more people moved into London for the winter, they opened daily until June, when the season ended. But during Lent, they played only four times a week, and theatres were closed for the Week of the Passion. After trying various curtain times – 5:00 p.m., 5:30 p.m., 6:00 p.m. – the theatres decided on 6:00 as the most acceptable. Though the play, or mainpiece, continued to be the centre of the evening's entertainment, the programme was likely to begin with three pieces of music (known as First, Second, and Third Music); to include – in addition to a prologue, the play, and an epilogue – between-the-acts music, dance and specialties not necessarily related to the play, either in theme or mood. As if this were not enough, it became more and more usual for an afterpiece to follow. It was a long evening.

Drury Lane could seat well over 700, and Lincoln's Inn Fields more than 1300, with the total number on any occasion determined by the willingness of the audience to be crowded on the backless benches in the pit and in the galleries above and behind it. There were also places in the side and front boxes, and on the stage itself. For really popular plays, like *The Beggar's Opera*, the managers would sell standing room to willing patrons. The Little Theatre in the Haymarket, where Fielding was later to mount his own plays, had a lesser capacity, but just what it was no one knows.[25] The price of admission might vary according to the lavishness (and hence the cost) of the production: costumes, scenes, decorations, music, afterpieces, and so on. The popularity of the programme also helped determine what the managers charged for a ticket. King's, in the Haymarket, limited the number of places sold in pit and boxes and set high prices to control the social status of the audience. In the 1720s, a typical scale of charges for Lincoln's Inn and Drury Lane might have been boxes 5s. (25p), pit 4s. (20p), first gallery 3s. (15p), and upper gallery 1s. (5p).[26]

Generally speaking, gentlemen and affluent citizens would occupy the pit, wits and beaux sat in the side boxes, and ladies in the front boxes. (In the first scene of *Love in Several Masques*, Lady Matchless is reported as having occupied a front box the night before, envied by the women and ogled by the men in the audience.) The galleries were filled with those less well-off. Sometimes servants came early to claim seats for their masters, who would arrive at a more convenient hour. As the century progressed, the social range of theatre-goers was enlarged, and so was their partisanship. Audiences might be very noisy, clapping at what they approved, hissing their dislikes, and sometimes calling out – all while the play was in progress. Politics (was the play somehow for or against party or faction?) or the theatregoer's personal taste (in actors and acting, the playwright, the play's qualities, the lavishness of the production) could determine the nature and intensity of the audience's response in the middle of things. Audience reaction might also be generated by partisan newspaper accounts of a play, with which the audience was already familiar. In this climate, actors and playwrights with thin skins were often uncomfortable. Fielding was bruised more than once. He seems to have been sensitive, but tough enough to bear his discomfort and carry on.

Theatres were expensive to run. Non-patent houses often operated at the margin or failed altogether. But successful theatrical entrepreneurs like John Rich and Henry Giffard had no trouble selling shares to raise money to build or refurbish a theatre.[27] We know that Drury Lane and Lincoln's Inn Fields enjoyed more than a few good years in the second and third decades of the century – 1712–13, 1713–14, and the early 1720s – posting profits of £3000 to £4000 a year. Obviously those with more than one source of theatre income benefited most. Cibber, for example, in addition to earnings as actor, playwright and manager, was entitled to an owner's share of Drury Lane revenue. Nevertheless high costs made it no easy thing to turn a profit. An early eighteenth-century estimate, which itemized anticipated costs for the 'Establishm^t of ye Company' for a year, came up with a figure of almost £10 000, much more money than most people then earned in a lifetime.[28] The figure would probably have been about right, perhaps a few hundred pounds low, for Lincoln's Inn Fields in the mid-1720s.[29] We have no good actual figures for Drury Lane. The estimate of anticipated annual costs for 'ye company' included payments to the shareholders, called rent (£600), tallow, wax and oil for lighting (£600), twenty actors (£1710) and eleven actresses (£800). The remaining £6000 or so was to pay apprentice actors, singers, dancers, musicians, a prompter and clerk, treasurers, doorkeepers, wardrobe keepers and other wardrobe personnel, scenemen, carpenters, candlemen, barbers, bill carriers, and three managers. To this total of about £10 000 should be added taxes (say, £25 a year) and the variable cost of repairs of the theatre building itself, and of printing, costumes, and properties.[30]

Though it was not until the Restoration, in 1660, that women acted on the public stage – their parts were earlier played by boys and young men – they quickly became an important element in the economics of the theatre. As Cibber says, 'The additional objects, then, of real, beautiful women, could not but draw a proportion of new admirers to the theatre.'[31] A few actresses like Elizabeth Barry and Anne Bracegirdle became famous and influential well before the turn of the century. Playwrights created roles with them in mind, audiences were eager to see them act, and managers were sometimes forced to take them into account in making policy. But women generally did not achieve equality with men in the theatre: 'They were paid significantly less than their male counterparts and not one of them became a theatre manager.'[32] It was an unusual woman – Barry and Bracegirdle were among the exceptions – who earned as much as the comparable men in the company and who acquired power enough, as shareholders or as dominant personalities, to have a say in the decisions of management. The breakdown of the prospective annual costs for 'ye Company', referred to above, says something about the uncertainty of their position, for it includes a list of men and women (identified by name) and the salaries they should be paid. One interesting point implied by the list is that actors outnumbered actresses by almost two to one, roughly the proportion of male to female roles in the dramas of the period. The four highest paid men – Betterton, Verbruggen, Powell and Wilks, all famous – were assigned £150 a year. (Betterton was assigned an additional £50 to teach apprentice actors.) The two highest paid women – Barry and Bracegirdle, at least as famous – were each assigned two estimates of salary, £150 and £120, apparently registering a sense for their worth – equal to the men – and yet leaving open the possibility that management might pay them the lower salary.[33]

Of a later generation of actresses was Catherine Raftor, after her marriage known as Catherine or Kitty Clive. Four years Fielding's junior, she was just coming into prominence when the young playwright turned professional. Her strengths were comedy and song, and in 1729 she enjoyed a great success in Cibber's ill-fated ballad opera, *Love in a Riddle*.[34] Cibber, Fielding, and later David Garrick made good use of Kitty Clive's talents, especially Fielding. He wrote many of his most distinctive, successful short pieces, sharp-edged burlesques, as vehicles for her.[35] She was a well-paid actress by the standards of the day, and she was sometimes influential in the internal affairs of Drury Lane. But like most other important women in the theatre, she exercised power unofficially, behind the scenes.

Only the foremost actors or actresses were well paid. Moreover the managers of all three patent theatres, including the opera house in the Haymarket, tried to hold members of the company to the letter of their contracts, sometimes withholding fees when actors were too ill to perform, and often enough provoking them to sue for redress.[36] There had been times, from the re-opening of the theatres in 1660, when income was too low for the payroll to be met. Management's inability (or unwillingness) to pay, at least to pay on time, and the actors' need for money, along with the power to bargain under certain circumstances, resulted in a compromise arrangement – the benefit performance – which gave the proceeds of ticket sales, less the cost of overheads, for a predesignated night to one, sometimes two, predesignated actors. The many variations on this plan were regularized in articles by the Lord Chamberlain, dated 17 April 1712, which included the stipulation that no benefit could be given until 1 March, after the height of the season.[37] To maximize their receipts on such occasions actors bought tickets, usually expensive tickets, in advance and sold them, at inflated prices when they could, to friends and acquaintances.

During the early eighteenth century no theatre had a playwright on its staff whose only duty was to write.[38] Managers like Steele and Cibber, who were also playwrights, could make ends meet reasonably well. But generally the incomes of freelance playwrights were poor. What money they made might come from three sources: author benefits, sale of the play's copyright for publication, and a gift from the play's dedicatee. Though negotiations between author and manager might result in unique arrangements for the benefit, the general practice by the 1720s was for the playwright to receive gross receipts less overheads (usually £50) for every third night during the first unbroken run, which was likely to be short. There were no benefits for later

performances.[39] Fielding's first play, *Love in Several Masques*, ran
for just four nights, which would have included only one benefit. It might have given Fielding £50 to £100 after house charges.[40]
Love in Several Masques was published by John Watts, London,
1728, but what Fielding got for it we do not know.[41] In the brief
dedication to his cousin, he compliments her on her intelligence,
which, he says, confutes those who would confine intellect to
men and the softer graces to women, and he tells us Lady Mary
saw two (of the four) performances of his play.[42] It seems reasonable to suppose that she attended the première and the benefit
and helped to pack the house on the third night.

Love in Several Masques is a comedy of intrigue, but quite without
the dark side, say, of Congreve's *The Way of the World*. Fielding
makes the pursuit of Helena by Merital, of Vermilia by Malvil,
and of the young widow, Lady Matchless, by Wisemore the chief
action of the play. He complicates the action by means of a psychologically plausible strategy. We learn that the women love their
men, but do not reveal their feelings, in part because it seems a
bad tactic and in part because they want to be sure they are
prized for themselves and not for their fortunes. Besides, the
women want constant lovers, and though they are doubtful that
even a sincere love can long survive the strains of matrimony,
they believe love to be the only acceptable basis of marriage.
Fielding uses the three men, from the start in doubt that their
women love them, and in farcically controlled turns in the plot
– farfetched but amusing – until their doubt becomes jealousy.
Similarly controlled turns make the men appear faithless to the
women. But the jealousies are undermined and so are the apparent
infidelities. The women admit their love and the happy couples
are united.

Though the play includes more than a few scoundrels and fools,
they are essentially powerless in the world of the work, both
because they are seen immediately for what they are by us and
by the ultimately moral characters on whom they try their mischief. Besides, they are not intelligent. And the lovers, who are
certainly smart and inventive enough to do real harm to one
another, are fundamentally charitable. In this context, the triumph
of goodness is never in real doubt, and the opportunities for
satire are limited. Hume says the play is an example of humane
comedy, which, without explicit debt, takes for its model many
of the comedies of the first quarter of the century (by Cibber,

Steele, Susanna Centlivre and Leonard Welsted, for example).[43]

Like most of Fielding's plays this one has genuine vitality, which typically finds expression when a character's radical nature is exposed by circumstance. So Lady Matchless, in a conversation with Vermilia about her widowhood, acknowledges her relief: 'Who would not wish her spouse in heaven, when it was the only way to deliver herself out of hell?' (II, i; Henley, I, 29). Helena, resisting her uncle, Sir Positive Trap, and her aunt, Lady Trap, who want her to marry the titled, wealthy fop of their choice, answers the charge of disrespect for her ancestors:

Sir Positive Trap: Do you ridicule your ancestors, the illustrious race of Traps?
Helena: No, sir; I honour them so far that I am resolved not to take a fool into the family. (II, vi; Henley, I, 36)

Sir Positive Trap, infuriated that his niece Helena defies him, says, 'I hope to see the time, when a man may carry his daughter to market with the same lawful authority as any other cattle' (II, vi; Henley, I, 37). All three speeches show the speaker's vitals, so that our approval of what we hear is made less important than our recognition of its truth for the character. And of course all three are funny, in a degree paradoxical, inverting or otherwise thwarting conventional expectation. Fielding cuts close to the bone, though less consistently in *Love in Several Masques* than in his later short pieces.

Hume seems right in wanting to make no more of the play's good qualities than they deserve. Its satire on rank, wealth, the law, politics and Italian opera, for example, is weak. And the play might have involved us more in the fate of its lovers if Fielding had made them face greater difficulties, building tension and suspense. In short, the play's structure is not strong.[44]

Fielding's satire on the marriage market, however, is effective, if not biting. And it is made to be consistent with his treatment of love and marriage throughout the play, where we are made to see that even though it may not survive matrimony, love is its only reasonable ('natural' and 'hopeful') basis. Fielding's most sympathetic characters, men as well as women, find marriage without love a violation of physical longing and a darkening of hope. The better they understand this truth, the more dramatic authority Fielding assigns them. Maybe at one level naive in its idealism, this view of marriage continues at the heart of Fielding's more extended treatments of the subject. He believed one may be taught morality, but at its best it operates for him less as acquired behaviour than as a complex reflection of our natural selves. Such a morality is neither static nor simple. For example, his ideal of love and marriage does not displace his tolerant treatment of loveless desire, especially when it reflects an aspect of human longing rather than the will to manipulate and possess.[45]

Nevertheless Fielding's first play, like all those to follow, is among other things an accommodation to the world of the theatre in which he worked. He wrote it either with Cibber, Wilks, Anne Oldfield and other first-rate actors in mind, or he modelled it so conventionally that these actors found characters ready-made for their well established specialties. Fielding is aware that he owes them a debt of gratitude, which he pays in the preface to the published version of the play. There, having thanked Cibber and Wilks by name, he goes on to express appreciation for 'how advantageously they and other personages set off their respective parts' (Henley, I, 9). In the same preface he also registers his professional sense for the competition that jammed his play, doing so in courteous and yet self-defending references to the 'just applauses' given to the piece that preceded his at Drury Lane 'for the continued space of twenty-eight nights' (Cibber's *The Provok'd Husband*), and to Gay's *The Beggar's Opera*, 'co-temporary with [*Love in Several Masques*], an entertainment which engrosses the whole talk and admiration of the town', and which had an unprecedented run of 62 performances beginning in February 1728 (Henley, I, 9).

Fielding's pragmatic sense for the exigencies of the the theatre world did not displace his artistic vision, but it certainly modified it. Getting Lady Mary to read his first play while it was yet unfinished, his dedication of it to her, her attendance at two of its four performances, Fielding's thanks to Cibber, Wilks, and the other actors, along with his references to *The Provok'd Husband* and *The Beggar's Opera* in the preface, all imply the young playwright's keen awareness of the context in which he worked. When he returned from Leiden in 1729, he seems to have had an unfounded expectation that Drury Lane would welcome another of his plays. But this misguided optimism notwithstanding, he was over the long run a pragmatist in business matters, developing his versatile talent with an eye on the real possibilities.

It is for this reason that critical judgments claiming to see in Fielding's first play only emphatic signs of what he was to become as playwright, essayist and novelist seem excessive. Albert J. Rivero, for example, says, '*Love in Several Masques* evinces what critics have identified as the quintessence of Fielding's art: its clear moral purpose, its conspicuous moral tone.'[46] This claim, in fact Rivero's entire discussion of the play, is within limits just, but it seems pat. 'Moral tone' is both generated and mocked by the play's principal moral characters, probably because there is fun in the mockery. Sometimes Fielding's 'clear moral purpose' is made to stand by, waiting out a babble of dialogue that helps fill *Love in Several Masques* without much furthering its purpose. All in all, a morality – the ideal of marriage based on love – stands confirmed by the end of the play, but it does so having survived the best Fielding can do to keep the action alive.

The second of Fielding's plays to be produced was *The Temple Beau*, staged at Goodman's Fields in January 1730. It was one of three plays he had worked on during the period of his student days at Leiden, the other two being *Don Quixote in England* and *The Wedding-Day*, both of which were not to be staged for some years (*Don Quixote* in 1734 and *The Wedding-Day* in 1743). Fielding tells us in the preface to *Don Quixote* that the play was 'begun at *Leyden* in the Year 1728' (Henley, IV, 9). And from his preface to the *Miscellanies* we learn that *The Wedding-Day* 'was the third Dramatic Performance [he] ever attempted'.[47] In 1729, Fielding offered an unfinished sketch of *Don Quixote* to Drury Lane, but Wilks and Cibber refused it. And John Rich heard *The Wedding-Day* for possible staging at Lincoln's Inn Fields, probably in late 1730; it was also refused there. Fielding seems to have been diffident about both plays[48] (Henley, IV, 9). Though his fourth play, *The Temple Beau*, may well have been turned down by both patent houses, it was accepted by Goodman's Fields (opened in October 1729), the first new play to be produced there, the acceptance being an early departure from what was to be its conservative repertory policy. Who accepted the play for Goodman's Fields is not known.[49]

Love in Several Masques and *The Temple Beau* have many elements in common. Both are comedies of intrigue and both turn on the marriage market and on its oppositions of youth and age, men and women, virtuous love and sexual self-indulgence. Though *The Temple Beau* is more complex in its intrigues than is Fielding's first play, both promote the ideal of love and marriage, showing money to be necessary for a happy marriage but bad as the primary reason for it. In oblique support of the ideal, both plays show some women to be at least the equal of men in intellect, the capacity for education, vitality, character, loyalty, affection and common-sense. Getting married is a gamble, but it promises – as an ideal – not only love between sexual opposites but a partnership between equals as well. Nevertheless, the ideal does not eliminate the double standard in Fielding's world, though he sometimes has a sympathetic male voice oppose it (like Heartfort in *The Wedding-Day*, for instance).

If we are attentive enough, we are able to infer that before the action of the play, Veromil and Bellaria – Fielding's principal lovers – have met, probably in France, fallen in love, and promised themselves to each other, with paternal approval for the match. But both fathers die and, cheated out of most of his inheritance by a shifty brother, Veromil is declared unsuitable as a husband by Bellaria's guardian uncle, George Pedant. She is worth £20 000 and he almost nothing. By the time we first meet the lovers, in England, they are separated and ignorant of each other's whereabouts, their letters to each other having been intercepted after their separation. Veromil is about to go to France, from London, in search of Bellaria, who in fact is in the city, having been sent there to a second uncle, Sir Avarice Pedant (to keep her from being found by Veromil at the family's country home, one infers).

The play's dramatic tension, such as it is, does not derive from the relation between the lovers, who soon meet and renew their vows after Veromil experiences a fleeting twinge of jealousy, which is understandable but unfounded as he soon realizes. He is the most truthful (Veromil), loving, attractive, understanding, energetic and self-controlled man in the world, and she is the most beautiful (Bellaria), loving, intelligent, educated, witty, virtuous and loyal woman. Despite their excesses of virtue, it is possible to like them. What tension the play generates comes from a complication of characters, all of whom have a stake in the marriage of heiress Bellaria: two fathers, greedy or otherwise eager for their sons and themselves (Sir Avarice Pedant and Sir Harry Wilding); two sons opposed or indifferent to the match, coerced into proposing (Young Pedant, who wants only to be a bookworm, and Young Wilding, the Temple Beau, who wants only to continue seducing women while he pretends to read law); two sisters (Lady Lucy Pedant and Lady Gravely), the first of whom has led Young Wilding on far enough to know what he is and the second, a prude with hidden appetites, who has fallen in love with him, so that each has a reason for opposing Wilding's marriage to Bellaria; and two lovers (Valentine and Clarissa) who get on less well with each other than do Veromil and Bellaria, largely because Valentine, Veromil's closest friend, has fallen in love with Bellaria before learning who she is.

Though the paired characters, like stock characters generally, are implicitly compared to each other through temperament and inclination – Lady Gravely is a nominal prude, Lady Lucy Pedant is an open flirt; Young Wilding is a rake (a rake manqué) and Young Pedant is a scholar (a feeble scholar); Sir Avarice is single-minded about money, impatient with his son, and Sir Harry is a blustering, amiable father; Valentine is an untrustworthy lover and Clarissa is steadfast – their predictable natures are not very interesting. But Fielding produces some tension between characters by means of the context in which he locates them: between Veromil and his absent brother, the wily disinheritor, proxied by Veromil senior's former servant Pincet; Valentine and his uncle, Sir Avarice Pedant, who owes his nephew money; Veromil and his friend Valentine, who both want Bellaria; and the two fathers and their sons, whose views of work and marriage are radically at odds. Fielding not only presents these tensions individually, he also assigns them to operate in relation to Bellaria as prospective bride, so that they are parts of a dramatic whole. Accordingly, Bellaria, always supported by her sympathetic lover, becomes the focal point of the tensions in the world of the play.

Though the dramatic structure of *The Temple Beau* is improved over that of Fielding's first play, it has some obvious weaknesses. The lovers are too nearly perfect to engage us in what is or ought to be their burdensome complication of distress. They are so sure of each other and of themselves that they are unassailable, however threatened by the loss of love, freedom and financial self-sufficiency. Still, Veromil and Bellaria are attractive enough that we wish them well.

If the goodness of the lovers is excessive, the evil of Valentine, Veromil's friend and vacillating rival, is doubtful. Fielding seems to have used him to introduce stress between the principal lovers where otherwise there was none, but he hardly succeeds. Valentine is compulsive, too unsure of himself to be convincing, and neither Veromil nor Bellaria takes him seriously as a threat for very long. When the vacillating scoundrel repents, and Clarissa forgives him, it is hard to accept their marriage, which is an unpleasant distortion of the ideal Fielding unselfconsciously promotes elsewhere in the play.

The Temple Beau, Young Wilding, is not much of a rake, and neither is he at the centre of the action, as the play's title implies he will be. He never beds Lady Lucy, whom he wants, or Lady Gravely, who wants him. Though he may have had successes before the action of the play begins, and he may even yield to Lady Gravely after it ends, he is not, as we observe him, a consummate lover. But he sometimes makes cuckolding old husbands and marrying for money joking matters, in an atmosphere that suspends morality where he is concerned. His most effective action is taken in conjunction with Pincet, his servant, formerly in the Veromil family. The two share a role like that of the wily servant of New Comedy, who makes his own rules at the same time that he is ultimately constructive on the side of youth, typically fleecing the father on behalf of the son, and in so doing, enabling the son to marry the woman of his choice. With Pincet's help, Wilding takes care of his own needs first, by duping his father into giving him an annuity of £500. It is a neat irony that instead of enabling his marriage, as it would in New Comedy, the annuity frees him from the obligation to court Bellaria, or indeed to marry at all, and reaffirms his status as the Temple Beau.

Quite incidentally Wilding's action is also the means of disclosing letters proving Veromil has been swindled by his brother. Wilding is immensely pleased to think himself a player in the restoration of Veromil's inheritance which makes possible the play's one important marriage.

Wilding: Dear Veromil, let me embrace thee. I am heartily glad I have been instrumental in the procuring your happiness; and, though it is with my mistress, I wish you joy sincerely. (V, xxi; Henley, I, 185)

Wilding is not at the centre of the play's action, but he is ultimately an effective comic character, with an important part in its culmination.

The Temple Beau ran for nine consecutive nights, giving its author three benefits, and it was played four times thereafter during the season.[50] Though, as Hume points out, it may not have yielded as much money as Fielding might have made at Drury Lane or Lincoln's Inn Fields, it was quite a success.[51] His other two early plays, *Don Quixote in England* and *The Wedding-Day*, were less well received. The first, mounted in the Little Haymarket – while Fielding was in mid-career as dramatist – played eleven times over two seasons, typically with another piece on the programme, the first performance being on 5 April 1734 and the last on 7 October 1734, with three of the first four given in Passion Week. The old taboo against Lenten performances began to break down in 1728–9, with the production of legitimate plays at non-patent theatres – first at the Little Haymarket and then, about a year later, at Goodman's Fields – which meant greater competition for all the houses.[52]

Not produced until 1743, *The Wedding-Day* fared even less well, though the lead, Millamour, was played by David Garrick, who by then had begun his acting career at Drury Lane, having enjoyed a great success at Goodman's Fields in 1741.[53] The play was given six performances, but the run was broken, and Fielding tells us he 'receiv'd not £50. for it'.[54] He sold the play to the publisher Andrew Millar for an undisclosed amount. Trouble with the Licenser, followed by bad publicity and inadequate revision (owing to his wife's illness), could not have helped the play's chances, but it is a better crafted piece than is generally allowed.[55]

The Wedding-Day, an intrigue comedy in five acts, generates real energy, especially among its four principal lovers. Though it has weaknesses, as many have noted, its failure probably owes more to Fielding's disregard of certain of the audience's expectations than to poor dramaturgy.[56] The play opens *in medias res*; Millamour, a rake who is the male lead, is informed by a letter from Clarinda, whom he has attracted deeply, almost bedded, and refused to wed, that she has that morning married Mr Stedfast. Fielding discloses the feelings of the jilting lover jilted, which complicate his rakish past.

Millamour: Till this hour I never knew the value of Clarinda . . . Oh! couldst thou tell her half my tenderness or my pain, thou must invent a language to express them. (I, ii; Henley, V, 73, 74)

But he is not simply a downcast lover. We see that despite his unhappiness, he reads her letter closely enough to infer that Stedfast, Clarinda's new husband, is old and rich: 'two excellent qualifications for a husband and a cuckold', he says (I, ii; Henley, V, 74). For the rest of the play Fielding displays Millamour's double sense, which is not quite ambivalence. He loves Clarinda, but resists the idea of marriage because he knows he has a 'mind to tempt [him] to sin, and the . . . constitution to support [him] in it' (I, iii; Henley, V, 76). Of course Fielding also capitalizes on the comic mischief such a character can be brought to do. But to see him as a badly handled rake of reform comedy is to overlook the consistency with which Fielding draws him as both capable of love and unable to turn away from the destructive implications of his self-examined sexuality.[57] This notwithstanding, the play would have been more effective if Millamour's final decision to marry Clarinda when her unconsummated marriage to Stedfast proves to be invalid had been handled with less moral righteousness.

All four principal lovers are distinctive, and their psychologies promising for dramatic action. Clarinda is as complex as Millamour. An orphan, we early learn, she flees the convent in which she is being reared to be with her lover, but she marries Stedfast when she recognizes that Millamour will not come to the altar, half believing she has given him up, half hoping he will seduce her. Mr Stedfast's daughter Charlotte's love for Millamour also complicates the action; and so does Heartfort's love for Charlotte. Fielding sees to it that Charlotte permits Heartfort, who is everything his name implies, to court her, while she pretends to agree with her father's choice of a husband for her, Young Mutable. She plays a delaying game to give herself a chance with Millamour, a real chance now that Clarinda is married. Ostensibly obedient to her father, she behaves with brilliant independence before finally resigning herself to Heartfort, whose good qualities she has undervalued, but never overlooked.

Millamour generates much of the action. Helped by Heartfort and Young Mutable, who cares little for Charlotte, he pretends to be a rich lord with a sister willing to marry Young Mutable. Old Mutable, who cannot resist the bait, breaks off his son's engagement to Charlotte. But too much of the play thereafter relies on Mr Mutable's vacillation and on Mr Stedfast's single-mindedness. The opposition of their fixed temperaments can be amusing, but it also grows wearisome. They are not always effective humour characters.

Some quick moving complications of plot succeed. Millamour, whom Stedfast catches with Clarinda, explains her presence in his house by pretending to be a physician obliged to minister to Mrs Stedfast, who was taken ill, he says, just outside his door. Millamour's deft control of the encounter is engaging. Later, when Stedfast believes Clarinda ill again (she is, of course, only trying to delay consummation of the marriage), he calls for Millamour to attend her and insists ('stedfastly') that doctor and patient be left alone in her bedroom. Other complications are less satisfying. Near the end of the play, we learn that Mr Stedfast is Clarinda's father. In his youth, he fathered her by Mrs Plotwell who, though she has been introduced to us early in the play, is known to us only as the friend of Lucina, a woman Millamour has seduced and jilted. The late recognition of long-lost daughters of upper-middle-class citizens is a hallmark of New Comedy, but apart from telling us early on that Clarinda is an orphan, Fielding uses none of the attendant elements of the convention to prepare the way for the recognition. We are also assured later of what we might have surmised earlier (that the marriage has not been consummated), so Clarinda and her father are saved from incest, and she and Millamour are free to marry.

However, the greatest trouble with the play is Millamour's reliance on a procuress, Mrs Useful, a character Kitty Clive categorically refused to play because she found the part reprehensible.[58] We learn that she helped Millamour get Clarinda out of the convent and helped him in the seduction of Lucina. She is unscrupulous and clever in manipulation; she is also partial to Millamour. His long-term connection with her was offensive to many in Fielding's audience, it seems, but even those who may find her acceptable as a comic character must wonder at her abrupt dismissal by Millamour, late in the fifth act. As I have said, Millamour's decision to become a husband is well foreshadowed, but not his dismissal of Useful. In addition to being abrupt, the dismissal is self-righteous, like Millamour's final comment on the rakes of the world.

Fielding's plays are almost always sympathetic to the conjunction of love and marriage. In fact *The Wedding-Day* is no exception if we view it from the perspective of Heartfort and its women. He is sympathetically treated for his unselfish love for Charlotte and for his efforts to get Millamour to see the destructive implications of his sexual behaviour. In fact, he batters the double standard.

Heartfort: . . . what can be more ridiculous than to make it infamous
    for women to grant what it is honourable for us to solicit? (V,
    iii; Henley, V, 131)

Clarinda, Charlotte, Lucina and Mrs Plotwell are all sympathetically treated for wanting to marry the man they love. Even Millamour comes to the conclusion, however slowly, that love should be joined to marriage. Of course his conversion – if it is that – fulfils a dramatic convention. Late reformations from rake to loving husband in eighteenth-century comedies were an old story when Fielding wrote *The Wedding-Day*, Cibber's *Love's Last Shift* (1696) and *The Careless Husband* (1704) having fairly begun the vogue. But at one level Millamour may be regarded as Fielding's (comic) means of exploring certain important elements of one kind of young man: strong sexuality, the power to attract, ranging appetite, the capacity to love, and considerable, though spotty, self-knowledge. The exploration, a difficult undertaking, is in places clumsy, but it is not naive.

Fielding's third play to be produced, *The Author's Farce*, on 30 March 1730, marked an important departure. It was his first experiment with farce and burlesque, and it was played at the New Theatre in the Haymarket. The unlicensed house was apparently without the usual kind of company; it may rather have been staffed, intermittently, by a small nucleus of regulars, with additional actors hired *ad hoc*. And it was perhaps without a manager. Even if it had a skeletal permanent staff, it seems that the details and costs of production were typically the responsibility of whoever rented the theatre from the owner (an author or a travelling troupe, for example).[59] In this venue, Fielding – any playwright – would experience the maximum of both risk and freedom. With the cooperation of the others involved, he could control the production, and unless there were a special arrangement, profits would go to him, the entrepreneur.

The Author's Farce is usually regarded as the beginning of Fielding's discovery of his true talent, farce and burlesque, which he would later have the chance to develop at the Little Haymarket, liberated from the conservative repertory policies of the patent theatres. The conclusion seems correct within limits. I happen to believe that *The Wedding-Day* and *The Modern Husband*, quite different plays from each other, show rare, perhaps unique promise, given the youth of their author. He was not 25 when he wrote them. Both are flawed, but both display a deep knowledge of human nature, a capacity for wit, and a complex moral integrity. Fielding wrote farce and burlesque and played them at Little Haymarket when he did simply because that is what the London theatre world made possible. Trying to get new five-act plays accepted or producing them oneself was a risky business. But in these circumstances, his great success at burlesque is hardly proof that writing finished conventional comedies was beyond him. Burlesque and comedy both require talent, but the comic art is long.

Fielding had his first great success with *The Author's Farce*; it was also the first of his rehearsal plays, which include a play within the play.[60] It was so well received that it was performed 42 times from its opening on 30 March to 3 July, the season having been extended to accommodate eager theatre-goers. The run, not unbroken, was the longest since *The Beggar's Opera*. After 24 April, the play was helped by Fielding's *Tom Thumb*, which was offered on the same programme.[61] In *The Author's Farce* Fielding parodies himself in the central character, Luckless, a playwright who is down and almost out, unable to get a play accepted or to pay his rent. Drawing on his first-hand knowledge of the London theatre and the whole literary scene of the day, Fielding writes full of fun and energy, giving us a Luckless so far from despair in his desperate predicament that he carries us with him.

Mrs Moneywood, Luckless's landlady, presses him hard for the rent, but she would forgive it if he would give her his love instead. Luckless, however, loves and wants to marry Harriot, Moneywood's daughter.

Mrs Moneywood: Do but be kind and I'll forgive thee all.
Luckless: Death! Madam, stand off. If I must be plagued with you, I had rather you should afflict my eyes than my touch.[62]
(I, ii)

When Witmore, a sympathetic old friend who sees the world for what it is, visits Luckless, he offers grim advice.

Witmore: If thou wilt write . . ., get a patron, be pimp to some
  worthless man of quality, write panegyrics on him . . ., and
  don't pretend to stand thyself against a tide of ill nature that
  would have overwhelmed a Plato or a Socrates. (I, v; Woods,
  p. 16)

Witmore's dark appraisal and his satirical advice are appropriate in a play attributed to Scriblerus Secundus who, according
to the title-page of the published version, wrote *The Author's Farce*.
Fielding of course derived the name from the distinguished
members of the Scriblerus Club, Swift, Pope and Gay among
them, who wrote satires on the world's follies, especially its literary
and political follies: *Peri Bathous: Or the Art of Sinking in Poetry*,
Gulliver's Travels and *The Dunciad*, for example.

Witmore is not only the Voice of Satire, however; he is also
the Hand of Charity. He privately pays Mrs Moneywood his
friend's back rent. When Luckless finds out, he steals the money
with the help of his servant, Jack, and they leave Moneywood's
house. Just as the context of farce allows civility to be suspended
when Luckless cruelly tells his landlady he would rather see her
than touch her, so it allows larceny. Instead of feeling the righteous urge to censure Luckless, we see his behaviour as allow-
able self-indulgence, somehow understanding that 'in farce as
in dreams, one is permitted the outrage but is spared the
consequences'.[63]

In Act II we find Luckless reading his play to Marplay (Colley
Cibber) and Sparkish (Robert Wilks), who offer obviously bad
advice for its improvement, especially Marplay. No doubt Fielding enjoyed making Cibber and Wilks look like rascals and fools.
They had turned down *The Temple Beau* for Drury Lane, and he
was unhappy with the refusal, which was owing at least in part
to their extremely conservative repertory policy. Besides, they
both had a reputation for humiliating dramatists whose plays
they rejected.[64] When Fielding revised *The Author's Farce* in 1734,
he had to write out Sparkish because Wilks had died, but he
introduced and satirized Theophilus Cibber, Colley's son, who
had led a rebellion of Drury Lane actors against their new
managers, with whom Fielding sided against the rebels. But the
new version had little success.[65]

The second act also includes scenes satirizing 'Grub Street',
the actual place in London, near Moorfields, where hack writers

were hired by publishers to produce 'literature' on assignment, at low wages – histories, dictionaries, apt quotations, translations, Greek and Latin tags, poems, political essays, letters – whence the term came to apply to all such activity. Fielding is supposed to have said to his cousin Lady Mary that he had 'no choice but to be a Hackney Writer or a Hackney Coachman'.[66] Whether or not he did, he was certainly poor when he wrote *The Author's Farce*. In satirizing Grub Street and its representative entrepreneur, Bookweight, who is 'as great a friend to learning as the Dutch are to trade' (II, vi; Woods, p. 32), Fielding mocks the degradation of literature in a good-humoured way. But he also shows us the world to which Luckless (Fielding's other self?) must turn for money. His play rejected by Marplay and Sparkish (as one of Fielding's had been by Drury Lane), Luckless rushes a lowly puppet show to 'the playhouse opposite to the Opera in the Haymarket' and simultaneously offers it for sale to Bookweight, who accepts it (II, vii; Woods, pp. 34–35). But fun, not sorrow, marks Luckless's literary descent. Besides, though Bookweight's name seems to imply that he buys books by the pound or that he merely props them, indifferent to their content, he is a shrewd business man, whose purchase suggests, ironically, that Luckless will succeed.

The nominal puppet show, *The Pleasures of the Town*, with the parts played by men and women, not puppets, fills Act III of *The Author's Farce*. It is an energetic and daring combination of farce, ballad opera and 'burlesque', a term Fielding defines in the preface to *Joseph Andrews* by referring it to *caricatura* (caricature) in the pictorial arts, where nature is exaggerated to produce the ludicrous or grotesque.[67] A play within the play, *The Pleasures of the Town*, has a double logic of action. Luckless, as Master of the Puppet Show, directs the players who perform his Nonsense ('Who would not rather eat by his nonesense [*sic*] than starve by his wit?' he asks: III; Woods, p. 39), mocking Bookweight's view of the arts and yet acknowledging its power.

The action of Luckless's play within the play, which he directs, figures the selection of the arch-poet by the Goddess of Nonesense, who will choose among the many dunces representing debased art (opera, tragedy, poetry), an action reminiscent of Pope's *Dunciad* (first versions, 1728, 1729), which celebrates the triumph of Dullness. Having chosen her favorite dunce, the Goddess will marry him. The setting is the far side of the River Styx, access to which is controlled by the boatman Charon; but the time is concurrent with that of *The Author's Farce*. The action is overloaded with characters, many of whom were easily identified by Fielding's audience, both old friends and new targets of satire: Punch, Joan, Poet, Bookseller, Mrs Novel, Signor Opera, Don Tragedio, Sir Farcical Comic, Dr Orator, Monsieur Pantomime, Somebody, Nobody, Murdertext, and others, including characters from the world of *The Author's Farce*. Like the dark world of Pope's *Dunciad*, in which the Prince of Dullness is crowned, Fielding's is so populated with fools and rascals that the Goddess's final choice ought not to be easy.[68] But she has no trouble because she loves the pea-brained Signor Opera to distraction. Nonesense, with a universe of compatible dunces to choose among, compulsively prefers the singer.

Fielding's invention is, matter-of-factly, imperious and breathtaking. It includes not only the world beyond Styx, but intermittent intrusions into it from the 'real life' of the first two acts, and from two other discrete places, Bantam and Old Brentford, which Fielding abruptly summons into existence without explanation. One may well consider the narrative line mad. In 'real life', before Styx, Signor Opera fathered a child by Mrs Novel, a secret that is exposed only in the world beyond Styx. The Goddess of Nonesense is so angered by the disclosure of her Signor Opera's ante-Styx betrayal that she repudiates him. But she soon relents and awards him the arch-poet's chaplet. Then Murdertext and Constable appear from 'real life' with a warrant for the arrest of Luckless for the abuse of Nonesense. Will the play be halted?

Mrs Novel's charms move Murdertext. The play is allowed to continue. But it is interrupted by Bantamite – from Bantam, a land unknown to us – who informs Luckless that he is Prince of Bantam, separated from home and father years before. Then another messenger arrives and announces the death of the King of Bantam. Luckless is the King. Mrs Moneywood turns out (on swiftly arriving information) to be the Queen of Old Brentford. Her daughter Harriot is therefore a princess. Everyone we care about is Royal! Comic recognition has been entirely liberated from antecedent events. Low becomes high; failure, success; 'nonesense', truth. In order to satirize the Pleasures of the Town, the playwright invents and controls new worlds. But under his pen the objects of satire are more amusing than reprehensible, perhaps because he pretends (or does he make us see?) that the farcical disorder of the world beyond Styx is not unlike the farcical disorder of London, and he has zest for both.[69]

On 24 April 1730, Fielding added *Tom Thumb*, a two-act afterpiece, to *The Author's Farce*, which by then had been played nine times.[70] It was an instant success. The demand for places was so great that Fielding was able to charge as much for a seat in the pit as in the boxes. Nominally *Tom Thumb* satirizes heroic tragedy, which had become a parody of itself, as many of Fielding's predecessors knew.[71] Tom Thumb, the hero, is a midget, no bigger than a thumb. Fielding would have relied on his audience's general recognition of the character, who figures in a widely known folktale.[72] But actually seeing him played by a small, adolescent girl, modestly confident of his fiery-tempered prowess as military commander, praised by King Arthur as a giant-killer, desired by both the Princess Huncamunca and her mother the Queen, and envied by the courtier Grizzle, must have surprised them.[73] A mock-heroic tone is struck in the opening line, which echoes Macbeth's first words: 'Sure such a day as this was never seen' (I, i; Morrissey, p. 23). And throughout the play, Fielding uses inflated language to represent small matters. The effects are ludicrous. But as Hume points out, the play does not owe its primary success to the reduction of heroic drama. It succeeds because its personations, incongruities and exaggerations surprise and tickle us, though one or two direct shots at Cibber might not be recognized for what they are.[74]

Fielding's invention and control of non-possible events stagger and cheer us. Tom is falsely reported dead after two physicians, Church-yard and Fillgrave, mistakenly treat (maltreat) a monkey dressed in the midget hero's clothes. Princess Huncamunca, a lusty young woman, is chided by her maid for wanting Tom, 'that little insignificant Fellow': 'If you had fallen in Love with Something; but to fall in Love with Nothing!' (II, iii; Morrissey, p. 31). At the height of his career, Tom is swallowed by a large cow. Grizzle, furious that his revenge on Tom is thwarted by the cow, stabs Tom's ghost so that the hero is twice slain. And the short play ends in a litter of the dead – Huncamunca kills Grizzle, Doodle kills Huncamunca, Queen kills Doodle, Noodle kills Queen, Cleora kills Noodle, Mustacha kills Cleora, King Arthur kills Mustacha, and then the King dispatches himself – eight corpses, counting Tom's, in eight lines.

Between the time of Fielding's great success with *The Author's*

Farce and *Tom Thumb*, in the season of 1729–30, and his expansion of the Tom Thumb play into *The Tragedy of Tragedies* (first staged at Little Haymarket on 24 March 1731), *Rape upon Rape* was produced at the Little Haymarket, on 23 June 1730. Later, on 4 December 1730, the same play was mounted at Lincoln's Inn Fields, but with a new title, *The Coffee-House Politician*.[75] During this period Fielding was also at work on *The Modern Husband*, written, he tells his cousin Lady Mary, 'on a Model I never yet attempted'.[76] It was indeed a new kind of play for Fielding, turning on a husband's sale of his wife, her complicated acquiescence, and their ultimately naked hostility towards each other. For reasons unknown, it was not produced until 14 February 1732, at Drury Lane.[77] Finally, he wrote *The Letter Writers*, which was first produced as an afterpiece on the same bill as *The Tragedy of Tragedies* on its first night.[78]

Fielding's revision of *Tom Thumb* enlarges it, complicating the plot and transforming the original play – a burlesque of heroic drama – into an extensive parody of the genre. To do so, he echoes turgid lines from dozens of plays, especially those of Dryden, John Banks and Nathaniel Lee, the best known writers of heroic drama in the late seventeenth century; he also mined bombast from Shakespeare, and from a few eighteenth-century playwrights as well, including Gay and himself. Finally, he provided the published version of *The Tragedy of Tragedies* (March 1731) with an elaborate pedantic apparatus – preface and footnotes – which he attributed to H. Scriblerus Secundus, probably taking Swift's fifth edition of *A Tale of a Tub* (1710) and Pope's *The Dunciad Variourum* (1729) for models. As J. Paul Hunter's acute discussion of *The Tragedy of Tragedies* demonstrates, the play, for all its satire on false learning, is not only clever and funny, it is also immensely learned.[79]

In lengthening the acting play, Fielding adds several characters who enable him to complicate the plot and enlarge the burlesque of heroic drama. Chief among these are 'GLUMDALCA, of the Giants, a Captive Queen', the 'Ghost of *Gaffer Thumb*', 'Merlin, A Conjurer, and in some sort Father to *Tom Thumb*', and 'Foodle, A Courtier that is out of Place, and consequently of that Party that is undermost' (Dramatis Personae, Morrissey, pp. 47–48). In addition to burlesqueing the captive noblewoman of heroic drama, Glumdalca, whose past includes twenty Giant husbands, parodies Dollalolla and Huncamunca, who are inex-

plicably overpowered by their love for tiny Tom in the earlier
version. Fielding expands Grizzle's opposition to Tom, as a rival
for the love of Huncamunca and for glory in war, by giving him
the restless Foodle as an ally in rebellion. The Ghost of Gaffer
Thumb fills two scenes that include predictions of the King's
'yet impending Fate', during which Arthur threatens him with
various deaths, forgetting the Gaffer is already a ghost. And Merlin,
the magical sponsor of Tom's birth in some versions of the folktale,
appears to the little hero portentously, amidst thunder and light-
ning, to retell 'the mystick Getting of *Tom Thumb*'. Hume's
conjecture about productions of the new play seems just right: 'I
would guess that in performance *The Tragedy of Tragedies* remained
pretty much what *Tom Thumb* had been, a travesty of heroic drama
to be enjoyed for its sheer silliness.'[80] In support of this opinion,
Hume offers several items of production history, including the
fact that 'John Harper (the most notable Falstaff of the day) was
cast as Huncamunca' when the play was staged at Drury Lane
in May 1732.

The full title of the play, *The Tragedy of Tragedies; or The Life
and Death of Tom Thumb the Great*, includes a hit at Walpole, who
was generally recognized as 'The Great Man', an epithet earlier
applied to him by opponents. But scholarly opinion about the
nature and intensity of the play's political content varies enormously. Cleary reviews the history of this opinion in a study
that appeared in 1984.[82] Four years later, Hume recapitulates and
extends the review, locating it in a shrewd discussion of political drama of the 1730s. There, he distinguishes between topical
plays – which may hit political persons and events discretely, in
order to be funny, without much partisan intent (or effect) –
and application plays, which analogize a well known political
past and current political events, with partisan intent (and effect).[83]
In this way he clarifies the view that plays with political content
need not be motivated by partisanship. At the same time, he
makes it clear that the subject of political drama is far from simple and, as I have said, competent drama historians often do not
agree. For example, Morrissey believes *The Tragedy of Tragedies*
contains extensive political satire against Walpole, which he regards
as a clarification of the political satire in *Tom Thumb*. Goldgar
finds no partisan content in either play, pointing out that one
may find in them ridicule of the opposition as well as of the
government, if one chooses to do so, and stressing that Fielding's

contemporaries did not find the plays political (including Walpole, who attended three performances of *Tom Thumb*). It is Cleary's opinion that *The Tragedy of Tragedies* (but not *Tom Thumb*) is politically partisan for reasons that go beyond those offered by his predecessors, including Morrissey. Hume's view seems most balanced; he acknowledges in *The Tragedy of Tragedies* the probable hit at Walpole in the title and the chance of political implication in descriptions of the dramatis personae added for publication and in a few references to Walpole and the court, but he does not believe the play is partisan.[84]

Rape Upon Rape; or The Justice Caught in his own Trap, a five-act comedy staged at the Little Haymarket in June 1730, was Fielding's fourth play of the season, following *The Temple Beau*, *The Author's Farce* and *Tom Thumb*. The title implies not only 'one rape after another' but also 'the rape of raping', both of which meanings are represented by the action, although literally the play includes 'no Rape at all', as the epilogue reminds us (Henley, II, 157). It is hard to be sure of Fielding's central concern. The relation between the lovers, Hilaret and Constant, provides no tension; they never really doubt each other, and they quickly control the forces that might keep them apart. The play's intrigues are complicated and nominally dangerous to the lovers, but they are obviously contrived to give Fielding opportunities for fun. Even the satire on corruption in the administration of the law loses some of its bite when the one evil character, Justice Squeezum, is made to talk affectionate nonsense as he is about to be tricked by Hilaret into an attempted rape. Nevertheless the play is energetic and amusing, fast-paced, intricate, appropriately improbable, and emphatic in its happy resolutions.

We know that Hilaret, Politick's daughter, is in love with Constant, who loves her faithfully. Unfortunately, her father is so obsessed with reading the news of the world's affairs that he neglects his daughter's wish to marry. Encouraged by her maid Cloris, Hilaret leaves home at night to marry Constant, but she is overtaken by Ramble, who, a little drunk, supposes her to be a woman on the make. When she cries, 'a rape, a rape', Staff and Watch appear, and they take both to Justice Squeezum because Ramble claims Hilaret set him up.

Meanwhile, Constant, a good man, is arrested by mistake when he rescues Justice Worthy's sister, Isabella, from rape by Fireball (offstage). Fielding reduces and then confines what dramatic tension there is by having Constant, Ramble and Hilaret, in detention, quickly sort things out and leaving them to contend not with each other, but only with Justice Squeezum. It is soon apparent that he is not interested in seeing to justice, but in what his prisoners can pay him. He solicits bribes, rigs juries, protects bawdyhouses, and makes and breaks the law.

Complications follow thick and fast. Squeezum's rapacity cannot be checked, except by his wife, who blackmails him daily with threats of exposing his crimes. He, meanwhile, appears to wink at her flirtation with Ramble, hoping to catch her in the act, so that he may have her brought to justice. Hilaret seems to return Squeezum's interest in her, but only to entrap him. Isabella, saved by Constant, turns out to be Ramble's lost wife, whom he thought dead; he regains her and her £80 000. Then we learn that Ramble, who has been in the Indies, is Politick's son. Ramble and Hilaret are brother and sister! Finally, we see Justice Worthy, Isabella's brother, oversee the triumph of the law upon Squeezum, in a non-comic excess of morality. Worthy says that 'the crimes of a magistrate give the greatest sanction to sin' (V, xi; Henley, II, 156). Fielding seems unwilling to complicate either Hilaret's and Constant's mutual love or Worthy's goodness, but the play's energy elsewhere makes up for this moral self-indulgence.

In February 1730, a certain Francis Charteris had been found guilty of raping his maidservant. Just two months before *Rape Upon Rape* was staged, in April 1730, Charteris was pardoned by the Crown. This lapse in the law's rigour was widely deplored, the general sentiment being that Charteris had found his way out of a corrupt system by means of political influence and bribery. Fielding no doubt knew that his play would be associated with the Charteris affair, but it is hardly an anti-government piece.[85] To the extent that it is satirical, its target is the general corruption of the law's operation, which he hits by means of Squeezum's rapacity and, closely related, by means of the injustices attaching to the two abortive rapes, which land two innocents, Hilaret and Constant, in jail. All Squeezum's actions (until he becomes a doting old lover, at least briefly) are like rape in that he assaults the integrity of those in his orbit: Hilaret, Constant, Mrs Squeezum, Ramble, and less directly Isabella and Worthy. But the satire is also blunted. On Hilaret's initiative, the third rape, also 'abortive', catches the Justice in his own trap. By that time, however, Squeezum has been made a little silly and a little human. Then, too, the heavily moral Worthy has been standing by all the while to show us that the law is in good hands after all. As I have suggested, the play misses chances for real satiric bite, and its potential love interest is barely explored.

The Letter-Writers: Or, a New Way to Keep A Wife at Home, a three-act afterpiece written to follow *The Tragedy of Tragedies*, is a merry farce. The two old husbands (Mr Wisdom and Mr Softly) and their two young wives (Mrs Elizabeth Wisdom and Mrs Lucretia Softly) are of course mismatched. The women want more in the way of love and excitement than their doddering husbands can offer. Both are secretly interested in young Rakel, who is interested in them. In fact, he has already enjoyed a flirtation with Mrs Softly. The husbands, suspecting the worst, agree that each will send a letter to the other's wife threatening death if she leaves her house. The letters do not alter their behaviour. Mrs Softly goes out, as usual, taking the dramatic precaution of carrying a gun and adding guards to her retinue. Mrs Wisdom stays at home, as usual, where she welcomes her lovers when her husband is away (often). Their nephew Commons, a young man about town, soon to accept a Church living in the country, has no calling. But he needs an income. He mischievously encourages Rakel to have a go at his aunts.

Seduction, woman's marital infidelity, and the marriage of age and youth are all handled with a light touch. Such treatment is aided by the fact that the men – Rakel the rake and Commons the worldly man of the cloth – and the women – Elizabeth and Lucretia the flirts – are amiable and decent. The play, nominally about seduction and adultery, includes neither. Even the old husbands, whose letter-writing sets up and (when their forgeries are discovered) winds down the action, are not bad. In fact the only subject taken seriously is a perennial one in Fielding's plays: the male seducer's obligation to protect the woman who has granted favours. So Rakel, discovered in Mrs Wisdom's room by her husband, has his servant quietly break the windows right away, making it look as though the motive for entry had been robbery.

The Letter-Writers was not a success. It opened on 24 March 1731, and it was performed only four times. Despite the happy idea of the husbands' letters and the possibilities they generate, the play misses as farce or burlesque, because the outrageous behaviour we have been promised, at least implicitly, never comes to pass. A certain audacity is wanting. The faithless wives are only flirts, and their husbands only foolish old men; the rake is no rake, and the clergyman without vocation is no scoundrel. But maybe its chief reason for failing is that it followed *The Tragedy of Tragedies* as an afterpiece. It would have taken a very strong play indeed to hold the audience after they had been shown Tom Thumb's rollicking universe. Nevertheless *The Letter-Writers* is often droll and always merry.

Mr. Wisdom: While in your husband's arms you keep your treasure,
  You're free from fear of hurt . . .
Mrs. Wisdom: Or hope of pleasure. (II, xiii; Henley, II, 191)

Always a pragmatist about plays that did not succeed, Fielding replaced *The Letter-Writers*, on 22 April 1731, with *The Welsh Opera*, by Scriblerus Secundus, as an afterpiece to *The Tragedy of Tragedies* at the Little Haymarket. A ballad opera, it is an outrageous burlesque of the royal family and the ministry. Though clearly topical satire, the play seems not to be partisan. Having fun as it does with the King's household, in caricatures of its members easily recognized by Fielding's audience, it is more playful than censorious, and apparently it did not in any immediate sense move the government to action.[86] *The Welsh Opera* was performed a total of ten times that spring, five as an afterpiece to *The Tragedy of Tragedies*, and five as afterpiece to *The Fall of Mortimer*, a play by an unknown hand that clearly attacked the ministry and the Queen. The government began to move the forces of law against *Mortimer*, eventually prohibiting its performance. The actors at Little Haymarket, threatened with arrest, escaped.[87]

At this point Fielding enlarged his ballad opera, increasing the number of songs from 31 to 65, improving plot and characters, and renaming it *The Grub-Street Opera*. But the expanded play, intended as a mainpiece, was never performed. No one knows why, exactly, but it is not unreasonable to suppose that Fielding was paid to withhold it.[88] In the revised play, *The Grub-Street Opera*, the royal family, barely disguised, are located in the Welsh household of Squire Ap-Shinken (George II), who is perfectly content to have Madam Ap-Shinken (like Queen Caroline) rule the roost, provided he may rest easy and smoke. Their son, Master Owen Ap-Shinken (the Prince of Wales), whom his parents (like the King and Queen) do not like, wants to make love to every woman in sight, but he is (like the Prince?) not a successful lover.[89] The ministry and the opposition are represented by the servants, though not very consistently. One of these is the butler, Robin (Robert Walpole), who steals methodically from the household, but who is deeply in love with Sweetissa, another servant; she returns Robin's love. William the Groom (William Pulteney, opposition leader) is Robin's rival for power in the Ap-Shinken household. Susan, another servant, and William are in love.

As he does in numerous of his plays – *The Temple Beau*, *Rape Upon Rape*, and *The Letter-Writers*, for instance – Fielding makes use of the written word in *The Grub-Street Opera* (letter writing) to generate and resolve the action. Master Owen longs to seduce Sweetissa, Robin's betrothed, even though he is loved by the virtuous, adequately born, but poverty stricken, Molly Apshones (whom Owen does not love in return; he is dead against marriage). His forged letters, one from William to Sweetissa, implying that they have been lovers, and the other from Susan to Robin, implying that she has been Robin's mistress, breed exactly the jealousy and doubt Master Owen hoped for. But we find him to be a maladroit seducer, and Fielding contrives to have the forgeries quickly discovered and the couples reunited. When Sweetissa rebuffs Master Owen, he is left to settle for Molly Apshones. Fielding's burlesque of late recognitions and family realignments brings the play to an end in a cluster of marriages, which is an irrepressible mockery of the unforeshadowed discoveries that wrap up bad comedy.

The government kept the Little Haymarket effectively closed for legitimate productions between 1 July 1731 and 10 February 1732. Fielding, in need of a theatre in the autumn of 1731, turned to Drury Lane, where Cibber welcomed him. The shrewd manager must have been aware that audience taste was moving away from conventional comedy and even away from mainpiece ballad opera, which had enjoyed an intense but brief vogue, beginning with *The Beggar's Opera* (1728). Topical subjects, in farce or burlesque, were proving more popular.[90] Cibber, probably attracted by the chance to profit from Fielding's demonstrated ability to write successful plays, seemed willing to overlook the ludicrous personation of him in *The Author's Farce*, and Fielding spent a season and a half at Drury Lane, during which time seven new plays of his were produced.

The first two mounted during this period at Drury Lane – *The Lottery*, 1 January 1732, and *The Modern Husband*, 14 February 1732 – were a farcical ballad opera afterpiece and a five-act satirical comedy. Each was in its own way topical and, although very different from each other, each was unmistakably Fielding's. *The Lottery* satirizes the abuses of private brokers who buy and manage the secondary sale of tickets in a government lottery.[91] Taking advantage of his audience's knowledge of the English State Lottery of 1731, Fielding ridicules the insane futility of gambling, largely through Chloe, a caricature of the comic romance heroine, who has left the dull country and her faithful suitor Lovemore for the exciting city; she is so certain she holds the winning lottery ticket for £10 000 that she claims quite sincerely that she is already worth the money. It is a neat turn that Stocks, an unscrupulous ticket broker, should be so taken in by Chloe's claims of wealth that he encourages his brother Jack, disguised as Lord Lace, to woo and marry her. When Chloe's ticket comes up blank, Jack drops her, accepting £1000 from Lovemore 'to resign over all pretensions in her' to him (sc. iii; Henley, I, 294).

Though the play was successful, with an initial unbroken run of seven nights, and another eight performances during January, Fielding revised it, changing and adding songs and a new scene 'representing the Drawing of the Lottery in Guild-hall, and mounting the new version just one month after the opening, on 1 February'.[92] The play enjoyed a continuing success in its revised form. In the new scene, Chloe is on stage for the drawing, and when her ticket comes up blank, she faints. Her husband is briefly solicitous, but when Chloe tells him the truth, he curses her. Lovemore is ready at hand, still loving, but hardly optimistic: 'That the world is a lottery, what man can doubt?/When born, we're put in, when dead, we're drawn out' (Air XXII, Henley, I, 296). Chloe is not converted into Lovemore's grateful, loving partner. She has been delightfully inane at every turn: in dropping Lovemore in the first place, in her empty-headed flight to the city, in believing a recurrent dream (and a fortune-teller's prediction and the tracings in a coffee-dish) that she holds the winning lottery ticket, and in her hasty marriage to a sham lord, which ends abruptly, giving her a new status, that of kept woman. Fielding takes care that Chloe's vacant mind survives her defeat as blank-ticket holder and deserted wife, as we learn from the Epilogue she speaks: 'Who'd trust to Fortune, if she plays such

pranks?/Ten thousand – and a lord! and both prove blanks?/
Piteous case! and what is still more madding,/To lose so fine a
lord before I had him' (Henley, I, 297).

The Modern Husband, produced at Drury Lane in the winter of
1732, has been a controversial play from the beginning. Not as
successful as his shorter plays, *The Author's Farce* and *Tom Thumb*,
The Modern Husband nevertheless had an unusually long unbroken initial run for a mainpiece. It was performed thirteen times
from opening night, 14 February, giving Fielding four benefits
at least. But it was staged only once again, on 18 March. As his
references to the play in the correspondence with Lady Mary
and in the Prologue itself make clear, Fielding believed he had
written a new kind of play, with a serious purpose, and in fact
he had. The Prologue's last four lines epitomize his view: 'Though
no loud laugh applaud the serious page,/Restore the sinking
honour of the stage:/The stage, which was not for low farce
designed,/But to divert, instruct, and mend mankind' (Henley,
III, 10). 'Mend' may be misleading. Fielding must have had no
more idea that *The Modern Husband* would eradicate the world's
vices than Swift did that *Gulliver's Travels* would do so. *The Modern
Husband* does not 'mend' the immorality it discloses. It rather
invites us to share the dramatist's view of it and, in the long
run, perhaps, make that view our own.

Fielding's 'serious social purpose' is embedded in the view
that human life is a struggle between the predators who exploit
others for the sake of wealth, pleasure and authority, and the
people of charity, for whom money and position are subordinate to loving relations, especially marriage. (In this regard, Shaw,
despite his complicated treatments of marriage, is strikingly like
Fielding, from *Major Barbara* to *Back to Methuselah*.) On the title-
page of *The Modern Husband* (1732), Fielding quotes a passage
from Juvenal's Satire I, the gist of which is this pair of related
questions: 'Should I view these things as worthy of Horatian
treatment and yet not have a try at them? in an age when the
willing husband looks the other way, if his wife gets money from
her lover?'[93] The quotation points to the heart of the play and
its mode. It is satirical, combining the dark vision of Juvenal
with the light mockery of Horace; and its subject is marriage,
ideal and prostituted.

We come to understand early that Mr and Mrs Modern have
agreed to her becoming Lord Richly's secret mistress for as much

money as she can get from him. Fielding introduces us to the adulterers just as Lord Richly makes it clear to Mrs Modern that he is tired of her. Unscrupulous and greedy, Mr Modern suggests that his wife seduce Richly once more, before witnesses, so that he may be sued for 'Criminal Conversation'.[94] At some level, her outraged refusal marks the limit of her willingness to degrade herself. Nevertheless, the play's adulterous texture thickens. Richly wants Mrs Modern's help in seducing Mrs Bellamant, who is happily married to Mr Bellamant, an essentially good man who has been Mrs Modern's lover. It is telling that Richly's leverage with both women is money; to repay a debt, Mrs Modern helps him arrange a meeting with Mrs Bellamant, who agrees to the meeting because she also owes Richly money.

Despite such marital depredations as these, accomplished or intended, the play includes an ideal marriage in-the-making: that between Mr Bellamant's daughter, Emilia, by a previous wife, and Gaywit, Lord Richly's nephew. Emilia and Gaywit are good people, deeply in love with each other, but money threatens their happiness, for, by the terms of Richly's will, Gaywit must marry his cousin Charlotte or be disinherited. It is notable that both Gaywit's and Bellamant's past affairs with Mrs Modern are made forgivable liaisons in the world of the work; in fact Mrs Modern's favourable recollection of them implies a dimension of feeling in her we would otherwise miss. It also implies that these lovers were considerate of her, unlike her husband and Richly. There is no doubt that the play accepts a double standard. No such liaisons as Gaywit and Bellamant enjoyed would be allowed to either Emilia or Mrs Bellamant. But then Fielding is not without good feelings for Mrs Modern, whose side he favours against Richly and her husband. No simple sexual morality dominates the play, though selling oneself for money is made repugnant, and yet slightly more acceptable than selling one's wife.

Both predators, Modern and Richly, are drawn economically, but not simply. If we read or listen carefully, we understand that Mr Modern comes step by step to the point of asking his wife to allow herself to be caught in bed with Richly as a basis for suing or blackmailing him (I, iv; Henley, III, 15–18). In the process, we learn that he blames her for failing to hold Richly and that he resents her having agreed to become his mistress in the first place. In fact, it is not clear whether he really wants her to be caught with Richly or whether he is just finding a new way to be cruel to her. He hates his wife, and she hates him. In the context, her angry refusal to be caught with Richly is plausible, despite her past, and it increases her complexity. Modern backs off, but through this one brief scene, we learn that he is cruelly intelligent, manipulative, and resentful, and also that she is no simple tool of her husband either. The Moderns live a prostituted marriage from first to last, but the fact does not prevent her from loving Gaywit and respecting Bellamant, her former lovers.

Lord Richly also prostitutes marriage. But we meet him first at his levee, where he makes promises he never means to keep. In his view of the world, he is very like Modern, except that he has the wealth and position to indulge himself. Accordingly, we see his sadistic intelligence first as an expression of worldly power.

> *Lord Richly*: Depend upon it, I'll take care of you. – What a world of poor chimerical devils does a levee draw together? All gaping for favours, without the least capacity of making a return for them.
>
> But great men, justly, act by wiser rules;
> A levee is the paradise of fools. (I,ix; Henley, III, 24–5)

In the world of the play, however, he uses his power chiefly to debase marriage. He buys Mrs Modern, who with her husband more or less willingly sells herself; he tries to seduce Mrs Bellamant, taking advantage of Bellamant's reduced circumstances, for which Richly is responsible; and by means of his will, he presses his nephew Gaywit to marry Charlotte, Richly's own daughter, though the cousins do not love each other and in fact have given their hearts elsewhere. Finally, throughout the play, Fielding leaves Richly without a wife, living or referred to, though presumably a wife bore Charlotte.

It is perhaps a weakness that the subtlety of the play's dark characters, the two Moderns and Richly, can easily be missed. Maybe it is a play better read than acted. In addition, the genuinely sinister powers of the Moderns and Richly may seem too easily thwarted. Fielding uses some comic modulation to cover the distance between the power of evil and its fortunate subduing, but not enough to free us from the sense that more darkness abides than his bright deliverance has accounted for.

Nevertheless the comedy concludes along well foreshadowed lines. Mrs Bellamant is of course not seduced by Richly, who thought her a pushover; and Bellamant, seeing that his wife is loyal, confesses and is forgiven his own connection with Mrs Modern. Modern fails to entrap Richly, and the Moderns are left penniless. Finally, Richly is undone by his own will: that is, Gaywit, giving up his uncle's estate, marries Emilia, daughter of Bellamant, whom Richly by then hates. But Bellamant's son by a former marriage, Captain Bellamant, marries Charlotte, Richly's daughter, lining up Richly's money for inheritance by a Bellamant. Justice is ironically accomplished.

Fielding has skilfully planted expectations in each of his characters by this point in the play, so that pleasure or pain is everywhere intense, and we have a good idea of each character's portion. Loving marriage triumphs. And so did Fielding, perhaps earning close to a thousand pounds for *The Lottery* and *The Modern Husband*.[95]

Fielding dedicated the published play to Walpole, probably hoping for support in return. But his praise of the minister apparently marks no turn in political allegiance, only a conventional means of winning favour. Most scholars consider whether Fielding's fulsome references to Walpole may not be ironic: 'Sir, – While the peace of Europe, and the lives and fortunes of so great a part of mankind depend on your counsels, it may be thought an offence against the public good to divert by trifles of this nature any of those moments which are so sacred to the welfare of our country' (Henley, III, 7). But there is wide agreement that despite his avowed dislike of excessive dedicatory praise, Fielding merely conforms here to the conventions of the genre.[96] There is no evidence that Walpole gave Fielding the response he hoped for.

During the remainder of his connection with Drury Lane, Fielding wrote five plays, all mounted there: *The Old Debauchees* (June 1732), *The Covent-Garden Tragedy* (June 1732), *The Mock Doctor* (June 1732), *The Miser* (February 1733), and *Deborah* (April 1733); the last is a lost play, apparently never published.[97] Of these, the *Covent-Garden Tragedy* failed badly on its first night, and it was only occasionally thereafter performed; but both *The Mock Doctor*, an afterpiece, and *The Miser*, a five-act mainpiece, had a lasting success.[98]

The Old Debauchees, a three-act play, turns on the farcically treated tension between generous and open sexuality (with or without love) and sexual hypocrisy, constraint and guilt, in various ways associated with the Roman Catholic Church.[99] The Old Debauchees are the vastly energetic Laroon, champion of desire over restraint, who has had two wives and 2000 other women, without ever being in love, and the guilt-ridden Jourdain, who is superstitiously – obsessively – bound to priests and the Roman Catholic Church because he fears damnation for the heinous sins of his youth, which include murder and rape. Young Laroon is as energetic as his father, but unlike him in being in love, with Isabel, whom he wants to marry. Isabel (Jourdain's daughter), who returns Young Laroon's love, is, unlike her father, joyously disdainful of Church constraint, as the opening words of the play make clear.

Isabel: A nunnery! Ha, ha, ha! and is it possible, my dear Beatrice, you can intend to sacrifice your youth and beauty, to go out of the world as soon as you came into it?
Beatrice: No one, my dear Isabel, can sacrifice too much, or too soon, to Heaven!
Isabel: Pshaw! Heaven regards hearts and not faces, and an old woman will be as acceptable a sacrifice as a young one. (I, i; Henley, II, 283)

The Jesuit Father Martin, Jourdain's (and Isabel's) confessor, is an unscrupulous manipulator, who commands Isabel to postpone her marriage to Young Laroon and persuades her father to send her to a nunnery, where he plans to seduce her. Far from being intimidated by Father Martin, Isabel guesses his intentions and resists her father's decision to give her to the Church, saying, 'Lud! papa! Do you think your putting me into Purgatory in this world will save you from Purgatory in the next?' (II, i; Henley, II, 295).

In arranging for Isabel and Young Laroon to entrap Father Martin, Fielding sets up a complicated process that includes numerous farcical moves, like visits to Jourdain by both Laroons, separately, dressed like priests, to counter Martin's influence on the religiously superstitious old man; engineering Martin's mistaken conclusion that he has lost Isabel's virginity to Young Laroon; Martin's repeated (utterly futile) instruction to the irrepressible Isabel to be passive in all things; Young Laroon's disguise in women's clothes, pretending to be Isabel waiting for Martin; and Isabel's ridiculous seductive disclosure to Martin that she dreamt she was 'brought to bed of the pope'. Inevitably Martin is trapped, and the young couple are free to marry.

The play may not be thoroughly anti-Catholic, including as it does a 'good' priest, who is one of the witnesses against Father Martin in his attempted rape of Isabel. But it ridicules the celibacy of priests and nuns, Confession, and the Jesuitical Priesthood, besides scoring other nasty hits at Catholicism. Fielding was not alone in this practice. Other playwrights, including Dryden, in *The Spanish Friar* (1681), just a few years before his own conversion to Catholicism, shaped humour out of the same context of bigotry. One might claim that Fielding makes impersonal professional use of anti-Papist sentiment as an available basis for humour, but in fact one finds his intense dislike of Roman Catholicism in his later works, including his very last, *The Journal of a Voyage to Lisbon*, in which we hear one of his autobiographical voices.[100] Without defending him, I think it right to say that anti-Catholic feeling was woven into the fabric of English society in Fielding's day. The threat that a Catholic monarchy might undo the work of the Glorious Revolution, a threat that did not end until after the dangerous Jacobite Rebellion of 1745, does not account for all of this feeling, which had an old and complicated genesis, but the threat helped to keep it alive.

One might say that Fielding lightens our sense of Father Martin's evil nature (and by implication, the evil of the Church he represents) by having Old Laroon set a comic punishment for the Jesuit, however painful in reality: being washed in a horse pond and tossed in a blanket. It was sheep stealer Mak's punishment in *The Second Shepherd's Play*. But, then, he has Martin threaten retaliation and remain sinister to the end. For all its vitality, especially in its celebration of sexuality, in and out of marriage, and in its farcical management of Father Martin, *The Old Debauchees* includes a dark element which its comic force controls only fleetingly.

The Covent-Garden Tragedy, a burlesque of tragedy in blank verse, takes life in a whorehouse for its subject, and the precept that whores should never go to bed for love, only for money, as its moral. But it turns out that its moral is only its ideal moral, thwarted by the reality of love, which sometimes leads the most principled whores astray. Fielding mocks tragedy both in his perverse choice and treatment of the subject matter – the fall of whores from professional dispassion into a life of love and marriage – and in his caricature of heroic language. One hears burlesque echoes of Pope in many lines: 'Sooner Fleet Ditch like silver Thames shall flow' (*Covent-Garden Tragedy*, II, ii; Henley, III, 123); 'While lasts the Mountain or while Thames does flow' (*Windsor Forest*, l, 266); 'Rushed I tremendous on the snotty foe' (*Covent-Garden Tragedy*, II, ii); 'Thus march'd the Chief, tremendous as a God' (*Iliad*, VII, 255).

The character who brings about the fall from strict whoredom is Lovegirlo, who will not be persuaded by Gallono that drinking is a fitter occupation than wenching. Lovegirlo loves Kissinda, a whore who will give up her honest work to be kept by him, saying in rapturous iambs, 'I shall forget my trade and learn to dote' (I, ix, Henley, III, 119). For a time we are led to believe that Stormandra may be faithful to her principles. When Captain Bilkum asks her to give him her love on trust of future payment, she declines with ferocity, in damaged lines from *Macbeth* that unfortunately foretell what they deny.

Stormandra: Trust thee! oh! when I trust thee for a groat,/Hanover Square shall come to Drury Lane. (II, i; Henley, III, 122)

We soon learn that she too loves Lovegirlo, and would give herself to him gratis, but he will not have her.

Not only the whores fall; the Madam herself shows the way, early in the play. She is Mother Punchbowl, who runs an amiable house on sound business principles, but not without exceptions: For, after a scene of mock heartbreak, during which she imagines herself taken by the law to be hanged, and is comforted by her favourite customer, Captain Bilkum, who says he would rather be hanged himself, she agrees out of gratitude to supply him with a wench and the loan of half a crown.[101]

I doubt that Fielding meant to satirize tragedy, except incidentally, in *The Covent-Garden Tragedy*. He seems rather to have chosen his favourite subject (love between the sexes) confined it to an improbable venue (a whorehouse), mocked it in mischievously resurrected blank verse, and watched it (made it?) move inevitably towards the next best thing to marriage in his world: extra-sacramental heterosexual permanence. After Lovegirlo is reported dead by the sword, and Stormandra dead by suicide, and the two then reappear miraculously, it is agreed that Lovegirlo will 'keep' Kissinda and Bilkum will 'keep' Stormandra, for as long as they will. The play is incredibly clever in its re-sounding of old heroic lines and in its invention and varied use of an inverted morality, to the effect that whores must never give it away. But the fun of burlesque rather than the ridicule of tragedy controls the piece, right up to the last lines of the Epilogue, spoken by Miss Raftor (later, Kitty Clive), who on the same night played both Isabel in *The Old Debauchees* and Kissinda in *The Covent-Garden Tragedy*: 'For prudes may cant of virtues and of vices,/But faith, we only differ in our prices' (Henley, III, 134).

The Mock Doctor: or The Dumb Lady Cur'd is an adaptation of Molière's *Le Médecin Malgré Lui*, in which Fielding follows the structure of the French model, but avoids literal translation in favour of an energetic, conversational English appropriate to comedy. He also makes the play his own by introducing nine songs into the action to make it a little ballad opera; by dropping one of Molière's scenes and adding one of his own; and by reversing the psychological authority of one character over another, giving it to Dorcas, the wife, rather than to her husband, Gregory (the mock doctor). Despite the debt to Molière, which Fielding acknowledges in his preface to the published version (1732), *The Mock Doctor* is unmistakably Fielding's play.

The Mock Doctor satirizes quacks, both the well known London practitioner, John Misaubin (d. 1734), to whom Fielding mockingly dedicates the play, and the character Gregory, a woodcutter tricked by his wife into attending, as physician, at the home of Sir Jasper, whose daughter Charlotte has duped him into believing she has been stricken dumb. It is an adroit touch that after the dedication, Misaubin is left behind long enough that we are pleasantly surprised when he is given to us in a transformed state in scene xiii, where Gregory pretends to be a French physician, Dr Ragou. Gregory's quackery is comic, in part because it is medically irrelevant; Charlotte, who loves Leander, is of course only pretending to be dumb in order to avoid marrying the old man of her father's choice. The fun of the play is in the farcical treatment of family relations: Sir Jasper/Charlotte/Leander's, Gregory/Dorcas's, and connections between the two. The *The Mock Doctor* is like the *Covent-Garden Opera* in making its nominal subject subordinate to a different purpose: writing a funny play about something else. Neither play forgets the object of its satire – quackery and tragedy – but neither keeps it uppermost, as does (for example) *The Modern Husband* in its treatment of prostituted marriage, the sense of which persists beyond the play's happy ending.

A couple of Fielding's departures from Molière will illustrate ways in which he makes the French play his own. He typically saves Molière's jokes, but when he can, he relocates them in England. For instance, when Gregory (scene ix) finishes a lecture on the causes of Charlotte's dumbness, which includes an anatomy lesson, he leaves Sir Jasper puzzled.

Sir Jasper: But, dear sir, there is one thing – I always thought till now, that the heart was on the left side, and the liver on the right.

Gregory: Ay, sir, so they were formerly; but we have changed all that. [Here Fielding leaves Molière.] The College [of Physicians and Surgeons] at present, sir, proceeds upon an entire new method. (sc. ix; Henley, III, 158)

Later, Sir Jasper is curious about strange drugs in one of the Mock Doctor's prescriptions – 'a dose of Purgative Running-away mixt with two drachms of pills Matrimoniac' – and Gregory explains, 'They are . . . lately discovered by the Royal Society' (sc. xvii; Henley, III, 170). Scene xiii, which has Gregory pretending to be a French physician, speaking with a preposterous accent, in an attempt to keep his wife Dorcas from recognizing him, replaces one of Molière's: 'Come hider, shild, letta me feela your pulse' (Henley, III, 164). Fielding gives their marital relation an inventive twist: as the scene progresses, with Dorcas resisting her husband's ministrations, he decides to cuckold himself; but she recognizes him just in time and turns the tables. In scene xx, the final one, Gregory tries, like Molière's Sganarelle (the physician *malgré lui*), to have the last word. But in keeping with Dorcas's initiatives (Fielding's preferences) throughout the play, the last word is the wife's prerogative.[102]

In the preface to *The Mock Doctor*, Fielding says, 'One pleasure I enjoy from the success of this piece is a prospect of transplanting successfully some others of Molière of great value.' Then he invites his reader to check his work against a recently published literal translation of the play into English, an expression of confidence that the comparison would reveal not only his debt to the French playwright but also Fielding's originality in handling the subject (Henley, III, 139–40). In writing *The Miser*, his most successful five-act play, Fielding fulfils the 'prospect of trans-planting' another Molière, this time *L'Avare*, and he once more displays originality and skill in reworking the material. His revisions change both the structure of the French play, and some of the characters as well. Still, there is no denying the great debt to his French predecessor.

Despite the title-page, which says the play was 'Taken from Plautus and Molière', it is hard to see that Fielding owes much besides an indirect debt to his Latin predecessor, whose Miser, Euclio, is an altogether different character from Molière's (Harpagon) and Fielding's (Lovegold).[103] Euclio is essentially a hard-working poor man whose life becomes burdensome when he suddenly acquires the gold his grandfather hid on the family property years before. He is anguished when the gold is lost, but we know – even though most of the last act of Plautus' *Aulularia* is missing – that after he recovers it, he gives it to his daughter and son-in-law. We also know he says, 'I have never had a moment's peace by day or night; now I am going to sleep.'[104] Harpagon, by contrast, is a greedy old man of wealth, ultimately checked, but in no sense cured, by the fact that his plans for his own and his children's marriages go hopelessly awry, though things go well for the children. Disappointed, he yields to circumstance and goes off to gaze at his beloved gold.

Fielding's miser, Lovegold, is even worse; he is an avaricious, unyielding old man, only slowly whittled down by a clever and resourceful Mariana, who looks like a witty coquette to the world while, with her servant's help, she systematically undercuts the old miser's desire to marry her by playing on his greed, all the while preparing the way for her marriage to Lovegold's son, Frederick. The last sentence in the quotation from Juvenal's Satire XIV, on the title-page of Fielding's play, points the way to his miser's repugnant pathology: 'But for what end do you pile up riches through torments such as these [acts of self-deprivation], when it is plain madness and sheer lunacy to live in want that you may be wealthy when you die?'[105] Lovegold can be amus-ing, but he is single-minded and without humanity. His repeated compulsion to visit and look at his gold reveals and emphasizes what it is he loves, more than he loves Mariana or his children. 'I would as soon hang my son as another – and I will hang him, if he does not restore me all I have lost', he says in the extremity of frustrated greed. (V, xviii; Henley, III, 271).

Besides intensifying the miser's character, Fielding devises several other radical changes that make the play his own. Molière opens with scenes that introduce the miser's marriageable daughter and son; Fielding opens with a scene between two servants: Lappet, maid to Harriet, Lovegold's daughter, and Ramilie, servant to Frederick, his son. (Lappet, played by Miss Raftor, is a complex version of Molière's Frosine, a go-between with a mind of her own, who often tries to manipulate her clients for profit; Ramilie, a new character, is her realistic and capable lover.) Fielding not only acquaints us early with these very clever, sparring members of the Lovegold household, who will contribute much to sustaining the tension between the Lovegold's greed and his financially burdensome desire to marry Mariana; he also assigns them the job of recapitulating for our benefit information about members of the Lovegold family, and (through their fellow servant Wheedle) about Mariana's family as well. These characters enlarge the world of the play and provide an additional perspective on its action.

Though all the principal lovers are lively and attractive, with minds of their own, it is Mariana who stands out among them. We get to know her only slowly. Frederick, who loves her, tells his sister that Mariana is a card-playing coquette; but he believes she has more character than she reveals. Though we have no reason at first to trust the lover's judgment, we credit him with insight when it turns out that he has spoken prophetically. But Fielding discloses her only slowly, for good dramatic reasons. When Harriet tells Mariana that Lovegold wants to marry her, we are left uncertain about how far towards matrimony Mariana may allow things to go, though it is clear she thinks Lovegold as a lover is ridiculous. Shortly after we see her rebuffing Frederick, Harriet assures her brother that Mariana is not his worst enemy, but we cannot be sure. Finally, Mariana and Harriet quarrel over Frederick, with Mariana left angry enough to say she will marry Lovegold, who signs a contract agreeing to forfeit £10 000 should he back out.

Unlike Molière, Fielding has given Mariana an interior life he deliberately and plausibly obscures by her behaviour, so that we do not know her. As a result we are surprised, then fascinated, during the first ten scenes of the fifth act, by her calculated displays of extravagance, which frighten the miserly Lovegold as nothing else could. Imagine marrying such a woman! Torn between losing the £10 000 and losing all his fortune to a spend-thrift wife, he ultimately decides against the marriage and forfeits the contract money, which Mariana promptly hands over to Frederick. Lappet's manipulations contribute to the dramatic conclusion; at one point she turns the screw and Lovegold speaks like Job: 'Why was I begotten! Why was I born!' (V, xii, Henley, III, 265). But it is Mariana who controls the miser's undoing.[106]

Fielding's lost play *Deborah; or, A Wife For You All* was performed once, on 6 April 1733, as a one-act afterpiece to *The Miser* at a benefit performance for Miss Raftor. We know from Genest that *Deborah* included a Justice Mittimus and a Lawyer Trouble among its characters.[107] And we learn from other sources that Handel's oratorio *Deborah* had opened at the King's Theatre in the Haymarket on 17 March 1733, charging inflated prices.[108] On the basis of this information and his sense of what Fielding might write for Miss Raftor's benefit, especially to show off her musical talent, Cross suggests that 'very likely the afterpiece [*Deborah*] was a ballad-opera laid in a justice court and mildly burlesquing the libretto of Handel's "Deborah", a new oratorio which was not succeeding very well at the Opera House, though patronized by the King and Queen'.[109] In a persuasive article, E. V. Roberts cites the few facts we have about Fielding's *Deborah*, and offers his conjectures on them in an attempt to reconstruct the play, building on Cross, but amplifying and refining in the process.[110] He offers the view that Fielding shaped the part of Deborah, played by Miss Raftor, to show off her fine singing voice, which her audience would have expected on her benefit night; she was not called upon to sing in the role of Lappet in *The Miser*.[111] He locates the action in a courtroom and, from the play's subtitle, infers that Deborah is guilty of prostitution, for which she is tried. But on the basis of trial scenes in other works by Fielding, Roberts concludes that a corruptible court found her innocent. Among his other conjectures is the view that Fielding probably meant to call Handel-Humphrey's oratorio to mind, maybe to burlesque it. Hume seems right to ask, 'Would Field-ing have risked overt parody of a biblical story?'[112] He suggests other kinds of ridicule, like a take-off by Miss Raftor of the eminent castrato, Senesino, one of Handel's performers, and mockery of the high price of tickets at King's, which had angered the town.[113] No one knows why Fielding never published the play.

In the summer of 1732, the Drury Lane patent was renewed for 21 years, to Cibber, Wilks and Booth, on terms that allowed them to sell or otherwise assign their shares. In July 1732, Booth sold half of his share (with full power of the whole) to John Highmore, an amateur with no real theatrical experience. Wilks died in September 1732, and his wife appointed the portrait painter, John Ellys, her deputy.[114] Cibber, about to retire, temporarily assigned his share to his son, Theophilus, for a fee, but then in March 1733 he sold it to Highmore. The Younger Cibber was understandably angry. The other actors, hardly feeling secure under the inexperienced managers, sided with Cibber in revolt. By the end of the season, the late spring of 1733, Drury Lane was fragmented by civil war, with the practical results that the rebellious actors went to the Little Haymarket, managing their own affairs, and the Drury Lane management mounted plays with a few veteran actors doubtfully assisted by a scratch company. What had been for decades a stable institution under Colley Cibber and his colleagues became a risky business for all concerned, not least for Fielding, who must have wondered which way to turn. Matters at the Little Haymarket were also in doubt. Both sides tried to mount plays, and at the same time to influence the outcome of the actors' lawsuit, which sought to obtain possession of Drury Lane.

In January 1734, the courts decided that the actors indeed held a valid lease to the theatre.[115] In the interim, Fielding had remained with the new management at Drury Lane, for reasons one cannot be sure about. He dedicated a new two-act afterpiece, *The Intriguing Chambermaid* (which, with a revised *Author's Farce*, was apparently his first programme offering of the 1733–4 season, on 15 January), to Kitty Raftor, by then Mrs Clive. In the dedication, he compliments her for having 'looked on the cases of Mr. Highmore and Mrs. Wilks with compassion, [and for having supported] the cause of those whom you imagined injured and distressed' ('An Epistle to Mrs. Clive', Henley, III, 278). And in the new epilogue to the revised *Author's Farce*, Fielding laments the sorry condition of the English stage and the thin audiences at Drury Lane and asks whether 'a brave, a generous, town/Will join to crush us, when we're almost down' (Henley, III, 284–5). At this time he especially hoped for support from Walpole, but it was not forthcoming.[116] It hardly needs saying that after the court's decision Fielding, who had satirized Theophilus Cibber as Young Marplay in the revised *Author's Farce* and had praised Kitty for her loyalty to the Drury Lane management in 'An Epistle to Mrs. Clive', was *persona non grata* there when the younger Cibber and his victorious actors returned. The unpopular managers quickly sold out to a single owner, Charles Fleetwood, who came to an agreement with the actors and made Theophilus deputy manager. For a time at least, Fielding was without a real choice, and he turned to the Little Haymarket to find a venue for his plays.[117] There, on 5 April 1734, his *Don Quixote in England* was produced. Although within a year he was back at Drury Lane, where his afterpiece, *An Old Man Taught Wisdom*, was produced on 6 January 1735, Fielding would thereafter enjoy his greatest triumphs at the Little Haymarket.

The Intriguing Chambermaid, a farce written with Kitty Clive in mind to play Lettice, a chambermaid, is an adaptation of Jean François Regnard's *Le Retour Imprévu*. As was the case with his plays after Molière, Fielding makes *The Intriguing Chambermaid* English. The action turns on Lettice's protection of her young master, Valentine Goodall, who has been left in charge of certain family affairs during his wealthy father's trip to the East Indies. Unfortunately the handsome Valentine spends money hand over fist and falls into debt. He also falls in love with Charlotte, who loves in return, but whose aunt has other marriage plans for her niece.

Having thus set the stage, Fielding is in a position to make comic hay by having the trusting father return unexpectedly, so that the playwright may call upon clever Lettice to save Valentine from acute embarrassment (he is throwing a wild party that must be adding to his debt). We have already heard her fiercely defending her young master against Charlotte's aunt, Mrs Highman, in the opening scene; we find it entirely plausible therefore that she should intercept old Goodall on his way home and invent an ingenious (and delightfully improbable) story to explain why a bill collector is outside his house and why loud noises are audible from within. It is nevertheless a jolly surprise to hear her claim that Valentine has borrowed £1000 to buy Mrs Highman's house, worth £4000, because she has gone mad and offered it for £2000. To keep Goodall from going into his own house and discovering his son in the midst of profligacy, she tells him Valentine has had to sell it because it is haunted. Strange sounds from within confirm her message. Goodall is gulled.

Under the circumstances his visit to Mrs Highman, whom he is prepared to find mad, is in a ridiculous way also plausible. Before the two meet, Fielding has Lettice give her invention a final twist by telling Mrs Highman that Goodall's losses in his recent voyage have driven him out of his mind. A sequence of farcical misunderstandings follows, ingeniously derived from the intriguing chambermaid's fabrications, which allow the truth to emerge only slowly.

In the happy world of the play it is inevitable that the father should forgive the sorrowful Valentine and settle money on him, so that he and Charlotte, whose aunt has done the same for her, may marry and live happily ever after. Fielding's conclusion here – a burlesque of comic reconciliations – is almost as liberated from the antecedent action as is the conclusion of *The Author's Farce*, where Luckless and Harriot are discovered to be of royal blood at the last instant.

The Intriguing Chambermaid had a fairly good success to begin with, and it went on to become part of the repertory for years. But the revised *Author's Farce* was not a success. *The London Stage* reports the 'cast not listed'.[118] It seems unlikely there were enough good actors left at Drury Lane to do a proper job with the many parts the play called for. Besides, Fielding's loss of heart, so evident in the new epilogue, may have been contagious. He had tried to reduce the chances that the evening's programme would fail by withholding his five-act satire, *The Universal Gallant*, which was ready for production, and revising *The Author's Farce* for the occasion instead. The decision may have forestalled an outright failure, but it did not bring him the success he needed then.

Fielding revised and added to the *Don Quixote in England* he had drafted by 1729, he tells us in his preface to the published version (1734). It was first performed at Little Haymarket on 5 April 1734. Included in the additions are election scenes, which satirize both the political management of elections and the corruption of the electorate. But whether to find in them evidence of partisanship or only general mockery of the contemporary political climate, however topical, is not a settled question, even though Fielding dedicated the play to Chesterfield, an influential member of the opposition since his dismissal by Walpole in 1733.[119]

The play in its published form remains 'the few loose scenes' Fielding said it was from the start. It has sparks of Fielding's vitality, but its three actions are unconvincingly hung together. We can well accept the notion that Don Quixote and Sancho Panza have come to England and are staying at an inn, where they run up a bill which Don Quixote refuses to pay because he thinks himself in a castle, ready to do knightly service (freeing a princess) for which he believes he is owed the hospitality of his host. And we may sympathize with the two lovers who want to marry (beautiful and sensible Dorothea and handsome and sensible Fairlove), especially given that their plans are threatened by her father, Sir Thomas Loveland, who wants his daughter to marry Squire Badger (an ugly lout, repulsive to Dorothea) because he has £3000 a year and Fairlove only £1000. And the play's election scenes are amusing. But when Don Quixote is encouraged to stand for Parliament against the local favourite, Sir Thomas Loveland, in part to provide opposition enough that Loveland will have to bribe his constituents for votes and, once elected, will repay his obligations with political favours, and in part so that the voters can get bribe money from the Don, we come to the end of Fielding's comic control. Don Quixote is made to abandon foolishness and talk serious morality.

Don Quixote: Ha! caitiff! dost think I would condescend to be patron of a place so mercenary? . . . Gods! to what will mankind degenerate! where not only the vile necessaries of life, but even honours, which should be the reward of virtue only, are to be bought with money. (II, iii; Henley, IV, 35)

Comedy may well make a serious point, but it must not do so seriously.

The Don is also made to play moralist in the play's matchmaking. Dorothea, piqued that Fairlove has not reached the inn ahead of her – it is their place of rendezvous – decides to have some fun by drawing Don Quixote into her orbit and teasing him about Dulcinea. (It is curious that she is the only person who recognizes him.) There is fun in this exchange, but the telling result of the Don's getting to know Dorothea is that he tells her father to choose Fairlove over Badger for the good reason that the young man is palpably better than the rich squire: 'is it possible you can prefer that wretch, who is a scandal to his very species, to this gentleman, whose person and parts would be an honour to the greatest of it?' (III, xiv; Henley, IV, 65). Again, in assigning the role of heavy moralist to Don Quixote, Fielding undercuts comic possibilities.

One might argue that *Don Quixote in England* is a play about madness. Everyone, including Sancho, thinks Don Quixote is mad, but the knight overturns the judgment, saying:

> Each man rises to admiration by treading on mankind . . . Why, one who, seeing the want of his friend, cries, he pities him! Is this real? no: if it was he would relieve him! His pity is triumphant arrogance and insult: it arises from his pride, not from his compassion. Sancho, let them call me mad; I'm not mad enough to court their approbation. (II, i; Henley, IV, 32)

By the end of the play there is sympathy for this view of Don Quixote's. Loveland says: 'I don't know whether this knight, by and by, may not prove us all to be more mad than himself' (III, xvi; Henley, IV. 70). Fairlove agrees, and then he and Dorothea end the play with a song on madness, which begins,

> All mankind are mad, 'tis plain
>   Some for places,
>   Some embraces;
> Some are mad to keep up gain,
> And others mad to spend it.
> Courtiers we may madmen rate,
>   Poor believers
>   In deceivers;
> Some are mad to hurt the state,
> And others mad to mend it. (Henley, IV, 70)

The implication, here and elsewhere in *Don Quixote in England*, is that we are driven to succeed by compulsions: compulsions that have become ways of the world, acceptable because of their familiarity, without reference to their sanity. But the play is uncertain in its treatment of Don Quixote, and it misses the comic vitality that would make criticism of its weak structure irrelevant.

An Old Man Taught Wisdom; or The Virgin Unmask'd, an afterpiece written for Kitty Clive, performed at Drury Lane on 5 January 1735, had an enormous success that lasted through the century. The very simple musical farce, left undivided into acts or scenes, turns on the happy idea that Lucy, a maiden of sixteen reared by her father, Goodall, to know little or nothing of the world, speaks and acts as she will, utterly unencumbered by her father's longlived effort to educate her. In addition to Lucy's compulsive candour as a basis for comedy, Fielding assigns the father a ridiculous expectation, namely that his daughter will settle down with one of the men of his choice, her five cousins (a dancing master, a singing master, a bookworm, an apothecary, and a lawyer).[120] Goodall may seem realistic in planning to attract the cousins as suitors with his fortune of £10 000, which eventually will go to the married couple, but he shows himself a fool in misreading Lucy. She is guided entirely by her own feelings, which are not only unchecked and indiscriminate, but undisguised. We observe her as that moving toyshop, her heart, compels her to fall in love with Tom, a handsome, sensible, and well mannered footman, and also to experience desire for two of her ridiculous cousins, and to be repelled by a third, also ridiculous.

Lucy would be what Bookish calls her, 'contemptible', if she were not naive (in a sense innocent) as well as self-indulgent. Urged by Blister, her apothecary cousin, to admit what she really thinks of him, she says, 'I hate you and I can't abide you' (Henley, III, 334). She is also openly attracted by the idea that Blister would require her fidelity for only the first two weeks after marriage. In short, she is a comic character whose status exempts her from simple moral judgments. Besides, the action is brought to a satisfactory resolution in that regard for when Lucy marries Tom without her father's permission, Goodall comes to prefer his daughter's choice to his own: her 'booby relations', as he calls his nephews (Henley, III, 349). The last joke contradicts the play's title since the old man has not been taught wisdom; he has only approved the fortunate compulsion of his intractable daughter.

Probably Fielding worked on *The Good-Natur'd Man* during the year in which *The Universal Gallant* was staged, 1735. It was not performed until long after his death, in 1778, at Drury Lane. In 1743, at Garrick's request, Fielding worked at revising it, but he was not satisfied with the results. According to Cross, Fielding gave it to Charles Hanbury Williams for criticism, probably in 1753, after which the play was lost for years.[121] Garrick got hold of it in 1776, and it may be that he and Sheridan revised it slightly, renaming it *The Fathers*. Despite this complex provenance, the play is clearly Fielding's.[122]

The Fathers contrasts not only two fathers, the good-natured

Boncour and the deceitful Valence (each of whom has a marriage-able son and daughter), but also two siblings, the same good-natured Boncour and his practical-minded bachelor brother Sir George. It is initially through the contrasting brothers that the play explores its first theme – the role of discipline in child-rearing – about which the brothers differ, Sir George urging strong measures and Boncour practising unusual leniency. (Fielding drew on Terence's *Adelphi*, which is itself closely modelled on a play by Menander, for the contrasting brothers. He also drew on Molière's *L'Ecole des Maris*, in which love-and-marriage triumphs over parental constraint, a theme after Fielding's own heart.) The exploration of the theme – the proper exercise of parental auth-ority – continues through the contrast between the fathers, and includes a test of their four children, who are paired for marriage.

Boncour's son and daughter at first show all the signs of a too-indulgent upbringing, and Valence's children display their father's rascality in conniving to win advantageous terms for marriage. But when wily Sir George, the bachelor, brings matters to a head by reporting (falsely) that his brother has lost his money, Boncour's children behave splendidly, the son giving his father that portion of his mother's fortune assigned to him. Now ineli-gible for the marriages they had anticipated, he and his sister accept their new status. All too predictably, the Valence chil-dren are utterly bad: the sister calls Young Boncour a fool for giving up his inheritance, and then she leaves him for a rich suitor already in the wings; the brother tries (and fails) to seduce the ineligible Miss Boncour, having coolly discussed his inten-tion with his sister.

The play has strengths and weaknesses that are hard to sepa-rate. Crucial to the effectiveness of the action is the way in which we percieve the four Boncours: the lenient father, his hard-nosed bachelor brother, Miss Boncour, and Young Boncour. Despite the actively contrasted philosophies of the brothers and the distance between the apparently spoiled children and their father and uncle, it is possible to read early signs that all are unusually amiable members of a family, deeply concerned for each other. As a result, the exploration of the contrasted parent–child relations becomes less important than effective drama requires. Add to this that the Valences are too simply evil, and dramatic tension about how to bring up children is further reduced. Good fathers have good children, and bad fathers have bad ones, the play seems to say.

Several things make the play effective, however. It is hard not to like the Boncours: the children are strong-minded and decent, the uncle is cleverly supportive of the family's interests, and the older Boncour is loving and constructive but not weak, a fact we learn by degrees and gradually come to admire him for. In addition, as the original theme of paternal discipline gives way to the theme of the good family's survival, Fielding's favourite subject (marriage) takes centre stage. Given the soured relations between the young Boncours and young Valences, the comedy must end without marriages or quickly reinvent itself. Fielding pointedly rejects a happy ending for Miss Boncour, even though she has been wooed by a loving young man from the country; he is rich enough and well-meaning, but, alas, oafish. Sir George explains the impossibility of her accepting the proposal: 'Wedding directly! what, do you think you are coupling some of your animals in the country?' (V, v; Henley, V, 229). We learn too that Young Boncour may have a possible bride in view, but she is a long way off in time. Wedding bells before play's ending – too soon after the painful discoveries of cold-blooded duplicity in both Valence children – would have violated the Boncours' integrity, making a mockery of loving relations in the good family. Even though the play transforms its theme, it does so without loss of continuity, at least for those who may find the four Boncours and their interests engaging.

Fielding, perhaps in collaboration with Garrick, wrote a sequel to *An Old Man Taught Wisdom* called *Miss Lucy in Town*, first produced at Drury Lane on 6 May 1742.[123] The action turns on Lucy's coming to London shortly after her marriage to Tom, as full of appetite as she was in *The Virgin Unmasqued* and as lacking in judgment and conventional sense. For their London visit, Fielding chooses to locate the couple in a house whose owner, Mrs Midnight, is a bawd fallen on hard times. Among her few clients are Lord Bawble, who does not pay for what he buys, and Mr Zorobabel, who does. As soon as Mrs Midnight sizes up Lucy and concludes that her fresh country beauty and her brainless desire to live a life of fashion make her a perfect victim, she sells her; first to Bawble, who does not come up with the cash, and then to Zorobabel, for twice the original amount. Amusing complications show Lucy to be unselfconsciously desirous, unscrupulous, acquisitive and ambitious.

Fielding pushes her self-indulgence to the limit. He heightens the ridiculous with a musical competition between an Italian opera singer and an English singer of ballads; and Lucy, for whose favours they vie, chimes in. Fortunately (or otherwise), Fielding has Tom return before Lucy's infidelities of imagination can be translated to the flesh. The playwright means them well. Though husband and wife argue, we understand that they will return to the country where married life affords great natural pleasures. The play had a good run of eighteen performances during the spring and autumn of 1742.

The Universal Gallant, a serious satire in five acts, was produced at Drury Lane on 10 February 1735. Though it ran for three nights, it was a painful failure. Fielding found it hard to accept the audience's unmistakable verdict, as his complaint in the published version makes clear: 'What could incense a number of people to attack it with such an inveterate prejudice, is not easy to determine; for prejudice must be allowed, be the play good or bad, when it is condemned unheard' (advertisement, Henley, IV, 77). But the play probably failed because it was not sound.[124]

The Universal Gallant has some of Fielding's most winning qualities – wit, knowledge of human nature, the sympathetic treatment of intelligent women, even moments of comic vitality – but it fails to give us engaging, or even consistently interesting, characters, whose fate and fortune we care about, because it fails to locate them in a comprehensive morality of whatever hue. In *The Modern Husband*, the treatment of marriages (both blessed and corrupted) may move us to appreciate broad ranges of human fulfilment and devastation, guided as we are by an ideal and its complex violation. But *The Universal Gallant* leaves us without such evaluative access to its action.

Mondish is the universal gallant and, as his name suggests, a worldling. He has had an extended affair with Mrs Raffler, wife of Colonel Raffler, who is mistakenly complaisant about his wife's fidelity. Sir Simon Raffler, the Colonel's brother, is by contrast mistakenly convinced that his wife has cuckolded him. Of these, only the Colonel's wife is once or twice sympathetic or interesting, as when she makes it clear she is not a hardened adulteress (which Mondish believes her to be, and which Fielding, at one point, inconsistently suggests she may become).

Besides these, there are two other principals: Clarinda, a marriageable young lady, and Gaylove, who loves and wants to marry her. Clarinda is attractive for openly returning Gaylove's affection, and for her independent spirit and intelligence as well. But we never get to know her well because she is located at the fringes of the action. And Gaylove, who might have been a moral contrast to Mondish, is in fact manipulated by him into attempting a seduction of Mrs Raffler. (Mondish suspects Gaylove of replacing him in Mrs Raffler's affections and he thus tests the suspicion.) Like so much in the play, the upshot of the encounter is not comic, only morally casual. Gaylove's attempt on Mrs Raffler, which we are left to believe may have succeeded but for an interruption by Lady Raffler, is not well developed. Gaylove simply tells us he is unable to deny a fine woman, and we are left to accept the fact. And it does not help us to understand these contradictions of earlier established motivation, in Gaylove and in Mrs Raffler, that Clarinda says she does not expect a young man to be proof against all temptations, because she means her words to apply to Mondish, not to Gaylove, though for a moment just whom she has in mind is in doubt (IV, i; Henley, IV, 134). Here and elsewhere the play is without effective use of plot and character; no person or theme or comic mode controls the world of the work.

Fielding had five more plays produced before the licensing act effectively forced him to give up his profession as playwright: *Pasquin, Tumble-Down Dick, Eurydice, The Historical Register* and *Eurydice Hiss'd*. Of these, only *Eurydice* was performed at Drury Lane, on 19 February 1737. The others were played at the Little Haymarket. Before turning to these last plays, which combine burlesque and topical satire, I think it useful to consider briefly Fielding's place in the theatre at this time. He was deeply disappointed over the failure of *The Universal Gallant*, and for the wrong reasons. He thought the world had been unfair.[125] Probably he and his wife went to the country, where Fielding must have taken stock of his predicament. He must have known that his return to Drury Lane without an intervening success was not a likely prospect. He would have to recover his pre-eminence at the Little Haymarket or another lesser house. Meanwhile London's non-patent theatres were being threatened by legislation against them in the form of the Barnard Playhouse Bill, which sought, among other prohibitions, to confine acting to those who performed under Royal patent. Though not without opposition, the bill had wide-ranging support and probably would have passed, except that

Walpole offered an amendment to give the ministry authority to censor all plays. Finding this attempt to increase ministerial power unacceptable, the drafters dropped the bill. But the groundwork had been laid for the passage of the Licensing Act two years later. Instead of regarding the close call as a warning, however, the non-patent theatres were apparently encouraged by the bill's failure to produce plays they should have known would offend the ministry. Fielding's last plays no doubt contributed their share to this offensive material.[126]

We have no evidence for knowing just when Fielding returned to London, or what he may have attempted before deciding to become the producer of his own plays at the Little Haymarket, or how and on what terms he was able to arrange things there. Our most informed conjecture comes from Hume:

> I hypothesize that Fielding returned to London around December 1735 or January 1736, was rebuffed by John Rich [manager of Lincoln's Inn Fields and Covent Gardens] (and perhaps by Fleetwood [of Drury Lane] and Giffard [of Goodman's Fields] as well), and decided that he must turn entrepreneur. The first clear reference to Fielding as 'Great Mogul' at the head of his 'Company of English Comedians' is in the *London Daily Post and Advertiser* advertisement of 24 February, promising *Pasquin* for 5 March.[127]

Pasquin, performed on 5 March, at the Little Haymarket, enjoyed an immense success, being acted 39 times in succession and 62 or 63 times altogether.[128] It is a play in two parts, as Fielding explains on the title page of the edition of 1736: '*Pasquin. A Dramatick Satire on the Times: Being The Rehearsal of two Plays, viz. A Comedy call'd The Election; And a Tragedy call'd, The Life and Death of Common-Sense*' (Henley, IV, 163). *The Author's Farce*, which in its 'The Pleasures of the Town' (Act III) includes internal reflexive commentary on the play in progress, in some ways anticipates *Pasquin*, a full-blown rehearsal play. But Fielding's target in *Pasquin* is less the theatre world than his society, and the political and social abuses of his times, although he takes opportunities for exposing the woes of dramatists and their idiosyncracies as well.[129] *Pasquin's* first play within the play is a comedy by author Trapwit, who oversees its rehearsal in the presence of Fustian, author of the tragedy which is to follow.

Their give and take provides amusing commentary on Trapwit's play. When the comedy ends, Trapwit, who dislikes all plays but his own, finds a way to excuse himself, leaving Sneerwell, a critic, and Fustian to comment on the rehearsal of the tragedy. Fielding times Sneerwell's arrival and Trapwit's departure to provide opportunities both for satirizing critics and playwrights and for introducing a variety of perspectives on the two plays within.

Both plays are chiefly social satire, the comedy ridiculing corrupt elections, and the tragedy the triumph of ignorance over common-sense. The two are joined by a general theme, which is that narrow self-interest (self-interest unbalanced by long-term perspective or ideology) so threatens the structure of society that it may not survive. Scriblerian in its view of the forces of social destruc-tion, Fielding's play is probably more even-handed politically than Pope, Swift or Bolingbroke would have liked, giving no preference to the country party over that of the court in the election scenes, though it scores many topical hits against the ministry.[130]

In *The Election, Pasquin*'s comedy, members of the court party, Lord Place and Colonel Promise, without disguising their action, offer to buy votes, and voters sell them; members of the country party, Sir Henry Fox-Chase and Squire Tankard, do the same (somewhat less candidly) and again, voters cooperate. Politicians and their constituencies (everyone), in the country and the town (everywhere), are corrupting or corruptible or both. In Fustian's tragedy, *The Life and Death of Common-Sense*, Firebrand (a Priest of the Sun), Physic (a physician), and Law (a lawyer), through their professions, work to control the lives of those around them, and so they give their support to the forces of Queen Ignorance in her war with Queen Common-Sense, ignorance being the state they prefer in their clients. In the comedy, narrow self-interest operates through the electorate at precisely the socially appointed time for serving the common good: an election. In the tragedy, narrow self-interest operates at the level of daily life, where the souls, the bodies, and the rights of the many are subverted by the greed of socially authorized professionals and by the igno-rance of their dupes, the people.

Pasquin is immensely funny, but dark elements inform its comic vitality. It is hardly optimistic. The comedy, in which narrow self-interest and silly private choices abound, ends in an ironi-cally unforeshadowed marriage between Miss Mayoress, the

corrupted Mayor's daughter, and Colonel Promise, a court-party
corrupter. It is a foolish marriage, without a past in love or courtship and without hope for the future. In the tragedy, which
displays the vicious triumph of self-aggrandizing professional-
ism over social responsibility, through the destruction of common-sense, hope is also lost. Queen Ignorance kills Queen
Common-Sense, who survives, but only as the Ghost of Common-Sense, a sorry wraith whose presence reminds us of her
demise.

Is it ironic that *Pasquin*'s comedy repudiates its own comic
nature by ending in a silly marriage between unmediated selves,
in which both intelligence and fecundity, comedy's hallmarks,
are undone? And is it ironic that its tragedy, in killing common-
sense, leaves the world unequipped to understand its own predicament and, incidentally, mentally unequipped to come to its
own comic defence against death? After all, Fustian's tragedy is
a comedy.

In fact, Fielding is audacious and clever enough to have it both
ways. We see from another perspective that he has mischievously
misled us in naming Trapwit and Fustian to make them sound
incompetent and in having them subvert the nature of comedy
(and tragedy). In the world of the work they are – as men –
vain, quarrelsome, and self-indugent; but as playwrights, they
are highly effective. Their plays are hilarious; they are miraculously complementary pieces (thanks to Fielding), which ironically (and comically) stand comedy on its head.

On 28 February 1736, Drury Lane had staged a pantomime,
The Fall of Phaeton, of which *The London Stage* reports, 'Invented
by Mr Pritchard. Music composed by Mr Arne. Scenes painted
by Mr. Hayman'.[131] Fielding could not resist a take-off of the
Drury Lane play, in which he retells the story of Phaeton, who
in Greek mythology is teased by his fellow mortals because his
mother Clymene cannot support her claim that Apollo rather than
some nobody has sired her son. Unsettled by the doubtful
paternity, Phaeton visits Apollo, who immediately acknowledges
his son and grants him a wish. Against his immortal father's
advice, Phaeton insists on driving the Chariot of the Sun for a
day. Unequal to the task, he plunges to his death. *Pasquin* played
40 times alone, but on 29 April, the night of the forty-first
performance, it was followed by Fielding's take-off of *The Fall of
Phaeton*. He named it *Tumble-Down Dick: or, Phaeton in the Suds*.

('In the suds' is a slang term meaning 'in deep trouble'. 'Tumble-Down Dick' is another, meaning 'a fellow prone to getting into trouble'.) Like *Pasquin* and the other Fielding plays produced in 1736 and 1737 – *Eurydice, The Historical Register for the Year 1736*, and *Eurydice Hiss'd* – it is a rehearsal play.[132] The characters Fustian, Sneerwell and Prompter are carried over from *Pasquin*. Instead of Trapwit, Mr Machine is the comedian who writes and explains the play within, typically stimulated by the questions and comments of others. Fielding takes opportunities to burlesque both the myth and the Drury Lane pantomime.

The nominal action, which begins in a round-house (a lock-up for holding arrested persons), has Phaeton, whose mother says he is the son of Phoebus Apollo, pay a visit to the god to quash the claims of the boys in the parish, who say he is the son of a 'Serjeant' of the Foot-guards. Though Phoebus does not explicitly acknowledge his paternity, he kisses Phaeton in welcome and allows him a wish. But Fielding's Phoebus has no Chariot of the Sun in which to make his daily journey, only a watchman's lantern (a glaringly unheroic vessel of light) which Phaeton mounts before disappearing from our view, never to return. We learn, however, that he falls asleep on his mission and, coming too close to the earth, dries up the oceans and scorches the land, as a result of which Jupiter himself intervenes and destroys him for doing a sloppy job.

Like many of Fielding's plays, this one is punctuated by airs, five of them, which have no apparent connection to the play's narrative line. But these are only some of the farcical irrelevancies to the action, which is otherwise subverted. Phaeton, Clymene, Phoebus, and other principals are made ridiculous; the hero disappears *in medias res*; and the play, along with the play within, is interrupted by the exigencies of the rehearsal form. Fielding leaves himself free to invent ridiculous moments that give *Phaeton in the Suds* a special comic vitality, as his characterization on the title-page of the first published version suggests: 'A Dramatick Entertainment of Walking, in Serious and Foolish Characters: Interlarded with Burlesque, Grotesque, Comick Interludes, call'd Harlequin A Pick-Pocket'.[133]

Fielding's next play, *Eurydice; or, The Devil Henpeck'd*, also a rehearsal, as I have said, was produced at Drury Lane on 19 February 1737, and was an afterpiece almost certainly written for Kitty Clive. Hume argues persuasively that Fleetwood, for sound business reasons, must have commissioned Fielding to write the play, offering him not only the prestige of a Drury Lane production at the same time that his career at the Little Haymarket went forward, but a first-night benefit, which doubtless earned Fielding a handsome sum, even though *Eurydice* failed dramatically.[134] Unfortunately a major disturbance in the gallery interfered with the first performance, and the play was hissed off the stage, perhaps for reasons having nothing to do with its quality.[135] In *Eurydice Hiss'd* (13 April 1737, Little Haymarket), a complex political satire against the ministry as well as a spoofing exercise in self-ridicule, Fielding has Spatter, a playwright, say about *Eurydice*, 'You will allow I have chosen my subject very cunningly, for as the town have damned my play for their own sakes, they will not damn the damnation of it.'[136] *Eurydice* is in fact a good burlesque.

The setting is Hades, which in Fielding's play turns out to be a place very much like earth in that individual human appetites continue to dominate the behaviour of the dead, except that their compulsions are more obvious below. Shaw's Hell in *Man and Superman* is in this regard like Fielding's, and so is Shaw's Devil like Fielding's Pluto, a suave old rascal, unabashed by vice, though quite unlike him in being married to Proserpine, who rules the roost. The action, which turns on the admission of Orpheus to Hades and his failed attempt to get Eurydice back to the world of the living (which can only be Fielding's London) is made ludicrous by a variety of means. It is overseen and commented on by Pluto and Proserpine, he astonished that a husband should want his wife back and she protective of Eurydice's right to decline the invitation to leave the underworld. We soon learn that Eurydice needs no help. Having said, as Shaw's Anna in the Hell scene was to do, 'O you great creature, you. You are a man, and I am a poor weak woman', she goes on to trick Orpheus into looking back and losing her (though it was Proserpine who set up the possibility, having arranged the proviso against a backward glance: Henley, IV, 281, 282). The 'women' stick together.

Throughout the piece, Kitty Clive (Eurydice) and Charles Stoppelaer (Orpheus), both known for their good voices, interfere with the audience's settling into the narrative action by mocking Italian opera, in melody and recitative. To reinforce this musical-burlesque fragmentation of dramatic continuity, Fielding calls on two pairs of observer-participants, who comment on the action: Author and Critic, who oversee the play's rehearsal; and two beaus, Captain Weazel and Mr Spindle, eighteenth-century Londoners who have crossed the Styx only to continue their improbable ways on the other side.

I have already said that *Eurydice* may have failed through no fault of its own, but reasons other than the gallery riot have been sought to explain why the play was produced only once. Genest cites the '[glaring] impropriety of calling Pluto the Devil' as an instance of Fielding's want of good sense. Battestin, among others, recalls Fielding's hint in *Eurydice Hiss'd* that the character of Captain Weazel 'was taken as an affront to the military'. Hume suggests that the music might have presented a difficulty; but Cleary may provide the best reason, pointing out that Pluto's dominance by Proserpine mirrors King George II's dominance by Queen Caroline (recall *The Welsh Opera*), so that the play would have been 'in the worst taste after Queen Caroline's death on November 20, 1737'.[137] Certainly the combination of *Eurydice's* widely publicized first-night failure, possible difficulties with the music, and the Queen's death would have given any manager reason enough to avoid the play.

Despite the bad luck at Drury Lane, Fielding continued to be active in his capacity as playwright and manager, moving ahead with plans to build a new theatre, probably somewhere in Westminster, and to produce plays at the Little Haymarket that would offer real competition to the patent theatres and Goodman's Fields, which with few exceptions confined themselves to mounting plays with a history of success. From mid-March 1737 until his dramatic career ended on 23 May, with the pending enforcement of the Licensing Act, Fielding's company produced eleven different plays, most of them new. As Hume points out, he 'was running a company genuinely devoted to contemporary plays. Nothing of the sort had ever been tried in the modern history of the London theatre.'[138] During this period, the plays mounted at the Little Haymarket, those by Fielding – *The Historical Register for the Year 1736* and *Eurydice Hiss'd* – and probably many of those by other authors as well, were politically partisan, anti-ministerial plays. The reason may have been Fielding's desire (or willingness) to cooperate with his friends in the opposition, the Broad-Bottoms, or perhaps it was his professional sense that the kind of play he had succeeded with, topical farce and burlesque, would be improved with the added bite of explicit partisanship. Both reasons may have contributed to his decision. Like author Medley of *The Historical Register*, Fielding must have wanted most 'to divert the town and bring full houses' (Act I, Appleton, p. 15).

The Historical Register for the Year 1736 was first performed on 21 March 1737. The title is pointedly ironic. As Appleton points out, Fielding took it from an annual publication of that name, begun in 1716.[139] It claimed to do for foreign and domestic transactions what the term 'register' implies: to report such matters by the year, impartially and systematically. Fielding's play, which is neither impartial nor systematic, is about as far from objective exposition as one can imagine. The name of its designated author, 'Medley', in a way forecasts his work, which Morrissey refers to (along with *Pasquin*) as a *melange*, 'held together by the imposed form of a rehearsal'.[140] But in fact even the rehearsal form succumbs to uncertainty in that the action of the play within more than once intrudes into the play itself, as when 'All ladies' of the play within say to Medley, 'Don't interrupt us, dear sir' (Act II, Appleton, p. 24). *The Historical Register* is consistent only in violating the limits of its title, unless one were to find that its chaotic mischief better represents England, especially London, of 1736, than any cut-and-dried Annal could.

Medley, the playwright, Sourwit, the critic, and Lord Dapper, a light-brained beau, attend the rehearsal. The nominal action centres on three meetings: politicians who gather in Corsica (which for various reasons had been associated with England in 1736); English ladies (all in love with the Italian castrato Farinelli), who attend a London auction; and Patriots, who also convene in Corsica.[141] These meetings and the comments on them by Medley, Sourwit and Dapper – to which are added comments by Banter, who insults everyone, Dangle, who encourages everyone to trivial activity, and Mr Hen, the auctioneer – satirize the world of English politics, the theatre and society, often with effective shots at Walpole, Colley and Theophilus Cibber, Fleetwood of Drury Lane, and others.

The satire on society runs the length of the play, but it is most intense at the auction, where foolish men and women, Mrs Barter, various officers and beaux, and Mrs Screen, bid and withhold bids on abstract items as they come up: Political Honesty, Patriotism, Three Grains of Modesty, Courage, Conscience, Interest at Court, All the Cardinal Virtues, Wit, and Common-sense. Little eagerness is shown for any of the items except Interest at Court, which brings £1000. This already heavy-handed satire on ethical values is given a new dimension when Lord Dapper, one of the spectators at the rehearsal, intrudes into the play within, unable to resist a bid. He chides himself for the slip, and Medley comforts him, saying, 'It's a sure sign it's Nature, my lord, and I should not be surprised to see the whole audience stand up and bid for it too' (Act II, Appleton, p. 34).

The theatrical satire centres on the Cibbers and on Fleetwood for his management of Drury Lane. Colley, as the character Ground-Ivy, is ridiculed especially for his revision of *King John*. Shakespeare's plays 'as now writ will not do', he assures us (Act III, Appleton, p. 42). Theophilus, as Pistol, a role for which he was famous, makes outrageous claims about the Cibber family dynasty. Fielding sets up Cibber for a fall by having him (Pistol) propose, towards the end of Act II, that his wife, Susanna Cibber, replace Kitty Clive in the role of Polly in *The Beggar's Opera*. (Fleetwood had actually proposed the change in 1736, causing a public furore.)[142] The suggestion is hissed fiercely by the mob in the play, but Theophilus–Pistol perversely understands their hiss to signify assent.

Fielding uses Corsica as the meeting place of Politicians at the beginning of the play and of Patriots at the end as a way of capitalizing on a publicly understood metaphor that in 1736 had connected England and the troubled Italian island, where a certain Baron Neuhoff, a patriot-adventurer with questionable credentials, worked to secure Corsica's liberty from Genoa. Presumably England, another island, under the yoke of the Walpole ministry, also needed liberation. Fielding makes Walpole–Politics the subject of his severest satire in the play, sometimes by showing theatrical and political subjects to be types of each other. When at the end of Act II Pistol parades himself as 'Prime Minister theatrical', Fielding hits the first target: Theophilus Cibber, long associated with the role of Pistol, a part he played broadly, with extreme braggadoccio. But 'Prime Ministerial', especially as it is coupled with 'great Pistol' in the same speech, also hits the second target, Walpole, widely known as 'the Great'. Such double-scoring quickens one's sense of the satirical hunt. Sometimes Fielding freshens his target by pointing away from Theophilus and towards another 'Walpole'. In Act III, Quidam, whose name means 'a certain thing, known, but not necessarily named', joins the Corsican meeting of the Patriots (Walpole's opposition) and succeeds in bribing them and recovering his money into the bargain. The double success of the financial transaction makes it clear that Quidam is none other than the corrupt and efficient Walpole himself.

Fielding goes on, however, in Act III, to make the Prime Minister seem a ubiquitous evil power by associating him with yet two other characters through their authority over 'houses': the play-house and the House of Commons. Ground-Ivy (Colley Cibber) and a bastard son of Apollo are said to be in charge of 'all our playhouses and poetical performances whatsoever' (Act III, Appleton, p. 40). Both show themselves to be part Walpole by reinforcing each other's contempt for public opinion, both in the playhouse and in Commons. After Ground-Ivy says, 'I have seen things carried in the House against the voice of the people before today', Apollo's bastard adds, 'Let them hiss and grumble as much as they please, as long as we get their money.' Then Ground-Ivy cinches the Walpole connection by pronouncing Apollo's statement 'the sentiment of a Great Man' (Act III, Appleton, p. 43). *The Historical Register* hits the Prime Minister very hard.

Though undoubtedly partisan, the play was highly successful because of its inspired handling of topical material. Fielding's contemporaries enjoyed it, and so do ours. Appleton says it is 'Fielding's most entertaining play', and Hume, after naming Fielding's principal targets, observes that his 'handling of this melange is simply brilliant'.[143] We know that the government's plans for some kind of Licensing Act were well developed long before Fielding became explicitly anti-ministerial, but his earlier spoofs of the royal family and his biting partisan plays of 1737 must have helped to keep the pot boiling.

Eurydice Hiss'd, Fielding's last play, was produced as an afterpiece to *The Historical Register*, on 13 April 1737. In its use of certain characters, Sourwit and Lord Dapper, and in its explicit attacks on Walpole, it is a continuation of the mainpiece. But it is also about the failed play *Eurydice*. Once again, Fielding complicates the rehearsal form by having the author of the play within, Spatter, invent a second author, Pillage, who is made to be both Fielding (the poet who wrote *Eurydice*) and Walpole (author of the failed Excise Bill and related actions that had led to riots in 1736). In this double identification, Fielding is daring, seeming to invite the view that he, like the Prime Minister, has been guilty of poor professional conduct. But in fact, his self-deprecation is facetious, although to make it so, Fielding comes precariously close to confessional sincerity.

Spatter gives us the first clue that Fielding's self-ridicule is disingenuous by telling Lord Dapper that he is about to see a tragedy – 'ten times as ridiculous' as Medley's comedy – about the fall of an immensely successful playwright, Pillage, as a result of an abrupt change of fortune (Appleton, p. 54). The setting for the play within the play within is the theatre, on the day Pillage's farce *Eurydice* is to be performed. We see Pillage with the weight of the world on his shoulders as he is not only the playwright but the theatre manager as well. His first words are a lament in heavy iambs: 'Who'd wish to be the author of a farce.' Obviously Fielding mocks Pillage's (his own) predicament, by not treating it seriously.

Spatter changes gears swiftly after the mock lament, however, assigning Pillage to do the work of a political minister (receiving petitioners at a levee). There, Fielding's self-satire apparently takes a serious turn. Pillage appears more and more like Walpole, hearing pleas from his dependants: actors who sound like men begging for political preferment and, in exchange, promising such favours as joining the audience to applaud plays, or whatever Pillage may require. The distinction between the illicit solicitation of support for plays and for parliamentary bills evaporates. Pillage–Fielding and Pillage–Walpole seem to be equally unscrupulous.[144] Then the supremely righteous Honestus, whose applause cannot be bought, joins the levee, and his presence seems to corroborate the serious moral tone.

Can Walpole be thus censured and not Fielding, when the two are one? In a sense, yes. Fielding turns away from the Walpole allegory, and through Splatter brings Muse to visit Pillage. She declares she cherishes the union that brought forth their *Pasquin*, before accusing Pillage of siring *Eurydice* by another. But Muse's fury over the betrayal is made ridiculous: 'I, whose fond heart too easily did yield/My virgin joys and honor to thy arms/And bore thee *Pasquin*', she declaims (Appleton, p. 63). A bit later, after *Eurydice* is hissed (offstage, following Horace's advice concerning matters too horrible to be shown), Honestus rejoins the miserable Pillage, parading a dispassionate mercy for the fallen playwright: 'When *Pasquin* run and the town liked you most,/And every scribbler loaded you with praise,/I did not court you, nor will shun you now' (Appleton, p. 67). But Pillage needs comfort, not rhetoric, so against Honestus's advice he gets drunk, and then he says of *Eurydice*, 'By Jove, there never was a better farce'. (Appleton, p. 68). *In vino veritas.* Maybe Fielding finds he has a little bit of Walpole in him, but it does not keep him from thinking well of the failed *Eurydice*, or from making the unpleasant congruity between himself and the Minister comically pleasant.

On Monday, 23 May 1737, Fielding's company gave their last performance, a bill made up of *The Historical Register* and *Eurydice Hiss'd*. But the Ministry, having tried and failed to pass a bill to control the theatres in 1735, was bringing things to a head once more. 'On 24 May, the Licensing Act was introduced in Commons, beginning a progress through both Houses that was inexorable, though there were many protests.'[145] Once passed, the Act did not become law until 21 June, when it received the royal approval, but Fielding had to give up his advertised plan to produce other anti-ministerial plays because Walpole had reached the owner of the Little Haymarket, John Potter, and got him to take 'down the scenes & decorations so that the theatre was Rendered Incapable of haveing any Play or other performance'.[146]

Opinions vary as to the extent of Fielding's reaction, which one might have expected to be strong, given his temperament, the abrupt loss of his access to the Little Haymarket, and the long-term implications of the Licensing Act on his career as dramatist. Cross says that Fielding 'submitted quietly to the law'; Cleary believes he was silent except for a 'reasoned valediction to the theatrical and censorial wars of 1737' he wrote for *The Craftsman* of 4 June; Lockwood says Fielding wrote a letter to *Common Sense*, over the name of 'Pasquin', published on 21 May 1737, in which he defends his plays of the season, and then 'fell silent for a year'; Hume remarks Fielding's 'rather astonishing public silence about [the Licensing Act]'; but Battestin, both in his biography and in another study with Michael G. Farringdon, claims that Fielding contributed several anti-ministerial pieces to *The Craftsman* during the months after the Little Haymarket closed.[147]

This divergence of opinion is interesting in that Lockwood, followed by Hume, wonders that Fielding did not take strong action against the ministry; for instance, by writing a Patriot play, having it censored, publishing it, and making a pot of money from the publicity.[148] Both scholars are surprised by his untypical restraint. But they take this and other available evidence into account (which includes a reference by Fielding, to Walpole and himself, in which he talks about his silent muse and a politician who bribes people to hold their tongues), and they conclude that Fielding accepted a bribe from Walpole in exchange for silence.[149] Battestin, however, confident that Fielding indeed wrote anti-ministerial pieces in the months following the Licensing Act, makes nothing of Lockwood's claim, simply observing that he must not have known about Fielding's contributions to *The Craftsman* during this period.[150]

In fact, whether Fielding accepted a bribe from Walpole need not turn on whether he was silent after the Licensing Act was passed, though both Lockwood and Hume argue as if that were a crucial matter. And if indeed Fielding wrote against the minis-try at that time, as Battestin on good evidence concludes, it need not follow that Fielding simply took the bribe and then disre-garded the obligation to keep quiet. It is much more likely that the briber and the bribed did not long believe themselves bound by their contract because the issue it was supposed to fix proved to be very much alive. Lockwood, though intent on another issue, instances this possibility nicely, quoting from an essay by Fielding in the *Champion* of 11 December 1739:

> [Walpole] . . . is known to have given money for any thing; . . . [to have] given money to suppress abuses against himself, and afterwards with as great Truth as Modesty, after many breaches of his Word, . . . [to have] accused the person who received it of Ingratitude for exposing him.

Lockwood points out that Fielding makes similar accusations elsewhere.[151]

It is reasonable to think that Walpole's bribery of Fielding is very much an open question. Critics and biographers generally agree that Fielding needed money at this time. Though his theatre earnings for 1736 and 1737 must have been considerable, both his own habits of spending and his growing family obligations would probably have eaten them up. His wealthy friends in the opposition may have helped him, and something may have been left of his wife's inheritance of £1500, which she received on the death of her mother, Elizabeth Cradock, in 1735. But it seems very likely that Fielding would have needed more money in 1737. Then there is the fact that Fielding says a good deal about Walpole and the bribery question, showing it to have been an emotionally complicated issue for him, very much alive in his mind for a long while. Even the matter of his anti-ministerial publications immediately after the passage of the Licensing Act leaves room for conjecture. Why did he did not write a Patriot play and bring it to publication, as Gay had done and Henry Brooke was to do, both very profitably?[152] Finally, the scholar with the most broadly informed sense of Fielding the man, Martin Battestin, considers that Fielding was not above taking a bribe from the ministry, which he seems to have done in 1731, for example, in return for withholding *The Grub-Street Opera* from production and publication.[153] If Fielding indeed took a bribe at this early date, for the explicit favour of withholding a play, it is reasonable to suppose that a subsequent bribe, paid in 1737 (say, to keep Fielding from writing a Patriot play and publishing it after it was censored), should have been understood by both parties to be a contract with no more scope than its terms specified. Accordingly Fielding would have felt free to continue to write against the ministry in *The Craftsman*, and Walpole (who might have hoped for a more general silence from Fielding) no doubt took new initiatives to stop him.

Whatever the truth, Fielding lost no time in readjusting his professional ambition. On 1 November 1737, he was admitted to the Middle Temple to study law at the inn of court where his cousin Henry Gould had recently been called to the bar and where, long before, in 1660, his mother's father, another Henry Gould, had been admitted. Called to the bar in 1667, the older Henry had enjoyed a full career in the law, being knighted in 1694 and made Judge of the King's Bench in 1699. His son Davidge, Fielding's uncle, also a lawyer of the Middle Temple, helped his nephew to qualify for the bar. What Fielding may have felt about this shift to the maternal family calling we can only guess. His plays suggest that he had no great respect for the practice of the law; but, even if his satirical treatment of lawyers there reflects a personal view, he may have looked forward to joining the profession for any number of reasons, both practical and idealistic.

Nevertheless, in making the change, he gave up his income and two professions, theatre manager and dramatist, each of which brought him money. His reasons for doing so are not altogether clear. Had Walpole threatened Fielding somehow? Recall that the minister had shown how ruthless he could be when he secretly coerced Potter, owner of the Little Haymarket, to gut the theatre, rendering it useless for performance. Did Walpole supply Fielding with an income while he read law in the Middle Temple? No one can say. Surely Fielding found it hard to give up his work as theatre mogul, which he seemed to enjoy and, until the last moment, gave every sign of expanding. And he must have found it hard to turn away from his ambition at the time to succeed as an Aristophanic comedian, satirizing social and political vice, and as an author of traditional five-act comedies with a serious social purpose.

His genius as a playwright was in topical burlesque, and it was in his short pieces, brilliant and full of energy, that he won his great successes. The vitality and audacious individuality of these plays are strong indications that however much Fielding may have preferred to write conventional comedy, he enjoyed using his burlesque eye and pen. But with the Little Haymarket and other theatres like it effectively closed to him, he had no venue for such work. Neither was there any real chance to earn money with new five-act comedies, given the patent theatres' practice of staging plays in the established repertory, with few exceptions, especially after the Licensing Act renewed their monopoly.

It seems reasonable to suppose that Fielding's wish to write conventional comedy was in some measure a longing for solid success and lasting reputation, which he did not associate with burlesque. Five-act comedy is a venerable form, the fivefold division traceable to classical comedy, according to a doubtful Renaissance view.[154] For all his libertarian vivacity, Fielding was an institutional conservative – proud of his birth, his maternal family's tradition in the law, his classical learning – who was eager to find a prominent place for himself. The London theatre prohibited the success he wanted, but the law was a possibility, especially as it offered a status that his family could help him to achieve, although not without his own very hard work; and it was a status the world would recognize.

As I said earlier, I believe Fielding's five-act plays have been undervalued, especially *The Modern Husband*. Battestin and Rivero think well of the play, largely for its moral vision, but many modern critics, from Cross onwards, have serious reservations as to its quality.[155] It has been censured for bad taste and for poor structure and character development, and praised chiefly for its serious purpose in exposing the deliberate corruption of marriage. It is of course a play about marriage (another of the institutions that energized Fielding's conservatism). But his strength in this play, like Molière's generally, lies in the exposure of character more than in his efforts at social reform, though he does both. In this regard, he anticipates Shaw's Plays Unpleasant, especially *Mrs Warren's Profession*, which have 'serious social purpose', but which are, more deeply, penetrating character studies.[156] In a way, both plays are about corrupt marriages. 'Why not sell your wife to a rich buyer if you are poor?', Fielding asks. 'Why not become a prostitute, like Mrs. Warren, given the oppressively limited job market for women?', Shaw asks.

Both dramatists become fascinated with the consequences for the abused women, Mrs Modern and (not Mrs Warren, vulgar enough to thrive, but her highly educated daughter by a sire unknown) Vivie. Fielding and Shaw let us see them, gradually exposed in various ways, but chiefly in a confrontation with a brutal male whose degrading proposals move them to murderous revulsion.

This concluding praise of *The Modern Husband* is meant to take nothing from Fielding's brilliance as a writer of topical burlesque, the heart of his immense success as dramatist, but only to claim that he is a more 'complete' comedian than is often allowed and that his preference for writing comedies with a 'serious purpose' was no idle wish, supported as it was by a genuine talent he expected to develop. Arthur Murphy's life of Fielding is not always trustworthy, but some of what he says about Fielding's playwriting is worth pausing over. He makes the point that Fielding wrote with 'extreme hurry and dispatch', and that generally 'his judgment was very little consulted'. But Murphy also says that Fielding's plays show a 'strong knowledge of life, delivered indeed with a caustic wit, but often zested with fine infusions of the ridiculous'. Amidst his two-sided appraisals, Murphy quotes Fielding as having said 'he left off writing for the stage, when he ought to have begun'.[157] It may be futile to ask what time and practice would have done to improve Fielding's dramatic craft. But what he accomplished as a very young playwright, in a short span of years, was promising to say the least.

3

The Novels and Other Prose Fiction

Long works of prose fiction have been written from classical antiquity to the present; but the English novel is widely accepted as a genre important elements of which one does not see until the seventeenth and early eighteenth centuries. It is also understood to be a genre not fully recognizable until Defoe, Richardson and Fielding each provided a unique model of the form. Though at one level accurate, this simple view needs heavy qualification because the shape of the novel and its origins are both complicated matters. For a solid understanding of the issues that comprise this difficult subject, one must read the relevant literature, important works of which I cite below. Here I have space enough only for a glance at some of the problems.

There is something like general agreement that the English, indeed the European novel, explores the individualism associated for the past 300 years with the sense of self that locates significant existence increasingly in one's own consciousness rather than in one's conformity with, or departures from, the traditional values of the community. It is also widely agreed that the novel explores the effects of the interplay of individual consciousness and the forces of the community. Finally, there is general agreement that the novel treats this individualism and its interplay with the community in the terms of formal realism, by inventing characters who are uniquely themselves, 'real human beings', located in psychologically recognizable relations with other 'real' persons, in settings taken from the 'real' world.

Every reader can think of exceptions to these broad generalizations. Fielding's Thwackum is at least named as if he were the type of a character and not a unique being. In *Pamela* the relation between the heroine and her parents is so thin psychologically as to be a parody of familial rectitude. The physical and

social setting for *Robinson Crusoe* is real in one sense, but uncom-
promisingly reduced. I simply ackowledge and pass over the
obvious possibility that these 'exceptions' may well be strategies
of the novelist's art for, despite them and more radical departures from the norm, the general statement that the subject of
the novel is the operation of individual consciousness and its
interplay with the 'real' world, including 'real' people, holds well
enough. Ian Watt elaborates the view in the first chapter of his
seminal study of the development of the novel. Though Northrop
Frye concentrates on archetypal forms, he makes the same point,
for example, as he differentiates the novel from romance: 'The
novel tends to be extroverted and personal; its chief interest is
in human character as it manifests itself in society.' In a recent
essay on the status of criticism of the novel as a genre John Richetti
makes the same point and says it is not in dispute. Even Michael
McKeon, who raises questions about Watt's critical method,
acknowledges that formal realism is the novel's lowest common
denominator.[1]

Other views about characteristics of the novel are hardly open
and shut, however. Is D. H. Lawrence right to claim that the
novel represents the fullness of life as nothing else can, including other forms of art?[2] Is every novel constituted by a range of
competing ('dialogic') voices, such that it is both a multi-faceted,
historically valid, dynamic work and an instance of an ever-
developing genre that alone provides access to modern experience as a function of its escape from fossilized literary forms?[3]
Does the novel (in addition?) generate a new epistemology and
new standards of acceptable behaviour at a time of intellectual
and socio-ethical crisis (the early modern period, 1600–1740)?[4]

At another level of inquiry, one might ask how the novel differs
from the confessional prose of the Protestant reformation – indeed
from Augustine's *Confessions* – with its intense focus on interior
being?[5] And what kinds of writing best display individual
consciousness (interiority): letters, diaries, and journals (self-
revelation by the first person), description and analysis by an
outside voice (omniscient story-telling by a third person), or some
other mode or combination of modes? And just how do the novels
of Richardson and Fielding, which (like most novels) have a strong
love interest, differ from the amatory fiction of their immediate
predecessors of the late seventeenth and early eighteenth centuries, Aphra Behn (1640–89), Mary Delariviere Manley (1663–1724)

and Eliza Haywood (1693?–1756)? And given their significant
differences from each other, in what sense are both Richardson's
and Fielding's novels examples of a single genre? These and other
questions and opinions should prove useful in the search for
access to Fielding's novels. They will almost certainly not lead
to finished critical positions, but they can help to generate an
informative body of conjecture.

By the time *Joseph Andrews* appeared in 1742, Defoe had written
numerous long works of prose fiction, including *Robinson Crusoe*
(1719), *Captain Singleton* (1720), *Moll Flanders* (1722), and *Roxana*
(1724); Richardson had produced *Pamela* (1740). And as one may
see in W. H. McBurney's checklist, hundreds of works of English
prose fiction had by then been published.[6] Given all this activity,
it is surprising that except for specialists in the eighteenth-century
novel, even sophisticated readers generally pay little or no attention
to the debt Defoe, Richardson and Fielding might owe to the
dozens of authors of prose fiction who came before them. Part
of the reason is that these three were so successful that they
effectively displaced their predecessors over time.

As the work of John Richetti and J. Paul Hunter tells us, it is
not easy to define the various predecessor forms. Dismissing the
'root meaning of fiction – a *false* story' – as an inadequate basis
of definition, Richetti describes the chief categories of this early
prose. These include narratives about rogues and whores; travel-
lers, pirates and pilgrims; scandal; and pious tensions between
vice and virtue. But he is careful to point out that the clarity of
his distinctions is rarely illustrated by any given work, which is
likely to draw on the subject matter of more than one category
and perhaps to be otherwise *sui generis*. At one point he calls
these works of prose fiction 'fantasy machines, which must have
appeared to the educated literate elite of the eighteenth century
precisely what comic books and television seem to the contemporary guardians of cultural standards'.[7] Popular taste and expectation no doubt helped to determine the content of these works.

Similarly sceptical that a compact formal definition (an 'essen-
tialist' definition) of the novel and its predecessor forms is possible, Hunter argues that:

the emerging novel must be placed in a ['broad'] context, [and
he 'insists'] that popular thought and materials of everyday
print – journalism, didactic materials with all kinds of religious

and ideological directions, and private papers and histories –
need to be seen as contributors to the social and intellectual
world in which the novel emerged.

Hunter goes on to argue 'that readers, publishers, and other bit
players in traditional literary history played a powerful role in
creating a new textual species responsive to human concerns about
the structure of everyday life as well as about the feelings that
flow from – and inspire – ordinary actions'.[8]
Hunter's view that the shape of the novel derives from an
interest in the human concern about the structure of everyday
life and about the feelings that flow from and inspire ordinary
actions may seem too general a description to be really useful.
But in fact his identification of this emerging, broadly held desire
among readers and writers alike has real critical value. Obviously the works thus produced would vary enormously. As I
have mentioned, they included amatory prose fiction, examples
of which owed much to romance: the exciting adventures of separated lovers (usually stereotypical characters) in exotic settings
like a magical or idealized world. But some of these amatory
pieces might, like the novel, suggest the unique interiority of
one or more of its principals; as is the case, for example, with
Eliza Haywood's character Placentia in *Philodore and Placentia Or
L'Amour trop Delicat* (1727). In addition to the amatory pieces
that sometimes moved away from romance and towards the novel,
there was other prose fiction that combined the use of established
literary kinds – like narratives of travel, diaries of self-examination,
and the last-hour statements of condemned criminals – with treatments of character and setting that suggested real life.

  Paradoxically, in order to stress its concerns with everyday life
and the feelings associated with ordinary actions, this fictional
literature typically claimed to report actual occurrences, using
suggestive words in its titles to reinforce the claim, such as 'history',
'memoirs', 'life', 'voyage' ('trip', 'travels', 'discovery'), 'adventures',
'tale', 'letters' and 'account' ('journal', 'relation'). 'All [of these
terms], with the exception of *tale*, were borrowed from purely
factual types of publications and used as authenticating devices
to avoid the stigma of a "meer Fiction or Lye". All were applied
indiscriminately by authors and booksellers to widely varying
fictional work.'[9] Sometimes the word 'novel' occurred on the title-page, side by side with one of the terms just quoted.

A handful of items taken from W. H. McBurney's list of titles will illustrate this usage and imply something about the subject matter of this early prose fiction, on which I shall comment briefly in a moment: *The Amours of Edward the IV. An Historical Novel* (1700), Anon.; *The Adventures of Lindamira, A Lady of Quality* (1702), by Thomas Brown; *The Perfidious P – Being Letters from a Nobleman to Two Ladies under the Borrow'd Names of Corydon, Clarinda, & Lucina* (1702), Anon.; *The Secret History of Queen Zara, and the Zarazians* (1705), by Mary Delariviere Manley; *The Scotch Rogue: or the Life and Actions of Donald Macdonald A High-Land Scot* (1706), Anon.; *The Golden Spy: or, A Political Journal of the British Nights Entertainments of War and Peace, and Love and Politicks* (1709), by Charles Gildon; *The Tell-tale; or the Invisible Witness: Being the Secret Observations of Philologus, Upon the Private Actions of Human Life* (1711), Anon.; *The Voyages, Dangerous Adventures, and imminent Escapes of Captain Richard Falconer* (1720), by William Rufus Chetwood; *The British Recluse: or the Secret History of Cleomira, Suppos'd Dead. A Novel* (1722), by Eliza Haywood; *The Reform'd Coquet. A Novel* (1724), by Mary Davies; *Friendship in Death: In Twenty Letters from the Dead to the Living* (1728), by Elizabeth Singer Rowe; *The Ungrateful Fair, a Tragi-comic Novel by Capt. Stephens* (1731), by John Stevens; *The History of Clorama, the Beautiful Arcadian or, Virtue Triumphant* (1737), Anon.

At least some of the authors of early amatory fiction, which replaced the long complicted heroic romances of seventeenth-century France, theorized – maybe they only claimed – that they had improved the older form through brevity and clarity of narrative and through characters who were realistically and consistently drawn. And it should follow that the realism achieved by such a method might leave readers to draw their own moral and ethical conclusions about the actions thus represented. But in fact the general tendency of this fiction was to involve readers in the passionate engagements of its heroines. 'By and large, the popular amatory novella quickly disregards its claims to domestic moral realism and constructs a world of sexual fantasy and thrilling moral melodrama, a world where persecuted female innocence is exploited by male corruption, sexual and financial.'[10]

Another kind of early prose fiction, which like the amatory novella often claimed or implied its basis was biographical when it was obviously fictional, are the lives and exploits of criminals, rogues, prostitutes, pirates, and other marginal figures. Before such fictional narratives became popular, actual reports of crimes, criminal trials, executions, and so on enjoyed an avid readership. Stories about criminals and other outsiders, both journalistic reports and fictional narratives, fascinated their readers, probably because of the individualities of these self-determining adventurers. They behaved with a liberty that disregarded social norms and risked society's ultimate sanction: execution. In their fictional representation they seemed 'splendidly wicked' and might therefore be dangerously attractive to young readers, Dr Johnson was to warn in *Rambler*, No. 4. But the market welcomed them.[11]

Writers of prose fiction who in some sense modelled their criminal characters on the desperate and daring spirits actually living on the fringes of society could claim their historical authenticity. Paradoxically, such authenticity strengthened the author's fictional control of characterization and narrative action so that art was in a degree free to invent or reinvent life. Obviously there are limits to such fictional management of 'reality': primarily the attractiveness of the author's invention in some conjunction with the reader's willingness to accept it. An author's calling on life for the ground of fiction and then using fiction to reshape life (like the author's unselfconscious faith in his or her own artistic will, modified somehow by a sense for the reader's expectations) requires a talent few possess. The work of just about all the writers of these early prose narratives turned out to be ephemeral. But a few eighteenth-century authors, notably Defoe, Richardson and Fielding, succeeded in interpreting 'experience' to produce an order of truth beyond the capacity of the mere observer and reporter of 'things as they are', real or invented.[12]

Books about travels were another kind of seventeenth- and early eighteenth-century literature that often mixed fact and fiction. Works like Addison's *Remarks on Several Parts of Italy* (1705) and Defoe's *A Tour Thro' the Whole Island of Great Britain* (1724–7) were for the most part based on the author's observation and interpretative reporting. Such books explored a spatially controlled range of the traveller's experience as traveller. He reported what he saw and offered opinions about what he had observed, but he was not typically inward looking, and neither did he speculate about the interior lives of people he met on his travels. But when authors combined travel with the lives of socially marginal characters, like pirates or rogues, as Defoe did in *Captain Singleton* (1720) and *Colonel Jack* (1722), the chief focus of attention would shift from places to individual criminal character and criminal adventure, more personally engaging subjects for most readers. And the characters and adventures the author had invented would be authenticated by the claim that they were taken from real life, however obvious it was that they were fictional. Indeed the author might claim, brazenly or sincerely, that his book of immoral characters and adventures had a moral purpose, as Defoe does in his preface to *Colonel Jack*: 'Every wicked reader will here [like Colonel Jack] be encouraged to a change, and it will appear that the best and only good end of a wicked and misspent life is repentance.' Questions about Defoe's moral reassurance come readily to mind. If only some of Defoe's readers are wicked, what good will his book do the others? And more to the point, why would the others be interested in Defoe's wicked narrative? Or are all his readers wicked?

These are twentieth-century queries, historically off the mark. Defoe, like his fellow authors of prose fiction, wrote with an eye to the market. Having concluded by trial and error that his readers would be attracted by the unremittingly acquisitive individualism of a criminal character, he would not have supposed that they had put aside their expectation that literature should serve a moral purpose, which he was forced by his treatment of his subject to locate in a deferred repentance. In this, he did not so much patronize a shallow readership as satisfy its need to find literature instructive. The reader's taking pleasure in individual criminal activity – being so fascinated by it as to imply an affinity for it – did not preclude the same reader's moral expectation.[13] To be sure, writers like Manley and other authors of persecuted female innocence were among those who shifted from 'moralizing discourse toward a proto-sentimentalism that is in practice as morally confused as it is emotionally intense and ideologically coherent'.[14] Nevertheless, authors of the age generally felt obliged to exonerate the means by which their literary methods achieved a moral purpose: less and less by precept, it seems, and more and more by example that left the reader to infer his or her own conclusions. Some of these exonerations were no doubt offered *pro forma*, not to say cynically, but they continued to be a requirement felt by almost all concerned.

I have stressed that early prose fiction was dominated by the study and revelation of individual characters. They were unique, and yet not so far astray from common humanity that the reader could not recognize and love or hate them. A way of suggesting the nature of this interest is to say it was satisfied through the literary exploration of numerous individuals whose selves taken together helped to clarify a widely experienced Individualism: the latent seventeenth-century status of Everyone, alone in the midst of others, left to cope with a world not often friendly or understandable. The individual struggling for wealth, power, social recognition, the fulfilment of sexual longing or a marriage part-ner – within or outside the limits of accepted behaviour – were good subjects. So were military adventurers, rogues, criminals, male (and sometimes female) sexual predators, and others at or beyond the limits of acceptability; such characters were fascinat-ing because they suggested something about the reader's own interior complexity, while at the same time they might entice and warn as well.

Telling the story of such a character, in the third person, as if he or she were a real human being, with a real history, was one way to engage the reader's interest, inviting that reader to share in the written reconstruction of a real past, even though it might be patently fictional. Defoe and Fielding used this general method, as had countless writers of prose fiction before them. Another method was to locate the reader in the very interior of principal characters by means of their personal letters to parents or close friends, which revealed their thoughts and feelings with a crucial immediacy. Though far and away the most effective author of epistolary prose fiction, Richardson was hardly the first.[15] These two methods of story-telling are among only the most obvious techniques with which early authors of prose fiction experimented. They also experimented with setting, especially in relation to character; theme; point of view; levels of language; representa-tions of time's passage; and competing systems of value (for example, in familial and other human relations, in religion, in politics, and in general social activity).

Along with Defoe and Richardson and Fielding, Tobias Smollett (1721–71), Laurence Sterne (1713–68), Jane Austen (1775–1817), and the other important novelists of the century used literary techniques employed by authors of prose fiction written prior to 1740. Like their predecessors, they individualized their charac-ters, located them in the workaday world, and gave them recog-nizable aspirations and problems. In addition, the love interest of many of the early works was taken up by the later novelists, though it was typically modified. And characters living at the margins of society or beyond the limits of accepted morality continued to appear in the later novels. Yet one looks in vain for signs that the novel evolved by degrees out of the earlier material: 'English fiction developed irregularly before 1740 and . . . notable works appeared sporadically, with little evidence of what is usually meant by literary influence.'[16]

In Richetti's view, no evolution of the novel can be demonstrated; the force and originality of the major novelists seem rather to have burst upon the world. But he goes on to explain that prose fiction before 1740 anticipates the work of Defoe and Richardson by providing:

> an over-simplification of the structure of society and the moral universe which allowed the reader to place himself in a world of intelligible values where right and wrong were clearly and unmistakably labelled. To read these popular narratives was, at least for the moment of belief and participation that even the most inept narrator can induce, to submit to an ideology, a neatly comprehensible as well as comprehensive pattern of reality.[17]

Robert Day sees Richardson's work as 'the culmination of a process of development rather than as a literary eruption', and yet 'so striking a phenomenon as to obliterate the memory of what had gone before'.[18] Nevertheless he denies that elements of the epistolary novel assembled themselves for Richardson's brilliant use: 'To look for development or evolution in this era of English fiction shows an ill-considered rage for order.'[19] It seems fair to conclude that the great eighteenth-century novelists enriched and complicated a fictional pattern of 'realism' generated by earlier fiction writers, who had themselves modified their work to meet the changing expectations of their readers. But just how the later novelists made use of their predecessors it is not possible to say. Ian Watt argues that the forces controlling the development of the novel were a growing reading public and a rising middle class with increasingly secular and self-regarding interests. Taking exception to Watt, Michael McKeon urges the view that the novel has an identifying characteristic – unresolved dynamism – owing to the radical instability both of literary genres and social categories brought about by the upheavals of secularization and reform that changed early modern Europe. Students of the novel should read both of these critics. It may be that the alternatives they offer are not mutually exclusive theories, but radically different orders of inquiry and that inescapable function of the shape of inquiry: the nature of conclusions.[20]

*   *   *

Richardson's *Pamela* enjoyed an incredible success, having been greeted with 'an epidemical phrenzy' of approval as soon as it was published on 6 November 1740.[21] Within five months, three editions had been printed. As I have said, it was by no means the first extended prose narrative told in letters; and neither was its conclusion, the marriage of a low-born woman to a gentleman, unheard of in eighteenth-century England. Though the reason for such alliances was typically financial – to restore an aristocratic family's fortune by joining the impoverished male heir to a wealthy commoner – there were also many unequal love matches, more often of high-born men to their social inferiors than of high-born women.[22] Even the story of the household servant, at first beleaguered by her master and later married to him, is not original.[23] Though Richardson's success with *Pamela* may owe something to an abiding interest in the various forms of this well known story, it doubtless owes more to his way of handling it, especially his unequivocal approval of his heroine, implicit in his having her speak for herself, in combination with her triumph, marriage to her would-be seducer, which in one sense at least fulfils the book's title, *Virtue Rewarded*. Richardson guides his darling Pamela's pen and approves of everything she tells us about herself: her good looks, her amiable nature, her single-minded intelligence, her courage in adversity, her loyalty to her parents, her ambivalent feelings for Mr B., and above all the remorseless accounts of her sexual resistance, the success of which she measures by her intact virginity (her virtue). Richardson believes he knows her inside out, and he allows us to share this intimate knowledge, through her letters, the mirrors of her heart and mind, completely confident that we will like her as much as he does.

Those who with Richardson saw her as an attractive fellow human, fighting for virtue and respectability against heavy odds, were pleased that her implacable resistance moved Mr B. to propose marriage. Others found her less winning, Fielding prominent among them. His first published criticism of *Pamela* was *Shamela*, a heavily ironic correction of Richardson's novel.[24] One of his motives was probably money. Although as I have said, he was admitted to the bar in 1740, he was still between professions in the matter of income, writing short pieces for pay whenever he could. He also had an artistic reason for producing *Shamela*. Having seen that Pamela was actually Shamela, a scheming sexual manipulator, Fielding the satirist was moved to tell the world the truth.

I doubt that Fielding, who incidentally did not then know Richardson had written the book, believed *Pamela's* author was consciously hypocritical in his invention of 'virtuous' Pamela, nor that Pamela 'herself', as she was invented, was conscious of an ultimate goal: marriage to Mr B. And in fact *Shamela* does not rebuke simple hypocrisy; it rather unmasks a delusional self-righteousness centred on an equation made doubtful by Pamela's persistent repetition of it. 'Virginity is Honour!' Richardson's heroine declares over and over. It is not hard to imagine that any woman's integrity would call for fierce resistance to rude addresses like Mr B.'s. It was not Pamela's resistance but her repeated protestations of virtue that Fielding objected to. Consider his mockery in having Shamela say to Mrs Jewkes, 'I value my vartue more than I do anything my master can give me; and so we talked a full hour and a half, about my vartue.' Besides the preposterous duration of the talk, Fielding reduces Shamela's claims of virtue by having her pronounce it 'vartue', the seldom used (and ugly?) eighteenth-century variation spelled 'vertue', and probably pronounced 'vartue', or something like it, as a glance at the *Oxford English Dictionary* makes clear. If Shamela's choice of word is off the mark, can the thing it refers to be genuine?

Pamela's remorseless dwelling on the preservation of her honour or virtue can be both tiresome and laughable; it is also suspect. And yet her compulsive rhetoric is genuine enough at one level. The fanatical self-congratulation suggests that she feels the strain of the unequal contest with Mr B., but it may also imply her fundamental unwillingness to quit the field. Can she be enjoying herself? Often dangerously close to defeat, she one way and another persists in the game, and then triumphs in marriage. There is indeed something engaging about the combination of her physical vulnerability and her persistent, rock-bottom courage. But her dangerous engagement with Mr B. is more akin to war than it is to love. It has little if anything to do with virtue, and it flirts radically with sin. She arouses Mr B.; rebuffs him by turning down his terms, not his person; and stays on for the next encounter. Richardson's Pamela is a sexual warrior, not a saint. Her battles against Mr B. in the marriage market may make good sense; they have little to do with virtue. But neither Richardson nor his admirers saw things quite that way.

It was not only its general popularity that made *Pamela* a book in need of satiric correction, but the moral authority of some of its champions. Formal guardians of virtue, including clergymen, were drawn to Pamela. Among them was the Reverend Josiah Relph of Cumberland, who wrote verses of extravagant praise to Richardson, including these lines: 'Thy pages like thy wondrous theme/Artless and undesigning seem,/Yet warmth to each beholder lend,/And fix him their and Virtue's friend.'[25] And Dr Benjamin Slocock, shortly after *Pamela's* appearance, 'recommended the book from the pulpit of St. Saviour's, Southwark'.[26] Other, non-clerical, readers, widely influential, also praised the book, in print or by word of mouth, including Alexander Pope, William Warburton, Ralph Allen, Aaron Hill and George Cheyney (1671–1743), mathematician and physician. These and others helped to establish the cult of *Pamela*. It is perhaps no surprise that the ordinary residents of Slough might gather at the smithy to hear their own Pamela's story read aloud, but quite another thing that clergymen and men of letters should be drawn to her.[27]

Fielding handles the issue of misguided clerical approval of *Pamela* by introducing three distinctive clergyman into *Shamela*. The first two are his own inventions, and the third is *Pamela's* dutiful Mr Williams turned upside down: a vice-ridden hedonist who has been and continues to be Shamela's lover, even after her marriage to Mr B. The other two are Parson Tickletext, who is taken in by Pamela's 'vartue', and Parson Oliver, who like Fielding sees that the true lesson of *Pamela* to servant-maids is 'that if the master is not a fool, they will be debauched by him; and if he is a fool, they will marry him'. Fielding controls his use of these two clergymen by having them exchange letters, which frame *Shamela*. Accordingly, wise Oliver takes exception to Tickletext's approval of Pamela; he describes her unscrupulous ways and sends his fellow clergyman copies of her 'actual' letters, which are the substance of *Shamela*. After reading the genuine letters, Tickletext closes *Shamela* with a letter of gratitude to Oliver for the truth about Pamela and the news that 'Mr Booby [Richardson's Mr B. truly named] hath caught his wife in bed with Williams; hath turned her off, and is prosecuting him in the spiritual court.' At one level, this framing correspondence represents Fielding's true vision of *Pamela* and the false vision of a reader ultimately converted by the demonstation of Pamela's duplicity.

Fielding's Parson Williams is a much more complicated character than these two. He is the willing Shamela's seducer, and he is interesting enough, physically and intellectually, to attract her 'always'. Having made it clear that he is a well endowed male animal who satisfies her, she reinforces her appraisal by later comparing Williams and her husband as lovers: 'To confess the truth, I might have been well enough satisfied too, if I had never been acquainted with Parson Williams' (*Shamela*, p. 347). While making Williams a seducer, the obverse of the Good Shepherd, Fielding extends the clergyman's concerns beyond the flesh, to matters of the spirit; Williams provides Shamela with theological arguments intended to allay any guilt she might feel about fornication. In excusing Shamela's illicit sexuality, Williams obviously excuses his own. She is of course in no need of such reassurances; it is ironic that she nevertheless approves of his solicitude on her behalf.

The reassurances offered by Williams to Shamela turn on a theological position Fielding distrusted. His satirical strategy is to assign to Williams a point of view so palpably self-serving as to inspire in us amused distrust. To some extent distorting the ideas of John Wesley (1703–91), the founder of Methodism, and his fellow evangelist George Whitefield (1714–70), Williams separates things of the flesh from those of the spirit, and in emphasizing that salvation is the reward of faith and repentance, and not of good deeds, reduces the importance of human choices and actions. Accordingly, sinful behaviour is no obstacle to salvation, provided one repents, which for Williams and Shamela is only a formality. Fielding probably distrusted Methodism because of its stress on religious 'inner feeling', on the need for conversion, and on grace as prerequisites to salvation. Though Wesley in fact stressed (and his life exemplified) the religious value of works, Fielding was sceptical of the effects of Methodism, with its spiritual intensity, preferring his own latitudinarian ease about religious forms. Deeds are more important to society than repentance; good works rather than grace nourish the community, he believed.

Despite his unsavoury characterization of Williams and his satirical treatment of Methodism, Fielding is hardly anti-clerical in *Shamela*. Parson Oliver sees through Pamela–Shamela as unerringly as Fielding does after all, and if Parson Tickletext needs Oliver's help to recognize the truth about her, he clearly acknowledges the error of his first appraisal. In drawing Williams as evil and in giving him a much larger role than Richardson does, Fielding is rather stressing the unfortunate fact that those in the best position to further the moral and ethical well-being of the community are too often themselves blind or wilfully destructive. For his own artistic reasons, Fielding leaves no room for Williams's redemption in *Shamela*. Though theoretically he may be saved, evil Williams is a fixed character. At one level he discerns the truth about Pamela as acutely as Fielding does; but Parson Williams is no moralist. He takes Shamela as he finds her, in more ways than one.

Other influential persons who, wilfully or otherwise, lead their followers astray are men of letters and courtiers and those politicians whose first concern is to maintain their power. Fielding hits these corrupters in various ways. Before I turn from the concern with religious error to his other targets, a word is in order about some of the directions of Fielding's satiric art in *Shamela*. Is it aimed at the readers Fielding believes are misled by the author of *Pamela*? Is it aimed at the author himself, who blindly leads his flock? Or at misguided leaders like Wesley whose good intentions, in Fielding's view, pave the way to error and disorder? Or perhaps at those rare shepherds who like Fielding's Williams exploit individual members of the flock ruthlessly?

Fielding believes good morals are a function of good taste.[28] In this formulation taste is not merely one's preference for a particular painting or book or person or course of action; it is rather the human sense or faculty by which the essential quality of a thing is discerned. Building on this distinction, one might suppose that Richardson wrote *Pamela* believing himself to have said a thing; then Fielding, whose discernment of essentials (whose taste) was more acute than Richardson's, wrote *Shamela*, a book that *Pamela* both implies and conceals, in order to show that

Richardson had written something else. Putting the matter in late twentieth-century critical parlance, one might say Fielding believes that *Shamela* is the crucial sub-text of *Pamela*, a dialogic voice too few can hear.

The extended revelation that Pamela is actually Shamela implies that Fielding the moralist's chief aim (at least the effect he achieves) is to correct the false discernment of others. (As I have already implied, it is also the effect achieved by the novel's frame.) Fielding wants Richardson's readers to see what they may have sensed only dimly or missed altogether. If Richardson's vision is incidentally improved also, so much the better, but I doubt that Fielding's moral expectations ran that high. It is probably closer to the truth to say that as a reader of *Pamela*, he found himself unable to remain passive. His counteraction to the book was his own satiric vision of it, *Shamela*. His need to write it probably included his need to share it and so convince others to see things as he did, at least in some degree. But his 'intentions' must have been complex, including not only the 'correction' of *Pamela*, the need to share his revision of it, and the moral impulse to fire shots at malfeasant persons in high office, but also to make money, to enjoy the operation of his own comic mastery, and to stay in the limelight. Morally considered, however, the targets of his satire are representatives of literary, religious and social disorder; and his chief aim is to correct the visionary ineptitude of those who cannot see that Pamela is Shamela.

Fielding hits Colley Cibber on *Shamela's* title-page by using words and a format that parody the title-page of *An Apology for the Life of Mr Colley Cibber, Comedian, and Late Patentee of the Theatre-Royal*, the autobiography which had appeared in April 1740, about a year before *Shamela*, and by naming Mr Conny Keyber as *Pamela's* author. ('Keyber' was a widely known variation of 'Cibber'.) He also has Keyber write and put his name to *Shamela's* dedication, addressed 'To Miss *Fanny*, &c.' This game of words and names had wide-ranging implications in Fielding's day. They are best discussed after we recall a little about Fielding's target here, Colley Cibber.

Cibber had been appointed poet laureate in 1730, probably as payment for political favours to the Walpole ministry. An effective playwright and theatre manager, Cibber was hardly a good poet. His *Apology* is full of such information and practical wisdom as only an insider of the London theatre could have gathered over a professional lifetime. But it is also flamboyant and self-aggrandizing, quite without the sensitivity and learning one might expect of England's laureate. In part at least, Fielding satirizes Cibber because he is an emblem of the corruption of letters; he does not have the requisite talent for the laureateship, so that his incumbency implicitly mocks the value of poetry. It also implies that political power buys and sells the arts.

In what ways are Fielding's parodic title-page and dedication satiric hits? At the most obvious level, the parallel titles – *An Apology for the Life of Mr Colley Cibber* and *An Apology for the Life of Mrs Shamela Andrews* – with the words of both titles distributed on the page in just the same way, imply mischievously that the books themselves are parallel lives, both written by the same hand. Beyond that, questions beg to be formulated. Why did Keyber write *Shamela*? (Why did Fielding decide to assign *Shamela's* authorship to Cibber?) Does Keyber feel an affinity for Shamela and her way of life? (Does Fielding think Cibber and Shamela – or Cibber and Richardson – have much in common?) If the meanings of 'shame' and 'sham' inhere not only in Shamela's name but in her nature, should we assign them to Cibber (and Richardson) as well, and if so, in what degree? These and other such questions need not produce answers to have their effect. Perhaps they need not even be formulated. The satire gives them a potential existence, which without having to rise very high in the reader's consciousness, constitutes a qualitative indictment of Shamela/Cibber.

Some topical information is necessary for understanding Keyber's dedication of *Shamela* to Miss Fanny, &c. 'Lord Fanny' was a derisive name assigned by Alexander Pope to John Hervey, Baron of Ickworth, a poetaster and courtier who worked for Walpole and was a confidential adviser to Queen Caroline; having been friends, Hervey and Pope quarrelled in print.[29] 'Fanny', Pope's nasty sobriquet, is an accurate enough translation of 'Fannius', the name of a second-rate classical author of whom Horace says (*Satires*, I, iv) that he 'delivered his books unasked'. Though some of Fielding's contemporaries must have caught the slighting classical allusion, all would have understood 'Fanny' as suggesting effeminacy and homosexuality, which in Fielding's view were distortions of natural behaviour.[30] In addition, many would have recognized that the fulsome dedication itself was a paragraph by paragraph parody of another fulsome dedication, that to Lord Hervey by Conyers Middleton, the author of *History of the Life of*

Marcus Tullius Cicero (February 1741). And they might well have recognized that Keyber's first name, Conny, which itself has derrogatory connotations, was remarkably like Middleton's (Conyers).[31]

What Fielding's parodies suggest, then, is that the author of *An Apology for the Life of Mr Colley Cibber* is also the author of *An Apology for the life of Mrs Shamela Andrews* (Conny Keyber). They further suggest that the author of *Shamela*, who dedicates his book to Miss Fanny (Hervey), has much in common with the author of *The Life of Cicero*, who also dedicates his book to Hervey; in fact the authors have so much in common that their names, Conyers/Conny, suggest each other. In short, Fielding's parodic logic encourages us to imagine that a certain foolish and effeminate Conny has written three lives, one of himself (Cibber's own), another of Shamela, and the third of Cicero, and all three within the space of a year, April 1740 to April 1741. Lest we forget, a fourth book, whose title rhymes with 'Shamela', was also published during this period. About its author, shall we suppose that he too is a Conny?

Obviously Fielding's serious moral purpose in writing *Shamela* did not get in the way of his having fun as he went along. Indeed his amused and amusing control of parody is unremitting throughout *Shamela*, the front matter containing only the opening shots. For example, he sustains Richardson's fiction that he is the editor of Pamela's letters by having Parson Oliver claim he has got hold of the genuine correspondence, which he tells us Richardson had doctored. He also follows *Pamela's* author, who prefixed his second edition with many pages of complimentary letters, by using the same device, including a laudatory letter from *Shamela's* editor to himself. Most important, Fielding comically reworks Richardson's most important scenes, as a simple comparison of the two books will show. So, for example, Pamela's pretended drowning, Mr B.'s invitation to Williams to sit next to Pamela in their carriage, and numerous of Pamela's and her master's encounters in the bedroom are all mischievously distorted to show us a cunning, sex-loving Shamela. Fielding's parodic inspirations throughout *Shamela* give comic pleasure. At the same time they invite us to conclude that Pamela is energetically prurient, not virtuous, and that the representatives of social disorder – Richardson (Pamela), Wesley, Whitefield, Cibber, Hervey, Walpole, and Middleton among them – are legion.

* * *

Shamela did not exhaust Fielding's interest in *Pamela*. In *The History of the Adventures of Joseph Andrews, and of his Friend Mr Abraham Adams* (February 1742), he returns to the subject, but he comes at it this second time in quite another way. As Battestin points out, in *Shamela* Fielding amusingly exposes Pamela, but in *Joseph Andrews*, he offers an alternative form and purpose of the novel.[32] In addition, he offers an alternative view of love and marriage. *Shamela* is devastatingly parodic, using burlesque actions and language to make its point. Though *Joseph Andrews* is incidentally parodic, it is generally comic, and according to Fielding, nature is the model for its actions, though he has 'sometimes admitted' burlesque in his diction. He goes on to explain that:

> no two Species of writing can differ more widely than the Comic and the Burlesque: for as the latter is ever the Exhibition of what is monstrous and unnatural, and where our Delight, if we examine it arises from the surprising Absurdity, as in appropriating the highest to the lowest, or *è converso*; so in the former we should ever confine ourselves strictly to Nature from the just Imitation of which, will flow all the Pleasure we can this way convey to a sensible Reader. (*Joseph Andrews*, Preface, 4)

With this observation Fielding prepares the way for an important claim; *Joseph Andrews* is comic (it is often uproariously funny), but it is nevertheless a serious representation of life.

As he continues his critical observations on comic art in the Preface, placing burlesque or caricature outside its limits and telling us that the ridiculous is its true subject, he implies that he will write fiction controlled by what we in the twentieth century might think of as the psychological appraisal of human actions. Fielding thought of himself as observing and writing about 'manners'. He identifies his critical interest in human behaviour when he claims that the ridiculous – the true comic subject matter – occurs only in instances of affectation, expressed either as vanity or hypocrisy (*JA*, Preface, 7–8).[33] Obviously to write about affectation, one must recognize and anatomize it.

It is important that Fielding's discussion of the ridiculous suggests that he will be working with the 'outside' of his characters

– the expression of their affectations – in order to imply what is 'inside': the motivating forces of vanity or hypocrisy. Both motivations involve one's wearing a mask, assuming a spurious identity. Vanity, he tells us, is the affectation of *'false* Characters in order to purchase Applause; [and] Hypocrisy sets us on an Endeavor to avoid censure by concealing our Vices under an Appearance of their opposite Virtues' (*JA*, Preface, 8). His interest in interiority runs deep, but the method of his art is generally to imply how the mind is working by the close regard of the behaviour it compels. He sometimes characterizes motives but, unlike Richardson, whose characters draw us into their mental operations as they occur, Fielding keeps his readers outside, showing us their ridiculous behaviour and leaving it to us to infer what lies beneath. To charge him with not knowing the human heart as well, say, as Richardson is to misunderstand the nature of his comic art.

Good examples of his management of behaviour as a method of implying interiority occur early in the novel. Lady Booby, recently widowed, lying naked in bed, is attended by Joseph, whom she tries to seduce by exposing 'one of the whitest Necks that ever was seen' and by offering warm hints that she would welcome his lovemaking (*JA*, I, v, 30). Joseph's effective rejection of her advances is followed by her wrath, coupled with incredulity, and then by tears of frustration, ostensibly caused by his innocent mention of her deceased husband. At this point she orders him angrily out of her sight forever. Joseph retreats 'in a most disconsolate Condition' (*JA*, I, v, 30) and writes a letter to his sister Pamela, telling her about his encounter with Lady Booby. Having sealed and addressed his letter, Joseph goes downstairs, where Mrs Slipslop, the chambermaid, whom we are told is past childbearing and ready to indulge her appetite for love, tells Joseph of her passion for him. Unwilling to wait for him to make the first move, she prepares like a 'hungry Tygress ... or voracious Pike ... to lay her violent amorous Hands on the poor Joseph, when luckily her Mistress's Bell rung, and delivered the intended Martyr from her Clutches' (*JA*, I, vi, 33–4).

In both these scenes we have a very good idea of what the characters feel from their behaviour. Lady Booby affects politeness, tenderness and concern for Joseph, but it hardly disguises her compulsive desire for him, which his resistance transforms to fury. Mrs Slipslop, painfully ugly and vain, utterly misapprehends her power over Joseph, and after an amatory prelude full of misused and new-coined words, attacks him. And Joseph, at first confused by these unlooked for advances, pretty quickly understands them. But to be sure we can have no doubts about the feelings of the women, Fielding has them meet quite plausibly while they are still hot with frustration, when the Lady rings for her maid. Then their anger and jealousy prompt an irrational exchange in which Mrs Slipslop bears false witness against Joseph, Lady Booby several times instructs her maid to dismiss him only to countermand her own order, and Slipslop divines her mistress's infatuation. What need is there for Fielding to carry us into the minds of his characters when their words and actions show us what they are? Fielding himself answers the question. Having explained briefly that Lady Booby was miserable, despising herself for her passionate suit and Joseph for rejecting her, he tells us that she spoke 'many Soliloqies, which, if we had no better Matter for our Reader, we would give him' (*JA*, I, vi, 34).[34] Fielding elsewhere observes similarly pointed omissions; for example, he tells us about a confrontation involving Joseph, Mr Adams, Mr Barnabas, and the Surgeon that 'A Dispute arose on this Occasion concerning Evidence, not very necessary to be related here' (*JA*, I, xv, 67). Joseph's soliloquy while he is ill is given verbatim (*JA*, I, xiii, 58–9), but in the telling Joseph becomes a parody of Richardson's Pamela, ironically inflating his view of himself as a virgin. Unless Fielding has a special purpose like this one, he keeps us outside the minds of his characters and conspicuously censors their speech.

Concerning this strategy, Fielding sounds confident that his reader will have no trouble inferring the interior condition of his characters from his handling of their speech and actions; at the same time, he amuses himself and us by relishing the obvious. For example, he says of Slipslop's evaluation of Lady Booby's mercurial reversals of decision concerning Joseph's place in her household, 'This Wavering in her Mistress's Temper probably put something in the Waiting-Gentlewoman's Head, not necessary to mention to the sagacious Reader' (*JA*, I, vii, 36). And soon after, Fielding invites his reader to infer, as soon as the author has provided 'hints' enough, that Joseph makes haste to leave London late at night to get to his beloved Fanny as soon as possible (*JA*, I, x, 47–8). Though in *Joseph Andrews* and elsewhere Fielding's faith in his reader's powers of inference is genuine, his adoption of the role of observer and narrator of exterior events leaves him in control of the evidence on which inferences may be drawn. Of course a narrator who presents a character's stream of thought is also in control of such evidence. But Fielding's narrator is a hovering consciousness, behaving as he will, observing, reporting, omitting, repairing an omission, predicting, moralizing, apostrophizing, and above all interrupting the nominal line of the narrative.

Not all of Fielding's informed readers find his narrative method in *Joseph Andrews* entirely congenial. Michael Irwin, for example, believes his prose has 'an alienating effect [on the reader]', the result of his 'schematic approach which derives from Fielding's moral intention'.[35] By pointing out that Book I, indeed the whole novel, retells the story of the Good Samaritan (the epitome of Fielding's morality), showing us, in a series of episodes unconnected by narrative continuity, men and women who do or do not measure up to its high standard, Irwin prepares the way for claiming that Fielding's characters are two-dimensional and unrealistic, endowed only with those qualities Fielding needs to illustrate his morality. Fielding himself admits as much in the introduction to Book III, Irwin believes: 'I describe not men, but manners; not an individual, but a species.'[36] The argument that leads to this conclusion does not explicity refer to Fielding's avoidance of interiority, but it often suggests that Fielding stays outside his characters (as, for example, the statement that 'Joseph is so stylized and idealized a figure that there is no personal involvement in his plight').[37]

Irwin makes a real point in saying that Fielding's approach is schematic. But the claim that the method produces discordantly artificial results may be wide of the mark insofar as it implies artistic failure or the glaring subordination of art to moral intention. Mr Wilson's story – his past – is not just a narrative interruption that gives Fielding the chance to repeat familiar social criticisms; it is among other things a way of providing Joseph with a temperate and charitable father whose understanding results from the self-examination of an early life misspent. Fielding generally presents his characters from the outside, giving us as much evidence about them as he chooses; at the same time he both guides us to conclusions about them and leaves it to us to imagine their interior natures. He never surrenders control of the narrative, but rather demonstrates his right to interrupt it, change its direction, and introduce into it, often late in the day, powerful elements – persons or hard facts – that affect it radically.

There is an undeniable pleasure in reading about characters from the inside, privy to their deepest feelings, as we are moved along by a seamless narrative that gives the impression of incontovertible completeness. Fielding's narrative art is different, but it is none the less finished. Its effect is comic, with the narrator engaging our minds 'outside' the story, where we may laugh at, play with, and judge both character and action moment by moment. (I shall only mention and pass over the encouragement this method gives the reader to sense and evaluate the looming novelist through the medium of his frisky narrator.) Perhaps one should not suppose that Fielding's precise aim was to distance his readers from the world of the narrative, charging them with the responsibilty for judging it from the outside, but that is the effect of his comedy. Indeed it is the general effect of comedy that its audience is not 'drawn into' the world of the work but stimulated to regard and evaluate it.

I see the reasonableness of saying that Fielding may alienate his reader; at times one may not be in the mood for surrendering to his comic control, the narrative enforcement of which often makes the Storyteller more palpable than the Story. But at other times one may find the Storyteller's ubiquitous consciousness the gateway to the pleasure of laughter and understanding. If not at each reading of *Joseph Andrews*, certainly in the mind's residual content of multiple readings, most readers are likely to experience the submergence of Fielding's narrative disjunctions under the narrative current, probably because of its many integrative elements: chiefly its moral themes and their representations by Parson Adams; the endlessly engagaging story of love and marriage; and the Storyteller's humour, full of vitality, along with his unqualified support of Adams and the lovers and what their lives stand for. And during any single reading, readers may also enjoy Fielding the Storyteller: the creator-historian, the unembarrassed narrative manipulator, and the authoritative ironist who invites us to measure the distance between a character's public side and interior state.[38]

The moral themes of *Joseph Andrews*, to be discussed in a moment, are illustrated by the action, which Fielding tells us in the Preface he has given the form of comic epic in prose: 'Now a comic Romance is a comic Epic-Poem in Prose; differing from Comedy, as the serious Epic from Tragedy: its Action being more extended and comprehensive [than that of comic drama]; containing a much larger Circle of Incidents, and introducing a greater Variety of Characters' (*JA*, Preface, 4).[39] Even modestly educated eighteenth-century readers would have known that epic poetry, along with tragedy, was regarded traditionally as the most elevated and serious of the literary forms, and that its structure is characterized by long narrative, unified by a single large action, and dominated by a hero who is at once representative of his people and yet larger than life. Generally the scope of epic action is greater than that of classical tragedy, first because it takes up a considerable span of time and typically ranges over a wide geography, whose dimensions are indicated by the travels of the hero upon land and sea (and a journey to the underworld), by the swift and unhampered movements of the gods across the vast reaches of the heavens and the earth, and by the poem's sweeping shifts in setting. The action is also enlarged by the cultural – social, ethical and religious – importance of the hero's undertaking; one understands that if he fails to accomplish his purpose, the world he represents will perish. Though the hero may be renowned for his nobility, his perseverance or his sagacity, he is invariably put to the final test in battle; in short, his honour – on which the fate of his culture depends – is ultimately measured in martial terms, though never limited to such measurement.

In the course of its action, epic fulfils certain other formal requirements. According to a standard neoclassical view, it teaches by presenting the behaviour of noble characters in adversity, and it pleases by engendering a sense of wonder, chiefly through its use of the machinery of the gods. Moreover, in formulaic passages, often ritual in manner and tone, the poet proposes his subject; invokes the aid of the heavens; comments on the action; offers as history certain traditions about his country and countrymen; sends vital information to his hero by means of supernatural characters, sometimes in a dream; arms his warrior characters (occasionally with special armour and weapons); permits them to boast of their prowess; and sends them into battle, which he often describes with epic simile. As they triumph and live or fail and die, they are elevated to the realm of permanent things. At one level, at least, epic may be thought of as the sanctified history of one's ancestors.[40]

Every reader of *Joseph Andrews* will recognize at least some correlations between these elements of epic and Fielding's novel, part of the comic pleasure the book affords. It has a hero or heroes; they are in certain important ways representatives of their culture; they cover a significant geography to accomplish a purpose; and they are tested in many encounters, some of them martial, before they reach their physical and ideational destination in triumph. The book also uses overblown epic similes: for example, 'As when a hungry Tygress' and 'As a person who is struck' (*JA*, I, vi, viii, 33, 39). The weapons Joseph and Adams use, fist and cudgel, are given special (comic) attention. And though the chief deity in the world of the work is an intangible 'Providence', the Pedlar is a palpable Godsend, a providential emissary who twice intervenes to save the hero Adams (like an earth-roving god of epic, or a magician of romance?) and later witnesses to the truth of Fanny's parentage, which raises the bar of incest between the lovers before leading to the discovery of Joseph's origins. Though *Joseph Andrews* includes romance elements, as well as elements of the picaresque, it is in significant ways a 'comic epic'.

Though comic – mischievously comic – *Joseph Andrews* is also a serious book in that it proposes and illustrates a morality of temperance (reason's control of the passions) and charity (love), which survives temptation and hostility. Martin Battestin argues persuasively that the theme and structure of *Joseph Andrews* were affected by the opinions of latitudinarian Christians like Isaac Barrow (1630–77), John Tillotson (1630–94), Samuel Clarke (1675–1729) and Benjamin Hoadly (1676–1761), whose work Fielding knew and found congenial in that it stressed, in optimistic terms, the perfectibility of our inner natures and the natural tendency of good people to help each other and to work to improve human society. Battestin suggests that to understand the ways in which Joseph Andrews and Abraham Adams are made to represent the twin virtues of temperance and charity, one does well to recognize Fielding's special debt to Barrow, whose:

> sermons present four points of special significance: (1) the depiction of the good man as hero; (2) the notion that the sum of his goodness is *chastity* (or virtue or temperance, the control of reason over the passions) with respect to himself, and *Charity* with respect to society; (3) the choice of [Old Testament] Joseph

[represented by the novel's Joseph] and his rejection of Potiphar's wife [Lady Booby] to exemplify the former, and of the [Old Testament] pilgrim patriarch Abraham [Parson Adams], the epitome of human faith expressed in works, to represent the latter; and (4) the analogy of the good man's life in a world of vanity and vexation to a pilgrimage through strange lands to his true home.[41]

Given the complicated history of critical views about the kind of book *Joseph Andrews* may be – comic epic, comic romance, or perhaps comic epic or comic romance with the stress on 'comic'? – it will be useful to say a word about the marriage of morality and comedy before discussing one or two of the implications of Battestin's views concerning the contribution of religious ideas to the themes and structure of the novel.[42] Comedy has traditionally, if not universally, generated laughter and moral allegiance at the same time. Aristophanes, Terence and Molière before Fielding, and Shaw after him, are among the comedians who enrich this tradition. Throughout *Joseph Andrews*, we are made to laugh at Parson Adams, sometimes at Joseph. But while we laugh, we earnestly cheer them on because we want the causes they represent to triumph. This reader-loyalty to them and what they stand for is borne out explicitly in numerous episodes. We want Fanny saved from rape, we want the squire who turns his dogs loose on Adams to be doused and brought almost to his death by fever, and we want Beau Didapper's rude sexual advances to Fanny brought to an end by Joseph's sound box on his ear. Fielding sees to it that our amusement is hardly impartial.

His claim that *Joseph Andrews* is a comic epic in prose is well supported by the structure of the book. But so is Battestin's view that the structure no less than the themes of the novel draw on Biblical characters and actions, especially as they are interpreted by latitudinarian divines. There is no necessary contradiction in these claims. Fielding the comedian plays games with both epic and Biblical sources. Though his literary manipulations in *Joseph Andrews* are less obviously daring then they had been in *Pasquin*, for example, they are daring nevertheless. At the same time, he makes use of the themes of temperance and charity to give his novel a moral edge, which his humour confirms, often viscerally.

Indeed Fielding's appetite for appropriating and giving a comic turn to diverse genres does not end with epic and Biblical structure.

Joseph Andrews makes use of romance elements too. Baker seems right to say, 'the mystery of identity, father, and station, the agony of unfulfilled love, all culminating surprisingly at the triumphant end', are characteristic of romance; but he appears single-minded in claiming that the 'mystery and wonder [of romance] have replaced [the] traditional knowledge [of epic] in *Joseph Andrews*'.[43] If in *Joseph Andrews* the 'central story of mysterious origin and courtly love [along with the] . . . discovery of fathers, identity, . . . and the happy ending in marriage' derives from romance, comically treated, its narrative of morally representative heroes who encounter and overcome the enemies of their culture as they make the troubled journey home (the sacred locus of that culture) derives from epic, comically treated.[44] Baker's claims for romance are one-sided.

Parson Adams and Joseph, the two heroes of *Joseph Andrews*, are spiritual allies. Distinct by virtue of age, appearance, education, vocation and the nature of their consciousness, they are nevertheless indivisible in their unselfconsciously constructive social behaviour; it is the workaday expression of their religion, which it would not occur to them to confine to Sundays. Their goodness of charity and temperance is deep and brave, as is their attractive ferocity on behalf of the good. They behave as if they were both members and guardians of a blessed community too often marred by the selfish acts of others. Though they sometimes deviate from their own ideal of behaviour, their errors are technical (the result of their loving too well). For example, Joseph, when he believes he is dying, fixes his attention on the loss of Fanny more than on the life to come; and because the thieves who beat him have brought him to his death bed (and the loss of his beloved), he finds it impossible to forgive them (*JA*, I, xiii, 59–60). He is also irreligious in his haste to marry Fanny without banns, against Adams's advice, which ultimately prevails (*JA*, IV, viii, 307); rejecting the consolations of Providence, he sinks into despair when Fanny is abducted (*JA* III, xi, 264–7). And Parson Adams is shown incapable of following his professed belief concerning faith in adversity when he is informed (mistakenly) that his son has drowned (*JA* IV, viii, 308–9). These frailties do not reduce them in our estimation any more than do Fielding's comic treatments of their characters. We do not mind that Adams finds the truth of human nature in books rather than in his own experience because, when the chips are down, he is a man of action, not a theorizer. We may agree with Lady Booby that Joseph's claim of virtue as a reason for rejecting her is ridiculous, but we are serious in approving his fidelity to Fanny.[45] Fielding's management of charity and temperance in Adams and Joseph is enriched, not reduced, by their forgivable inconsistencies and their other comic actions.

Joseph Andrews is an account of the journey from London to the country: to Adams's parish (sacred) rather than to Lady Booby's estate (profane). Adams and Joseph share the experience of other epic characters who travel physically and spiritually towards home, such as Odysseus and Aeneas. Despite the variations in their journeys, all are radically interrupted by circumstances understood to be evil so that reaching their objective, the place of fulfilment and rest, becomes something of a religious quest, a pilgrimage. The heroes and the sacred locus they aspire to are mutually defining. Joseph and Adams, and Fanny as well, have been in different ways dislocated from their home in the country and drawn towards London. Though only Joseph reaches the city, all three are implicated in the evils associated with the town and with the journey home.

Essentially good people – innocents – they are practically speaking ill-equipped to cope with the fallen world through which they travel. Having predetermined a stark moral distance between them and their less scrupulous fellows, Fielding puts it to very good use. His ingenious pen makes it both the cause of much of the novel's comic adventure, especially episodes in which Adams figures, and the basis of the physical and spiritual survival of all three principals. For example, Adams's innocence appears as naivety during the early moments of his meeting with the mean-spirited pig farmer, Parson Trulliber: '*Adams*, whose natural Complacence was beyond any artificial [sic], was obliged to comply [with Trulliber's invitation that he handle the hogs] before he was suffered to explain himself, and laying hold on one of their Tails, the unruly Beast gave such a sudden spring, that he threw poor *Adams* all along in the Mire' (*JA*, II, xiv, 163). Trulliber laughs, and we may do so too. A bit later, however, when the parsons' discussion takes a theological turn and they argue the relative values of faith and works – belief in the scriptures as opposed to charitable deeds – the intensity of Adams's conviction on the side of good actions is amusing, but it also makes us see that he speaks in support of a living principle that governs his whole

life. Indeed his expectation that Trulliber will provide the where-
withal for discharging the debt for food and lodging is only at
one level naive; it is also an expression of Adams's unselfconscious
commitment to the ideal of charity. In Adams the spirit and the
flesh are one (almost always one). This rare conjunction makes
for comic turns, but its value to the life of the community in the
world of the work is palpable.

From the beginning of the novel until Joseph and Fanny are
united in a promising marriage and Adams is given an adequate
living, the good shepherd continues his comic and yet serious
representations of charity. It is important that both culminations,
the young couple's secure marriage and the Parson's adequate
living, are in different ways confirmations of the stabilty and
permanence of home, the object of their pilgrimage. But it is also
important that both fulfilments – marital and financial – are
achieved within the sacred limits of temperance and charity. These
virtues have been tested over and again, in London and on the
journey home. We come to expect that Joseph's temperance, shown
principally through his loyalty to Fanny, and Adams's charity,
exemplified in his treatment of Joseph, Fanny, and numerous
others, will never fail. But the troubles mount so that we may
wonder for a moment whether Adams's charity can survive the
double jeopardy of an impatient wife (*JA*, IV, viii, 306–7) and a
furious mistress, Lady Booby (*JA*, IV, ii, 281–4), the one scorn-
ing his charity because it does not begin and end at home and
the other forbidding him to publish the wedding banns for Fanny
and Joseph on pain of having his curacy taken from him. But
even the threats of losing the comfort of the hearth, and the hearth
itself, do not weaken his commitment to the young couple, here
the objects of his loving work.

We may also wonder for a moment whether Joseph (and Fanny)
can possibly respond temperately to the abrupt transformation
of their status to that of brother and sister. It is no fate for intensely
heterosexual lovers who are also intensely moral! But they do
so, deciding to live together Platonically, having 'vowed a
perpetual Celibacy' (*JA*, IV, xv, 335), choosing not to part as if
awaiting other marital prospects. The continuity of the heroes'
trials is thus brought to a pitch as the novel nears its conclusion. First Fielding enlarges the earthly difficulties Adams and
Joseph face as they uphold the virtues they embody; then he

shows their integrity to be consummate. But these culminations are heavily involved in yet others before *Joseph Andrews* ends.

To consider the novel's resolution, energized by the complex recognitions of the Pedlar, Gammar Andrews and Mr Wilson, one does best to look at the frame of *Joseph Andrews*; that is, to the role of Lady Booby, chiefly at the beginning and the end of the book; to the curtailed parodic element in the characterization of Joseph as Pamela's brother; and to the appearance of Squire Booby and Pamela, Gaffar and Gammar Andrews. It has been widely observed that *Joseph Andrews* is different from *Pamela*, both in kind and in the nature of its morality. Generally speaking, it does not parody *Pamela*; it provides an alternative to it. But Fielding's novel indeed begins with a parody of Richardson's, reminding us of Pamela by making her brother Joseph seem for a moment sanctimonious about his virginity, like his sister. Though, as I have said already, Fielding quickly transforms this laughable prudery into Joseph's entirely sympathetic loyalty to Fanny, he does not simply cut off the Richardson connection when he launches into his alternative novel of morality. He carries on with it to the very end.

By the beginning of Book IV, Fielding has prepared the way to assimilate his borrowings from *Pamela* into elements of his own narrative, converting them to his own non-parodic purposes. Reduced and schematized, Fielding's narrative turns on Joseph who loves Fanny and who is Pamela's brother; Parson Adams, who is Joseph's spiritual guide and Fanny's; Fanny, whose parents are unknown; the beneficent Pedlar, who carries the threat of incest; Mr Wilson and his past, which includes a lost son who has a unique birthmark; and Lady Booby, Fielding's transsexual conversion of Mr B. from *Pamela*. Fielding begins the merger of Richardson's material and his own early on in the characters of Joseph and Lady Booby. And he continues the mischievous art, using his Pedlar first to make Fanny Joseph's brother, but ultimately, Pamela's sister; he also transforms Richardson's Gammar Andrews into a woman with a secret past, however innocent. But his appropriation of Mr B. and Pamela, and his transsexual conversion of Richardson's Mr B. into Mr B.'s aunt, Fielding's own Lady Booby, are vitally important to the conclusion of *Joseph Andrews*. These mischievous uses of certain of Richardson's formal elements may at first appear to be unmanageable self-indulgences by Fielding the comedian; but in fact he exercises masterly control, integrating them into his complex narrative.

The Richardsonian characters Fielding appropriates and transforms support three lines of action that dominate Book IV of *Joseph Andrews*. The first centres on Lady Booby's passion-driven attempts to win Joseph; the second, on Squire Booby's plausible wish to elevate his wife's family, especially Pamela's brother Joseph, so as to close the social distance between them and himself, for his own and his wife's sake (and, as it turns out, quite unintentionally, for Lady Booby's sake as well); and the third, on relocating Fanny and Joseph, each with a new identity by the end of the novel, so that we at last see them married and settled in an appropriate setting. All three actions in different ways enable Fielding to compare and contrast Fanny's (Fielding's) and her sister Pamela's (Richardson's) idea of marriage. A passion-driven Lady Booby, a mean-spirited but conventional Pamela, and a generally proper and ostensibly reasonable and generous Squire Booby are essential to this fictional strategy.

Throughout the novel Fielding makes use of one of Richardson's chief actions: the attempted seduction of a servant by a master. His Lady Booby schemes fitfully to possess Joseph, carnally and then in marriage, from the beginning through to the penultimate chapter. Her machinations in this regard become extensive and intense in Book IV, where they include threats to Adams, manipulations of the law and other social pressures against Fanny to drive her from the parish, and finally the enlistment of her nephew to dissuade Joseph from marrying Fanny, using reasons that have nothing to do with her real motives. Lady Booby's frenetic behaviour throughout the novel's final Book is reminiscent of Mr B.'s in *Pamela*; like her nephew of *Pamela*, she will do almost anything to have her way with the object of her desire. Threatening Adams and employing Lawyer Scout are only the most egregious examples of the nasty work. By intruding herself dishonourably into the issue of Adams's appointment as curate and into the operation of the poor laws, a communal expression of charity, she threatens the well-being of the parish. But Adams continues to be the steadfast shepherd. Taken altogether, her behaviour, very like Mr B.'s in *Pamela*, is out of joint with the moral basis of marriage foreshadowed in the love of Joseph and Fanny, supported by Parson Adams, and illustrated by Mr Wilson. It is by assimilating Mr B. as Lady Booby into his own fictive universe that Fielding reveals an important aspect of Richardson's moral inadequacy.

He continues the revelation by assimilating Mr B. as Squire Booby, whose first business when he visits his aunt is to locate Joseph, arrange for the trumped-up legal charges against him to be dropped, dress him in gentleman's clothes, and bring him to Lady Booby and Pamela (*JA*, IV, v, 288–93). In befriending Joseph as he does, Squire Booby plays into his aunt's hands: she wants a gentrified Joseph for obvious reasons of her own. And even though she thinks her nephew a fool for marrying Pamela (*JA*, IV, vi, 297), his example provides the precedent for her to marry down, a possibility both attractive and painful for her to consider, simply because Joseph prefers Fanny. The fact that her nephew claims his brother-in-law as part of the family makes Joseph a tantalizing prospect for marriage. But the deep sense that she cannot seduce him divides her between the wish to possess and the wish to destroy him. She is not remotely temperate or charitable, which is to say she is unable to understand the nature of marriage as Fielding sees it.

Squire Booby's apparently generous behaviour towards Joseph is not surprising if we realize that he is not the thwarted lover of *Pamela*; Fielding instead introduces us to a post-marital Squire Booby, an apparently reasonable man and loving husband, who wants to help his wife's brother. But when we learn that Joseph's elevation must include his separation from Fanny, we see that his motives are ruthlessly self-serving. They do not take Joseph's feelings into account, and Fanny is utterly disregarded. Joseph of course refuses to give her up, and as the exchange between the two men becomes heated, we recognize signs of the self-willed Mr B. in Squire Booby (*JA*, IV, vii, 301–2). At this point Squire Booby's wife takes her husband's side against her brother. To be sure we recognize that the 'happily married' Pamela has changed only the direction of her sanctimonious rectitude, not its nature, Fielding has her urge Joseph to separate himself from Fanny; when he resists, she tells him to pray for the 'Assistance of Grace' (*JA*, IV, vii, 302), a bit of advice that reminds us of Trulliber, the pig-parson. Pamela and her husband are similarly self-righteous in other ways; for example, he, with Lady Booby, chides Joseph for protecting Fanny against Didapper (*JA*, IV, xi, 321), and '*Pamela* chid her Brother *Joseph* for the Concern which he exprest at discovering a new Sister. She said, if he loved *Fanny* as he ought, with a pure Affection, he had no Reason to lament being related to her' (*JA*, IV, xiii, 330).

Until it is finally clear that Joseph and Fanny are to be married, Fielding limits Squire Booby's and Pamela's actions to their concern for Joseph's separation from Fanny, a step essential to their need (Joseph's social elevation). In handling them in this way, he satirizes them, but he does not test credulity; he rather presents them realistically. As the Squire and his wife work to disguise Joseph's (and Pamela's) humble origins, they remind those of us who know *Pamela* of their own mating game: on Mr B.'s side, an intemperate, unilateral passion (resurrected in his aunt), and on Pamela's, an unspeakable prudence. The contrast between this couple and Fanny and Joseph, who join in a mutually passionate, temperate and generous love, could hardly be more stark.

Fielding makes yet another use of the assimilated Pamela and the Squire. After the disclosure of the 'whole truth' about Fanny's and Joseph's parentage, various portions of which are known to the Pedlar, Gammar Andrews and Mr Wilson, he describes the consequences of the discoveries. Joseph, convinced that his new identity is genuine, begs his father's blessing (*JA*, IV, xv, 339). Realizing Joseph is out of reach, Lady Booby bolts from the room 'in an Agony' (*JA*, IV, xv, 339), and in a few days departs for London. And Fanny, after being indifferently welcomed by her parents (*JA*, IV, xvi, 339–40), receives a kiss from Squire Booby, who calls 'her Sister, and introduce[s] her as such to Pamela, who behave[s] with great Decency on the Occasion' (*JA*, IV, xvi, 340).

These largely predictable actions have important implications for the novel's conclusion. Beyond committing himself to his father, who is on the scene, Joseph defers his marriage until he sees his mother, by which time the banns can be published for 'the third and last Time' (*JA*, IV, xvi, 342) in Adams's parish. In this way Joseph is gathered into his heretofore unknown home, adding the dimension of familial continuity to that which Abraham Adams has wished for all along: the continuity of religious tradition represented by a church wedding. And poor Fanny, claimed only conditionally by her parents, and supported by her new-found sister and brother-in-law only for those reasons of self-interest that moved them to support Joseph when they thought he was Pamela's brother, is left with Joseph as her only refuge. Fielding of course knew his readers would understand that she was safe since Joseph's love for her is boundless. He nevertheless modifies her dependency by having Squire Booby provide a gift of £2000 to her, with which she and Joseph buy 'a little Estate in the same Parish with [Joseph's] Father' (*JA*, IV, xvi, 344).[46] The Squire also grants a generous living of £130 a year to Parson Adams; and he manages the Pedlar's appointment as Excise-man.

In all this, Fielding assigns Booby a circumscribed generosity, giving him no more than a worldly pre-eminence in family affairs. This limitation is emphasized when during the wedding ceremony Adams publicly rebukes the Squire and Pamela 'for laughing in so sacred a Place, and on so solemn an Occasion' (*JA*, IV, xvi, 342). Their laughter, especially reprimanded as it is, seems to imply the Boobys' disengagement from the holy union; neither understands the sacramental nature of marriage any more than does Lady Booby. It is Parson Adams, Fanny's and Joseph's spiritual father, and Mr Wilson, the groom's father, who are the true genial spirits presiding over the ceremony and the married life it heralds. (Though at one level important, Mrs Wilson is not given a strong presence. The world of *Joseph Andrews* is patriarchal.) Once joined by Adams, God's emissary, Joseph and Fanny will live near his parents, in a union that implies the continuity of the older couple's marriage, while it further suggests the eternal nature of the conjugal union, with its physical and spiritual dimensions, 'based on love and merit and characterized by mutual trust'.[47] Fielding's complex ending of *Joseph Andrews* does not parody *Pamela*, but it contrasts Richardson's characters and his own with brilliant effect.

* * *

In April 1743, Fielding published his three-volume *Miscellanies*, which include two important works of prose fiction: *A Journey from This World to the Next* (in Volume Two) and *Jonathan Wild* (Volume Three). The *Journey* is an interesting narrative, but not entirely successful, most agree. During the time that Fielding prepared the *Miscellanies* for the press, probably beginning in 1741 when he is likely to have begun taking subscriptions for the work, he was on hard times, despite the success of *Joseph Andrews*. Desperately in need of money, he was sued and briefly imprisoned for debt. As a young lawyer, he was largely unsuccessful in finding legal work; he was disillusioned enough with the Patriots, and financially desperate enough, to change the nature of his political writing; he endured the death of his daughter Charlotte, in 1742, and the severe illness of his wife, who died in 1744; and he himself began to suffer chronic ill-health. There were delays in the publication of the *Miscellanies*, and their quality is uneven, in part no doubt because of his personal troubles, but also because he decided against including certain works he had written earlier, probably for a variety of reasons.[48]

A Journey from This World to the Next is written in the tradition of Fielding's favourite classical author, Lucian (*c.* 125–*c* 190 AD), a Syrian rhetorician, whose works, written in Greek, included satiric dialogues of the dead which were intended to represent conversations between inhabitants of Hades. Though Lucian is the oldest known writer of such dialogues, narratives about travelling to the realm of the dead are much older, as the journeys to the underworld in the *Odyssey* (XI), in the vision of Er in *The Republic* (X), and in the *Aeneid* (VI) make clear. Though strictly speaking dialogues of the dead are satirical conversations overheard by us, the living, without the speakers' knowledge, they are part of a large body of work concerning historical and fictional characters whom we hear, or hear about, from the other side of the grave.[49] These closely related genres were popular in seventeenth- and eighteenth-century England and France, so that Fielding contributed *A Journey from This World to the Next* to a considerable context of similar literature written in the age. Charles Gildon's *Nuncius Infernalis: or, A New Account from Below* (1692), William King's *Dialogues of the Dead* (1699), John Sheffield, first Duke of Buckingham's 'A Dialogue between Augustus Caesar and Cardinal Richelieu' (1723), and an anonymous work appearing in *The Gentleman's Magazine*, November 1738, 'A Dialogue between the Queen of Sweden and the Czarina', are among these works published in England.[50] In France, Bernard de Fontenelle wrote *Dialogues des Morts* (1683) and François Fénelon published a series of such dialogues under the same title (1700–18). Fielding was familiar with these sources, both classical and modern, but the *Journey* draws most from Lucian's style (the comic-satiric treatment of serious matters) and from Plato's theme in the vision of Er (that only goodness can bring true happiness).

Lucian and Fielding demonstrate that the subject of life after death can lend itself to satirical comic treatment, in conjunction with a moral purpose. Lucian's *Menippus*, for example, begins with the return of Menippus from Hades, which he has visited to acquire wisdom. The first thing he wants to know is what is going on in Athens. 'Oh, nothing new', his friend Philonides answers, 'extortion, perjury, forty per cent interest rates'. After this satirical reintroduction into the terrible world of the living, Menippus gives an account of his trip to the underworld, full of amusing turns, but he never loses sight of his chief interest: the waste of human life in vain ambition, especially among the avaricious rich. Having completed the story of his journey down, he tells Philonides the substance of a law recently passed by the Assembly in Hades against the unscrupulous wealthy. When they die, their bodies are to be punished like those of other malefactors, and their souls are to be sent back to Earth, where they are to live as donkeys, for 250 000 years (donkeys' years), transmigrating from donkey to donkey during all that time! *Menippus* ends with the sympathetically treated opinion, spoken by the blind prophet Teiresias, that the life of the ordinary man, who does what his hand finds to do, is best.[51]

Fielding's *A Journey from This World to the Next* also finds matter for satiric comedy and moral teaching in Hades, chiefly among the dead who have not yet been judged by Minos or who, after judgment, are assigned by him to be born again. Like *Joseph Andrews*, *A Journey* ridicules affectation; 'its overriding theme is the same as that of portions of Volume One [of the *Miscellanies*] and of *Jonathan Wild*: the excoriation of "false greatness" and overweening ambition'.[52] It is in the fifth chapter that he makes the point most clearly, first by describing the ugly, dangerous road to Greatness and the beautiful road to Goodness; then by having great numbers choose the first road and almost none the second. But among these few is a responsible, virtuous king, whose socially active goodness represents a moral norm against which the vainglorious behaviour of the many in the *Journey* may be judged.

Fielding introduces topical allusions, often satirical, into his treatment of the other world in the *Journey*. The canals of the Hague give off a terrible odour (*JWN*, I, ii, 13); shortly after the good king begins to walk the road to Goodness, his Prime Minister (Walpole) limps after him to 'fetch him back' (*JWN*, I, v, 28); William Warburton is hit for claiming that the Eleusinian Mysteries are represented in the sixth book of the *Aeneid* (*JWN*, I, viii, 38–9); Tom Thumb, Fielding's cow-devoured midget, talks to his spirit-author in Elysium (*JWN*, I, ix, 41); the political abuses of patriotism are scored (*JWN*, I, xxiii, 102–4), reminding us that Fielding disapproved of the practices of some of those he had earlier supported in the opposition. These references to his own world – like Menippus's 'What is going on in Athens?' – in a sense interrupt the narrative set in Hades, but they also serve as comic reminders that an important aspect of the *Journey* is its application to the real world.

The sixteen chapters devoted to the reincarnations of Julian the Apostate (*JWN*, I, x–xxv, 45–111) provide opportunities for learned humour, but they also allow Fielding to examine the characters of various historical figures and types of men, and to review (and revise) historical material from the fourth to the sixteenth centuries. In all this he finds ways to illuminate his theme of false greatness. But most readers have found these narratives unrewarding. In fact *A Journey from This World to the Next* is not one of Fielding's most satisfying works.

> [it] gives the impression of something fresh and promising that went wrong. Inspired by Plato's Myth of Er and attempted in the satiric manner of his favorite Lucian, the *Journey* is another of Fielding's imaginative renderings of the theme that goodness alone can bring happiness. But in 1742 he could summon neither the cunning nor the will to carry out the experiment successfully.[53]

His recently deceased daughter, Charlotte, and his sister, Sarah, are both shadowy witnesses to the trouble he was having when he wrote the *Journey*. When the spirit-author first enters Elysium, he tells us:

> I presently met a little Daughter [Charlotte], whom I had lost several Years before. Good Gods! what Words can describe the Raptures, the melting passionate Tendernesss, with which we kiss'd each other, continuing in our Embrace, with the most exstatic Joy, a Space, which if Time had been measured here as on Earth, could not be less than half a Year. (*JWN*, I, viii, 36–7)

Obviously Fielding felt the loss of his daughter deeply. Her death at the least must have contributed to the flagging energy with which he wrote the *Journey*. Because of the complicated history of the manuscript, it is hard to know the significance of his telling us in the Introduction that the text of the *Journey* is a fragment. Perhaps Fielding's leap from the last chapter on Julian (*JWN*, I, xxv, 111) to '*Wherein* Anna Boleyn *relates the History of her Life*' (*JWN*, XIX, vii, 113) is a playful return to the spirit of H. Scriblerus Secundus, whom he had called on more than a decade earlier in *The Tragedy of Tragedies*. The textual hiatus is reminiscent of Swift's *A Tale of a Tub*, where gaps in the narrative are mischievously explained as having resulted from the Bookseller's use of a 'surreptitious Copy'. In neither work – *Tale* or *Journey* – does the 'loss' of text interfere with its thematic completeness. Even the Boleyn chapter clearly supports the idea that striving for false greatness is a waste of life. Nevertheless the ebbing vitality of the interminable Julian passages and the serene storytelling of the final chapter, written almost certainly by Fielding's sister, suggest the possibility that he sought relief from Sarah, finding himself for once too tired to get on with his work.[54] Did he at some level of imagination travel from this world to the next to visit his daughter Charlotte, find himself burdened with Julian almost as soon as he had reached his destination, and call upon his sister to complete the journey when he could no longer carry on?

*   *   *

The Life of the Late Mr Jonathan Wild the Great filled the third volume of Fielding's *Miscellanies*. Over a decade later, in 1754, a considerably revised version of the work was published. It is this second book that I shall comment on here, with a historical reference or two to the first. *Jonathan Wild* is a complicated piece of prose fiction, at once a psuedo-history of the real-life criminal Jonathan Wild, who was hanged at Tyburn on 24 May 1725; a political and a social satire; a study of evil represented by a man who repudiates, exploits and corrupts binding human relations; and a serious comic-sentimental treatment of marriage, which serves as a foil to the evil Wild, who works to destroy it.

The historical Jonathan Wild was probably born in 1683, in the village of Wolverhampton, Staffordshire. Though by 1700 he had been apprenticed to a buckle-maker for some years, he left his master abruptly then and went to London, at the same time deserting his young wife, probably to avoid prosecution for a crime. He was soon arrested and imprisoned for about five years in the Wood Street Compter, where he met and bigamously married Mary Milliner, a thief and a prostitute, who became his partner in crime. By 1708 he had given up common robbery to become a manager in his chosen profession. And by the time he was hanged, in 1725, Jonathan Wild was famous for working both sides of the law. He had behind him a long career as the leader of a band of thieves who took all the risks of robbery and got almost none of the profits. After Wild received the property his men had stolen, he would pretend to have located it by innocent means; then he would negotiate its return to the owner for a 'gift' of money. He was also a thief-catcher, who was paid £40 each for criminals brought to trial, convicted of felony, and hanged. In this last role, he managed to make himself acceptable enough to the law that no one interfered with his declaring himself Thief-Catcher General of Great Britain and Ireland and moving into showy quarters near the Old Bailey, the chief criminal court of London. Wild was without conscience in securing indictments against guilty and innocent alike by bribing or coercing witnesses to lie. He also kept recalcitrant members of his gang in line with threats of prosecution, which they knew were not idle. Long believed to be invulnerable, he was finally brought down by two members of his own gang and the victim of one of his robberies, who together witnessed to his crimes. Public opinion, which turned against him only late in the day, was brought to a pitch by Wild's unscrupulous treatment of a fellow criminal. When Wild was hanged, a pitiless London mob cheered.[55]

Shortly after Wild's death, Defoe published *The Life and Actions of Jonathan Wild*, in June 1725. Beginning in 1718, there had been periodical references to Wild and pamphlets about him, some of which which claimed to detail his illicit activities. This essentially ephemeral literature contributed to the shift in public opinion against him, but Wild probably would have been forgotten, despite Defoe's more substantial life, if Walpole's Opposition had not been looking for an effective symbol to represent the prime minister. On 12 May and 19 May 1725, there appeared an essay in two parts in the recently established *Mist's Weekly Journal*, in which Wild is satirically venerated as a Great Man, the effective beginning of the often used Wild–Walpole, Thief–Statesman parallel, though the association of pejoratively treated 'great men' and criminals is much older.[56] Gay gave new dimensions to the parallel in *The Beggar's Opera* (1728), and by the time Fielding began *Jonathan Wild*, probably in 1739, the identification of Walpole as the 'Great Man' and Wild as a satiric proxy for the minister were widely recognized connections.

At the heart of Fielding's social and political satire in *Jonathan Wild* is the distinction between greatness and goodness which, his speaker says ironically, 'sages or philosophers, have endeavoured, as much as possible, to confound'. Then he drops the irony as he expains that 'no two things can possibly be more distinct from each other, for greatness consists in bringing all manner of mischief on mankind, and goodness in removing it from them' (*Jonathan Wild*, I, i).[57] The mischief brought on mankind results chiefly from blind ambition striving for success without considering the consequences to others or, in the long run, the consequences to oneself.

In addition to the general identification of Wild and Walpole as equal exemplars of the Great Man, *Jonathan Wild* includes other social and political allusions that Fielding's contemporaries would have recognized immediately. By the time the first version of the book appeared (7 April 1743), Walpole had already been forced to resign (2 February 1742). Well before the resignation, Fielding had separated himself from the opposition and had written pro-ministerial propaganda.[58] Elements of both political stances appear in *Jonathan Wild*: satire against Walpole and against the former opposition. In his Preface to the *Miscellanies*, Fielding comments, in a degree disingenuously it seems, on the nature and scope of his satire in his life of Wild: 'as it is not a very faithful portrait of *Jonathan Wild* himself, so neither is it intended to represent the Features of any other Person. Roguery, and not a Rogue, is my subject' (*Miscellanies*, I, 9). But indeed it is true that in addition to hits at Walpole and the triumphant opposition, *Jonathan Wild* includes less personal targets of satire: unjust applications of the law, insensitive members of the clergy, corrupt prison officials, and perversions of sacred human ties like friendship and marriage. It also mocks the abortive criminal brotherhood in which Wild lives his life, a dark context of rapacity and social unpredictability.

Ultimately it is Wild's psychology that is Fielding's chief subject. Wild, a lone wolf, is unwilling to be anyone's friend. In fact he is a sociopath without the capacity for friendship. Quite apart from the long, complex history of his exploitative dealings with all around him, Fielding associates Wild with sinister emblems. He is baptized by Titus Oates (*JW*, I, iii, 9); he echoes Milton's Satan when he says, 'I had rather stand on the summit of a dung-hill than at the bottom of a hill in Paradise' (*JW*, I, v, 15); he is praised by Fielding's ironic narrator for his 'double method of cheating . . ., [which falls] very little short of diabolism itself' (*JW*, II, ii, 51); he often retires to a night cellar, which is a transparent surrogate for hell (*JW*, I, v, 18; I, xiv, 41; II, iv, 57; II, ix, 72); and, finally, his maxims epitomize an efficient, satanic hypocrisy (*JW*, IV, xv, 173–4).[59]

Fielding uses two general means of displaying Wild's solitary diabolism. He locates him in the underworld of cheats and murderers, where dog eats dog, and he contrasts Wild's failure at marriage with Mr and Mrs Heartfree's happy union. We learn from the beginning that there is no honour among thieves. La Ruse and Wild set the standard for criminal behaviour by pretending to be amiable at the same time that they work to undo each other. Even their plan to cooperate for the sake of a joint venture at theft turns out to be only the setting in which first one and then the other secures the booty. Wild thrives in this context of duplicitous striving. When Straddle lifts £900 from him and La Ruse runs off with Heartfree's jewels, having left paste imitations behind, Wild regrets the losses, of course, but finds in the occasion an opportunity for rejoicing in his real gift, 'his mind: 'tis the inward glory, the secret consciousness of doing great and wonderful actions . . . Let me then hold myself contented with this reflection, that I have been wise though unsuccessful, and am a GREAT though an unhappy man' (*JW*, II, iv, 58–9). Pausing only to refresh himself with a sneaker of punch, he sets out bravely to recover what is rightfully his.

Fielding gives us countless instances of Wild's criminal activity and his aloneness, which are in some sense part of each other. His crimes are depredations against any other human (potentially every other human), acts that inevitably isolate him socially. That is the nature of his criminality, which Fielding deplored both as the subversion of life – which for him is fulfilling only when it is socially constructive – and ultimately a threat to the country at large, as he explains at length in *An Enquiry into the Causes of the late Increase of Robbers* (1751). Though *Jonathan Wild* allows us to imagine that a dark underworld corrupts the life of the nation, its chief attention is on Wild's irredeemable predatory aloneness.

An equation operates throughout *Jonathan Wild*; it is that conquerors, absolute princes, statesmen and thieves are equally great. This realignment of social roles overturns a commonplace view by implying among other things that conquerors, tyrants and statesmen are thieves. But it leaves us to decide in what (ironic) sense thieves, including Wild, may be great. Fielding helps us with his associations of Wild and Satan, the long history of Wild's lone depredations, and with any number of pithy sentences like 'the highest excellence of a [thief is to] convert those laws which are made for the benefit and protection of society to [his] single use' (*JW*, I, xiv, 43).

Fielding adds to our sense of Wild by telling us what he is not, namely a loving and beloved husband. His unswerving commitment to false greatness distorts his opinion of women.[60] In his view they are inferior to men, not only physically but mentally, and he patronizes them accordingly, offering gifts and promising marriage with equal insincerity (*JW*, I, ix, 26–7). His chief interest in them is their availability at moments when he wants relaxation from the demanding life of crime (*JW*, II, iii, 53). And he comes to them not with friendly passion, but with lust, which he expresses in brutal physical actions. His attempt to rape Mrs Heartfee is foiled only by the intervention of the French captain (*JW*, II, x, 75), and Laetitia Snap escapes by ripping his cheeks with her nails (*JW*, I, ix, 28) in a display of ferocity that anticipates the quality of their marriage. The 'dialogue matrimonial' between Wild and Laetitia, which takes place a fortnight after their wedding, is an exchange of hate-laden recrimination. Its conclusion is that they agree 'never [to] live like man and wife; that is, never to be loving nor ever quarrel' (*JW*, III, viii, 106). What should have been the sacrament of their union is reduced to an inhuman neutral separateness.

When the narrator introduces Heartfree at the beginning of Book II, he tells us that his character 'will serve as a kind of foil to the noble and great disposition of our hero' (*JW*, II, i, 46). Though the contrast between the two covers a wide range, it is ultimately in their marriages that the differences signify. Ronald Paulson points out that 'love stands as a norm of ordinary human

activity; indeed, throughout Fielding's novels it signifies goodness'.[61] Whereas Wild and Laetitia are meanly self-constrained –
in no important sense available to each other – and sexually
promiscuous, the Heartfrees are open-hearted (as their name
implies) and mutually accessible, a deeply loyal couple.[62] At one
level they are each other. Even when Heartfree is in prison and
his wife threatened by rape abroad, we understand that they are
sustained by their marriage, a given that survives Fielding's comic
treatment of her dangerous travels.

The extended comparison of these marriages culminates in
Wild's late discovery of Fireblood in Laetitia's willing arms. Fielding's narrator times the cuckolded husband's bull-roar so that it
interrupts Mrs Heartfree's long narration of her adventures abroad,
which are testimony to her marital fidelity. This fictionally
controlled coincidence of Wild's publicly displayed discovery of
his wife's infidelity – the involuntary bull-roar – and Mrs
Heartfree's narrative celebration of her marital loyalty – she tells
the world her story – dramatizes the distance between the
marriages.

It is possible that Mrs Heartfree's apparent vanity about her
power to attract men may amuse or disappoint us. We may also
feel that Fielding strains our credulity with the frequency and
intensity of her sexual encounters. But her story is in fact a comic
recapitulation, made so in part by her super-animated pleasure
in recounting her unlikely adventures *after* she and her husband
are out of danger. Fielding has prepared the way for this animation with Heartfree's surprise reprieve, the narrator's mock
diffidence concerning his ability to describe the family's joy, and
its mischievous surgical aftermath: 'It would be very imperti-
nent to offer a description of the joy this occasioned to the two
friends, or to Mrs Heartfree, who was now again recovered. A
surgeon, who was happily present, was employed to bleed them
all' (JW, IV, v, 139).

Mrs Heartfree's sanguine humour survives the phlebotomy and
contributes an element of irrepressible joy to her narrative which,
however hyperbolic, is the account of her fidelity recited in the
context of Heartfree's reprieve. Its flow is significantly interrupted
by Wild's bestial complaint, the voiced symbol of his and Laetitia's
brutalized marriage; but it is renewed and concluded with the
happy wife's expression of faith 'THAT PROVIDENCE WILL
SOONER OR LATER PROCURE THE FELICITY OF THE

VIRTUOUS AND INNOCENT' (*JW*, IV, xi, 161). Fielding almost certainly had reservations about such optimism, but he must have been pleased to have Mrs Heartfree express it.

When 'the history returns to the contemplation of GREATNESS' (*JW*, IV, xii, 161), we see a tortured Wild who has been 'sentenced to be hanged by the neck' (*JW*, IV, xii, 162). Though Fielding's narrator continues his praise of Wild's greatness, his dispassion is droll: 'For my own part, I confess, I look upon this death of hanging to be as proper for a hero as any other' (*JW*, IV, xii, 162). Thereafter the claims for the condemned man's greatness are undercut by Wild's incapacity to bear his predicament. He fears the malice of his enemies and so takes to the bottle; the ordinary tells him that he is an angel of the devil who must reconcile himself to everlasting fire, and Wild dreams so confoundedly of hanging that his sleep is disturbed; he takes a dose of laudanum to escape the public honour of hanging but does not succeed; as Laetitia, his wife, recapitulates the list of her husband's faults, he catches her by the hair and kicks her heartily out of his prison room. The evidence for his despair is weighty enough that it overpowers both his claim that he does not fear death and his nominal assurance that he will be given a reprieve. Fielding's narrator displays Wild's disintegration, hyperbolically, just as he had the Heartfrees' renovation, ironically solemnizing his hero's greatness all the while. Wild's final reduction occurs at the gallows where, having been stoned by the crowd, he performs an action that 'serves to show the most admirable conservation of character in our hero to the last moment – [he] applied his hands to the parson's pocket, and emptied it of his bottle-screw, which he carried out of the world in his hand' (*JW*, IV, xiv, 171).

This late intensification of the narrator's irony, which continues through the final chapter, is only the last instance of his tendency to modulate his point of view throughout *Jonathan Wild*. Generally he satirizes greatness, implicitly directing his readers to correct their confusion of greatness with goodness or to recognize that the successes of ambition and avarice are inane. But this typically controlled irony is sometimes overstated and occasionally suspended altogether; and between these extremes there are many nuances. For example, he uses an almost literal voice to say:

> When I consider whole nations rooted out only to bring tears into the eyes of a GREAT MAN . . . because he hath no more nations to extirpate, then truly I am almost inclined to wish that Nature had spared us this her MASTERPIECE, and that no GREAT MAN had ever been born into the world.

But he recovers his ironic tone in the very next sentence, saying that he will proceed with his 'history, which will . . . produce much better lessons . . . than any we can preach' (*JW*, I, xiv, 41). Letting his true voice break through the ironic surface on rare occasions may give moral reassurance to the reader without weakening the satire; indeed, the contrast may strengthen it.

At the other end of the satirical scale, the narrator first describes Mrs Heartfree with a jarring vulgarity as 'a mean-spirited, poor, domestic, low-bred animal, who confined herself mostly to the care of her family' (*JW*, II, i, 46). After its initial shock, the hyperbole hints to the reader attuned to the narrator's irony that Mrs Heartfree is a rare genial spirit, the obverse of self-serving 'true greatness', a conclusion supported by everything that follows. Indeed it is into his treatment of the Heartfrees and their family, including Friendly, that Fielding most often introduces brief praises, in a 'true voice', followed by dismissive scorn for their lack of greatness. One may suppose that the author, behind the narrator, is tense between his approval of these benevolent people and his obligation to sustain the satiric mode. But I believe Fielding measures his suspensions of irony effectively. 'Inconsistency' does not seem the word to apply to these shifts of voice.

At times throughout the book, especially in the last chapter, which includes Wild's maxims, the hero is made to speak for himself: 'A man of honour is he that is called a man of honour; and while he is so called he so remains, and no longer' (*JW*, I, xiii, 38). At one level, we hear Wild unmediated in the great man's own words; at another, we enjoy Fielding's inventive vocal control, which in this modulation he uses to satirize Wild by implying facetiously that his soliloquies and maxims are to be taken seriously. Wild's longish speech on honour (*JW*, I, xiii, 37–8), which includes several ineluctable sentences like the one quoted above, is intended most immediately to bluff his henchman Bagshot into submission. It serves a practical purpose, showing Wild to be unscrupulously effective in dealing with his fellows. But in offering us the maxims as if they were the distilled wisdom of a teacher who has left us the essence of his philosophy, Fielding implies ironically that Wild has a worldview, the maxims being its presumptive theoretical basis.

All of the maxims one way and another shadow forth Wild's implacable greatness and contempt of goodness, but the fifteenth is especially effective in this regard: 'The heart [is] the proper seat of hatred, and the countenance of affection and friendship' (*JW*, IV, xv, 174). The sentence mockingly represents not only Wild's satanic wisdom, but the nature of his being and of his life as well: he hates, he is a conscious hypocrite, he subverts friendship. That the maxim completely disregards his utter failure as a man is a signal irony, which Fielding reinforces with that last image of Wild when we see him pickpocket the Newgate ordinary's bottle-screw and carry it out of the world with him; this is a final compulsive gesture, which like the rest of his life is barren.

* * *

Tom Jones's complex and abundant goodness, along with the goodness of his friends, dominates the novel and makes him ultimately an ideal lover and husband.[63] At the same time, the narrator's understanding and management of that goodness encourage our friendly respect for the storyteller; he may surprise us with twists and turns of action, but he is comfortingly predictable in his moral outlook. He early allies himself with Tom, Sophia and Allworthy, whose strength of character lies ultimately in their prudent goodness, the capacity for practical, socially constructive behaviour, and he shows himself to be at odds with characters like Blifil and Thwackum who, as far as we know, will not, perhaps cannot, be redeemed. In addition, he champions a human fulfilment that cannot be: a perfectly happy marriage, which for him and for the Toms and Sophias of the world is an indispensable ideal they live to foster, even as it fosters them. These commonplace observations on *Tom Jones* are sound enough, but except for my implicit identification of the narrator as a character to be reckoned with, they fail even to suggest the complex formal strategies Fielding invents to dramatize his related themes of goodness and its fulfilment in marriage. If we take a critical look at the narrator's methods of storytelling in conjunction with the novel's unfolding action, centred on marriage, both 'actual' and ideal, we should come away with a useful sense of *Tom Jones*. Obviously nothing approaching a thorough criticism of the vast book is possible here.

In an often quoted statement, Coleridge praises *Tom Jones*: 'What a master of composition Fielding was! Upon my word, I think the Oedipus Tyrannus, the Alchemist, and Tom Jones the three most perfect plots ever planned.'[64] Many have agreed and not a few have disagreed with this high praise. Austin Dobson, for example, observes that 'progress and animation alone will not make a perfect plot, unless probability be superadded. And though it cannot be said that Fielding disregards probability, he certainly strains it considerably.'[65] And F. R. Leavis is peremptory in his correction of the praises of Fielding's plot: 'The conventional talk about the "perfect construction" of *Tom Jones* . . . is absurd. There can't be subtlety of organization without richer matter to organize, and subtler interests, than Fielding has to offer.'[66] R. S. Crane changes the ground of critical discourse by rejecting the tendency to consider the mechanics of plot in isolation from such other elements of the novel as characters and their interactions, which in his view affect their moral natures and states of mind, and from the novelist's linguistic medium (the manner and technique) used to represent these interactions. Crane obviously directs the criticism away from simple plot – what happens in the novel? – and towards the means by which the novelist makes things happen. Having claimed that plot is a complex synergy, which must engage the reader's interest if it is to succeed, Crane argues that the particulars of the novel's action dovetail in complicated ways, with remarkable plausibility. He also acknowledges that the plot to some extent succeeds with the assistance of Fortune.[67]

This acknowledgment that Fortune sometimes controls the details of Fielding's plot in no way diminishes the novelist's control of its rich synergism. In fact the operations of Fortune in *Tom Jones* allow us to see Fielding through his narrator managing the plot's more than occasional improbabilities. Tom just happens to be at the home of the Man of the Hill in time to rescue him and, later, Mrs Waters; Squire Western appears just in time to save Sophia from Lord Fellamar; Sophia meets her cousin Harriet as both women dash cross-country to escape tyrannical males, a father and a husband; Tom is miraculously freed from prison; and so on.

Both Coleridge and others who praise the novel's superb control of plot and those critics who express reservations about it because Fielding too often relies on improbable coincidence to further the action seem to have a point. Martin Battestin reconciles these contradictory opinions by calling on an eighteenth-century religious view of human experience: 'the fortunate contingencies and surprising turns which affect the course of events in *Tom Jones* are neither the awkward shifts of incompetency nor the pleasant fantasies of romance; rather, they have an essential function in the expression of Fielding's Christian vision of life'.[68] In an historically grounded argument, Battestin makes the case that Fielding believes in and draws on the idea of a benevolent Providence which operates in the world of its making; the world *Tom Jones* imitates. In further support of his claim, Battestin calls on numerous contemporary theologians, including John Tillotson (1630–94): 'God generally permits things to take their natural course'; nevertheless 'God hath reserved to himself a power and liberty to interpose, and to cross as he pleases, the usual course of things; to awaken men to the consideration of him, and a continual dependance on him.'[69] In a novel that imitates a Christian universe overseen by a benevolent Providence which intervenes as it will, apparent coincidences may be divinely directed action at one level. But they are also part of the comic scheme of things, mischievously controlled by the narrator. To the extent that we like him and trust him, we may allow him to indulge himself with improbabilities that seem to give him pleasure. In fact the success of *Tom Jones* depends on our willingness to do so, as a close look at Tom's character, especially in his affair with Lady Bellaston, will make clear.

It has often been observed that Tom is fundamentally good from the beginning, but that he needs to learn prudence. The need is certain, but the learning is in one sense built into Tom's nature. When Tom is first introduced to us (*Tom Jones*, III, ii, 118–23), we learn that his most serious crimes are his virtues: he conceals the truth about the poaching incident only to protect Black George. The poaching itself might have had serious consequences, but in the world of the novel it is not taken seriously. Tom's sexual escapades, except that with Lady Bellaston, are expressions of his physical and social health, which include his sense of responsibility for the consequences of his lovemaking. In the universe of *Tom Jones*, his behaviour is accepted as natural, especially given his spontaneous unwillingness to regard his gratification as the end of the game. Perhaps his relief at discovering Molly's ranging sexual appetite seems less complicated than it might have been; why should he feel altogether relieved of the burden of paternity? But he never forgets her. When in the end Black George disappears, Tom settles money on the family, giving Molly 'much the greatest Share' (*TJ*, XVIII, xiii, 980). The gift, along with Sophia's mediation of Molly's marriage to Partridge, implies, among other things, Tom's continuing interest in her. It is generally his way with all who have become part of his life, even Blifil. (Lady Bellaston and Thwackum are likely exceptions.) Tom's heart is in the right place. His sense of responsibility – the charitably shaped continuity of his relations with the men and women who are part of his life – suggests that no radical conversion is needed for him to become prudent; time and experience will bring him to that condition. Nevertheless the matter raises interesting critical issues.

When Tom meets Lady Bellaston, he is down and out, without money (except Sophia's), banished from home and Allworthy's loving protection, and most important, bereft forever, he almost believes, of his Sophia. It is in these circumstances that he accepts Lady Bellaston's implicit offer to become her lover for pay; and even so, he acquiesces on condition that she arrange a meeting with Sophia, at which time he will say goodbye to his love forever. Tom's aim is both to return Sophia's money and to ascertain her feeling for him following the episode with Mrs Waters at Upton. Lady Bellaston's aim is to enjoy Tom's person and to get him to end his relation with Sophia. Despite his motivations, some of them extenuating, Tom soon regrets prostituting himself, and we see him divided between a distorted sense of responsibility to Lady Bellaston – second nature for Tom – and the desire to be rid of her.

Is his affair with the Lady in some sense a base act, leaving us to face a new Tom, as Crane suggests?[70] Our hero has taken money for making love to a woman who does not attract him. And he feels terrible guilt when he thinks Sophia will learn about the affair, as of course she does. On the other side, his loyalty to Sophia, far from being adversely affected by the affair, is its very reason for being. Lady Bellaston knows the way to Sophia, and paradoxically, the wages of Tom's prostitution enable him to return her money intact. It seems wrong to sweep aside his taking money to make love to a woman he does not care for, but it would be unreasonable to say the connection affects his love for Sophia. And yet he should have found another way of locating Sophia, one may claim; the way he chose was base (uncharacteristic of the Tom we knew) or imprudent or both. But it was not improbable.

Tom's marriage proposal, in writing, begging to be disclosed to Sophia by Lady Bellaston, is something else. Would the Tom we know have written it? The intrusive, wilful narrator works hard to make the hero's sending the letter seem probable to the reader because the narrator has a lot of explaining to do. Tom's act is not only egregiously risky, it is cheeky, and not really his kind of thing. The narrator, realistically enough, makes Tom uncomfortable with it in the prospect. Moreover a good deal of the energy for the deed is assigned to Nightingale. It is he who first suggests and then dictates the proposal, and he advises Tom with the second letter to Lady Bellaston. On top of this the narrator assures us that Tom remains uncomfortable with the duplicity after the fact, however pleased by its success, because he 'utterly detested every Species of Falsehood or Dishonesty: Nor would he, indeed, have submitted to put it in Practice, had he not been involved in a distressful Situation, where he was obliged to be guilty of some Dishonour, either to one Lady or the other' (*TJ*, XV, ix, 821). Finally, Nightingale is made to speak for the appropriateness of the scheme: 'Dear *Tom*, we have conferred very different Obligations on each other. To me you owe the regaining of your Liberty; to you I owe the Loss of mine [in marriage]' (*TJ*, VX, ix, 821).

The narrator's devices for claiming the plausibility of Tom's action seem numerous in proportion to its deviation from Tom's well established behaviour. It is hard to resist the sense that the narrator is pulled two ways. He wants to arrange for this missive hostage to Fortune so he can have Sophia hit Tom with it when our hero is already almost down and out. And he recognizes that Tom's writing the letter has taxed his, the narrator's, rhetorical ingenuity for making the implausible plausible. Undeterred by this palpable tension, the supremely confident storyteller decides to risk implausibility. Tom writes the letter, but with what consequences to the narrative?

Throughout the brief chapter that opens Book XVII, the narrator mockingly, and yet affectionately, taunts the reader with his utter power to control Tom's predicament and the novel's outcome.

First he says that 'it would be difficult for the Devil, or any of his Representatives on Earth, to have contrived much greater Torments for poor *Jones*, than those in which we left him in the last Chapter' (*TJ*, XVII, i, 875), where Tom, in prison, is led to believe he has mortally wounded Fitzpatrick just before he receives a letter from Sophia, in which she says she has seen his proposal of marriage to Lady Bellaston in his handwriting! To this the omnipotent narrator adds ironically, once again calling attention to his control of invention, '[It is a hard task] to bring our Favourites out of their present Anguish and Distress, and to land them at last on the Shore of Happiness.' Then in the very next sentence he says, 'the Calamities in which [Tom] is at present involved [are] owing to his Imprudence!' (*TJ*, XVII, i, 875). How seriously can we take this charge of Tom's imprudence? Given the narrator's reader-taunting voice in the first chapter of Book XVII and the concatenation of Tom's miseries, all brought to a head just before the marvellous reversal, one may well smile at the suggestion that the decision to write a proposal of marriage to Lady Bellaston is simply an instance of Tom's imprudence.

The chief issue is not that the narrator is improbable in having Tom propose to Lady Bellaston (and to do so in writing), it is rather that matters are complicated by the confluence of the narrative's integrity and the narrator's comic intrusiveness and control. What are we to make of this creature of Fielding's, the narrator, who revels in his control of events and then solemnly tells us that Tom is imprudent? In the midst of this critical uncertainty, generations of readers – not all readers – have experienced the pleasures of a happy surrender to the autonomous narrator who, like his hero, has his heart in the right place. In such a fictional context we can readily understand that the morality represented by Allworthy, Tom, Sophia and especially the narrator is the basis for a life well lived, and we sympathize with all four of them. It is less clear that Tom's imprudence needs systematic correction. In fact the narrator implicitly encourages us to understand that with the help of his comic-fictive guidance, which we know to be loving as well as autocratic, Tom will more or less 'naturally' find his way back to Allworthy and Sophia.[71]

Fielding's narrator very seldom lets us forget that he is present, deciding what portions of the whole truth known to him he will let us have, and when. Like his characters in *Joseph Andrews*, those in *Tom Jones* are not immediately available to us; we do not encounter them directly, and neither are we privy to their internal struggles. By contrast Defoe and Richardson generate fictions which sustain the illusion that Robinson Crusoe and Clarissa, for example, are self-reflexive individuals working hard to cope with the dangers in a fallen world. As Leopold Damrosch, Jr, informs us at length, such soul-searching characters are integral to the Puritan tradition, obsessively burdened with their individuality.[72] To put the matter simply, one might say that the Puritan imagination, which conceives of each man and woman as alone, confronting an alien universe, fosters the kind of fiction that implies reality to be the details of such confrontations. As readers, we are encouraged to accept the self-evaluating self, interior and mysterious, struggling for fulfilment, as if it were the primary reality, unmediated. From the perspective of the author of such fiction, we would unselfconsciously receive the narrative as true. Fielding's narrator, on the other hand, claiming to write history, reminds us by a hundred means of his authorial presence. It is part of the fiction of *Tom Jones* that the truth about its universe requires the narrator's mediation. Such a requirement need not lessen the verisimilitude of the narrative, which Fielding believes is true to nature in treating its men and women as universal types to be described rather than as individuals whose interiors need to be explored. Time and place will inevitably alter certain exterior features of such types, but their essential qualities survive from age to age, he tells us (*Joseph Andrews*, III, i, 189). His narrator allows us to see them re-enact aspects of human existence rather than alter their souls by self-examination.

Indeed few characters in *Tom Jones* experience a deep change of heart. The Man of the Hill in one sense sees the error of his ways but, in condemning his own past, he condemns the whole world and withdraws from it into isolation and despair; he is not socially constructive in either mode of his life. Nightingale wobbles on a moral fence until Tom gives him a firm, benevolent shove in the direction of goodness. Square experiences the most radical change of any character in the novel, but he does so only on his deathbed. Generally, the good characters, not without faults, are good from the beginning, consistent in their fundamental morality, as are the bad – like Blifil and Thwackum – in their immorality. Between these are various characters, more good than bad, like Western (who can be very cruel nevertheless), and more bad than good, like Mrs Fitzgerald, all with their own psychological (if not moral) integrity. In the universe of *Tom Jones* characters are essentially stable, revealed rather than transformed, including, of course, the character of the narrator. To this it may be added that the bad characters are compulsively self-serving, and the good are moved to support others, without much reference to self-knowledge. They instinctively understand and practise charity.

Until now I have stressed the narrator's control of character and event in *Tom Jones*; indeed, not only his control, but his display of it and the pleasure he takes in it, effectively requiring us to accept his strong, sometimes arbitrary – in appearance arbitrary – intrusions or drop the book. But Fielding can make the narrator as subtle as he is bold for, paradoxically, he can exercise fictional control by appearing to suspend it. Three such apparent suspensions reveal a good deal about Fielding's art of storytelling, and they lead us to the heart of the novel as well. These three are the histories of the Man of the Hill (*TJ*, VII, xi–xiv, 451–83) and Mrs Fitzpatrick (*TJ*, XI, iv–vii, 581–602), and the monologue/dialogue of the Gypsy King/Tom (*TJ*, XII, xii, 663–71). These episodes are at one level significant instances of the narrator's surrender of his declared authority as historian and fiction maker: he lets others speak extensively, without interruption, especially the Man of the Hill and Mrs Fitzpatrick. But in fact these new voices tell stories integral to the rest of *Tom Jones*, supplying oblique as well as direct reinforcement of its subject matter. That subject matter, schematically represented, is Tom's and Sophia's journey from the country, both having experienced the unjust displeasure of their fathers, through a world of hard times (including London), which tests them until their socially constructive energies (love, goodness, faith that human society is or ought to be a justice-loving community) and certain turns of good fortune (a benevolent Providence) bring them together in a fulfilling marriage. All three episodes 'outside' the main narrative, told by a voice nominally independent of the narrator's, in different ways converge on the same problem: that of establishing and maintaining a good marriage in a congenial social context. To be sure, these episodes and the 'main narrative' have other subjects in common, like government, religion, morality and politics. But the most basic common element is marriage and its contexts, to which elements of the foregoing list of subjects may themselves contribute. The narrator, who has the audacity to parade himself as both the historian and the inventor of the novel's action, is also (under Fielding's guidance) capable of surrendering centre stage to another speaker.

The episode of the Gypsy King is a circumscribed adventure that shows us the gypsy community celebrating a wedding. Within the temporal limits of the celebration, their king characterizes his people as a loving society for whose well-being he is lovingly responsible; then he adjudicates in the case of a husband and wife who have prostituted their marriage. It is significant that except for the king's brief description of his society and its governance, the episode is made up entirely of the wedding celebration and his swift punishment of the couple who prostitute their marriage. It is also significant that the only instance we have of the king's capacity to administer justice in the interest of social order is this one about a corrupted marriage. It is as if the whole business of the gypsy community were to celebrate marriage and preserve its sanctity in the face of a cupidity that profanes the holy union. The combination resonates with the treatment of marriage (and the relations between the sexes) throughout the novel, where it is presented ideally as the sanctified union of lovers well-suited to each other, and treated practically as an affair controlled by the market-place or by some self-indulgent appetite.[73]

Along with the gypsy episode, the histories of the Man of the Hill and Harriet Fitzpatrick in different ways turn on marriage and marital failure. Every reader will recall Harriet's bad marriage and her adulterous intrusion into another. The same subject frames the life of sin of the Man of the Hill. In his youth, he was bent on marrying his mistress even though he knew 'half [his] Acquaintance' had slept with her (*TJ*, VIII, xi, 457). After his father reclaims him and brings him home, however, he will hear nothing of the subject: 'My Father now greatly solicited me to think of Marriage; but my inclinations were utterly averse to any such Thoughts' (*TJ*, VII, xiii, 470). This 'utter aversion' to marriage is in Fielding's universe the radical expression of the old man's misanthropy, an unwillingness to perpetuate the race, a negation of humanity which requires biological and social continuities; indeed it is the ultimate transgression against God's will in its denial of the life He created.

A closer look at connections between the stories told by the Man of the Hill and Mrs Fitzpatrick and the rest of the novel illuminates Fielding's treatment of marriage and its moral contexts. The Man of the Hill tells his story to Tom (Partridge is pointedly interested only in its ancillary elements, and he falls asleep before the important resolution of the old man's history). Mrs Fitzpatrick tells her story to Sophia. Both storytellers deliver 'elaborate negative analogies to the moral state of the listeners'.[74] Tom is outgoing, compassionate, optimistic, and full of the love of life. The Man of the Hill is reclusive, self-absorbed, pessimistic, and suspicious of everyone. Sophia is both socially conservative and independent-minded: unwilling to marry without her father's consent and yet unwilling to marry just any man of his choice. She is a loving woman whose desire, though physical, is informed and directed by her understanding of the moral nature of others, most relevantly Tom's and Blifil's. Mrs Fitzpatrick defies her family to marry the man of her choice, whom she has utterly misread; after the failure of the marriage, she is willing to become, and to continue to be, the secret mistress of her good friend's husband.

In addition to obvious differences, Tom and the Man of the Hill have surprisingly much in common. Both have loving fathers from whom they are separated in young manhood, mothers who in different ways abandon them, greedy brothers who dislike them, and imprudent early loves. Both have close calls with the law. Both are born in the country, and both are well educated; both travel to London, the corrupting city. Both are embarrassed by the want of money. Both their mothers die, and both enjoy reconciliations with their fathers. Both are earnest members of the Church of England and anti-Jacobites. The remarkable similarities make the differences between them seem all the greater.[75]

There is no need to detail the obvious here: the Man of the Hill is defeated by a life in some ways reminiscent of Tom's. But the old man has none of our hero's energetic optimism and resilience. Having been reclaimed by his father, he rejects the idea of marriage and turns away from society altogether. Apart from the obvious conclusion – active goodness and faith in humanity is right, and withdrawal from society because it seems evil is wrong – are there matters to consider in the Man of the Hill's story? It is in ways tedious, a history that from its beginning can only provide the nominal reasons for what we already know (that the old recluse is an utterly despairing misanthrope). But the episode in fact illuminates the moral and social distance between Tom and the Man of the Hill.

His story is more an exemplum than a biography, its precept being that humans are so treacherous that living away from them is the only reasonable course. Tom briskly counters this Bad-Angel view, pointing out that the recluse has taken 'the Character of Mankind from the worst and basest among them . . . [which is] as unjust as to assert, that Air is a nauseous and unwholesome Element, because we find it so in a Jakes' (*TJ*, VIII, xv, 485). The vulgar energy and scorn of Tom's counterargument, unusually if not uniquely robust for him, epitomizes his complete rejection of the old man's view. At the same time, he continues to behave with deference and charity towards one who is almost too much like him, except for the crucial difference of worldview, intensified by the context.

The Man of the Hill seems consciously to explain his misanthropy by telling the story of the mistress and the friend who betrayed him. But he seems also to suspect, however subliminally, that his predicament may be accounted for in another way. A current of verbal clues running through his tale suggests his sense that a malevolent Fortune may account for his hard times. 'It was my Misfortune to fall', the old man says early in his tale (*TJ*, VIII, xi, 453). Thereafter, he refers to himself as an 'unfortunate Pupil' (*TJ*, VIII, xi, 454), one whose 'mind [has] grown as desperate as [his] Fortune' (*TJ*, VIII, xi, 455), one who begins 'to reflect . . . on the Misfortunes . . . [he] had brought on [him]self' (*TJ*, VIII, xi, 457). He also claims it was his 'Fortune to be destitute' (*J*, VIII, xii, 461), complains of 'all the Freaks which Fortune, or rather the Dice, played' (*TJ*, VIII, xii, 465) at the gaming table, observes that study hardens 'the Mind against the capricious Invasions of Fortune' (*TJ*, VIII, xiii, 470), and says finally that 'Fortune at length took Pity on me' (*TJ*, VIII, xiv, 479). I have not quoted quite all of the old man's references to the goddess.

Sometimes the recluse feels responsible for the bad turns of Fortune, but more often he seems to attribute them to an intrusive force over which he has no control. Is this an unconscious exercise in self-exculpation? One may suppose that if Fortune is responsible for his predicament, then he himself is not. Tom's final words on the subject do not exactly clarify the matter, though they may seem to place the ultimate responsibility on the old man. 'You might [have continued to believe "Men worthy of the highest Friendship, and Women of the highest Love"] if you had not been *unfortunate*, I will venture to say *incautious* in placing your affections' (*TJ*, VIII, xv, 485; my italics). Tom's statement is ambiguous. Is he just being polite? Does *'incautious'* displace *'unfortunate'* or only qualify it? It is hard to be sure about this dense play on 'Fortune' in the Man of the Hill's tale. Its lexical uncertainty (its providential untidiness) contrasts sharply with the clarity of Tom's fortune, which is, on the surface of the action, almost unbelievably bad until it becomes almost unbelievably good. Are we left rather too much with the sense that Tom is blessed and the old man is not? Or perhaps we should understand that the world of *Tom Jones* is so created that Tom's deliverance is the providential celebration of his largeness of soul, which mere circumstance cannot trammel. Would it be only perverse to suggest that if the Man of the Hill had somehow allowed the narrator to tell his story, he would have enjoyed the blessings of good fortune and escaped misanthropy?

Sophia and Harriet also have much in common. They are cousins, members of the same family; they have lived together with their aunt, Mrs Western; both are young and beautiful; both are at odds with their family over the choice of a husband; both flee tyrannical males; and when they meet fortuitously on the road and exchange recent histories, both omit any mention of the men who engage their hearts. As is true of the similarities between Tom and the Man of the Hill, those between Sophia and Harriet serve to intensify our sense of the differences, which are comically heralded by the nicknames the young women had earlier given each other: Miss *Graveairs* (Sophia) and Miss *Giddy* (Harriet).

Though Sophia is a much more passionate young woman than 'graveairs' suggests, her understanding and judgment are good, and her behaviour is prudent, given her circumstances. She acts so as to maximize her chances for fulfilment, which in the universe of *Tom Jones* is possible only if her family approves her marriage to the man she loves (a long shot). She escapes from her father with Tom very much on her mind, but her immediate reason for leaving home is to avoid marriage to Blifil. As I implied earlier, she is remarkable for having taken an accurate measure of both young men, and it is she alone who does so. Allworthy, who has watched the two from infancy and should be in a better position to judge, is hopelessly misled. Sophia is the penetrant one. She is also self-reliant, loving, faithful, honest and fair-minded.

By contrast, Harriet is taken in by Fitzpatrick, a blockhead whose good looks and superficial charm blind her to his primitive stupidity until it is too late. Imprudent in rushing into marriage, she continues to act imprudently in her efforts to escape it, relying on the 'protection' of a married lover. She not only makes a bad marriage for herself, but she contributes to the primal laxity of another. She is besides unscrupulous in trying to regain a place in the Western family by betraying Sophia's whereabouts to her aunt and uncle. Finally, she attempts to seduce Tom, or at least she aims at him. Clearly like Sophia in certain ways, she is also her cousin's antithesis, socially and morally.[76]

The episodes that compare and contrast Tom and Sophia with the Man of the Hill and Harriet are not exactly short, but both are compressed within the greater narrative, and they are essentially uninterrupted. Moreover their contexts, in addition to showing us characters who contrast with Tom and Sophia, are, as I have said, redactions of subjects treated expansively in the larger narrative. And finally the blessings of good fortune are withheld from them – by a narrator piqued at their independent storytelling? At some level of the reader's mind this concentrated duplication seems likely to resonate with what has already occurred in the novel, just as it may anticipate what is yet to come, generating comparisons that intensify and clarify understanding. For example, the old Man of the Hill's family is divided, the mother from the father, the brothers from each other; and its members are allied (the mother and older brother, the father and younger brother) and the pairs are bitterly opposed, as if primordially. Even if we recognize this symmetrical family disruption as a 'natural' condition, we also recognize that the Man of the Hill's family is 'imperfect'. I suspect Fielding would be pleased if we were to imagine and prefer a family in which such divisions and inimical alliances did not exist. Not the Allworthys, the Westerns, the Blifils, the Seagrims, the Partridges or, later, the Nightingales constitute such a family. It is left for Tom and Sophia and their children to achieve the ideal, and in a subordinate way, as we shall see, Nightingale and Nancy Miller as well, in a future beyond the novel's limits.

The narrative of *Tom Jones* begins with the end of a perfect marriage, Allworthy's; and it ends with the beginning of a perfect one, Tom's and Sophia's. The fulfilment of these marriages – the actual living of them – pre-date and post-date the action, though we have strong evidence of their satisfying nature, especially Tom's and Sophia's. With a few possible exceptions, the many other marriages and aborted courtships in the novel are one way or another blighted. The relation between the sexes, the basis of a flourishing society in Fielding's world, turns out to be the locus of its dysfunction.

Bridget Allworthy and Summer, Tom's parents, experience a short illicit liaison (about which we know almost nothing) before Summer's untimely death from smallpox; then Bridget marries Captain Blifil, a nasty fortune hunter who becomes a tyrannical husband. Dr Blifil, who introduces his brother into the Allworthy household, is himself disqualified as Bridget's suitor because he has a wife from whom he is separated for reasons unknown. Mrs Partridge foolishly bears false witness against her husband with premeditated malice. Jenny Jones, though she calls herself Mrs Waters, is not formally married to Waters, and she is no better than she should be: she seduces Tom, although not without his help. Molly Seagrim, who also seduces Tom, allows him to believe that he has seduced her; shortly thereafter she grants Square her favours for money, sharing the income with her mother, who would not otherwise permit the use of a room for their trysts. Squire Western has been an abominable husband, as Sophia, who takes her deceased mother's part, well knows. Mrs Western makes a fool of herself in a flirtation with the much younger Fitzpatrick, who courts and marries her niece without the family's consent, with results that include her sustained liaison with a married nobleman and her incidental attempt to seduce Tom. Tom prostitutes himself to Lady Bellaston, primarily to locate Sophia; the demi-rep's response to Tom's manipulative proposal of marriage makes it clear that she abhors the very idea of marital union, which she refers to as 'that monstrous Animal a Husband and a Wife' (*TJ*, XV, ix, 820). Young Blifil, moved only by the twin passions of greed and hate, courts Sophia against her will; assisted by Lady Bellaston, Lord Fellamar assaults her with unwanted attention too. Nightingale impregnates Nancy Miller and then writes to tell her he must obey his father, who insists upon his paying court to a 'Lady of Fortune' (*TJ*, XIV, vi, 763). After his disgrace and banishment, young Blifil converts to Methodism 'in hopes of marrying a very rich Widow of that sect' (*TJ*, XVIII, xiii, 980). And then there are the tyrannical elders who coerce their children into loveless marriages of convenience (the Westerns and the Nightingales) and the scheming women (Lady Bellaston and Mrs Fitzpatrick) who manipulate and sacrifice others in the marriage game for their own selfish reasons.

It is in contrast to this collection of destructive relations between the sexes, at the level of seduction, courtship and marriage, that we measure the ideal union between Tom and Sophia and its attendant social consequences.[77] The other good marriages in the novel have a negligible impact, for various reasons. Mrs Miller tells us she lived for five years with her husband in a state of perfect happiness (*TJ*, XIV, v, 758), but we know her only as a widow. Young Nightingale's uncle enjoyed a perfect marriage for 25 years, but we know him only as a widower; besides, he is so stubbornly bent on having his own way that we may suppose the marriage was 'perfect' only because of his wife's 'good Humour, of which she possessed a very large Share' (*TJ*, XIV, viii, 775). Harriet Nightingale may enjoy a happy marriage, but the narrator discloses what little we know about it largely to characterize her father's parental blundering. Her cousin Nightingale's marriage to Nancy Miller is indeed a happy one, but the narrator subordinates it in special ways to Tom's and Sophia's.

The episode of the Gypsy King, which presents marriage as fundamental to social order and the desecration of marriage as an occasion for the swift administration of justice, is an emblem of *Tom Jones*. Tom's and Sophia's union, which contrasts with the marital shambles of the rest of the novel, exemplifies what marriage should be. But unlike the swift justice of the Gypsy King, it is not offered as a correction of the terrible state of affairs. The narrator treats it as an ideal ending of the lovers' story. We readers may be made to feel that it is essential to its closure, a fact that places it beyond the limits of the narrative for the most part, 'ever after'.

The novel includes another marriage, however, which is indeed a correction of a relation between the sexes gone awry. Tom, like the Gypsy King, intervenes swiftly and pragmatically to correct its imminent failure. In an extended analogue of the Gypsy King's control of marital justice, Tom takes action on behalf of the Millers and, in the long run, on behalf of young Nightingale as well, to bring about a fulfilling marriage. Having read Nightingale's letter of farewell to Nancy, Tom comforts and reassures Mrs Miller; persuades Nightingale, well-intentioned but weak, to reconsider his decision to leave his sweetheart, by then pregnant; lies on behalf of Love, by telling Nightingale's father that his son is already married, in an effort to get him to accept their relation; and when Nightingale flees, drunk, from his suddenly coercive uncle, gets him to bed and next morning sees 'his good Offices to [Mrs Miller] and her Family brought to a happy Conclusion' (*TJ*, XV, viii, 815). In the midst of his own pre-marital troubles, Tom does not lose sight of the pre-marital troubles of others. Indeed it may be that the obviously sincere charity that moves him to help his friends to marry relieves his own frustrating inability to bring about his own marriage to Sophia. By helping them, he helps himself. Fortune or Providence plays some part in Tom's efforts to unite Nightingale and Nancy Miller, but his success is essentially the culmination of his efforts on behalf of a good marriage.

It is a piquant irony that the narrator should elect Partridge, along with Tom, to link the 'novel proper' to the episode of the Gypsy King on the subject of marital justice. We know Partridge as an innocent husband wrongly found guilty of adultery by Allworthy. But among the gypsies Partridge indeed becomes an adulterer, exonerated by the king because he has been seduced, while drunk, by a wife operating on her husband's fiscal behalf. That the Gypsy King has greater perspicacity than Allworthy need hardly be mentioned. A more important point is that Fielding, through his narrator, amuses us and himself with a comic moral contrast: Partridge-the-innocent found guilty, and Partridge-the-guilty found innocent. At the same time, he implies that the proper administration of justice requires, apart from a knowledge of the law, both a keen sense of right and wrong and the capacity to gather, sift and evaluate evidence, case by case.[78]

The relations between the sexes are at the heart of *Tom Jones*, and Tom (with Sophia and the good, sometimes blind, Allworthy) is the unofficial minister of Good Marriage. In this role, his function as the Gypsy King's analogue is only the most explicit of his works. His own unbroken focus on Sophia, despite the obstacles between him and his heart's desire, is more longlived and more important. In his lengthy quest for her, Tom is sometimes drawn or tempted into error, most prominently in his affair with Lady Bellaston. But his decision to leave the Queen of the Fairies, like his silent rejection of Mrs Fitzpatrick, shows us clearly where his heart is. Tom is also shown elsewhere to be the champion of that rarity in *Tom Jones*, a good marriage. For example, the terms of Arabella Hunt's proposal to him, like the terms of his kind refusal (*TJ*, XV, xi, 826–7), identify his special status in relation to marriage. The rich Widow Hunt recognizes his worth beyond male attractiveness, and he justifies her appraisal by telling her the truth about his commitment to Sophia (without naming her, of course). His assistance to the inept robber Enderson, 'who dares venture every thing to preserve his Wife and Children' (*TJ*, XIII, x, 727), is another example of his concern for marriage and its stable continuance.

When Tom and Sophia leave us at the end of their story, we find that as a complement to their own rich marriage they enjoy the marriage Tom worked diligently to bring about. Nightingale's father, we learn, has bought his son an estate 'in the Neighbourhood of Jones, where the young Gentleman, his Lady, Mrs Miller, and the little Daughter reside, and the most agreeable Intercourse subsists between the two Families' (*TJ*, XVIII, xiii, 980). Along with his own marriage to Sophia, the narrative carries the 'Conclusion' of Tom's 'good Offices', the Nightingales' marriage, into the realm of tranquil permanence: life beyond the book's ending. There the hero and heroine are blessed in their own marriage. At the same time they enjoy the life of the marriage Tom has wrought.

* * *

Amelia (1751), Fielding's last novel, 'was by its author intended to present a picture of durable matrimony and the beauty of virtue in woman'.[79] Though it is indeed a book about a woman, Amelia, as the title certainly makes clear, it has many interests. As Battestin points out, *Amelia's* subjects range 'from "the state of matrimony", that smallest unit of the polity, to the English "constitution" itself'.[80] Providence, fortune, love, barren lust, seduction, goodness, marriage, the family (husbands and wives, parents and children, brothers and sisters), friendship, the doctrine of the passions, religion, the clergy, politics, the government, the law, the military, debtor's prison, philosophy, education, medicine, the social classes, adultery, gaming, duelling, drinking, and theory of the novel are among the most obvious subjects in *Amelia*. This goldmine of opinion (often Fielding's own, delivered by Dr Harrison or another sympathetic character) was its author's favourite book.[81] Though fascinating as a source of his views, *Amelia* has been less well received than his other novels, from the time of its publication to the present.

It is an obvious but important point that *Amelia* is 'more serious and less high-spirited' than his other works.[82] One wonders why Fielding chose to write the novel without his gifted comic pen. Perhaps the serious tone is owing to his own troubles during the period of composition, or his wish to give the world his own version of Richardson's tragic Clarissa, or his earnest desire to embed the narrative in a context of social protest and reform.[83] Whatever the reason, *Amelia* does not have the comic vitality of *Joseph Andrews* or *Tom Jones*. And the absence of that vitality seems to have a negative consequence beyond our personal regret that Fielding has abandoned his most attractive and masterful literary mode.

It has been argued that many of the scenes include romance elements which, because they are realistically rather than comically treated, become sentimental.[84] How seriously Fielding drew on romance in the composition of *Amelia* is debatable, but few readers would deny that the novel's tender scenes, lacking comic treatment, are very sentimental. In the second chapter of Book III, for example, Booth recapitulates to Miss Matthews the long exchange with his pregnant wife, just before he leaves for military service on Gibraltar; though we are told '*Amelia* spoke but little [on that occasion]; indeed more Tears than Words dropt from her', she in fact speaks torrents, well represented by this short burst: '"Farewel, farewel forever: for I shall never, never see you more"' (*Amelia*, III, ii, 103–4). Later, while the couple enjoyed an ill-grounded expectation of preferment from Mrs Ellison's cousin, the noble Lord, Booth's and Amelia's 'Bosoms burnt with the warmest Sentiments of Gratitude' (*Amelia*, V, ii, 198). Amelia visits her husband during his last imprisonment:

> When *Booth* found himself alone with his Wife, and had vented the first violence of his Rapture in Kisses and Embraces, he looked tenderly at her, and cried, 'Is it possible, *Amelia*, is it possible you can have this Goodness to follow such a Wretch as me to such a Place as this – or do you come to upbraid me with my Guilt, and to sink me down to that Perdition I so justly deserve?' (*Amelia*, XII, ii, 497)

Such verbal excesses occur throughout *Amelia*.

The very characters of Amelia and Booth may also contribute
to the novel's problematic nature. After a long acquaintance, we
leave the heroine as we found her, an unexceptionable woman.
She is too good to be true; and her character is so constructed
that she can neither grow nor diminish in important ways. A
completed soul before we meet her, Amelia has no interior problems: hers are all outside herself. We may wish her well, but we
are not likely to identify ourselves with her deeply. In fact certain instances of her goodness may make us impatient if we do
more than accept them at face value. Just why does she conceal
her knowledge of Booth's infidelity? Is it only love for her husband that makes her a mute forgiving wife? Is the concealed
knowledge valuable as a reinforcement of her sense of herself?
Is it a source of strength and power? And after she has pawned
almost all her possessions to raise the £50 Booth needs to pay
off a foolishly contracted gambling debt that threatens him with
imprisonment, how can she possibly defer to his plan to use the
money to buy preferment from a stranger: 'In the Morning *Booth*
communicated the Matter to *Amelia*, who told him she would
not presume to advise him in an Affair, of which he was so
much the better Judge' (*Amelia*, XI, v, 476). Perhaps one does
best to recognize in Amelia an ideal woman conceived and nour-
ished by a longing man's imagination.[85]

Booth with his palpable imperfections is in many ways a poor
husband and father, despite his love for wife and children. Bad
judgment is his hallmark. His very weaknesses may engage our
sympathy for a while, but early on it becomes possible to grow
impatient with him, or at least to wonder how he can behave as
he does. For example, he and Miss Matthews offer each other
their sexual autobiographies in a mutual seduction (conscious
on her part, unconscious on his?) which takes up the first three
books, over one-quarter of the novel. By the time of their adultery, we know he loves Amelia deeply and that he ought to be
aware of the vixen-danger Miss Matthews represents. That his
highly imprudent and illicit sexual indulgence lasts 'A Whole
Week' (*Amelia*, IV, ii, 154) is notable, given the depth and per-
sistence of his guilt thereafter. Would such a Superego have deferred to Libido for so long a time without efficient interruption?

Fielding's narrator requires us to suppose it would; he expects
us to make allowances for the fact that Miss Matthews, an old
acquaintance, is very attractive, and that Booth, young and full

of energy, finds himself alone with her, a more than willing partner. Our extended exposure to Booth, whom we see as a polite male listener to a bitter and vindictive woman's sexual history, as an emotionally intense autobiographer of his own loving marriage, and as an adulterer who repeats his infidelity for a week, leaves us with a character whose conflicting tendencies are hard to reconcile with the attractive strong-man-manqué the narrator wants us to see in him. Booth often shows himself to be a good man, but his repeated errors indicate that he is missing more than prudence, which to be developed over time requires the innate capacity to read people and circumstances accurately. He often lacks good sense, a failing that makes both Amelia and Dr Harrison essential as Booth's complements.

Another problem is that his conversion from belief in the control of human actions by the moment's dominant passion to a belief in a benevolent Christian Providence has seemed to many inadequately foreshadowed. The matter is complicated in that Booth often behaves with brave charity, and he renounces essentially anti-Christian positions at two crucial junctures. His first arrest, for example, results from his intervention on behalf of a helpless man being beaten by two others (*Amelia*, I, ii, 24). He repudiates Miss Matthews's Mandevilianism because it attributes the passion of love to 'the base Impulses of Pride and Fear. Whereas, it is as certain that Love exists in the Mind of Man, as that its opposite Hatred doth' (*Amelia*, III, v, 115). And he rejects the stoical position of a fellow prisoner for essentially the same reason, that it omits the possibility of charity in its doctrine of reasoned self-sufficiency: 'we reason from our Heads, but act from our Hearts', Booth says in denying stoicism's 'Efficacy in Practice' (*Amelia*, VIII, x, 350). By no means as clear-sighted as Tom Jones, Booth is nevertheless a good man to the extent of his ability to judge well.

The issue is not whether Booth is ripe for conversion, however; it is rather that Fielding gives us no clues as to his state of mind in that regard until Dr Harrison visits him in prison very late in the novel and learns for the first time that Booth has had doubts as to the truth of Christianity, after having heard that his young friend has been converted by 'Dr. *Barrow's* Works, which then lay on the Table before him' (*Amelia*, XII, v, 511). We have no trouble accepting Booth's claim about his earlier state, which we recognize as accurate: 'Indeed I never was a rash Disbeliever; my chief Doubt was founded on this, that as Men appeared to me to act entirely from their Passions, their Actions could have neither Merit nor Demerit' (*Amelia*, XII, v, 511). Nevertheless he surprises us because we do not have evidence for the interior transformation that alone could allow us to appreciate his conversion, from doubter to Christian, for the significant thing it is.

The late discovery of the false will that leads to Amelia's and Booth's deliverance from poverty, the chief obstacle to their happiness, is also unforeshadowed. One may well feel it makes for an ending appropriate to comedy, not to the serious treatment of life we find in *Amelia*. But given the rich Christian texture of the novel, which by this time has included Booth's conversion, it is also possible to accept it as Dr Harrison does: 'Good Heaven! how wonderful is thy Providence' (*Amelia*, XII, vi, 517). On this view, it is Heaven (and not Fielding, the inveterate comedian, here inept) which enables the Booths to leave the evil city for the country where they live out their happy marriage.

One may see *Amelia* as a failed novel; one may at the same time think of it as a work in which Fielding takes off the comic mask and struggles to assess the world in which evil and its knaves flourish while the good are battered and left with little chance of enjoying life's most precious possibility: a shared geniality. For Fielding, marriage is the obvious locus of such geniality. Deeply in love and married before we meet them, the Booths are tried by poverty, geographical separation, adultery and seduction; Booth and, through him, Amelia are abused by unjust Justice in a Round-house, before Thrasher's bench, in Newgate Prison, and in Bondum's sponging-house; Amelia is betrayed by her sister, and both she and Booth are betrayed by friends. The dark social context in which the Booths' marriage is tested includes in addition unsavoury attorneys, bailiffs, turnkeys, surgeons, physicians, thieves, pawnbrokers and parasitic lords and ladies; it also includes bleak images of the underclasses, half-pay officers, betrayed women, hack-writers, and cardsharps; abuses in institutions like the army, the Church and the government; and bad practices (like touching for prison favours or for preferment, and pimping for relatives) also figure in the terrible world the Booths inhabit.

Like Sophia's and Tom's, the Booths' loving and potentially happy marriage is contrasted with numerous desecrated alliances:

those in which Miss Matthews figures, with Hebbers, Booth and
James; the Jameses'; the Atkinsons' (and before Mrs Atkinson's
marriage to the sergeant, her seduction as Mrs Bennet by the
noble Lord); and the Trents'. It is enough to say about them that
excepting the Atkinsons' they carnalize relations between the sexes,
to which one may add for emphasis that Mrs James pimps for
her husband (at his insistence) and that Mr Trent sells his wife's
favours. In addition to contrasting with the Booths' marriage,
these alliances, including the Atkinsons', actually invade it in
complex ways, and so become part of the dense social context
in which the Booths struggle. I shall here touch on only the most
obvious of these. Miss Matthews, intent on revenge over having
lost Billy, tries to destroy the Booths' marriage; and Colonel James
and the noble Lord utterly disregard its well-being in their lust
for Amelia. Trent, heavily complicit in the Lord's efforts to seduce
Amelia, lends Booth £50 of his patron's money in order to ruin
him, and then he urges Booth to allow Amelia to meet the nobleman: ' "D—n me if I don't wish his Lordship loved my Wife as
well as he doth yours, I promise you I would trust her Virtue;
and if he should get the better of it, I should have People of
Fashion enough to keep me in Countenance" ' (*Amelia*, X, vii,
441). Even Mrs Atkinson, who saves Amelia by warning her of
the Lord's true intentions and by taking Amelia's place at the
masquerade, endangers the Booths' marriage by risking Amelia's
reputation in order to secure a commission for her husband, the
sergeant (*Amelia*, X, viii, 442–8).

In a way the hostile world the Booths encounter is the same
one Fielding lives in. I do not refer primarily to the autobiographical elements in *Amelia*, though these are important.[86] I wish
rather to suggest that the novel's vision of a fallen world in which
good people are rare and evil abounds, and in which frightened
hope must look to love and a benevolent Providence for deliverance, is Fielding's own. Not that he would have us turn away,
passive, making no effort to reform people and institutions: in
fact, he had just published the masterly *An Enquiry into the Causes
of the Late Increase of Robbers, &c. with some Proposals for Remedy-
ing this Growing Evil* (6 March 1751). But I suspect that at some
level of mind he half believed that the general will of humankind, far from benevolent, is too intent on self-gratification for
the wisest message on behalf of social change to get much of a
hearing.

Fielding, and Amelia and Booth, repelled by the morally bank-
rupt world epitomized by the London he paints, look elsewhere
for refuge. For all three its immediate locus is human love. Fielding
has his Charlotte, kept alive, idealized, as Amelia; and the Booths
have each other. But they care about an eternal refuge as well.
They all need assurances from Heaven that the future will
include them. Dr Harrison, the intermediary Word, fulfils the
need. He carries a knowledge of the past, and he is the incarna-
tion of an informed faith in an eternal future. Though he can be
tedious in his displays of learning – as are Booth and Mrs Atkinson,
incidentally – his actions show him to be a thoroughly honest
herald of Providence, even when his judgment is hasty, as for
example it is when he has Booth arrested (*Amelia*, VII, x, 307).
Harrison is Amelia's 'father' and teacher, and he is Booth's
protector and guide; he is also Fielding the author's religious
spokesman in *Amelia*, and the representative of Fielding the man's
religious convictions as well.

Unfortunately for Fielding, his last novel was not well received.[87]
I doubt that he seriously expected his disclosure of evils committed by humankind and its institutions to result in reform or
even in the beginnings of reform. Clear-eyed satirists like him
are passionate in skewering and displaying vice and folly, but
hardly sanguine about effecting quick changes for the better. They
are likely to know the world too well. Gulliver, writing to his
cousin Sympson, makes the point ironically: 'Instead of seeing a
full stop put to all abuses and corruptions, . . . as I had reason
to expect: behold after above six months warning, I cannot learn
that my book hath produced one single effect according to my
intentions.'[88] It was less Fielding the reformer who was disappointed by the poor reception of his 'favourite child', *Amelia*,
than it was Fielding the novelist, who had exposed himself by
stepping out from behind the comic mask.

The voices of praise were few; Censure missed no chance to
speak. In *The Covent-Garden Journal*, No. 8, Fielding pleads for
his daughter *Amelia* before the Court of Censorial Enquiring, where
he concludes with the promise to write no more novels:

> I do not think my Child is entirely free from Faults. I know
> nothing human that is so; but surely she doth not deserve the
> Rancour with which she hath been treated by the Public. How-
> ever, it is not my Intention, at present, to make my Defence;

but shall submit to a Compromise, which hath been always allowed in this Court in all Prosecutions for Dulness. I do, therefore, solemnly declare to you, Mr. Censor, that I will trouble the World no more with any Children of mine by the same Muse.[89]

Fielding the novelist kept his word.

4
The Final Years: 1751–4

Fielding's last years were typical of his earlier life, full of energy well used, both in his work and in the pleasures and pains of living. Despite severe illness and other troubles, he never lost his zest for the day or his sense of humour. Nevertheless the vision which accounts for the serious regard of a wide range of social issues in *Amelia* also controls his last important works: *An Enquiry into the Causes of the Late Increase of Robbers* (1751), *The Covent-Garden Journal* (1752), *Examples of the Interposition of Providence in the Detection and Punishment of Murder* (1752), *A Proposal for Making an Effectual Provision for the Poor* (1753), *A Clear State of the Case of Elizabeth Canning* (1753), the revised *Life of Mr. Jonathan Wild the Great* (1754), and *The Journal of a Voyage to Lisbon* (1755). Though Fielding was never a pessimist, his view of the world took on a sober colouring as he kept watch over the human condition. His intense vision of things and his implicit belief that it was his responsibility to observe and to comment on what he saw were mutually nourishing aspects of his deepest being.

His life, private and professional, was full and demanding during these final years, sometimes painful. As was noted in the first chapter, his own health was failing. He suffered considerable discomfort from the gout, and he was ultimately to experience the symptoms of cirrhosis of the liver.[1] In addition, he suffered the loss of two children and three sisters. His sister Catherine and his only son by Charlotte, Henry, had died in the summer of 1750, and in the winter of 1750–1 sisters Ursula and Beatrice died too. And in May 1753, his five-month old daughter Louisa died. It is a tribute to the human spirit that he was able to continue to serve efficiently as magistrate as well as to write some of his best essays on social problems during this trying period.

From about the time of the riots involving Bosavern Penlez, London had become notoriously unsafe. Things reached the point that robbers boldly attacked men and women on the streets, choosing the fashionably dressed among them as most likely to be carrying money and jewelry. In response to this naked disregard of the law, Fielding organized the city's first police force, led by the High Constable, Saunders Welch; they came to be known as the 'Bow Street Runners', men trained and organized to respond to a crime quickly by using their knowledge of the underworld to discover and arrest the criminals in the shortest possible time.[2] By the winter of 1753, the rate of crime in Fielding's jurisdiction had been dramatically reduced.

During these years, Fielding was also occupied with that other aspect of his magistracy: the hundreds of cases that required his close attention from the bench in the Bow Street court. There he questioned persons accused of crimes, sifting evidence carefully and patiently before deciding on the appropriate action, to rebuke, indict, sentence or dismiss. Fielding gives us a good sense of both elements of his work – the active pursuit of criminals and his diligence and propriety as a legal examiner – in his Introduction to *The Journal of a Voyage to Lisbon*:

> Tho' my health was now reduced to the last extremity, I continued to act with the utmost vigour against these villains; in examining whom, and in taking depositions against them, I have often spent whole days, nay sometimes whole nights, especially when there was any difficulty in procuring sufficient evidence to convict them; which is a very common case in street-robberies, even when the guilt of the party is sufficient to satisfy the most tender conscience.[3]

It was not until January 1754 that Fielding, too ill to carry on, gave up his work as Court Justice, leaving his blind half-brother John, who had in 1751 been appointed by Lord Chancellor Hardwicke to the Commission of the Peace for Westminster, to succeed him.[4] By that time it was not only Fielding's efficient policing of criminals and his practice of scrupulous inquiry from the bench that had given new authority and dignity to the office of justice of the peace; so had his reasoned discussion of contemporary problems then being addressed by social and criminal legislation. As will become clear, his *Enquiry into the Causes of the late Increase of Robbers* was an especially effective sounding board for such legislation. Before I discuss this and his other late works briefly, a word about Fielding's attempt to improve his ever-precarious financial condition is in order.

In February 1749/50, Fielding and his half-brother John, joined perhaps by other shareholders, opened a business that about a year later came to be known as the Universal Register Office. Its purpose was to provide the services of a commercial go-between by listing, for a fee, buyers and sellers, servants in need of work and prospective employers, tutors and pupils, and numerous others in need of information that would enable business transactions.[5] Fielding, who was probably the major author of *A Plan of the Universal Register Office*, explains succinctly, 'the Design of [the Office] is to bring the World as it were together into one Place'.[6] Johnson praises this 'general mart of intelligence' in *Rambler*, No. 105, though not without satiric reservations; the accuracy of his view that the Universal Register Office would serve a useful purpose is borne out by its success during Fielding's few remaining years and for some time after his death.[7] Fielding's will, probably drawn up in the spring of 1754, directs his executor to sell all his property and to buy annuities with the proceeds, except for his twenty shares in the Universal Register Office (probably because they yielded more income than another investment was likely to provide).[8]

An important literary by-product of the Universal Register Office was *The Covent-Garden Journal*, a periodical that had a run of 72 issues from 4 January until 25 November 1752, being published on Tuesdays and Saturdays until 4 July, and from that time on Saturday only until the end of the run.[9] The *Journal* was intended to carry advertisements for the Universal Register Office, and it did so. But it also allowed Fielding, who wrote most of its lead pieces, to speak in a moral voice on social and moral issues as 'Sir Alexander Drawcansir, Knt. Censor of Great Britain'. The voice is typically witty and learned, and though it generally steers clear of politics, it is highly topical, 'strikingly rooted in the everyday life of mid-century London and unusually reflective of the most circumstantial details of the contemporary scene'.[10] In addition to the Censor, we meet Fielding the Magistrate, describing his work on the bench, and so enriching the topicality of the *Journal*.

About one-quarter of the *Journal's* numbers include a section entitled 'Proceedings at the Court of Censorial Enquiry'. As I pointed out in the preceding chapter, it is in this section of the *Journal*, No. 9, that Fielding defends himself against the charge that *Amelia* is dull and promises to write no more novels. The

indictment of *Amelia* is, like almost all the other pieces in the
Journal, comically treated. But also like almost all the other pieces
there, it registers the deep sense of something profoundly wrong
with the taste of the age, which for Fielding signified that something was profoundly wrong with the morality of the age, with
its faulted perception of the human condition, and its wasteful
use of life. Despite its Scriblerian manner – its irony and humour
– the *Journal*, like his late work generally, reveals Fielding's deep
concern with the ways of the world.

An Enquiry into the Causes of the Late Increase of Robbers is
Fielding's most ambitious social commentary. His discussion of
the causes of the increase is full and competent, rather than original, informed as it is by conventional attitudes towards the English
Constitution, the nation's social hierarchy, and mercantile economic
theory. Fielding's opening discussion of the 'little understood'
Constitution provides him with a basis for claiming that something is terribly wrong with England's social fabric. The Constitution, he tells us, ideally comprises:

> the original and fundamental Law of the Kingdom, from whence
> all Powers are derived, and by which they are circumscribed;
> all legislative and executive Authority; all those municipal Provi-
> sions which are commonly called *The Laws*; and, lastly, the Customs,
> Manners, and Habits of the People. These, joined together, do,
> I apprehend, form the Political, as the several Members of the
> Body, the animal Oeconomy, with the Humours and habit,
> compose that which is called the Natural Constitution.[11]

Simply put, Fielding believed the Constitution should be a synergy of the operations of law, custom and human behaviour.

He argues, however, that the synergy has been disrupted. The
once stable social hierarchy, in which the great population of
poor commoners was subordinate to the sanctified authority of
the few, has broken down. In Fielding's view the commonalty
have deserted their pre-ordained and fixed social role, which is
to provide the labour necessary to the health of the nation. For
their own good and for the good of England, they must be made
to return to their fixed place in the hierarchy. To the late twentieth century, such a view may seem insensitive to the rights of
the vast majority of the people, but it was widely accepted in
Fielding's day. Like Dr Johnson and others who understood society

to be in need of such 'subordination', Fielding could disdain a corrupt nobility and sympathize with the suffering poor; but he nevertheless saw no way of maintaining social stability except by stabilizing social inequality. In some earlier, happier time in English history, Fielding says, there had been a productive social balance among 'the Nobility, the Gentry, and the Commonalty'; all three have come to disregard the limits appropriate to their classes, but the greatest harm to society as a whole results from the abuses of the most numerous, the 'lower orders'.[12] 'The Power of the Commonalty hath received an immense Addition; and . . . the Civil Power having not increased, but decreased, in the same Proportion, is not able to govern them.'[13]

Fielding was familiar with mercantile doctrine, the leading economic theory of the day. One of its most important precepts was that a favourable balance of trade with other countries was essential to England's fiscal health, and that to maintain such a balance, exports must be inexpensively priced: that is, manufactured by a cheap labour force working at fixed prices. Perhaps as a result of such mercantile practice, England enjoyed a favourable balance of trade in the early eighteenth century, and dozens of items of luxury from abroad filled the shops of the nation. Had the cheap labour force done its job well? If so, it is ironic that Fielding should have attributed the seduction of the 'Commonalty' away from their proper roles to England's increasing prosperity: 'Nothing hath wrought such an Alteration in this Order of People, as the Introduction of Trade. This hath indeed given a new Face to the whole Nation, . . . more especially of the lower sort . . .; their Frugality [is changed] into Luxury; their Humility into Pride, and their Subjection into Equality.'[14]

Fielding makes plausible the view that the combination of 'the vast Torrent of Luxury which of late Years hath poured itself into this Nation', together with a large population of the unemployed or underemployed, in various ways has contributed to the increase in crime. Luxury leads the poor to financial distress, which leads to crime; society's failure to give the poor employment also leads to crime as an alternative source of income. In his search for a solution to the problem, he distinguishes between the consequences of an appetite for luxury among persons of fashion and fortune and that appetite among the commonalty. The wealthy merely kill time in voluptuousness, but the poor, for whom time is money, squander both, though they have little to spare of either.[15] By means of this distinction, he turns away from wealthy voluptuaries to his principal subject: the poor, for whom such luxuries as expensive public diversions, drunkenness and gaming tempt them both to debt and the avoidance of the labour they owe the nation, and ultimately tempt them to crime as well. Without omitting all censure of the self-indulgent wealthy, he uses the *Enquiry* primarily to consider what social policies and laws may return the commonalty to their proper place. Fielding's moral disapproval of their abdication of duty does not get in the way of his dispassionate treatment of the problem they represent. Despite his occasional ridicule of people of fashion in the *Enquiry*, Fielding pointedly avoids offending the powerful, whose authority is, in the view of the age, necessary to a healthy social hierarchy. Besides, he is aware that the voluptuous wealthy enrich the economy by spending, and that apart from setting a bad example, their excesses generally harm only themselves.[16]

In the longest section of the *Enquiry*, 'Of the Laws that relate to the Provision of the Poor', Fielding reviews the legislation and the reasons why it has proved ineffectual. His recommendations for putting the poor to work are likely to sound harsh to twentieth-century readers; nevertheless his realism and his command of legal detail lend authority to his suggestions even at the distance of 250 years. His argument combines a close knowledge of the law and his experience of the men and women who appeared before his bench in a display of informed pragmatism few could equal.

The paragraphs with which this section is concluded imply that Fielding was both confident of the accuracy of his judgments and suggestions, and doubtful that they would be quickly implemented. Indeed the subject matter of the later sections of the *Enquiry* all imply that the high rate of crime will continue, as a glance at their headings will suggest. Battestin points out that Fielding's older biographers, who thought him in some immediate way responsible for the criminal legislation of 1751–2, were incorrect; but he adds that there is 'every reason to believe that the *Enquiry* gave impetus to these reforms and that it served to identify areas in which specific legislation was needed'.[17]

Like robbery, murder increased dramatically during this period. It was a surprisingly rare crime in mid-eighteenth-century London, but during the six months between September 1751 and February

1752, the number of murders was more than double the average number per mayoral year.[18] Every reader of the *Enquiry* will be struck by the range of deterrents to crime Fielding recommends, from putting the poor to work to changing the nature of capital punishments from the raucous public affairs they were to solemn, private occasions, with the executions carried out immediately after sentencing, witnessed only by the judges, so as to deprive the condemned of the opportunity to play to the mob. Fielding's serious concern over the increase in crimes of physical violence, murder especially, led him to publish another work of deterrence, *Examples of the Interposition of Providence in the Detection and Punishment of Murder*, in April 1752. It is an anthology of 33 stories, culled from a range of classical, mediaeval, and seventeenth- and eighteenth-century sources, illustrating 'the divine vengeance against Murder', as Fielding tells us in his introductory essay.[19] In addition to collecting these examples – or perhaps having them collected – Fielding contributed an introduction and a conclusion to the *Interposition of Providence*.

The anthology is shaped to bring about both social and religious results, such as the deterrence of murder through the fear of God's wrath and the hope of salvation. The psychology on which Fielding relies is reminiscent of Dr Harrison's in *Amelia* (*Amelia*, XII, v, 511): 'if Men act, as I believe they do, from their Passions, it would be fair to conclude that Religion to be true which applies immediately to the strongest of those Passions, Hope and Fear'. One need read only the brief introduction to the *Interposition of Providence* and a few of the examples to recognize that Fielding's rhetorical formula is crude, probably because he intended it primarily for unsophisticated readers. Nevertheless, as his major novels in various ways imply, he himself believed in the immediate interposition of Divine providence; and indeed his mind 'reveals an increasingly religious bent in this period'.[20]

A Proposal for Making an Effectual Provision for the Poor may seem to be the fulfilment of an offer Fielding made in the *Enquiry*:

> Thus have I endeavoured to give the Reader a general Idea of the Laws which relate to this single Point of employing the Poor; and as well as I am able to discern, of their Defects, and the Reasons of those Defects. I have likewise given some Hints for the Cure, and have presumed to offer a Plan, which, in my humble Opinion, would effectually answer every Purpose desired.[21]

But in fact the plan he offers in the *Proposal* is not an extension of the explicit suggestions he makes in an *Enquiry*, which turn on improving the administration of the existing system of parish poor-laws; central to suggestions in the *Proposal* is the recommendation for large workhouses, with jurisdictions that exceed parish limits.[22]

One cannot say whether Fielding favoured the workhouse scheme even while he discussed the defects of parish poor-laws and their administration in the *Enquiry*, but whenever he began to formulate the workhouse plan, he aligned the *Proposal* with the House of Commons resolutions of June 1751 in adopting it. At the same time he was able to draw on the work of seventeenth- and eighteenth-century workhouse projectors, whose publications he knew. Generally speaking, these earlier proposals recognized that many of the parishes were too small and poor to handle the problem of the unemployed, especially in densely populated areas. The economies of scale of the large workhouses seemed an attractive alternative.

One of these early projectors offers three mottoes on his title-page, which imply a typicallly strict attitude towards the poor among those trying to help them: 'Industry brings Plenty/The sluggard shall be cloathed with raggs./He that will not Work, shall not Eat.'[23] Fielding's way of implementing the view that industry brings plenty was to make the government responsible for finding work for the poor and then requiring the poor to work. The strength of his conviction that labour must be compulsory is apparent in his provision for transporting those who 'absolutely refuse or neglect to labour, . . . to serve his Majesty in any of his Forces in the *East* or *West Indies*'.[24] It is easy enough to fault the strict discipline that informs Fielding's *Proposal* which, besides transportation, recommends corporal punishment for certain transgressions; but its relative harshness was not unusual for the age. Besides, anyone who recalls the thousands of discharged soldiers and sailors who had yet to be assimilated into the labour force – the London mob associated with the Penlez case – and 'the Late Increase of Robbers' will recognize that generating work for the many unemployed required a comprehensive plan that could provide '*Effectual* Provision for the Poor' only if everyone involved cooperated. The problem was massive and a solution elusive.

The twentieth-century reader should not be misled by the *Pro-*

posal's disciplinary austerities. Fielding's compassion for the wretches brought before his bench is well documented.[25] And his views concerning the private person's obligation to relieve the poor are emphatic:

> Those who want, have by the Laws of Nature a Right to a Relief from the Superfluities of those who abound; by those Laws therefore it is not left to the Option of the Rich, whether they will relieve the Poor and Distressed; but those who refuse to do it, become unjust Men, and in reality deserve to be considered as Rogues and Robbers of the Public.[26]

In the *Proposal*, however, Fielding expresses his deep concern for the poor from a broad social perspective, charting a detailed, comprehensive plan that takes into account his predecessors' views on the subject, the views of his contemporaries in public office, and his own pragmatic sense of human behaviour. He states his controlling premise succinctly:

> From what I have here advanced, it seems, I think, apparent, that among a civilized People that Polity is the best established in which all the Members, except such only as labour under any utter Incapacity, are obliged to contribute a Share to the Strength and Wealth of the Public. 2dly, That a State is capable of this Degree of Perfection, and, consequently, that to effect this is the Business of every wise and good Legislature.[27]

Fielding's comment in the final sentences of the *Proposal* – 'I am . . . sensible of my declining Constitution' – is clearly intended to disarm those he imagines may charge him with a selfish motive in dedicating his plan for the poor to Henry Pelham, who as first lord of the Treasury and chancellor of the Exchequer had established himself as Walpole's successor. But he was in fact increasingly ill, and though inverately cheerful, probably spoke the truth in saying '[I] have no further Design than to pass my short Remainder of life in some Degree of Ease, and barely to preserve my Family from being the objects of any such Laws as I have proposed.'[28] Unfortunately, he was not to find the degree of ease he hoped for.

A little more than a week after publication of the *Proposal* on 29 January 1753, Fielding found himself caught up in what was to become a notorious legal controversy. On 7 February 1753, he took a sworn statement at Bow Street from one Elizabeth Canning, a servant girl of about 18, who claimed to have been abducted and held captive for almost a month after refusing to become a prostitute. The accusation aroused great interest, in part at least because Elizabeth Canning was an unusually credible witness, well liked by many, who showed the physical effects of having spent a painful time away from employer, friends and family; on the other hand, the story she told included many improbabilities she could not prove true. This is no place to review the massive body of evidence that gathered around the case as a division grew between those who thought her story untrue and sought witnesses who might provide evidence against it, and those who more or less took it on faith that this young woman of established good character and artless demeanour was telling an essentially true story. Perhaps her claim that she had received a blow from one of her assailants and had lost her senses for several hours during the abduction helped to explain the weaknesses in her recollection. It is hard to know.[29]

That at least some of Canning's charges against those who ran and worked in the alleged bawdyhouse were untrue seems beyond question. But when she was charged with perjury, and after long delay brought to trial in the spring of 1754, the jury's verdict was that she was guilty, and yet innocent of the intent to mislead anyone: 'Guilty of perjury, but not wilful or corrupt.'[30] Unfortunately, the judge would not allow the verdict. Rebuffed, the jury that had probably responded accurately in its evaluation of the evidence, if not properly in the legal sense, thereafter found Canning guilty as charged. She was deported to Connecticut in 1754, and about two years later, in 1756, she married and had two children, a son and daughter.[31]

It may well be that Fielding, who could sift evidence very well, was disposed to take Canning's side for reasons very similar to those that prompted the jury's first verdict. True, *A Clear State of the Case of Elizabeth Canning* indicates that he thought her innocent not only in spirit but in the most literal sense. Even so, he makes it clear that his appraisal of her character is the basis of his faith in her innocence: 'As such a Behaviour could proceed only from the highest Impudence, or most perfect Innocence, so it seemed clearly to arise from the latter.'[32] Almost certainly in error about Canning's technical innocence, Fielding was probably right in thinking her free of guile. There may well have been a point at which he acknowledged to himself – but not to the world – that she was guilty, by which time the case had become so complicated that he was at odds with some of her defenders.[33] Perhaps he came to regret the support he had given the pitiable Elizabeth Canning, and yet it is just the kind of thing Fielding might have done again.

The winter of 1753, which was part of the long interim between Canning's story of abduction and her trial, was a period when Fielding suffered discomfort from his accumulated illnesses and yet continued his work: organizing and directing his police force, gathering evidence against known criminals, and dramatically reducing the crime rate. As I mentioned earlier, he was replaced by his half-brother John in January 1754; nevertheless, Fielding returned to Bow Street whenever he felt strong enough. But by May of that year he could no longer work, and he retired to Fordhook, his house in the country, on the Uxbridge Road in Ealing, Middlesex. He hoped for pleasant weather, we learn from his Introduction to *The Journal of a Voyage to Lisbon*, but 'in the whole month of May the sun scarce appeared three times'.[34] Fielding's dropsy-swollen belly was repeatedly tapped and quarts of water removed, fourteen quarts the first time and almost as much thereafter. Though he continued to speak as if he were recovering, and indeed found hope in brief remissions until very close to the end, he must have known his days were numbered. Concerned that he could not survive another English winter, he thought of travelling to a warmer climate. His first choice was Aix-en-Provence, but because he was unable to walk and the journey would require considerable land travel, he decided to go to Lisbon, which he could reach by sea.[35]

Late in June 1754, accompanied by his wife, Mary Daniels, his daughter Harriet, the only living child of his marriage to Charlotte, and his long-time friend and Mary's, Margaret Collier, Fielding left the house at Fordhook for Rotherhithe, a section of docks on the south bank of the Thames, to board the *Queen of Portugal*. Henry and Mary left behind them (in the care of Mary's mother) their three surviving children, William, Sophia and Allen. It was a sad occasion. Fielding was aware that he would never see his 'little ones' again, and Mary, a loving mother and wife, was stretched between her obligations to her children and to her husband. Fielding experienced indignities as well as sorrow. At

Rotherhithe, seated in a chair, he was lifted aboard with pulleys, exposing himself to the insults and jests of sailors and watermen nearby. Disavowing any personal resentment at their behaviour, Fielding nevertheless refers to it as an instance of 'that cruelty and inhumanity, in the nature of men, which I have often contemplated with concern'.[36] The day of his departure was hardly propitious. Though his natural good spirits and love of life soon reasserted themselves, his little remaining time inevitably included dark moods.

It was to be 7 August before they anchored in Lisbon, the trip having taken over a month because of delays in departure owing to the absence of favourable winds and bad weather. During these weeks, Fielding spent much of his time writing *The Journal of a Voyage to Lisbon*, nominally an example of travel literature, but actually an essay on a range of subjects of past and present interest to him, including the traditions, laws and customs of England; the British naval and merchant fleets; the monopolistic fishmongers of Westminster; medical practitioners, nostrums and quackeries; London thieves and London paupers; authors, ancient and modern; the tyrannies of supply and demand; and the healthy pleasures of food and drink.[37] Fielding makes it fairly clear that he is writing the *Voyage to Lisbon* to help provide for his family.[38] At the same time he continues to comment on the state of the world and to suggest remedies for its problems, in a voice that is still sometimes comic; absent, however, is the sound of romance one hears in *Tom Jones*, for example:

> If any merely common incident should appear in this journal . . . the candid reader will easily perceive it is not introduced for its own sake, but for some observations and reflections naturally resulting from it; and which . . . tend directly to the instruction of the reader, or to the information of the public; to whom if I chuse to convey such instruction or information with an air of joke or laughter, none but the dullest of fellows will, I believe, censure it.[39]

The *Voyage to Lisbon* reveals that Fielding had not lost his ability to delineate character. The skipper of the *Queen of Portugal*, Captain Veal, a tyrannical ex-privateer, who at the age of 70 was still a man of gallantry, emerges as a many-sided being who, for all his roughness of command and pretensions to more social status then he had, shows himself to be good natured, acting 'the part of a father to his sailors'.[40] Mrs Francis, the innkeeper at Ryde, is also well drawn, and less sympathetically than is Captain Veal. Fielding's extended satiric treatment of her turns deftly on her need to satisfy her vanity at the expense of her guests' comfort. She is the very antithesis of the good hostess, who emphasizes her inhospitality by overcharging her customers. It may have been Fielding's portraits of these two, potentially offensive if not libellous, that resulted in two quite distinct versions of the *Voyage to Lisbon*.[41]

It is remarkable that Fielding's literary productivity, which had been great during his professional lifetime, should have continued even while he was dying. The *Voyage to Lisbon* is not his best work, most would agree, but it is a strong representative piece that displays its author's keen satiric vision, his involvement in a range of social issues, his irrepressible sense of humour, and his zest for life. In addition to family, food, drink and conversation, all of which he required and enjoyed all of his life, one may suppose writing was also a necessity. In fact once he was in Lisbon, where he completed the *Voyage* by writing the Preface and the Introduction, he began to plan a work on Portugal (probably a history).[42]

Despite the author's sanguine expectation that he would continue to write, Fielding the man was dying. Even so, he occasionally enjoyed shortlived periods of well-being, when hope rebounded; but his body continued to weaken, and his mind was sometimes confused. It is unfortunate that towards the end, with financial prospects uncertain, he and his wife disagreed about the management of family affairs. Mary was intensely concerned about the children she had left in the care of her mother, who showed signs of increasing instability; indeed, she finally took her own life. And Henry felt himself to be struggling with their companion, Margaret Collier, to maintain control of his life. She had marital designs on the local English clergyman, John Williamson, designs impeded by Fielding because of her 'Bitchery'. As Fielding saw things, Margaret was trying to get Mary to declare her husband incompetent and to return to England and her children, while Miss Collier remained behind in charge of the household and near her target. Fielding wrote to his brother, explaining the situation and giving instructions for John's assistance. It is hard to appraise the accuracy of Fielding's charges; he obviously was deeply concerned that he would lose his independence. But in the midst of this unpleasant experience, he recovered his typical zest for life; he anticipated hearty meals with lively companions, he bought pets for his children, and he laughed at himself, his wife, and his daughter Harriet for a silly argument over which of two parrots was the better.[43]

Fielding died on 8 October 1754. Nothing is known about his final hours. He was buried in the cemetery, just outside Lisbon, which the non-Roman Catholic English shared with the Dutch, where his grave was identified by a small marker. Mary returned to England to take care of her children. As she had feared, Henry's debts were heavy, and everything had to be sold to meet them. But he had left a legacy of goodwill among his fellows more valuable than money. The benevolent Ralph Allen, of Prior Park, one of the models for Squire Allworthy; Andrew Millar, Henry's loyal publisher; and his brother John, all contributed in various ways to meet the continuing needs of Fielding's widow and children. The love he had generously given to family and friends survived his passing.

Notes and References

A note about eighteenth-century dates: my reader should recall that England had chosen not to adopt the Gregorian calendrical reform of 1582, with the result that it lagged behind the Continental calendar during the first half of the eighteenth century. England's calendar also differed from the Continent's in starting its legal year on 25 March instead of 1 January. The English calendar was brought to conformity with that of the Continent with the decision that 2 September 1752 would be accounted the 14 September of that year, and that England's year thereafter would begin on 1 January.

1 A Biographical Sketch, 1707–50

1. My debt to Fielding's earlier biographers is immense, especially that to Martin C. Battestin; I have also drawn on the work of Arthur Murphy, Wilbur Cross and Pat Rogers. I believe my notes will indicate explicitly in what ways I have relied on these and others.
2. W. L. Cross, *The History of Henry Fielding*, 3 vols (New Haven, Conn.: Yale UP, 1918), I, 1–4; M. C. Battestin *with* Ruthe R. Battestin, *Henry Fielding: A Life* (London and New York: Routledge, 1989–90), pp. 7–8.
3. See R. Halsband (ed.), *The Complete Letters of Lady Mary Wortley Montagu*, 3 vols (Oxford: Clarendon, 1965–7), I, v.
4. Cross, *The History*, I, 15–16; Battestin, *A Life*, pp. 11–12.
5. Battestin, *A Life*, pp. 4, 167–8.
6. J. Scott, *The Early History of Glastonbury, an Edition, Translation and Study of William of Malmesbury's De Antiquitate Glastonie Ecclesie* (Woodbridge, Suffolk: Boydell, 1981), pp. 43–5, 83. For conjecture about Glastonbury's (Avalon's) status as an island see B. Cunliffe, *Wessex to AD 1000* (London and New York: Longman, 1993), p. 143. But there is strong evidence – linguistic, geographical, and archaeological – that Arthur belongs to North Wales, not to England's south-west. See N. L. Goodrich, *King Arthur* (New York: Harper & Row, 1989), especially the Introduction and Part I.
7. J. P. Carley, *Glastonbury Abbey* (New York: St Martin's, 1988), pp. 72–3.
8. Cross, *The History*, I, 18–19; P. Rogers, *Henry Fielding: A Biography* (New York: Charles Scribner's Sons, 1979), pp. 14–15; Battestin, *A Life*, pp. 3–5.
9. Cunliffe, *Wessex*, p. 282.
10. D. D. Knowles, *The Religious Orders in England*, 3 vols (Cambridge: Cambridge UP, 1948–59), III, 379–82, 483–91.
11. Cross, *The History*, II, 165.

12. See Battestin, *A Life*, p. 5, for Fielding's incorporation of several features of the landscape from the estates of his friends, George Lyttelton (Hagley Park) and Ralph Allen (Prior Park).
13. The chief sources for reconstructing Fielding's boyhood are court records and other documents, the first of which were published by G. M. Godden, *Henry Fielding. A Memoir, Including Newly Discovered Letters and Records* . . . (London: S. Low, Marston, 1910); since then many more documents pertaining to the custody litigation and other important matters have been uncovered by Ruthe R. Battestin, as M. Battestin explains in the Preface to *Henry Fielding: A Life*, pp xiii–xiv. For aspects of Fielding's boyhood, see Cross, *The History*, I, 24–40, and Battestin, *A Life*, pp. 17–37, who offers solid conjecture about Fielding's fascination with the incest theme.
14. Battestin, *A Life*, p. 23, quotes these statements from the court records, and to them he adds the information about Sarah.
15. See M. Grace (ed.), *Arthur Murphy, The Lives of Henry Fielding and Samuel Johnson* (Gainesville, Florida: Scholars' Facsimiles & Reprints, 1968), pp. 10, 23, 26, 27, 28, 32–4. To make the point about good and great men, Murphy draws heavily on Fielding's own view, quoting liberally from *The Life of Mr. Jonathan Wild the Great*. Fielding also makes the distinction between the good and the great (and their combination as an ideal) elsewhere. For example, see H. K. Miller (ed.), *Miscellanies by Henry Fielding, Esq; Volume One* (Middletown, Conn.: Wesleyan UP, 1972), Fielding's Preface, p. 12, and the poem *Of True Greatness*, pp. 19–29.
16. Battestin, *A Life*, p. 14.
17. H. C. Maxwell Lyte, *A History of Eton College 1440–1875*, (London: Macmillan, 1875), p. 428, n. 1 provides a list of those whose busts were mounted there from time to time. Though Fielding's, which dates from the early nineteenth century, looks to me to have been modelled on Hogarth's likeness (the frontispiece to Fielding's *Works*, 1762), the sculptor makes him a much younger man, with a marked Habsburg lip.
18. Maxwell Lyte, *A History of Eton*, pp. 158–62.
19. Battestin, *A Life*, p. 39.
20. Maxwell Lyte, *A History of Eton*, p. 290.
21. Maxwell Lyte, *A History of Eton*, pp. 141, 311.
22. Maxwell Lyte, *A History of Eton*, p. 193–5.
23. Maxwell Lyte, *A History of Eton*, pp. 146–7, 314–18.
24. Grace, *Arthur Murphy*, p. 8.
25. Battestin, *A Life*, p. 41, gives the reference to Roger Strap.
26. Maxwell Lyte, *A History of Eton*, pp. 321–2.
27. T. R. Cleary, *Henry Fielding: Political Writer* (Waterloo, Ontario: Wilfrid Laurier, 1984), pp. 75–90, outlines the Broad-Bottom position and makes the point, among others, that in *Pasquin* Fielding depicts a corrupt England whose only hope is the foundation of a coalition of parties.
28. *The Covent-Garden Journal*, 10 (Tuesday 4 February 1752). See B. A. Goldgar (ed.), *The Covent-Garden Journal and a Plan of the Universal*

Register Office (Middletown, Conn.: Wesleyan UP, 1988), p. 74, for the praise of Lucian, Cervantes and Swift, and p. 74, n. 4 for Fielding's gradually developed exclusion of Aristophanes from the list of good comedians.

29. The only known copy of *Ralph Roister Doister* was discovered in 1818 by the Reverend Thomas Biggs, an Etonian, who presented it to Eton College in December of that year. For an outline of the play's early history see E. K. Chambers, *The Mediaeval Stage*, 2 vols (Oxford: Clarendon, 1903), II, 451–2. See also C. Leech, L. Potter, and T. W. Craik, *et al.* (eds), *The Revels History of Drama in English*, 8 vols (London and New York: Methuen, 1975–7), II, 34, 137–8, for brief discussions of Udall's use of student actors.

30. Maxwell Lyte, *A History of Eton*, pp. 340–1.

31. Battestin, *New Essays by Henry Fielding: His Contributions to 'The Craftsman (1734–1739) and Other Early Journalism*, with a Stylometric Analysis by Michael G. Farringdon (Charlottesville: Virginia UP, 1989), establishes the basis of the claim that Fielding witnessed Wild's execution when they attribute to Fielding the letter from 'A Moderate Man' in *The Craftsman* of 5 June 1736.

32. Miller, *Miscellanies*, I, 53–4, n. 4, demonstrates that '"Hog's Norton" is almost certainly derived from Hock [Hook] Norton, Oxfordshire, once proverbial for boorishness'.

33. Battestin, *A Life*, pp. 50, 632, n. 123.

34. Battestin, *A Life*, pp. 49, 52.

35. Battestin, *A Life*, pp. 51–2, locates Fielding in St James's, London, assaulting one Joseph Burt, probably one of his father's servants, on 4 November 1726; on pp. 185–90 Battestin discusses Fielding's stays in East Stour during this period.

36. R. D. Hume, *Henry Fielding and the London Theatre 1728–1737* (Oxford: Clarendon, 1988), p. 28.

37. In April 1729, Fielding left Leiden abruptly to escape the legal consequences of his debts. See Battestin, *A Life*, pp. 62–76, for the Leiden experience, the case against Fielding for debt, and the likely continental tour.

38. See Battestin, *New Essays by Fielding*, for a full treatment of Fielding's early journalistic essays and for the essays themselves.

39. Grace, *Arthur Murphy*, p. 9.

40. Battestin, *A Life*, p. 57.

41. These verses were not published until 1972, by I. M. Grundy, 'New Verse by Henry Fielding', *PMLA*, LXXXVII (1972), 213–45. As a Roman Catholic, Pope was ineligible to participate formally in the activities of the nation's social, religious or political institutions. He seems amused that he was mistaken both for a Tory and for a Whig: 'Tories call me Whig, and Whigs a Tory': *Imitations of Horace*, II, i, 68.

42. These dates of composition are given by Hume, *Henry Fielding*, p. 257.

43. See Battestin, *New Essays by Fielding*, pp. 510–24 for the poem and three essays.

44. See Grundy, 'New Verse', pp. 216–17. Fielding eventually made it

clear that he admired Pope's poetry, but he continued to object to Pope's libellous satire. Fielding himself was not completely innocent in this regard.

45. *The Musical Miscellany; Being a Collection of Choice Songs . . .*, 6 vols (London: John Watts, 1731), VI, 170–3.
46. Grace, *Arthur Murphy*, p. 14.
47. Battestin, *A Life*, pp. 161, 642, n. 248; Grundy, pp. 240 and 240, n. 15.
48. Battestin, *A Life*, p. 178.
49. Grace, *Arthur Murphy*, p. 27.
50. Cross, *The History*, I, 173–4; Battestin, *A Life*, pp. 179–80.
51. Rogers, *A Biography*, p. 77.
52. The approximate birth year for Henry is inferred by T. C. Eaves and B. D. Kimpel, 'Henry Fielding's Son by His First Wife', *N & Q*, n. s. XV (1968), 212, who note that he was described as eight years old at the time of his death on 3 August 1750.
53. Battestin, *A Life*, pp. 234–5, points out that the evidence for supposing these to be Fielding's daughters is not conclusive.
54. Battestin, *A Life*, p. 617.
55. Grace, *Arthur Murphy*, p. 48.
56. Battestin, *A Life*, p. 353.
57. Grace, *Arthur Murphy*, p. 38.
58. Battestin, *A Life*, pp. 384–5.
59. Hume, *Henry Fielding*, pp. 172–3.
60. See Hume, *Henry Fielding*, Chapter 4, 'The Years of Uncertainty', for a full discussion of this period in Fielding's professional life.
61. See W. E. Henley (ed.), *The Complete Works of Henry Fielding, Esq.*, 16 vols (New York: Croscup & Sterling, 1902; repr. New York: Barnes & Noble, 1967), X, 283.
62. Battestin, *A Life*, p. 175.
63. See Battestin, *New Essays by Fielding*.
64. B. A. Goldgar, *Walpole and the Wits* (Lincoln, Nebraska: Nebraska UP, 1976), pp. 150–6, and Hume, pp. 238–9, 255, for example.
65. Though Hume, referring to Battestin and Farringdon, acknowledges that Fielding may have contributed to *The Craftsman* 'as early as March 1734' and that we do not know 'when he first allied himself with the opposition', p. 184, n. 65, he maintains the view that only Fielding's very late plays are partisan.
65. Battestin, *A Life*, p. 370.
66. See H. Pagliaro (ed.), *The Journal of a Voyage to Lisbon* (New York: Nardon, 1963), pp. 91 and 146, n. 97. I no longer believe this reference to Walpole is ironic.
67. See Cleary, *Henry Fielding*, Chapters 1 and 3.
68. Hume, *Henry Fielding*, pp. 200–4, 254–5.
69. Hume, *Henry Fielding*, pp. 255–60.
70. The Barnard Playhouse Bill, proposed in Commons on 5 March 1735, sought primarily to limit the number of theatres in London to those with a Royal patent (Drury Lane, Covent Garden, and perhaps Lincoln's Inn Fields). It was defeated because Walpole offered an amendment that would have given his ministry the power

to censor plays, and Barnard, who framed the bill, opposed the idea. See Hume, *Henry Fielding*, pp. 195–9.
71. Hume, *Henry Fielding*, pp. 242–8. Also see V. J. Liesenfeld, *The Licensing Act of 1737* (Madison, Wisconsin: Wisconsin UP, 1984), pp. 191–3.
72. Hume, *Henry Fielding*, p. 240.
73. See Battestin, *A Life*, pp. 233–4 for the argument that Fielding himself – through his late plays – was an effective immediate cause of the Licensing Act.
74. Battestin, *A Life*, p. 238.
75. Grace, *Arthur Murphy*, p. 28.
76. See, for example, M. R. Zirker (ed.), *An Enquiry into the Causes of the Late Increase of Robbers and Related Writings* (Middletown, Conn.: Wesleyan UP, 1988), pp. xxviii–xxxi, where Zirker discusses Fielding's command of the law as it is displayed in his *A Charge Delivered to the Grand Jury* (1749).
77. Battestin, *A Life*, pp. 245. See also B. M. Jones, *Henry Fielding: Novelist and Magistrate* (London: Allen & Unwin, 1933), Part II, Chapter 1, 'Fielding as a Law Student', pp. 65–78, for a description of the academic requirements, which Jones says, p. 67, were then strictly enforced.
78. See Battestin, *A Life*, pp. ix–x, for identification and a brief discussion of four probable likenesses of Fielding, reproduced in Battestin as the frontispiece and Plates 36, 47 and 52.
79. For discussions of this tantalizing possibility, see C. B. Woods, 'The Miss Lucy Plays of Fielding and Garrick', *Philological Quarterly*, XLI (1962), 294–310; *Miscellanies*, I, 15; Hume, *Henry Fielding*, pp. 265–6; and Battestin, *A Life*, pp. 346–7. (Kitty Clive played Lucy in both *Lethe* and *Miss Lucy in Town*.)
80. Battestin, *A Life*, p. 407.
81. See L. W. Labaree, R. L. Ketcham, H. C. Boatfield and H. Fineman (eds), *The Autobiography of Benjamin Franklin* (New Haven, Conn., and London: Yale UP, 1964), pp. 89, 98–9. Franklin gives us amusing clues about Fielding's friend, among them the observation that Ralph borrowed £27 from Franklin during the period 1725–6, and did not repay it.
82. Labaree *et al.*, *Franklin*, p. 90.
83. Hume, *Henry Fielding*, pp. 205–6; Battestin, p. 203.
84. Battestin, *A Life*, p. 110.
85. Battestin, *A Life*, pp. 102–3.
86. G. Midgley, *The Life of Orator Henley* (Oxford: Clarendon, 1973), pp. 167–9.
87. Battestin, *A Life*, pp. 187–8.
88. Battestin and C. T. Probyn (eds), *The Correspondence of Henry and Sarah Fielding* (Oxford: Clarendon, 1993), p. 11. Battestin, *Life*, p. 311, shrewdly observes that Fielding's choice of the word 'expose' indicates his strong sense of privacy, which makes his willingness to yield to Harris's 'Power' a rarity that only a great friendship could account for.
89. Battestin, *A Life*, p. 285, suggests the book in question was *The*

Life of Mr. Jonathan Wild the Great, in which the deeds of the criminal, Wild, become the crimes of the minister, Walpole.

90. Jones, *Henry Fielding*, p. 76.
91. For differing explanations of this shift in Fielding's rhetoric, see
Battestin, *A Life*, pp. 316–24, and Battestin, 'Fielding's Changing
Politics and *Joseph Andrews*', *Philological Quarterly*, XXXIX (1960),
39–55; see also W. B. Coley, 'Henry Fielding and the Two Walpoles',
Philological Quarterly, XLV (1966), 157–78, and Coley (ed.), *The Jacobite's Journal and Related Writings* (Middletown, Conn.: Wesleyan UP,
1975), p. xlvii.
92. Battestin, *A Life*, pp. 295–6. See Jones, *Henry Fielding*, pp. 215–17,
for a brief but effective description of life in debtor's prison. Fielding
himself characterized aspects of debt as a crime and the treatment
of debtors, for example, in *Amelia*, VIII, i, ii, vi, and x.
93. Battestin, *A Life*, pp. 297–301.
94. *Miscellanies*, I, 14.
95. For a brief survey of Walpole's political survival and downfall,
see E. Cruickshanks, 'The Political Management of Sir Robert
Walpole, 1720–42', in J. Black (ed.), *Britain in the Age of Walpole*
(New York: St Martin's, 1984), pp. 21–43.
96. Whether or in what degree Fielding's esssays were political during the early years of this period is a matter of opinion, though
differing views may turn on no more than differing, implicitly held,
definitions of the word 'political'. Coley (ed.), *The True Patriot and
Related Writings* (Middletown, Conn.: Wesleyan UP, 1987), p. xxxvi,
says that with a 'single possible exception', Fielding wrote nothing political between *The Opposition* (December 1741) and *A Serious Address to the People of Great Britain* (3 October 1745); but Battestin,
A Life, pp. 343–5, 367–8, 387–8, argues that Fielding's *A Full Vindication of the Duchess Dowager of Marlborough* (1742), *Some Papers to
be Read before the R[oya]l Society* (1743), as well as Coley's 'single
possible exception' (*An Attempt towards a Natural History of the
Hanover Rat*, 1744, which Battestin attributes to Fielding) are all in
some sense political. For a discussion of Fielding's pamphlets and
essays on the Forty-Five, see Coley, *The True Patriot*, pp. xix–cvi.
97. Coley, *The Jacobite's Journal*, pp. xvii–lxxxii.
98. Battestin, *A Life*, pp. 440, 447.
99. Battestin, *A Life*, p. 417.
100. R. Paulson and T. Lockwood (eds), *Henry Fielding: The Critical
Heritage* (London: Routledge & Kegan Paul; New York: Barnes &
Noble, 1969), p. 6.
101. See W. J. Bate and A. B. Strauss (eds), *The Rambler*, in *The Yale
Edition of the works of Samuel Johnson*, vols III, IV and V, (New
Haven, Conn., and London: Yale UP, 1969), III, 23.
102. See G. B. Hill (ed.), *Boswell's Life of Johnson*, 6 vols, rev. L. F. Powell
(Oxford: Clarendon, 1964), 2nd edn, II, 174.
103. *Boswell's Johnson*, II, 49.
104. *Boswell's Johnson*, II, 174.
105. *Boswell's Johnson*, II, 495.

106. To Lady Bute, 22 September [1755]. See Halsband, *The Complete Letters*, III, 90.
107. To Lady Bute, 23 July [1754], Halsband, *The Complete Letters*, III, 66.
108. Halsband, *The Complete Letters*, III, 66 n.
109. *Boswell's Johnson*, II, 49. Anent the 'expansion in dissertation' of Richardson's characters, some found him prolix. Lady Mary calls attention to his wordiness in several letters: To Lady Bute, 8 December [1754], 22 September [1755], 9 August [1760]: Halsband, *The Complete Letters*, III, 70, 89, 244.
110. See G. A. Bonnard (ed.), *Edward Gibbon Memoirs of My Life*, (London: Nelson, 1966), p. 5. Bonnard, p. xvi, conjectures that Gibbon wrote this prediction in 1789–90.
111. *Miscellanies by Henry Fielding, Esq.* is printed in two volumes in *The Wesleyan Edition of the Works of Henry Fielding*. The first, 1972, cited above, was edited by Miller; the second, 1993, by Goldgar and H. Amory.
112. See M. Kelsall (ed.), *The Adventures of David Simple* (London, New York and Toronto: Oxford UP, 1969), p. 3.
113. Jones, *Henry Fielding*, pp. 91–2.
114. Grace, *Arthur Murphy*, p. 29; Jones, *Henry Fielding*, pp. 95–6; Battestin, *A Life*, pp. 383, 390–1, 505. For a compilation and transcription of the available fragments of Fielding's work on Crown law, see, H. Amory (ed.), *Henry Fielding. An Institute of the Pleas of the Crown. An Exhibition of the Hyde Collection at the Houghton Library, 1987* (Cambridge, Mass.: Harvard UP, 1987).
115. See Grundy, for one of Fielding's early hits at physicians (probably in 1729): 'Which of my Doctors would with safety kill/Should he not only write but taste the bill': 'New Verse', p. 227. For Fielding's praise of Ranby, see, for example, *Tom Jones*, VII, xiii, where the Man of the Hill assigns Ranby 'the first character in his profession'.
116. For the attribution to Fielding, see R. C. Jarvis, 'The Death of Walpole: Henry Fielding and a Forgotten *Cause Célèbre*', *Modern Language Review*, XLI (1946), 113–30.
117. Battestin, *A Life*, p. 411.
118. Preface to *Familiar Letters*, Henley, *Complete Works*, XVI, 19.
119. Two feminist studies of Fielding are A. J. Smallwood, *Fielding and the Woman Question: The Novels of Henry Fielding and Feminist Debate, 1700–1750* (New York: St Martin's, 1989); and J. Campbell, *Natural Masques: Gender and Identity in Fielding's Plays and Novels* (Stanford, Calif.: Stanford UP, 1995).
120. *Voyage to Lisbon*, p. 34.
121. Jones, *Henry Fielding*, p. 113.
122. See Battestin, *A Life*, pp. 448–50 for ways in which Bedford helped Fielding meet the property qualification for the Middlesex appointment. See also M. C. with R. R. Battestin, 'Fielding, Bedford, and the Westminster Election of 1749', *Eighteenth-Century Studies*, XI (1977/78), 143–85, for a discussion of an aspect of Fielding's service

to Bedford and for the relevant correspondence by Fielding. For the geographical limits of the City of London, see G. M. Trevelyan, *English Social History* (London, New York and Toronto: Longmans, Green, 1942), pp. 333–4.

123. Zirker, *An Enquiry*, p. xcix.
124. Jones, *Henry Fielding*, p. 149, and his entire chapter 'The Establishment of the First Detective Force in England', pp. 143–54. See also *Voyage to Lisbon*, pp. 32–3.
125. Zirker, *An Enquiry*, p. xxviii.
126. I spend some time on the Penlez case not only because it is fascinating in itself, but also because it is near the heart of 'one of the most colorful [episodes] in Fielding's political life': Battestin with Battestin 'Fielding and Bedford', p. 155.
127. P. Linebaugh, 'The Tyburn Riot Against the Surgeons', in *Albion's Fatal Tree* (New York: Pantheon, 1975), p. 93; for a full account of the riots, see Linebaugh, 'Tyburn Riot' pp. 89–102, and Zirker, *An Enquiry*, pp. xxxiii–lii.
128. Linebaugh, 'Tyburn Riot'; Zirker, *An Enquiry*.
129. See Battestin with Battestin, 'Fielding and Bedford' for Fielding's support of Trentham (a service to his patron, Lord Bedford).
130. Zirker, *An Enquiry*, p. 59.
131. Both Cross, *The History*, II, 236–40, and Jones, *Henry Fielding*, pp. 137–42, find Fielding's *Bosavern Penlez* competent and unimpeachable as a justification for the execution, and only incidentally a partisan argument. But Battestin with Battestin, 'Fielding and Bedford', pp. 165–6, and Zirker, *An Enquiry*, pp. xliv–xlv, are among more recent commentators who find the essay less unequivocal.
132. Zirker suggests a motive for the government's unwillingness to pardon Penlez: 'A drunken peruke-maker perhaps seemed a safer sacrifice to the principle of exemplary punishment than one of the sailors [in the riots of 1–3 July 1749], who were spared but none the less warned': *An Enquiry*, p. xlix. To this conjecture I would add that when the government indeed risked further rioting by hanging 13 sailors and a sailor's wife at Tyburn on 18 October 1749, Penlez was hanged with them, perhaps to temper the death of the seamen and the wife with the life of a civilian.
133. Battestin, *A Life*, p. 422.
134. Battestin, *A Life*, pp. 434–5.
135. Battestin, *A Life*, pp. 423, 463, 498, 576, 582, 615, 617, 618.
136. *Voyage to Lisbon*, p. 43.

2   Fielding in the Theatre

1. R. D. Hume, *Henry Fielding and the London Theatre 1728–1737* (Oxford: Clarendon, 1988), pp. 190–1.
2. See W. W. Appleton (ed.), *The Historical Register For the Year 1736 and Eurydice Hissed* (Lincoln, Nebraska: Nebraska UP, 1967), p. xi.
3. Hume, *Henry Fielding*, p. 259.

4. See Hume, *Henry Fielding*, pp. 14–20. Hume, *Henry Fielding*, p. 19, mentions pirating as another reason for not investing in new plays.
5. See, for example, W. L. Cross, *The History of Henry Fielding*, 3 vols (New Haven, Conn.: Yale UP, 1918), I, 58; P. Rogers, *Henry Fielding* (New York: Charles Scribner's Sons, 1979), p. 27.
6. Hume, *Henry Fielding*, pp. 1–14.
7. See R. W. Lowe (ed.), *An Apology for the Life of Mr. Colley Cibber*, 2 vols (London: John C. Nimmo, 1889), I, 320–2.
8. Italian opera, the rage for a few years, excited expectations for profits that rose and then fell. *Tatler*, 1 (12 April 1709), prefers a current benefit performance of Congreve's *Love for Love* for the ageing Betterton (1635?–1710) to Italian opera: the 'Late Apostacy in Favour of Dress and Sound'. Such disparaging citations are common in the age, though *Tatler*, 115 (3 January 1710), praises Nicolini at the same time that it scores lesser singers. See also Lowe, *Cibber*, II, 87–9 for an insider's comments on Italian opera, including references to the singer Farinelli.
9. Hume, *Henry Fielding*, p. 14.
10. J. Loftis, *Steele at Drury Lane* (Berkeley: California UP, 1952), pp. 244–5.
11. Hume, *Henry Fielding*, pp. 8–11.
12. A. Nicoll, *A History of English Drama, 1600–1900*, 6 vols (Cambridge: Cambridge UP, 1923–59; 4th edn, 1952), I, 361.
13. For discussion of the Little Haymarket's construction, see E. L. Avery (ed.), *The London Stage* (hereafter *TLS*), Part 2: 1700–1729, 2 vols (Carbondale, Illinois: Southern Illinois UP, 1960), I, xxxv–xxxvi. Avery also reports there a notice in the *London Journal*, 23 December 1721, which states that a patent had been issued during Anne's reign (in 1712?), but says no proof of this claim is known to exist. See Hume, *Henry Fielding*, pp. 55–9, for a discussion of operations at the Little Haymarket.
14. See M. C. Battestin *with* Ruthe R. Battestin, *Henry Fielding: A Life* (London and New York: Routledge, 1989–90), pp. 59–63 for a discussion of the acceptance and reception of *Love in Several Masques* and of Fielding's departure for Leiden.
15. Hume, *Henry Fielding*, p. 29.
16. Lowe, *Cibber*, II, 251–2.
17. Hume, *Henry Fielding*, p. 29.
18. Hume, *Henry Fielding*, p. 33; Battestin, *A Life*, p. 60.
19. In 1727, the year of George II's accession (in June) and of Walpole's new consolidation of power, Drury Lane would have been willing to oblige a powerful Whig, just as it had been in 1714. Lady Mary Wortley Montagu's warm friendship with Maria (Molly) Skerret, the mistress who bore Walpole a daughter in 1725, and whom he later married, seems to have involved the minister and Lady Mary in a common concern in the mid-1720s. See J. H. Plumb, *Sir Robert Walpole*, 2 vols (London: Cresset, 1960), II, 113. See also Battestin, pp. 56–61.
20. Battestin, *A Life*, pp. 72–6.

21. Battestin, *A Life*, p. 71.
22. G. M. Trevelyan, *English Social History* (London, New York and Toronto: Longmans, Green, 1942), pp. 330–31.
23. Battestin, *A Life*, p. 721.
24. I am indebted to *TLS* throughout the following discussion of the London theatre, especially to Avery's Introduction, Pt 2, I, and to Hume as well.
25. Lowe, *Cibber*, I, 321; II, 78–81, informs us that the Drury Lane stage was shortened to increase the seating capacity; and the bad acoustics of Queens, later King's, in the Haymarket, were improved, after which it was given over to music, though it was originally intended for straight drama.
26. Avery, *TLS*, Pt 2, I, lviii. We have no basis for calculating the real cost of a theatre ticket, but it may be helpful to know that in London in 1730, a very large, four-pound, loaf of bread cost about 4d. (2p), or one-third of the price of the cheapest place in the upper gallery. See B. R. Mitchell, *British Historical Statistics* (Cambridge: Cambridge UP, 1988), p. 769.
27. Hume, *Henry Fielding*, pp. 144–9.
28. Nicoll, *A History of English Drama 1660–1900*, II (3rd edn, 1952), pp. 276–7.
29. Avery, *TLS*, Pt 2, I, lxviii.
30. Nicoll, *A History of English Drama 1660–1900*, II; Avery, *TLS*, Pt 2, I, lxii–lxvi.
31. Lowe, *Cibber*, I, 90–1.
32. E. Howe, *The First English Actresses* (Cambridge: Cambridge UP, 1992), p. 171.
33. Nicoll, *A History of English Drama 1660–1900*, II (3rd edn), 276.
34. On the first night, there was a disturbance in the audience, planned by faction. But when Kitty sang, she was applauded. Though the play did not survive in its original form, Cibber cut and revised it, and the new version, named *Damon and Phillida*, became a standard. See Nicoll, *A History of English Drama 1660–1900*, II (3rd edn), 15–16.
35. Hume, *Henry Fielding*, p. 258.
36. Nicoll, *A History of English Drama 1660–1900*, II (3rd edn), 274–92: 'Summary of documents connected with the history of the stage, 1700–1750, preserved in the Public Record Office'.
37. Nicoll, *A History of English Drama, 1660–1900* II (3rd edn), 281. Also Avery, *TLS*, Pt 2, I, xcvi–cii. Lowe, *Cibber*, I, 161, says that Mrs Barry was 'distinguished by the indulgence of having an annual benefit-play, which was granted to her alone', during the reign of James II. But as Cibber's editor Lowe points out, E. Bellchambers (ed.), *An Apology for the Life of Mr. Colley Cibber* (London: W. Simpkin and R. Marshall, 1822), p. 172, says an agreement reached by Davenant, Hart, Betterton, and others on 14 October 1681, makes it clear that benefits for actors were by then in existence. This and other evidence suggests that various *ad hoc* arrangements were made for actor

benefits until the practice became regularized, in certain particulars at least, by the Lord Chamberlain, in 1712.

38. Hume, *Henry Fielding*, p. 21.

39. Avery, *TLS*, Pt 2, I, c–cii; Hume, *Henry Fielding*, pp. 23–8.

40. See Avery, *TLS*, Pt 2, I, c, for a detailed accounting of benefits for Philip Frowde's *The Fall of Saguntum* at Lincoln's Inn Fields in 1727. Though Frowde's was a more popular play than *Love in Several Masques*, his benefit receipts suggest a likely range. See also Hume, *Henry Fielding*, pp. 24–7.

41. J. Genest, *Some Account of the English Stage from the Restoration in 1660 to 1830*, 10 vols (Bath, 1832), III, 8, says *The Revenge* (1721), by Edward Young, was sold for £50 and *The Rival Modes* (1727), by James Moore Smythe, for £100. According to Hume, p. 26, anything over £40 would have been unusual. We know the prices Watts paid Fielding for some of his short pieces (on average, £10).

42. See W. E. Henley (ed.), *The Complete Works of Henry Fielding, Esq.* 16 vols, including *Plays and Poems* in 5 vols, I–V (New York: Croscup & Sterling, 1902; repr. Barnes & Noble, New York, 1967), I, 7–8. Hereafter references to Fielding's plays will include act and scene numbers, followed by the number of Henley's volume containing the play, and the page number; unless another edition is named, quotations from Fielding's plays are taken from Henley.

43. Hume, *Henry Fielding*, p. 31.

44. Hume, *Henry Fielding*, p. 30; Cross, *The History*, I, 53–4, suggests that Fielding drew much of the plot from his own failed attempt to marry the closely guarded young heiress, Sarah Andrew, of Lyme Regis.

45. C. J. Rawson, *Henry Fielding and the Augustan Ideal Under Stress* (London and Boston: Routledge & Kegan Paul, 1972) discusses Fielding's view, 'backed by the whole moral atmosphere of *Tom Jones*', that 'lewdness is better than no love at all', p. 15.

46. A. J. Rivero, *The Plays of Henry Fielding* (Charlottesville: Virginia UP, 1989), p. 16.

47. See H. K. Miller (ed.), *Miscellanies by Henry Fielding, Esq; Volume One* (Middletown, Conn.: Wesleyan UP, 1972), 4–5.

48. *Miscellanies*, I.

49. Hume, *Henry Fielding*, pp. 39, 51.

50. Avery, *TLS*, Pt 3, I, cxl, 34–5.

51. Hume, *Henry Fielding*, p. 51.

52. Avery, *TLS*, Pt 3, I, xliv–xlv, 384–8, 392, 407, 418, 420.

53. See *Miscellanies*, I, 5–7; Hume, *Henry Fielding*, p. 201; and Battestin, *A Life*, pp. 360–2, for discussions of Fielding's substitution of *The Wedding-Day* for the play he first offered Drury Lane, *The Good-natured Man*.

54. Avery, *TLS*, Pt 3, II, 1035–7; *Miscellanies*, I, 7.

55. *Miscellanies*, I, 7; Hume, *Henry Fielding*, p. 46; Battestin, *A Life*, p. 361.

56. Cross, *The History*, I, 373–5; Battestin, *A Life*, pp. 359–65.

57. Hume, *Henry Fielding*, pp. 48–9, raises the question of whether Fielding meant to burlesque reform comedy and then rejects the idea.

58. Battestin, *A Life*, 361–2.
59. See Hume, *Henry Fielding*, pp. 52–61 for an authoritative discussion of the workings of Little Haymarket at the time.
60. See D. Farnsworth Smith, *Plays about the Theatre in England from 'The Rehearsal' in 1671 to the Licensing Act in 1737* (London and New York: Oxford UP, 1936), pp. 140–50, for a discussion of *The Author's Farce* in the context of English rehearsal plays.
61. Hume, *Henry Fielding*, pp. 67–8.
62. Quotations are from C. B. Woods (ed.), *The Author's Farce (Original Version)* (Lincoln, Nebraska: Nebraska UP, 1966), p. 11.
63. E. Bentley, Introduction, 'The Psychology of Farce', in Bentley (ed.), *Let's Get a Divorce And Other Plays* (New York: Hill & Wang, 1958), p. xiii.
64. Battestin, *A Life*, pp. 77–8.
65. Hume, *Henry Fielding*, p. 63, points out that it was this later version, published in 1750, that was the basis for all reprints until 1966.
66. 23 July 1754, in R. Halsband (ed.), *The Complete Letters of Lady Mary Wortley Montagu*, 3 vols (Oxford: Clarendon, 1965–7), III, 66.
67. Battestin (ed.), *Joseph Andrews* (Middletown, Conn.: Wesleyan UP, 1967), p. 6.
68. Though Fielding drew on Pope, he had earlier satirized him, making sophisticated use of the older poet's own methods. See I. M. Grundy, 'New Verse by Henry Fielding', *PMLA*, LXXXVII (1972), 213–45, for the text and a discussion of Fielding's unfinished burlesque, a satire in heroic couplets, wherein Pope is made the favoured son of the Goddess of Dullness. Fielding set the poem aside, probably because it would have been imprudent to publish it.
69. I. Donaldson, *The World Upside Down* (Oxford: Clarendon, 1970), p. 188, says that 'Fielding often implied [that his] is an age which seems about to disintegrate into farcical disorder.' Donaldson associates this view especially with Fielding's work as Scriblerus Secundus.
70. The text I discuss is that of L. J. Morrissey, *Tom Thumb and The Tragedy of Tragedies* (Edinburgh: Oliver & Boyd, 1970). Morrissey's 'A Note on the Texts', pp. 13–16, gives a brief description of the early editions and printings of both plays.
71. See Rivero, *The Plays*, pp. 57–61, for an excellent discussion of heroic tragedy as self-satirizing.
72. K. M. Briggs, *A Dictionary of British Folk-Tales* (Bloomington, Indiana: Indiana UP, 1970), Part A, Vol. I, 531–3.
73. A Miss Jones played the part. See Avery, *TLS*, Pt III, I, 54; Hume, *Henry Fielding*, p. 68, n. 61.
74. Hume, *Henry Fielding*, p. 70.
75. See Battestin, *A Life*, pp. 104–5, for a discussion of the likely arrangements between Fielding and John Rich, manager of Lincoln's Inn Fields.
76. Halsband, *The Complete Letters*, II, 93.
77. Avery, *TLS*, Pt 3, I, 190; Hume, *Henry Fielding*, p. 128, who says one reason the play had a great success during its first run was that Drury Lane was able to mount a production of a high quality,

permits the inference that (perhaps among other reasons for delay in production) there was a need to wait for a suitable venue.

78. Avery, *TLS*, Pt 3, I, 125.
79. J. P. Hunter, *Occasional Form* (Baltimore, Md, and London: Johns Hopkins UP, 1975), pp. 23–46. For this discussion, Hunter acknowledges a debt to the pioneering work of J. T. Hillhouse (ed.), *The Tragedy of Tragedies* (New Haven, Conn.: Yale UP; and London: Milford-Oxford, 1918).
80. Hume, *Henry Fielding*, p. 89.
81. Hume, *Henry Fielding*, p. 89.
82. T. R. Cleary, *Henry Fielding Political Writer* (Waterloo, Ontario: Wilfred Laurier, 1984), pp. 32–45.
83. Hume, *Henry Fielding*, pp. 77–86. I have conflated Hume's secondary distinction between 'politicized plays and partisan plays' with his primary distinction, as he himself does to some extent.
84. Morrissey, *Tom Thumb*, pp. 4–6; B. A. Goldgar, *Walpole and the Wits* (Lincoln, Nebraska, and London: Nebraska UP, 1976), pp. 104–5; Cleary, *Henry Fielding*, pp. 32–45; Hume, *Henry Fielding*, pp. 89–91.
85. Goldgar, *Walpole*, pp. 105–10, argues that the allusion to Charteris and related matters are elaborately anti-ministerial; Hume, *Henry Fielding*, pp. 72–3, disagrees.
86. From one point of view, J. R. Brown, 'Henry Fielding's *Grub-Street Opera*', *Modern Language Quarterly*, XVI (1955), pp. 32–41, seems right to say, 'The whole thing is done in a tone of light-hearted banter, and it is apparent that Fielding was far more interested in writing a clever play than in carrying a flag for any political faction' (p. 37). Fielding's intention notwithstanding, the play may have disturbed the King, according to V. J. Liesenfeld, *The Licensing Act of 1737* (Madison, Wisconsin: Wisconsin UP, 1984): 'There is substantial evidence that some of these personal satires, which opponents of the Licensing Act also condemned, infuriated the king more than they did Walpole, and that Walpole hoped that the act would placate the king and thereby make his own position more secure' (p. 60). Though Liesenfeld apparently intends his comment to apply to later plays, the king's feelings of 1736–7 could well have been the culmination of a long-gathering rancour.
87. J. Loftis, *The Politics of Drama in Augustan England* (Oxford: Clarendon, 1963), pp. 105–6.
88. See Hume, *Henry Fielding*, p. 104. The play's publication and performance history is complicated. It was printed in three versions of uncertain authority: *The Welsh Opera*, London, 1731; *The Genuine Grub-Street Opera*, London, 1731; and *The Grub-Street Opera*, London, 1731? 1755? Discussions of various aspects of the history may be found in the following works among others: Brown's article, 'Henry Fielding's Grub-Street Opera'; E. V. Roberts (ed.), *The Grub-Street Opera* (Lincoln, Nebraska: Nebraska UP, 1968), pp. xi–xxv; L. J. Morrissey (ed.), *The Grub-Street Opera* (Edinburgh: Oliver & Boyd, 1973), pp. 13–24; Hume, *Henry Fielding*, pp. 93–104; and Rivero, *The Plays*, pp. 88–91.

89. Roberts, *Grub-Street Opera*, p. xxi, is among the critics who mention the Prince's rumoured impotence; so is Liesenfeld, *Licensing Act*, p. 17; but see also Liesenfeld, *Licensing Act*, pp. 107 and 222, n. 51, for evidence that Prince Frederick was cured.
90. Hume, *Henry Fielding*, pp. 104–110, provides a valuable discussion of the state of London theatre on the eve of Fielding's connection with Drury Lane.
91. Roberts, 'Fielding's Ballad Opera *The Lottery* (1732) and the English State Lottery of 1731', *Huntington Library Quarterly*, XXVII (1963), pp. 39–52, points out that 'The evils of the lotteries occurred not in the [government controlled] drawing, but almost exclusively in the manipulation of tickets by brokers or stockjobbers, like Fielding's Stocks' (p. 47). Brokers bought up huge blocks of the 80 000 tickets issued, 8000 of which were winners, and so marked in the government records. Each ticket, which cost £10, was also a stock share worth £7 10s., on which the government paid 3 per cent a year. Most prizes were small, but the grand prize was worth £10 000. At the designated time, which in 1731 was 11 October, the government began to draw stubs, in public, from large drums, until all 8000 winners were identified. The procedure took weeks. It was during this long period that brokers made money, by selling tickets at inflated prices as gambling fever grew and especially by renting them for short periods such as a week, a day, or just an hour.
92. Avery, *TLS*, Pt 3, I, 180–7; Hume, *Henry Fielding*, p. 120.
93. See *Juvenal and Persius*, trans. G. G. Ramsay (London: Heinemann; Cambridge, Mass.: Harvard UP, 1957), pp. xx.
94. D. M. Walker, *The Oxford Companion to Law* (Oxford: Clarendon, 1980), defines the term, often shortened to 'crim con', as follows: 'A common law action for criminal conversation formerly lay at the instance of the husband against one who had committed adultery with his wife, for damages. After the institution of judicial divorce in 1857 this was replaced by a claim for damages against a co-respondent' (p. 316).
95. The play has had a mixed reputation from the beginning. For reviews of its reception and related matters, see Woods, 'Notes on Three of Fielding's plays', *PMLA*, LII (1937), 359–73. See Hume, *Henry Fielding*, p. 126, for a brief appraisal of Fielding's likely earnings.
96. Cross, I, 121; Loftis, *Politics of Drama*, pp. 130–1; Goldgar, *Walpole*, p. 112; B. McCrea, *Henry Fielding and the Politics of Mid-Eighteenth-Century England* (Athens, Georgia: Georgia UP, 1981), pp. 59–60; Hume, *Henry Fielding*, pp. 115–18; Battestin, *A Life*, pp. 128–9.
97. Avery, *TLS*, Pt 3, I, 222, 224, 272, 285.
98. Hume, *Henry Fielding*, pp. 134, 136, 153; *TLS*, Pt 3, I, ccvi.
99. Cross, *The History*, I, 126, after recounting the incident that led to the trial, in October, 1731, of the Director of the Jesuit Seminary in Toulon, Father Girard, who was accused of practising sorcery to seduce the beautiful Marie Catherine Cadiere, to whom he was confessor, concludes that Fielding did not follow the French story very closely. Battestin, *A Life*, p. 134, comes at the matter another

way, saying that Fielding, like some of his contemporaries, tried tastelessly to capitalize on the sensational case.

100. H. Pagliaro (ed.), *The Journal of a Voyage to Lisbon* (New York: Nardon, 1963), pp. 27, 135, n. 12.

101. Fielding's audience would have been reminded of the real life Madam, Elizabeth Needham, known as Mother Needham, who died shortly after being pilloried, in 1731 (*Dictionary of National Biography*). Hogarth includes her in the first plate of *The Harlot's Progress*, and Pope refers to her in *The Dunciad, In Four Books*, 1743, I, 324, as 'pious Needham' because, as his own note makes clear, she hoped to make enough money to retire in time to make her peace with God.

102. Scenes were unnumbered until John Watts's second edition, London, 1732, which includes a few verbal changes by Fielding. See Hume, *Henry Fielding*, p. 138.

103. Both Molière and Fielding, however, lift Plautus' scene in which the miser and the young man who ultimately marries his daughter misunderstand the object of the young man's 'theft', the father believing it to be money, and the young man the daughter's virginity.

104. Plautus, *The Pot of Gold and other Plays*, trans. E. F. Watling (Harmondsworth and New York: Penguin, 1965), p. 9.

105. *Juvenal and Persius*, p. 275.

106. Hume, *Henry Fielding*, p. 153, details *The Miser's* great stage success, mentioning along the way that it 'was performed regularly for the rest of the century'.

107. Genest, *Some Account*, III, 371.

108. Avery, *TLS*, Pt 3, I, 279.

109. Cross, *The History*, I, 146.

110. Roberts, 'Henry Fielding's Lost Play *Deborah, or A Wife for You All* (1733)', *Bulletin of the New York Public Library*, LXVI (1962), 576–88.

111. Roberts, '*Deborah*', pp. 577–8.

112. Hume, *Henry Fielding*, p. 154.

113. Battestin, *A Life*, pp. 164–5, suggests that Fielding may well have played on the association between Handel and Walpole, whom the opposition press had 'linked as arrogant colleagues in oppression': the minister for introducing an excise bill on wine and tobacco (14 March), and the composer for doubling the cost of tickets at the Opera House (17 March).

114. One reason for the widow's appointing the painter her deputy may have been that she thought him powerfully connected. Ellys, 1701–57, a fellow student and later a colleague of Hogarth, had been consulted and employed by Walpole while the minister was buying his collection of paintings. For this work, presumably, Ellys was given a sinecure, Master Keeper of the Lions in the Tower, which he held for life. See Battestin, *A Life*, p. 157, and *DNB*.

115. Hume, *Henry Fielding*, pp. 155–85, and Battestin, *A Life*, pp. 167–73, cover this ground in detail from their special perspectives as theatre historian and biographer.

116. Battestin, *A Life*, pp. 170–1.
117. Hume, *Henry Fielding*, p. 182.
118. Avery, *TLS*, Pt 3, I, 358.
119. For discussions of this issue, see Battestin, *A Life*, pp. 173–5, and Hume, *Henry Fielding*, pp. 184, 209–12.
120. Fielding dropped one of the cousins, Bookish, because the audience objected to him. See Hume, *Henry Fielding*, pp. 187–8.
121. Cross, *The History*, III, 100.
122. For discussions of the play's history, see Fielding's Preface to *Miscellanies*, I, 5–7; Cross, *The History*, III, 99–109; Hume, *Henry Fielding*, pp. 263–4.
123. For a discussion of the play's history, see Woods, 'The "Miss Lucy" Plays of Fielding and Garrick', *Philological Quarterly*, XLI (1962), 294–310; *Miscellanies*, I, 15; Hume, *Henry Fielding*, pp. 265–6.
124. Avery, *TLS*, Pt 3, I, 459, quotes *The Prompter*, 18 February, as plausibly arguing a case against the play.
125. Battestin, *A Life*, pp. 181–3.
126. Liesenfeld, *Licensing Act*, Chapter 2; Hume, *Henry Fielding*, pp. 192–9.
127. Hume, *Henry Fielding*, p. 204; also see pp. 204–9 for an interesting amplification of the quoted conjecture.
128. Avery, *TLS*, Pt 3, I, cxliii.
129. See Farnsworth Smith, *Plays about the Theatre*, pp. 205–8, for a discussion of *Pasquin* as a rehearsal play.
130. Even critics who consider *Pasquin* to be an intensely political play – rather than a play about social disintegration – acknowledge Fielding's even-handedness in his treatment of parties, though they vary in the degree to which they believe Walpole to have been a partisan target. See, for example, Loftis, *Politics of Drama*, p. 133; Goldgar, *Walpole*, pp. 151–2; McCrea, *Henry Fielding and Politics*, pp. 73–4; Cleary, *Henry Fielding*, pp. 81–3.
131. Avery, *TLS*, Pt 3, I, 556.
132. See Hunter, *Occasional Form*, pp. 49–74, and Rivero, *The Plays*, pp. 127–38, for a discussion of Fielding's use of the rehearsal play as in various ways suited to his talents as playwright.
133. Cross, *The History*, III, 299–300.
134. Hume, *Henry Fielding*, p. 223.
135. Cross, *The History*, p. 213.
136. Appleton, *Historical Register and Eurydice Hissed*, p. 54.
137. Genest, *Some Account*, III, 492; Battestin, *A Life*, p. 214; Hume, *Henry Fielding*, p. 224; Cleary, *Henry Fielding*, p. 184.
138. Hume, *Henry Fielding*, p. 229. Also see Hume, *Henry Fielding*, pp. 224–34, for a discussion of Fielding's activities in the theatre world at this time.
139. Appleton, *Historical Register and Eurydice Hissed*, p. xiii.
140. Morrissey, *Tom Thumb*, p. 1.
141. Appleton explains the identification of Corsica with England: 'Like Great Britain it was a small island, struggling to free itelf from the burden of heavy taxes and a notoriously corrupt set of officials': *Historical Register and Eurydice Hissed*, p. xiv.

142. Appleton, *Historical Register and Eurydice Hissed*, p. xiii; Hume, *Henry Fielding*, p. 235, n. 90.

143. Appleton, *Historical Register and Eurydice Hissed*, p. x; Hume, *Henry Fielding*, p. 235.

144. Appleton cites the Earl of Egmont's diary entry on *Eurydice Hiss'd*, which says it is an allegory of Walpole's failed Excise Bill: *Historical Register and Eurydice Hissed*, p. xiii.

145. Cleary, *Henry Fielding*, p. 113.

146. From Potter's account of expenses, presumably submitted to the Government, as quoted in Hume, *Henry Fielding*, p. 246.

147. Cross, *The History*, I, 233; Cleary, *Henry Fielding*, p. 114; T. Lockwood, 'Fielding and the Licensing Act', *Huntington Library Quarterly*, L (1988), 379–93, 380; Hume, *Henry Fielding*, p. 251; Battestin, *A Life*, p. 235. See also Battestin, *New Essays by Henry Fielding: His Contributions to the 'Craftsman' (1734–1739) and Other Early Journalism*, with a Stylometric Analysis by Michael G. Farringdon (Charlottesville: Virginia UP, 1989).

148. Lockwood, 'Fielding', p. 382; Hume, *Henry Fielding*, p. 251.

149. Lockwood, 'Fielding', p. 385 and throughout; Hume, *Henry Fielding*, pp. 251–2.

150. Battestin, *A Life*, p. 650, n. 412.

151. Lockwood, 'Fielding', pp. 386–7. Battestin, *A Life*, pp. 282–5, refers these of Fielding's comments about bribery to the time of their writing, not to the past, arguing that Walpole tried to bribe Fielding to stop his writing partisan essays for *The Champion*.

152. Lockwood, 'Fielding', p. 382.

153. Battestin, *A Life*, pp. 112–23, considers bribery as a plausible reason for the suppression of *The Grub-Street Opera*. See also Battestin, *A Life*, pp. 282–5, 291, 324.

154. See P. W. Harsh, *A Handbook of Classical Drama* (Stanford, Calif.: Stanford; London: Geoffrey Cumberlege-Oxford, 1944), pp. 14–15, 331–2, for a discussion of the complicated classical origins of the division of plays into acts and the conclusion that 'the division into five acts found in the modern texts [of Roman Comedy] dates from Renaissance editions' (p. 332).

155. Battestin, *A Life*, pp. 127–33; Rivero, *The Plays*, pp. 112–26; Cross, *The History*, pp. 118–25; others who take exception to the play are, for example, Loftis, *Politics of Drama*, pp. 130–1; Cleary, *Henry Fielding*, pp. 63–5; Hume, *Henry Fielding*, pp. 121–9.

156. In a much quoted portion of his preface to *Plays Unpleasant*, Shaw says Fielding was 'the greatest practising dramatist, with the single exception of Shakespeare, produced by England between the Middle Ages and the nineteenth century'. See D. H. Laurence (ed.), *The Bodley Head Bernard Shaw*, 7 vols (London, Sydney and Toronto: Reinhardt, 1930–74), I (rev. 1970), 19–20.

157. M. Grace (ed.), *Arthur Murphy, 'The Lives of Henry Fielding and Samuel Johnson'* (Gainesville, Florida: Scholars' Facsimiles & Reprints, 1968), pp. 250–1.

3 The Novels and Other Prose Fiction

1. I. Watt, *The Rise of the Novel* (London: Chatto & Windus, 1957; repr. Berkeley and Los Angeles: California UP, 1964); see especially Watt's first chapter, 'Realism and the Novel Form', pp. 9–34. N. Frye, *Anatomy of Criticism* (Princeton, NJ: Princeton UP, 1957), p. 308. J. Richetti (ed.), *The Columbia History of the British Novel* (New York: Columbia UP, 1994), pp. xii–xiii. M. McKeon, *The Origins of the English Novel 1600–1740* (Baltimore, Md, and London: Johns Hopkins UP, 1987), pp. 1–4, points to the contextual nature of Watt's argument, questioning his close analogy between formal realism and philosophical realism and between individualism and the rising middle class, for example. See n. 20 below.
2. See Lawrence, 'Why the Novel Matters', in E. D. McDonald (ed.), *Phoenix: The Posthumous Papers of D. H. Lawrence* (New York: Viking, 1936), pp. 533–8.
3. The claim is argued by M. M. Bakhtin, 'Epic and Novel', in M. Holquist (ed.), *The Dialogic Imagination: Four Essays by M. M. Bakhtin*, trans. C. Emerson and Holquist (Austin: Texas UP, 1981), pp. 3–40.
4. The thesis is well argued by McKeon; see his Introduction and Chapters 1 and 2 in *The Origins*.
5. For a historical treatment of this and related questions, see L. Damrosch, Jr, *God's Plot & Man's Stories* (Chicago and London: Chicago UP, 1985), pp. 34–40 and elsewhere.
6. W. H. McBurney, *A Check List of English Prose Fiction, 1700–1739* (Cambridge, Mass.: Harvard UP, 1960) provides almost 400 titles.
7. Richetti, *Popular Fiction before Richardson* (Oxford: Clarendon, 1969), p. 9.
8. J. P. Hunter, *Before Novels* (New York and London: Norton, 1990), p. 5. In his Preface, Hunter pays tribute to Ian Watt for his 'courage' and 'prescience' in claiming 'the "sociological" basis of the English novel' and for his 'then [1957] defiant act of attributing creative power to readers'; Hunter claims that in the past thirty years [since about 1960], everyone writing about the novel 'has been engaged in rewriting Watt and . . . in renewing him'.
9. McBurney, *A Check List*, p. viii.
10. Richetti, 'Popular Narrative in the Early Eighteenth Century: Formats and Formulas', in J. M. Armistead (ed.), *The First English Novelists: Essays in Understanding* (Knoxville, Tennessee: Tennessee UP, 1985), p. 13. I am indebted to Richetti, pp. 12–17, for a discussion of the critical claims some of the authors of amatory fiction made about their own work, especially Mary Manley.
11. For a sample of eighteenth-century criminal biographies and a historical discussion of the form, see P. Rawlings, *Drunks, Whores and Idle Apprentices* (London and New York: Routledge, 1992).
12. For a historical and critical discussion of this complicated issue see L. J. Davis, *Factual Fictions: The Origins of the English Novel* (New York: Columbia UP, 1983), especially Chapter 3, 'News/Novels: The Undifferentiated Matrix', pp. 42–70, and Chapter 9, 'Daniel Defoe:

Lies and Truth', pp. 154–73.

13. See Hunter, *Before Novels*, pp. 225–302, for three informative chapters on the expectation of didacticism in seventeenth- and eighteenth-century readers.
14. Richetti, 'Popular Narrative', p. 13.
15. R. A. Day, *Told in Letters: Epistolary Fiction Before Richardson* (Ann Arbor: Michigan UP, 1966), traces the history and methods of using letters to tell a story, drawing on over 200 epistolary works written before *Pamela*.
16. Day, *Told in Letters*, p. 192.
17. Richetti, *Popular Fiction Before Richardson*, p. 11. In this context, Richetti refers to Fielding as an 'anti-novelist' (p. 1, n. 1), who, for example, consciously parodies 'the traditions of popular fiction' (p. 204, n. 1); but he also remarks on Fielding's debt to earlier fiction for the model of his heroines (p. 172), and on his interest in criminals, notably Jonathan Wild, whom Fielding, unlike his predecessors, handles with destructive ridicule (p. 58).
18. Day, *Told in Letters*, p. 9.
19. Day, *Told in Letters*, p. 192.
20. McKeon, *The Origins*, p. 10, and others have suggested a teleological bias in Watt's presumed sense of the novel's 'pre-existence', a bias buried in the premise that the new form was increasingly (over time) differentiated from other genres and accordingly could be formally defined. McKeon's approach avoids the conventional need to define the novel – the 'thing' we call the novel – by arguing its dialogic nature: that is, he claims the novel derives from dynamic elements and voices that reflect social and generic instability, problems which the novel both records and addresses, but does not necessarily solve; and he claims that as a result of its dialogic nature the novel is in the everlasting state of Becoming.
21. For these only slightly hyperbolic words, see Parson Oliver's letter to Parson Tickletext in M. C. Battestin (ed.), *Joseph Andrews and Shamela* (London: Methuen, 1965), p. 306. Quotations from *Shamela* are taken from Battestin's edition.
22. See Defoe's discussion of the matter in K. D. Bulbring (ed.), *The Compleat Gentleman* (London: David Nutt, 1890; repr. Folcroft Library Editions, 1972), pp. 259–62. See also A. D. McKillop, *Samuel Richardson: Printer and Novelist* (Chapel Hill: North Carolina UP, 1936; repr. Shoe String Press, 1960), pp. 29–30.
23. McKillop, *Samuel Richardson*, pp. 30–1.
24. *Shamela*, published on 4 April 1741, is the first of many eighteenth-century parodies and imitations of Richardson. Though *Shamela* was published anonymously and Fielding never acknowledged authorship, the book has been reliably assigned to him. See C. B. Woods, 'Fielding and the Authorship of *Shamela*', *Philological Quarterly*, XXV (1946), 248–72.
25. McKillop, *Samuel Richardson*, p. 46.
26. McKillop, *Samuel Richardson*, p. 47.
27. McKillop, *Samuel Richardson*, p. 45.

28. Fielding makes the point in one of his contributions to his sister's *Familiar Letters between the Principal Characters in David Simple*, Letter xl; and in *Amelia*, IX, ix. See Battestin, (ed.), *Amelia*, (Middletown, Conn.: Wesleyan UP, 1983), p. 394; hereafter my quotations from *Amelia* are taken from Battestin's edition. Also see *Amelia*, p. 394, n. 2 for a brief characterization of this eighteenth-century doctrine of the connection between taste and morals.

29. For an account of the quarrel, in which Lady Mary Wortley Montagu was Hervey's ally against Pope, see John Butt, Introduction, *Alexander Pope, Imitations of Horace* (London: Methuen; New Haven, Conn.: Yale UP, 1939), repr. with corrections, 1961, pp. xv–xxii. Pope refers first to Harvey as Fanny in 'A Master Key to Popery' (1732) and again in his *First Satire of the Second Book of Horace* (1733), l. 6.

30. In addition to 'backside', 'Fanny' signifies 'the female *pudenda*', according to Partridge; but how early this meaning was in use is not certain.

31. A 'Cony' is a silly fellow, a dupe or gull (*Oxford English Dictionary*). And 'coney' refers to the female sex organs, as the prostitute's cry 'no money, no coney' suggests (*Oxford English Dictionary*).

32. Battestin (ed.), *Joseph Andrews* (Middletown, Conn.: Wesleyan UP, 1967), p. xvi. Quotations cited hereafter are from Battestin's edition.

33. See *Joseph Andrews*, pp. 7–8, n. 4, for eighteenth-century treatments of the ridiculous.

34. For a discussion of Fielding's characterization of Lady Booby, see R. Alter, *Fielding and the Nature of the Novel* (Cambridge, Mass.: Harvard UP, 1968), pp. 73–5.

35. M. Irwin, *Henry Fielding The Tentative Realist* (Oxford: Clarendon, 1967), p. 74.

36. M. Irwin, *Tentative Realist*, p. 68; for the whole argument, see pp. 65–83. Irwin's discussion of *Joseph Andrews* also includes strong praise; for example, he sees Adams, for him the only full-drawn character, along with the novel's most obvious and remarkable quality – its humour – as elements that compensate for the narrative disjunction.

37. Irwin, *Tentative Realist*, p. 70. For a brilliantly argued alternative view that sees Fielding supremely aware of the status of his novels as artifacts, see Alter, *Fielding*, especially Chapter 4, 'The Architectonic Novel'.

38. For a discussion of Fielding's narrator of *Joseph Andrews*, see R. Paulson, *Satire and the Novel in Eighteenth-Century England* (New Haven, Conn., and London: Yale UP, 1967), pp. 100–10, especially. I have borrowed the terms 'creator/historian', 'manipulator' and 'ironist' from Paulson, *Satire*, pp. 103–5.

39. See Sheridan Baker, 'Fielding's Comic Epic-in-Prose Romances Again', *Philological Quarterly*, LVIII (1979), 63–81, for an extended argument in favour of using the term 'comic romance' rather than 'comic epic' to 'illuminate' Fielding's novels, a preference Baker believes to be Fielding's own.

40. For a brief discussion of connections between epic and comic epic, see H. Pagliaro (ed.), *Major English Writers of the Eighteenth Century*

(New York: The Free Press; London: Collier-Macmillan, 1969), pp. 602–3.

41. Battestin, *The Moral Basis of Fielding's Art* (Middletown, Conn.: Wesleyan UP, 1959), pp. 26–7.
42. For a summary of the epic-romance debate, see J. F. Bartolomeo, *A New Species of Criticism* (Newark, Delaware, London and Toronto: Associated University Presses, 1994) pp. 69–71.
43. Baker, 'Fielding's Comic Romances', p. 74.
44. Baker, 'Fielding's Comic Romances', p. 77. Heavenly sponsorship of epic causes and the religious dedication of the epic hero are commonplaces of the genre. There is no space here for considering the difficult question of Christian epic (and *Paradise Lost*). For discussions of the problem, see A. B. Giamatti, *The Earthly Paradise and the Renaissance Epic* (Princeton, NJ: Princeton UP, 1966), especially Chapter 6, pp. 295–351; and M. A. Treip, *Allegorical Poetics & The Epic: The Renaissance Tradition to 'Paradise Lost'* (Lexington, Kentucky: Kentucky UP, 1994); see also R. Folkenflick, 'Tom Jones, the Gypsies, and the Masquerade', *University of Toronto Quarterly*, XLIV (1975), 224–37.
45. J. P. Hunter, *Occasional Form* (Baltimore, Md, and London: Johns Hopkins UP, 1975), pp. 98–9, points out that Fielding mitigates Joseph's declaration of virtue – 'the oration of a fool' – by swiftly exposing him to a very different seductress, Slipslop, and in doing so, prepares the way for us to recognize that Joseph does not respond uniformly to all women, and thus to recognize that he is not chiefly a parody of Pamela.
46. For a discussion of feminist issues in Fielding's novels, see A. G. Smallwood, *Fielding and the Woman Question* (New York: St Martin's, 1989); and J. Campbell, *Natural Masques: Gender and Identity in Fielding's Plays and Novels* (Stanford, Calif.: Stanford UP, 1995).
47. M. B. Williams, *Marriage: Fielding's Mirror of Morality* (University, Alabama: Alabama UP, 1973), p. 62. See also pp. 43–70 for a discussion of marriage in *Shamela* and *Joseph Andrews*. The novel's ending, which stresses the male-secured home, representing religiously endorsed survival and continuity, is a dominant characteristic of epic. Fielding continues to mix romance and epic elements to the very end. For a view of the farcical bedroom scenes in which Adams figures as the novel's resolution of its 'major themes and passions [chastity and lust] through benevolent humor' (*Joseph Andrews*, IV, xiv, 330–5), see M. Spilka, 'Comic Resolution in *Joseph Andrews*', in H. Bloom (ed.), *Modern Critical Views: Henry Fielding* (New York, New Haven, and Philadelphia: Chelsea House, 1987), pp. 7–16.
48. For detailed accounts of Fielding's preparation of the *Miscellanies*, see H. K. Miller (ed.), General Introduction, *Miscellanies, Volume One* (Middletown, Conn.: Wesleyan UP, 1972), pp. xi–xlix, and B. A. Goldgar and H. Amory (eds), General Introduction, *Miscellanies, Volume Two* (Middletown, Conn.: Wesleyan UP, 1993), pp. xvii–xxiii.
49. For a discussion of dialogues of the dead and related genres, see F. M. Keener, *English Dialogues of the Dead* (New York and London: Columbia UP, 1973), especially pp. 3–24.

50. See the full checklist of such works in Keener, *English Dialogues*, pp. 277–95.
51. *The Works of Lucian of Samasota*, 4 vols, trans. H. W. Fowler and F. G. Fowler (Oxford: Clarendon, 1905), I, 156–67.
52. *Miscellanies*, II, xxv–xxvi.
53. M. C. Battestin *with* Ruthe R. Battestin, *Henry Fielding: A Life* (London and New York: Routledge, 1989–90), p. 371. For an excellent essay on the *Journey*, see C. J. Rawson, 'Introduction', in Rawson (ed.), *A Journey from This World to the Next* (London: Dent, New York: Dutton, 1973).
54. For the attribution of the final chapter to Sarah, see Battestin, *A Life*, pp. 27, 371, 379, and Goldgar, *Miscellanies*, II, xxxiv–xxxv.
55. For a brief detailed account of Wild's life, see W. R. Irwin, *The Making of Jonathan Wild* (New York: Columbia UP, 1941; repr. Hamden, Connecticut: Archon, 1966), pp. 4–11.
56. Irwin, *Making of Jonathan Wild*, pp. 22–4, 43–79. For an account of the activities of the Opposition during this period, see Goldgar, *Walpole and the Wits* (Lincoln, Nebraska and London: Nebraska UP, 1976), pp. 29–63.
57. Quotations are taken from A. R. Humpreys and D. Brooks (eds), *Henry Fielding: Jonathan Wild [and] The Journal of a Voyage to Lisbon* (London: Dent; New York: Dutton, 1973).
58. For detailed discussions of this activity see Battestin, *A Life*, pp. 317–39, and Goldgar, *Walpole*, pp. 186–216.
59. A night cellar is 'a cellar serving as a tavern or place of resort during the night for persons of the lowest class' (*Oxford English Dictionary*.)
60. For a discussion of the treatment of women in *Jonathan Wild*, see Smallwood, *Fielding*, pp. 89–106.
61. Paulson, *Satire*, p. 80.
62. For comments on marriage in *Jonathan Wild*, see Williams, *Marriage*, pp. 63–9, 123.
63. Hunter, *Occasional Form*, p. 185. 'In making Tom Jones a nonmilitary, nonaristocratic, nonperfect hero, Fielding was creating not a "great" man in an old mold but a good man in a new one. In this sense, *Tom Jones* fulfills the promising distinctions of *Jonathan Wild*'.
64. See C. Woodring (ed.), *Samuel Taylor Colerdige: Table Talk* (London: Routledge; Princeton, NJ: Princeton UP, 1990), II, 295.
65. A. Dobson, *Fielding* (London: Macmillan, 1883), p. 126.
66. F. R. Leavis, *The Great Tradition: George Eliot, Henry James, Joseph Conrad* (New York: Stewart, 1948), pp. 3–4.
67. R. S. Crane, 'The Plot of *Tom Jones*', *The Journal of General Education*, IV (January 1950), 112–30. References to Fortune as an important factor of plot occur throughout the article: for example, pp. 117, 119, 120, 127.
68. Battestin, '*Tom Jones*: The Argument of Design', in H. K. Miller, E. Rothstein and G. S. Rousseau (eds), *The Augustan Milieu: Essays Presented to Louis A. Landa* (New York: Oxford UP, 1970), p. 306.
69. Sermon XXXVI, *Works* (1757), iii, 40, and Sermon XCVIII, *Works* (1738), i, 620, quoted from Battestin, 'Argument of Design', p. 308.

70. Crane, 'The Plot', pp. 120, 127.
71. W. C. Booth, *The Rhetoric of Fiction* (Chicago: Chicago UP, 1961), p. 217, points out that the narrator of *Tom Jones* is an important character in the novel. See also A. Wright, *Henry Fielding: Mask and Feast* (Los Angeles: California UP; London: Chatto & Windus, 1965), Chapter 1, which makes the point that Fielding's narrator 'demonstrates from the very beginning of *Tom Jones*, [that] he intends to be Master of the Revels' (p. 31).
72. Damrosch, *God's Plot*, pp. 263–303.
73. Many critics have dismissed the episode of the Gypsy King as an interruption of the narrative without much significance, but there are some interpretations which see strong connections between it and the rest of the novel, including Battestin, 'Tom Jones and "His Egyptian Majesty": Fielding's Parable of Government', *PMLA*, LXXXII (March 1967), 68–77, which argues that Fielding's apparent Utopia of the gypsies is an ironic attack on Jacobite absolutism; Folkenflik, '*Tom Jones*', pp. 224–37, which suggests that one best understands the episode in relation to the masquerade (*Tom Jones*, XIII, vii, 712–17) – to which Tom has been invited by the Queen of the Fairies, Lady Bellaston – and argues that the gypsy society is natural, warm, festive, moral and open, whereas high masquerade society is artificial, cold, calculating, immoral and closed; and Manuel Schonhorn, 'Fielding's Ecphrastic Moment: Tom Jones and his Egyptian Majesty', *Studies in Philology*, LXXVIII (Summer 1981), 305–23, which claims that the episode of the gypsy king (*Tom Jones*, XII, xii) represents the principle of genuine social order, and that it mimics and resolves the earlier episodes of the Man of the Hill (*Tom Jones*, VIII, xi–xiv) and the Master Puppeteer (*Tom Jones*, XII, v), which are both unsatisfactory analogues of order.
74. Crane makes the point – without at all characterizing the analogies – as a basis for claiming that the reader may infer 'on the eve of the most distressing part of the complication for the hero and heroine, that nothing that may happen to them will be really bad' ('The Plot', p. 130).
75. See *Tom Jones*, V, i, especially pp. 212–14, for Fielding's own comments on contrast.
76. In the same section of the novel, Fielding also dramatizes what his heroine is not by having Sophia mistakenly (and comically) identified as Jenny Cameron, the daughter of a Highland laird popularly believed to be the Young Pretender's mistress; see Battestin, *Tom Jones*, p. 578, n. 2. Sophia may indeed share high spirits, youth and beauty with the Jenny of popular imagination, but she is not a Scot, she is no one's mistress, and she is not a Jacobite.
77. I pass over the two marriages made appropriate, it seems, by the narrator's mischievous sense of fun – Mrs Waters to Parson Supple and Partridge to Molly Seagrim – though there may be something to the view that the pairs are intended to represent mutually correcting complements. For a discussion of the place of marriage in *Tom Jones*, see Williams, *Marriage*, pp. 71–94.

78. Fielding makes the same point at length in *Amelia*, I, ii, 17–25.
79. George Sherburn, 'Fielding's *Amelia*', *ELH: A Journal of Literary History*, III (1936), 1–14, p. 1. Not only the novel itself, but its title-page, which includes two lines from Horace and two from Simonides of Samos, indicates the theme. See *Amelia*, pp. 1 and 3 for a facsimile of the title-page and a translation of the Latin and Greek lines.
80. Battestin, 'The Problems of *Amelia*: Hume, Barrow, and the Conversion of Captain Booth', *ELH: A Journal of English Literary History*, XLI (1974), 613–48, pp. 613–14.
81. *The Covent-Garden Journal* for 28 January 1752, in B. A. Goldgar (ed.), *The Covent-Garden Journal and A Plan of the Universal Register-Office* (Middletown, Conn.: Wesleyan UP, 1988), p. 65.
82. Sherburn, 'Fielding's *Amelia*', p. 2.
83. See T. C. D. Eaves, '*Amelia* and *Clarissa*', in D. Kay (ed.), *A Provision of Human Nature: Essays on Fielding and Others in Honor of Miriam Austin Locke* (University, Alabama: Alabama UP, 1977), pp. 95–110 for the view that Fielding's known admiration for *Clarissa* led him to attempt the characterization of an equally moving heroine. See Battestin's Introduction to *Amelia*, p. xv, for Fielding's personal troubles while he wrote the novel.
84. S. Baker, 'Fielding's *Amelia* and the Materials of Romance', *Philological Quarterly*, XLI (1962), 437–49.
85. For discussions of Amelia's character by critics who are women, see Williams, *Marriage*, pp. 95–120; Campbell, *Natural Masques*, pp. 203–41, esp. 235–41; and E. Kraft, 'The Two Amelias: Henry Fielding and Elizabeth Justice', *ELH: A Journal of English Literary History*, LXII (1995), 313–28.
86. For the autobiographical elements in *Amelia*, see Battestin, Introduction, *Amelia*, pp. xvi–xxi.
87. For the early criticism of *Amelia*, see R. Paulson and T. Lockwood, *Henry Fielding: The Critical Heritage* (London: Routledge & Kegan Paul; New York: Barnes & Noble, 1969), pp. 286–336, 345–52, and elsewhere; for Fielding's own summary of the early criticism and his reply see *Covent-Garden Journal*, 25 and 28 January 1752, pp. 52–66. For a discussion of the early criticism, see Battestin, Introduction, *Amelia*, pp. xliv–lxi.
88. H. Davis (ed.), *Gulliver's Travels* (Oxford: Basil Blackwell, 1959), p. 6. *Gulliver's Travels* was published in 1726; the letter to cousin Sympson is dated 2 April 1727, but not published until 1735; when it was written is uncertain.
89. *Covent-Garden Journal*, pp. 65–6.

4 The Final Years, 1751–4

1. M. C. Battestin *with* Ruthe R. Battestin, *Henry Fielding: A Life* (London and New York: Routledge, 1989–90), p. 577.
2. See Battestin, *A Life*, pp. 499–502, 576–80 for a discussion of the Bow-Street Runners.

3. H. Pagliaro (ed.), *The Journal of a Voyage to Lisbon* (New York: Nardon Press, 1963), p. 33.
4. Battestin, *A Life*, pp. 525, 581.
5. For a full discussion of this venture see B. A. Goldgar (ed.), *The Covent-Garden Journal and A Plan of the Universal Register Office* (Middletown, Conn.: Wesleyan UP, 1988), pp. xv–xxii.
6. *Covent-Garden Journal*, p. 6.
7. *Covent-Garden Journal*, pp. xxi–xxii.
8. Battestin, *A Life*, p. 585.
9. *Covent-Garden Journal*, p. xxviii.
10. Goldgar, *The Journal*, pp. xxxii–xxxiii.
11. M. R. Zirker (ed.), *An Enquiry into the Causes of the Late Increase of Robbers and Related Writings* (Middletown, Conn.: Wesleyan UP, 1988), p. 66.
12. See Zirker, *An Enquiry*, pp. lix–lxxxiii, for Fielding's reliance on the social, historical and political arguments of his predecessors and contemporaries.
13. Zirker, *An Enquiry*, p. 73.
14. Zirker, *An Enquiry*, pp. 69–70. Zirker reminds us that Fielding 'shared his contemporaries' respect for the industrious merchant' (p. 69, n. 7).
15. Zirker, *An Enquiry*, p. 84.
16. Zirker, *An Enquiry*, p. 83.
17. Battestin, *A Life*, p. 519; see also Zirker, *An Enquiry*, p. lix and n. 2.
18. Zirker, *An Enquiry*, p. lxxxv.
19. Zirker, *An Enquiry*, pp. lxxxiii–xcii.
20. Battestin, *A Life*, p. 549; see also Zirker, *An Enquiry*, pp. xci–xciii.
21. Zirker, *An Enquiry*, p. 124.
22. Zirker, *An Enquiry*, pp. lxxii–lxxiv.
23. *Proposals for Raising a Colledge [sic] of Industry for all Useful Trades and Husbandry, with Profit for the Rich, a plentiful Living for the Poor; and a Good Education for youth: Which will be Advantage to the Government, by the Increase of the People, and their Riches, by John Bellers* (London: Printed and Sold by T. Sowle, 1696). Zirker, *An Enquiry*, prints 'Bellars', not 'Bellers', p. lxxvii and throughout.
24. Zirker, *An Enquiry*, p. 250.
25. Battestin, *A Life*, p. 565, n. 326, 327.
26. *Covent-Garden Journal*, p. 229.
27. Zirker, *An Enquiry*, pp. 226–7.
28. Zirker, *An Enquiry*, p. 277.
29. See Zirker, *An Enquiry*, pp. xciv–cxiv, for a full discussion of the case.
30. Zirker, *An Enquiry*, p. cx.
31. Zirker, *An Enquiry*, p. cx.
32. Zirker, *An Enquiry*, p. 294.
33. Battestin, *A Life*, p. 576; Zirker, *An Enquiry*, p. cix.
34. *Voyage to Lisbon*, p. 39.
35. *Voyage to Lisbon*, pp. 35–41.
36. *Voyage to Lisbon*, p. 45.
37. For a brief comment on travel literature, see Pagliaro, *Voyage to Lisbon*, pp. 7–9.

38. *Voyage to Lisbon*, pp. 34–5.
39. *Voyage to Lisbon*, p. 29.
40. *Voyage to Lisbon*, p. 116.
41. See Battestin, *A Life*, pp. 611–12, and Pagliaro, *Voyage to Lisbon*, pp. 17–18, 153–4, for conjectures about the unsolved mystery of the two journals, the 'Francis' version and the 'Humphrys' version.
42. Battestin, *A Life*, pp. 596, 601.
43. Battestin, *A Life*, pp. 597–605.

Index of References to Fielding's Works

General Index

Montagu, Lady Mary Wortley
(HF's cousin) 2, 17, 18, 19,
26, 36, 39, 47, 51, 52, 58, 60,
74, 82
Moore, Hannah 36
Morrissey, L. J. 75, 76, 110
Murphy, Arthur 9, 10, 12, 17,
19, 38, 118
on Fielding as husband and
father 21
on Fielding's law career 25

narrative method in Fielding and
Richardson 136–40
New Theatre (Haymarket) 50, 68
novel, the, its beginnings 119–28

Odell, Thomas 53
Oldfield, Anne 60
Oliver, John 10

parody 74, 136
partisan plays 30, 109, 112
patents 47–8, 48, 49, 50, 109,
117
Patriots 33, 151
Paulson, Ronald 160
Pelham, Henry 33–4
Penlez, Bosavern 41–3, 187
Pitt, William 11, 13, 23, 33
Plato 152, 154
Plautus 53, 91
Pope, Alexander 19, 27, 70, 105,
130, 134
Dunciad 18, 28, 71–2, 74
Potter, John 114, 116
Powell, George 56
Pulteney, William 80

Queen's Theatre *see* King's
Theatre

Ralph, James 25, 27–8, 31
Ranby, John 38
Regnard, Jean François 95
rehearsal plays 69, 107, 110, 112
Relph, Reverend Josiah of
Cumberland 130
Rich, John 26, 28, 55, 61, 104

Richardson, Samuel 120, 121, 147
Pamela 32, 35, 43–4, 119–21,
128–30, 132–3, 135–6, 138,
147–51
on *Tom Jones* 36
Richetti, John 120, 121, 127
Richmond Hill theatres 50
Riot Act 1715 41–2, 43
Rivero, Albert J. 61, 117
Roberts, E. V. 93
Rogers, Pat 4, 20, 51
Rowe, Elizabeth Singer 123
Royal Academy of Music 49

Salisbury 19–20, 29
satire 17, 18, 132
political 157
serious 102
social 46, 157
topical 23–4, 46, 79
topical political 17
Scriblerians 27
Scriblerus Secundus 70
Shakespeare, William 74, 111
Shaw, George Bernard 82, 108,
118, 143
Sheffield, John, first Duke of
Buckingham 152
Sheridan, Richard Brinsley 99
Slocock, Dr Benjamin 130
Smollett, Tobias 126
Sparrye, Elizabeth (HF's father's
fourth wife) 32
Stanhope, Philip Dormer 22
Steele, Richard 49, 52, 57, 58
Sterne, Laurence 126
Stevens, John 123
Stoppelaer, Charles 108
Strange, Sir John 37–8
Swift, Jonathan 18
Gulliver's Travels 82
Scriblerus Club 70
Tale of a Tub, A 74, 155

Terence 53, 100, 143
Theatre Royal 48
theatres in seventeenth- and
eighteenth-century England
47–58